MW00906096

A Glittering Chaos is wonderful, dark, witty and wild. Here is a writer who is willing to explore the darkest corners of the human psyche and expose life for all its beauty and depravity. Lisa de Nikolits is a master storyteller who takes the reader on an unforgettable ride that begins with Melusine and her husband, Hans, whose trip to Las Vegas unravels their lives in ways they never would have thought possible. Stories within stories. Poetry. Madness. Illicit love. A city's power to unleash forgotten selves. The real dangers of trying to get to the truth. *A Glittering Chaos* has it all. A completely riveting read that will engage the mind, body and spirit.
—LISA YOUNG, author of *When the Earth*

The adage about "what happens in Vegas" is funny precisely because we know it's wishful thinking. *A Glittering Chaos* is about what happens when "what happens in Vegas" comes home to haunt you. Melusine is a German librarian whose ho-hum world wobbles after she tags along when her husband Hans attends a Las Vegas optometry conference. A newly empty nester who speaks no English, Melusine's voyage of self-discovery is punctuated by the poetry of Ingeborg Bachmann, nude photos in the desert, a black dildo named Kurt, autoerotic asphyxia, and the unravelling of her husband's sanity because of a secret from his youth. Lisa de Nikolits manages to integrate all these surprising pieces into a jigsaw that is a poignant, at times even lyrical, story of sexual coming-of-age, and the sometimes hard price paid for the wisdom of middle-age.
—BEVERLY AKERMAN, author of *The Meaning of Children*

An innocent trip to Las Vegas sparks a series of commissions and revelations that unravel a couple's deepest beliefs about themselves and each other. Like Madame Bovary before it, *A Glittering Chaos*

illustrates with an expert synthesis of empathy and honesty the ways in which our fantasies can have very real, and potentially devastating, consequences.
—RICHARD ROSENBAUM, *Broken Pencil*

Lisa de Nikolits is a smart, sensitive and adventurous writer, and she pulls out all the stops in her third novel. Sometimes comical, sometimes touching, sometimes outrageous, *A Glittering Chaos* is a riveting read from start to finish.
—ROSEMARY MCCRACKEN, author of *Safe Harbor*

Expertly crafted, this twisted page-turner unfolds against a backdrop of arid desert and tacky pleasure palaces and carries us directly into the eye of a storm called "unrequited love." From the delicious heights of sexual awakening to the hellish depths of human depravity, *A Glittering Chaos* sure blasted a hole in my ozone! Call it required reading: You simply won't be able to put it down.
—KRISTIN JENKINS, *The Anglican Journal*

Filled with intrigue, excitement, anticipation and sexual diversity, *A Glittering Chaos* grabs its reader from the very beginning. Lisa de Nikolits shines a light on the reality of a family who seems so perfect on the surface. Digging deeper and deeper, de Nikolits takes you on a roller coaster ride of portentous realizations, consummate emotions, deep-seated secrets and sexual relationships spanning from the reckless abandon of a spontaneous affair to the dark recesses of a deranged mind. The biggest problem with *A Glittering Chaos* is whether to read faster to see what happens next or slow down in order to savor every word.
—PAM LOFTON, book reviewer and blogger at oneflewovertheemp-tynest.blogspot.ca

A Glittering Chaos provides us with just that: a maelstrom of drama, crises, self-doubt, self-discovery, failure, success and much more, against both glamorous and banal backgrounds. The characters are multi-faceted and deep, each struggling to come to terms with their

own flaws and weaknesses. It is possible to both despise and adore them in equal measure. As with *West of Wawa*, Lisa de Nikolits has created a central female character that you cannot help but fall in love with. Melusine has so much about her to make you shake your head in frustration but at the same time want to wrap your arms around her. She's lovely and lovable, yet frighteningly frustrating. Once again, Lisa de Nikolits proves she is a master at making a reader think and feel from page 1 to the very end.
—DONNA BROWN, book reviewer and blogger at tweedling.com

*A Glittering Chao*s assures de Nikolits of her rightful place in the Literati world. The perfect balance of the Yin Yang of writing shines through in every chapter.
—BETSY BALEGA, author, *Being Mystic*, producer/host of *Tuning in with Betsy*

In *A Glittering Chaos,* author Lisa de Nikolits has written a compelling, fast-paced story peopled with vivid characters who surprise and delight the reader. I couldn't stop reading until I reached the end.
—CAROLINE CLEMMONS, author of romance, mystery, and adventure

Canada Council   Conseil des Arts    ONTARIO ARTS COUNCIL
for the Arts   du Canada   CONSEIL DES ARTS DE L'ONTARIO

We gratefully acknowledge the support of the Canada Council for the Arts and the Ontario Arts Council for our publishing program. We also acknowledge the financial support of the Ontario Media Development Organization.

We are also grateful for the support received from an
Anonymous Fund at The Calgary Foundation.

Cover design: Lisa de Nikolits. Design direction: Jason Logan. Image: Getty Images.

From *Malina: A Novel* by Ingeborg Bachmann, translated by Philip Boehm. Copyright © 1990 by Holmes & Meier Publishers, Inc. Used with permission by Lynne Rienner Publishers, Inc.

All poems from *Darkness Spoken* by Ingeborg Bachmann. Copyright © 1978 by Piper Verlag GmbH, München for all poems taken from *Gesammelte Werke*, Bd. I Geditchte. Copyright © 2000 by Piper Verlag GmbH, München for all poems taken from *Ich wieiß keine bessere Welt*. Translation Copyright © 2006 by Peter Filkins. Used with permission by Zephyr Press.

Library and Archives Canada Cataloguing in Publication

de Nikolits, Lisa, 1966-
    A glittering chaos / Lisa de Nikolits.

(Inanna poetry and fiction series)
Also issued in electronic format.
ISBN 978-1-926708-92-8

    I. Title. II. Series: Inanna poetry and fiction series

PS8607.E63G55 2013   C813'.6   C2013-901783-6

Printed and bound in Canada

Inanna Publications and Education Inc.
210 Founders College, York University
4700 Keele Street, Toronto, Ontario, Canada M3J 1P3
Telephone: (416) 736-5356 Fax: (416) 736-5765
Email: inanna.publications@inanna.ca   Website: www.inanna.ca

A GLITTERING CHAOS

a novel by

Lisa de Nikolits

inanna poetry & fiction series

INANNA PUBLICATIONS AND EDUCATION INC.
TORONTO, CANADA

*To Bradford Dunlop
and the red rocks of the Nevada desert.*

One
carefree, be carefree

1.

THE MAN IS SAYING SOMETHING incomprehensible to Melusine. She is trapped in a hotel elevator in Vegas with a man pointing at her breasts and repeating something she cannot understand.

"German," she says, and she shakes her head. "German."

The man nods and carries on talking.

Melusine looks at him. He is waving his arms around as if his gestures might make his meaning more apparent.

She is so close to him she can smell his fruity chewing gum and she backs away as much as she can, hugging the tightly-wrapped bath towel to her chest with folded arms, and wishing once again that the hotel offered robes but the sprawling low-slung hacienda is just a three-star budget resort, tucked way off the Strip, up near the Mandalay Bay Hotel.

Melusine knows how far Hans has to travel to get down to the Convention Center and she cannot help but wonder if he deliberately chose a hotel at the opposite end to the conference after she insisted on joining him.

"Vegas will bore you," he had said, trying to dissuade her from coming. "You don't speak English, you won't understand what's going on, and you'll be bored."

"Nonsense. I don't know much about Vegas, but I do know that no one's ever bored there."

He shrugged. "As you wish. I'll change the reservations. Really, Melusine, you're so restless and unsettled lately. But if you think coming to Vegas will make you feel better, then fine."

And now she is in Vegas, alone in an elevator alongside a smiling gesticulating man.

The elevator door opens, and she rushes out to the swimming pool, noticing that the area is already crowded and that the other bathers have large blue and white striped towels; hers is the only bath towel. Maybe that's what the man was trying to tell her; he had not been interested in her breasts or in trying to have sex with her.

She laughs at the thought and settles down in her deck chair. She can't imagine anyone wanting to have sex with her.

She stretches out and takes stock of her body. Her legs are long, her breasts are full and firm, and she has managed to dodge the usual afflictions of age; her skin is unblemished and smooth. But none of this is about her body; it is her mind that's been causing her all kinds of concerns; her mind that has become so unruly of late.

She had tried to blame her unsettling discontent on the recent death of her parents and she'd also considered that her shiny new knife-edged tone was due to Jonas's departure, but none of it rang true in pinpointing the true source of her malaise.

Shortly before learning of the Vegas trip, standing in her kitchen and making the final preparations for a dinner party, she had acknowledged that her frustrations were not that easily explained away.

At work, earlier that day, she had taken a moment for herself among the quiet stacks of books in the library, and she had thought about those published works, questioning what she had to show for her life. She, who had dreamt of being a writer, poet or even madly, a philosopher, could only say that she had been a good daughter, an attentive, loving mother and a reproachless wife.

Ingeborg? Old friend, I near the age at which you died. And look what you had achieved. You know I'd never be so bold, or so foolish as to categorize myself alongside you but still, we both thought I'd achieve more? Even you thought I'd achieve so much more?

There was no reply.

Talk to me. Please, talk to me.

"You always do things so beautifully." A woman came into the kitchen and complimented her and Melusine smiled politely. Was this the answer to the questions that had been plaguing her? That she created beauty and order where she could?

"Your house is so perfect and you're such a great cook," the woman continued. "You're the envy of all of us. And your pastries are to die for. You could open a coffee shop, they're that good."

Melusine wondered if the woman had somehow read her mind. The list of her life's achievements was being offered at exactly the right time.

"Thanks," she said. "I do love cooking. Baking in particular."

"And Jonas, off to university. Do you miss him?"

"I feel as if I've lost a limb," Melusine started to say and then realized it would embarrass her to reveal that much to this casual acquaintance. "Not as much as I thought I would," she said, instead.

"That's good. It means that your life is full and rich and you're happy."

"Well, Jonas has always been so independent," Melusine said, feeling the need to justify something although she wasn't sure what. And she wanted to object and say that she wasn't happy at all, and that the woman couldn't be more wrong.

She discouraged further conversation by opening the oven and testing the venison. "Hans?" she called out. "Has your wine got enough oxygen into its system yet?"

It was an old joke between them.

"I would say just about, yes," Hans replied, his voice rising to be heard above the chit-chat.

Melusine carried the dishes through to the dining room and served dinner. She felt absent from the entire evening, dislocated, until she heard Hans say something about an upcoming trip to Las Vegas. It was the first she'd heard of it.

"Have you been before?" one of the men asked Hans.

"No. I've never understood the appeal but the conference looks top-notch, all the latest high-refraction lenses will be on display and I've been invited to give a talk."

"You'll come back a slot machine millionaire," one of the guests teased, "and never work a day in your life again!"

Hans pursed his lips. "The only thing on my mind will be business. I won't have any time for frivolities."

"You know what they say," the same man commented, "what happens in Vegas stays in Vegas. You could get up to all kinds of mischief and we'd be none the wiser."

"Not my style," Hans retorted. "Now, you on the other hand…" His expression suggested all kinds of mayhem and the group around the table laughed.

"Melusine," another man said, turning towards her, "what extraordinary confection do you have in store for our dessert tonight?"

"Just a simple Apple Walnut Bundt cake," Melusine apologized but her words were met with enthusiasm.

"That's one of my favourites of yours," one of the other men said.

"I told her, she could open a bakery or a coffee shop," the woman who'd been talking to Melusine in the kitchen piped up.

Hans snorted. "She studied Philosophy, Art and German Literature so she could be a baker? I don't think so."

"You're right," Melusine said, getting up and gathering plates. "It's much better that I check out library books and chase overdue fines instead."

The group laughed and Melusine went to make coffee and get the cake.

Later that night she loaded the dishwasher and tidied up.

She heard Hans come into the kitchen and she spoke to his reflection in the window, rather than turn around to face him.

"I'm coming to Las Vegas with you," she said, and she noticed that she wasn't asking.

She watched his reflection stiffen.

"You'll be bored," he said. "And I won't have time to entertain you. You'll be on your own. I'm going for nearly a week. You won't find enough things to do and I'll have to worry about you. And besides, what about Mimi?"

Mimi was Han's beloved black Riesenschnauzer. Jonas had begged his parents for a puppy for years and Hans had finally given in, telling the boy he could have a dog for his seventh birthday. But then Hans had fallen in love with Mimi and taken the lead in appropriating her affection.

"We can put her in a kennel. Or one of your friends could take her. Or Jonas can look after her; I know he'd love to. There are lots of solutions. But I'm coming with you, so get used to the idea."

She looked at the reflection of her husband's resigned face and then at her own flushed countenance. Hans turned and left the room and Melusine, still watching her own face against the blackened mirror of the night, saw her shoulders straighten slightly and the hint of a smile appear in her eyes.

2.

ON THE PLANE to Las Vegas, with Hans fast asleep beside her, Melusine felt a triumphant sense of accomplishment that she was there at all.

I step outside of myself, out of my eyes, hands, mouth, outside of myself I step.

She loved everything about the flight; the tiny oval window with the view of cotton clouds below, the neat little containers of food and she even loved the wine that Hans deemed worse than vinegar.

Melusine felt as if all her senses were heightened and the world seemed exciting again, in a way that it hadn't since she was a teenager with her veins filled with the rush of amphetamines and her heart ready to explode.

They arrived at midday and from the minute the plane landed, Melusine loved Las Vegas. She immediately wanted to go out and explore. Hans wanted to unpack, have a nap and work on his presentation.

"Well, I'm going out," Melusine said.

"Wait," Hans stopped her. He took out a map. He circled where they were and showed her how to get to the Strip from their hotel. He gave her a hundred dollars.

"But I brought my own money."

"Let me treat you," he replied with a lopsided smile she had once found so endearing. "A man's allowed to give his wife a treat."

She smiled and took the money.

"Check that your key card works," he said, "these new-fangled ones often don't and if it doesn't, you'll have to go back to the front desk and ask for a new one."

"Oh, Hans," she said, running out of patience, "it will work just fine."

"Off you go then, and have fun." He turned back to his suitcase. "Melusine…"

"Yes?" she asked sharply.

"Sunscreen," he said, and he threw a small tube at her, which she caught and put in her handbag.

"Drink lots of water," she heard him call out as she left. "We are in the desert."

She laughed and set off at high speed; a jerky walk that was almost a run.

She reached the Strip, stopped for a moment, and took a deep breath. A feeling of wild glee swelled in her chest like a balloon and she choked down a sob of joy.

It was the first week of October and back home, the world was wearing a drab coat of brown and gray but before her lay a vibrant scene of explosive colour. Melusine looked at the blue-green MGM hotel with its enormous golden lion standing guard and then over at the New York, New York, with its giant Statue of Liberty and skyscraper skyline. A rollercoaster wove up and down and around the hotel, and she could hear the screams of the tiny people on the ride as they flipped over and hurtled this way and that, and she hurried in their direction.

The Strip was much bigger than she had imagined and she had to walk a good few blocks to get from the street corner to inside the New York, New York hotel.

The interior was buzzing with tourists, food joints, and trinket vendors. Melusine realized that she was as good as mute since no one would be able to understand a single thing she had to say and, with her silenced tongue she found a freedom to censor neither word nor thought.

Deaf to all meaning, her ears had been liberated from their duties, and she made no effort to even try to understand the chatter around her or decipher the codes of words. The border of speech had become a tangible thing; she could not touch it but it stood between her and the rest of the world like a shield — she was a wordless conqueror.

Ingeborg! I'm the living embodiment of that which fascinated you. Perhaps this wordless experiment will help name the 'unspeakable' truth that is both transient and real. Or perhaps, for once, I'm simply to be carefree — if I can manage that...

She went down the escalator into the casino, gliding into the anonymous artificial night; outside it was only lunchtime. Everybody, it seemed, was carrying a drink and for a wild moment she wondered if she should get one too; get tipsy, get a buzz on.

She laughed at herself. She didn't use those kinds of words. She had never been drunk in Hans's presence although he swore there was a night when she returned from her best friend Ana's and he had to carry her up the stairs and undress her and put her to bed.

"I was simply tired," she argued. "I was just tired and you were kind."

The truth was that she and Ana had been drunk. They had been celebrating her fortieth birthday and she had wanted to get very, very drunk and Ana had obliged.

And now, looking at the holidaymakers, with their drinks in hand, she wanted to be drunk too. Not just tipsy, drunk.

But she cautioned herself. It was time to get back out into the daylight.

Need to calm down a bit.

She remembered something that her son had said to a friend on the phone; *no need to blow his wad in the first five minutes.* It came to mind now, that phrase that she had found so ugly; no need for her to blow her wad in the first five minutes.

She wandered slowly down the Strip, looking around her. She

was a miniature Gulliver in Brobdingnag; everything around her was huge—the hotels were cities; empires, each boasting a spaceship-sized façade, with limos and cabs circling the lobbies like birds of prey ready to snatch up carrion. Pedestrians were ferocious toddlers who ignored traffic signals and pushed forward in waves, and she wondered where everyone was going. She knew she was irritating those around her as she slowed down to look this way and that. She stared at the plethora of shopping bags; every pedestrian was laden. Should a tsunami inexplicably wash through the desert and rush down through the Strip, this lot would be buoyed to safety by the glossy bags. Perhaps she needed to get some too; balance Gucci with Yves Saint Laurent, throw credit card caution to the wind, wouldn't that be nice?

She watched a woman throwing coins into a fountain and she tried to imagine what the woman could be wishing for with such intense hope. She asked herself what she would wish for but could think of nothing. Her gnawing restlessness was quiet for the moment, uncomplaining.

She walked for five hours, zig-zagging, and she finally reached the Bellagio where she sank down onto a bench. It was close to six o'clock. She was starving and it was a long walk back to her hotel.

She regretted not curtailing her desire to explore and she felt angry with herself. She muttered under her breath, scolding herself as she would a child, and she felt a headache building. She tried to recapture her earlier feeling of exhilaration but she simply felt lost and exhausted and she hated herself at that moment, hated her aching body, her unreliable moods, her tiredness and her age. She wished she'd never come on the trip; and now she was stuck here for a week. Hans had been right, what had she been thinking?

She thought about hailing a cab; she could point to the hotel on the map that Hans had given her. She twisted around on the bench and turned to look back up the Strip in the direction of her hotel, trying to calculate how long it would take her if she walked straight back, with no detours into any of the shops or hotels.

But when she turned, she was filled with wonder and her punishing thoughts fell away; the Strip was glowing and flashing with electric beauty and the sky was liquid gold and it seemed to Melusine that a light was shining down from heaven and pouring into every nook and cranny, polishing the buildings and facades with a sharp gleam. The world was surreal, and the light was calling out to her because she was the only one who mattered. And it was telling her that she was welcome and that she was wanted and that she was in Vegas for a reason.

Melusine was not a religious woman. She had attended church to make her mother happy and she had followed the diocesan rules with diligence, but she'd never felt the strangely otherworldly comfort that she felt now.

There are, indeed things that cannot be put into words. They make themselves manifest. They are what is mystical. Ach me, with my dead philosophers and poets. I'm not alone. I've never been alone.

She felt her shoulders relax and she exhaled the tightness out of her chest. Her teeth had been clenched and her lips tightly pursed. She rubbed her jaw, not caring who saw her.

She sat turned towards the light until darkness fell.

And then suddenly, the night was filled with loud music and Frank Sinatra broke into song: *Luck Be A Lady.* Melusine recognized the tune, and she sat up in alarm. She hadn't noticed the crowds that had gathered around her and she wondered what was wrong; why had all these people stopped here?

Before she could question any further, the lake in front of her exploded into balletic fountains with jets of water shooting upwards with cannonball thrust, in time to the music.

Melusine was enthralled. She sat for another half an hour, for two more showings. Then she got to her feet and decided it was time to make her way back to her hotel.

She bought a bottle of water and a chocolate bar and ate as she walked, smiling at the costumed mimes that lined the way, waiting to be photographed with eager tourists.

She dodged dozens of stubby ugly men and women, all of them wearing bright orange T-shirts and snapping business cards at her. She accepted a few of the cards before she noticed that they were of nearly-naked, provocatively posed women.

Melusine studied the cards, not understanding the words but the message was clear. The young women hooked their lacy panties down with cheeky thumbs, or rubbed the taut nipples of full, round breasts, jutting their smooth bellies forward. Some of the girls were kneeling, naked, with their backs to the camera, spines curved and flawless buttocks thrust upward. Censor stars covered nipples, anus and vagina but in some places the stars had slipped and were strangely lodged; drunken adornments of blameless flesh. A few of the girls had their hands posed provocatively over their vaginas, or, as looks would slyly intimate, with fingers slipped inside. There were girls in swimming pools, on bicycles and chairs; there were girls wearing sheer lace thongs with their hands cupped behind their heads, and on some of the cards, girls were entangled with other girls; their lipsticked cherry mouths open, ready to give and receive, doe-eyes gazing at the camera.

Melusine threw the cards down in disgust.

But she was aroused.

When she and Ana were young and at school together, they'd tease each other, saying "was that a positively pant-wetting experience for you, my dear?"

Melusine knew that while she'd never tell Ana what had just occurred, it was without doubt, pant-wetting.

She felt excited, disturbed and ashamed; her groin was hot and tight and her lace panties rubbed roughly against the softness of her swollen flesh.

She caught sight of the Excalibur hotel, modeled like a Disney castle and she pushed her way inside. She was nearly hallucinating with tiredness but she was aching with a sudden and fierce longing that the cards had woken in her.

The interior of the Excalibur was shabby and Melusine wrinkled her nose at the casino aroma of powdered carpet freshener mixed with spilled alcohol, cigarette smoke, and cheap perfume.

She walked in a daze, not sure what she was looking for, but searching. She stopped to watch the tabletop showgirls; some were sensual and engaged, dancing as if they actually meant it, while others were bored in their feathered bikinis and one girl was even snapping gum. Melusine could imagine the girl on a grassy lawn in a small American town, swinging a hula-hoop at a family barbecue, with all the uncles watching appreciatively.

Melusine moved on and soon found herself transfixed by a poster for The Apollo Boys; a male revue group of muscle-bound young men who seemed to be looking directly at her and the hotness inside her grew and she could feel her tight nipples brushing against the lace of her bra. She did not care if the men were young enough to be her son; she imagined slipping her hand down into their tight underwear and feeling the hot solid hardness of smooth cock.

Then she noticed a group of women in their forties, spilling out of their clothes every which way, and tottering on high heels, already drunk with lust and alcohol and she felt a terrible shame for her thoughts and her desire. She told herself that she was not like them but she was still on fire and she rushed back to her hotel with a raw ache in her belly.

She was relieved to find a note from Hans; he was out with his colleagues and she wasn't to wait up.

Grateful that she didn't have to worry about his return, she shed her clothes and stood under the shower, masturbating with a fury she had not known in a long time, with the water a river of tears running down her face and her mouth an open silent scream as she came.

When she had finished, she leaned against the wall, wishing she had paid more attention to the sex toy novelty stores.

Tomorrow. I'll buy myself a treat tomorrow. Something to fuck me hard. I'm sorry, Ingeborg, to be so crass but this place has woken me from my coma and I feel as if I'm starving; I want to feast, rip flesh with my teeth and howl at the moon. I apologize, Ingeborg. You were the one with genius, I am merely a body.

Momentarily satiated, she stood in front of the bathroom mirror and studied herself. Her breasts were as fine as any of the card girls, despite her being twice their age, and her legs were better than most and her waist was tight and her stomach flat.

She caressed her body, knowing it would not be long before the all-consuming hunger returned, wanting more. She did not recognize her expression; she was angry, dark, fierce.

She checked the time. It was well after midnight.

She climbed into bed and took half a sleeping pill from the stash her doctor had given her for the plane ride. She knew she was too wound up to sleep without help and she lay awake with her hand between her legs, waiting for the pill to work.

3.

IN THE MORNING, it is too early to hit the Strip and Melusine heads for the pool, bumping into the man in the elevator on the way. She is half-hoping that the coolness of a swim will help her come to her senses while another part of her argues: let's not come to our senses at all, let's follow this path of awakened desire and see where it leads.

She makes a note to ask Hans where she is supposed to get the towels for the swimming pool.

She wades into the icy water. The pool area is crowded but she's the only one swimming. The cold feels wonderful, exhilarating.

She thinks about Hans who must have come back to the hotel while she was sleeping her drugged sleep. He was gone again before she woke, and he left her a note: *Enjoy your day. Don't wait up tonight.*

The sun feels glorious and she stretches out, wriggling her toes. When she looks up, she is startled to see a young man across the pool eying her with appreciation and she blushes. He's in his early thirties, with thick wild blonde hair and a large tattoo on the side of his arm. He is not nearly as hot as he thinks he is. She puts on her sunglasses and pretends to hide behind the German magazine she's brought but she watches the young man watching her. There is something sleazy about him; he is very clearly on the make, and she raises her magazine to block the view.

She reads and swims until noon, taking turns between the cold pool and the swirling hot tub but her yearning to be out on the Strip soon asserts its power. She goes back to the room, changes and heads out, making straight for the Excalibur. In spite of the language barrier, she manages to buy herself a ticket to the nine p.m. show of The Apollo Boys.

Positively pant-wetting. She smiles and wishes Ana was with her. She's certain that Ana would be game for some fun but nevertheless Ana would be astounded at Melusine's interest in such things.

She leaves the hotel, with her ticket a hot throbbing promise in her purse, and strolls down the Strip, taking a side street that leads her to a few high-end art galleries. She stops in at one featuring Richard MacDonald; sculptures based on the balletic, gymnastic and naked bodies of the Cirque du Soleil performers, with their musculature extreme and taut. The bodies are exquisite, with faces contorted in pain as they push themselves beyond their limits. The art pivots and turns on stands and the displays are huge, larger than life.

Melusine wishes she could touch them; wishes they would come to life and dance with her. The gallery owner attempts to engage her in conversation but she shakes her head. *German.*

She goes into the next gallery that is filled with glass sculptures by Dale Chihuly and the art is magnificent; glossy, lush and iridescent, but all she can see are gigantic penises and open vaginas, blood-red, engorged and pulsating with passion, ripe to explode.

She leaves the gallery and walks further down the Strip, finding a novelty store filled with sex toys. She examines the erotic fortune cookies but their messages are lost on her. She picks up cookie cutters in the shape of penises and wonders what her fellow librarians would say if she whipped up a batch of sugar-frosted chocolate cocks.

Delicious, nein? Ach, only joking...

She looks at shot glasses adorned with crude genitals, as if

. craft group had sculpted them in a hurry. She is only really interested in the dildos but she is too shy to approach that area of the store; when she notices that no one is paying her the slightest attention, she goes over to examine what is on offer.

Half an hour later she settles for a giant black cock that promises to pleasure her with three speeds. She purchases it with Hans's money and feels a confused sense of anger, triumph and nervous excitement.

She rushes back to her hotel room, rips open the packaging and lies down on the bed, ready to explode like a Chihuly wildflower. But she finds the dildo no more erotic than the handle of her hairbrush and the shuddering speeds bring her electric toothbrush to mind. She licks it experimentally, then she slaps it against the palm of her hand.

"I think I'll call you Kurt," she tells it. "Well, my friend, I guess I'm just not the right woman for you. Maybe we'll get on better after I've seen my show tonight."

She pulls the gold satin comforter over her and thinks about her marital sex life. She asks herself if she's the one to blame for the bland nature of their tepid physical forays. Perhaps she needs to be more take-charge and sexually aggressive but Hans has never seemed to encourage that kind of thing. She's fairly positive that their routine lovemaking has been dictated by him, as are his regimented, although not unwelcome, foot rubs.

Hans is a stickler for a foot rub. He insists on massaging her feet with unusual dedication.

A woman has to shelter her real feelings in the ones she's invented, just to stand the whole business with the feet, but above all to stand the greater part that's missing, for someone who is so hung up on feet is bound to be greatly neglecting something else.

No! Melusine had argued with Ingeborg. *He's not hung up on feet, he's not. It's his way of showing affection.*

"A long day standing?" Hans would say, which was their signal.

"Yes," she'd reply. She had learned early on that saying no was not an option; when she had said no, not realizing the importance of his request, he had given her the silent treatment until she acquiesced.

"Wash your feet then," he would say in response to her agreement, and she'd trot off to the bathroom, returning with a towel in hand and her feet clean and fragrant.

Hans rubbed her feet two to three times a week for at least an hour each time.

There had been one incident in the early years when Melusine had developed a hint of the callus on the third toe of her right foot. "You need to take care of that," Hans had said with distaste, badgering her to completely remove the thick and hardened skin so that the foot rubs might resume and Melusine had obliged.

It wasn't that she didn't enjoy the foot rubs; she loved the attention and she found whole thing wonderfully sensual and relaxing. She wondered how many men put that much effort into taking care of their wives and Hans was beyond skillful; he brought her to ecstasy.

"It's really quite orgasmic," she had said to Ana, some months into her married life. "The way he does it, my whole body vibrates with pleasure."

Ana had looked skeptical and Melusine had dropped the subject, feeling disloyal to Hans for having said anything to Ana about it at all. Right from the start, the foot rubs were a private, almost sacred thing between them.

Even Jonas had been taught not to disturb his parents when his father was rubbing his mother's feet. As a toddler, and later a teenager, he had known to leave them be, with their dim lighting and their soft classical music; his mother's feet in his father's lap and her head resting on a cushion.

Hans had forbade Melusine to have pedicures in any of the local nail bars. "You could catch all kinds of communicable diseases," he'd said.

So Melusine pedicured her own feet, becoming so artistically adept that she began to do Ana's feet also.

"If you ever give up your day job," Ana joked, "I'll be your most regular customer."

Melusine took to rubbing Ana's feet and the look of bliss that crossed Ana's face made her laugh.

"Ha!" Melusine said. "You see! How good does this feel?"

"It's better than sex," Ana said, "don't stop. Don't ever stop. Hans does this to you three times a week?"

"Two at the very least, but usually three."

"Dear god," Ana said. "The man is an angel."

Hans had won a convert.

But as great as the foot rubs were, Melusine had, over the past few years, felt a growing disinterest and separation from the intimacy of the moment. She could no longer completely relax into a state of mellow happiness but mentally ran through a list of chores or contemplated a menu for a dinner party as she lay there with her eyes squeezed shut.

And, these days, as soon as Hans was done, Melusine would leap up and resume the thread of her activities as if she had enjoyed a mild but quickly forgotten distraction.

Lying in her bed in Las Vegas, she pulls the gold satin comforter off her feet, and examines them, recalling the great distance they've walked the previous day and she wonders how many calluses she'll have by the end of the holiday. She does not care a whit.

She feels sleepy and has a nap, then she goes out for a slice of pizza, excited by the prospect of the night ahead. She feels like a teenager getting ready for a party that would be banned by parents, if only they knew. She joins the crowd of women forcing their way into the nine p.m. show of The Apollo Boys.

There are all kinds of women jostling to get in; every age, size, and ethnicity is accounted for. The women are all clutching large drinks and Melusine has hers, a long red bong-shaped container filled with vodka and orange juice. The women are dressed in a wide range of fashions from über-conservative to slut-maximized, and the make-up is thick and heavy.

Melusine's nostrils close, objecting to the many warring perfumes, not to mention the overpowering chemical stench of strong hair spray that fills the tiny corridor as the women file into the theatre. A woman's yellow feather boa floats into Melusine's drink and she plucks it out and wonders if the small corridor wouldn't be considered a safety hazard in the event of a fire. The corridor finally leads them to the theatre door.

Well, pseudo-theatre. Melusine's not sure what she was expecting but this conference-like venue is not it. The cavernous room is filled with rows of tables that remind her of the cafeteria at university. She had imagined herself sitting in a curved velvet banquette, with privacy to enjoy the show. Instead, she has to squeeze into one empty seat in between two groups of women, the one group evidently celebrating a divorce, and thrusting bare ring fingers at the bachelorette crowd opposite. The bride of the party, resplendent in a frothy veil and tight white mini-skirt is shouting insults back to the divorcees that Melusine is grateful she cannot understand.

She takes a sip from her giant-sized drink and hopes that the alcohol will help get her more into the swing of things. She has no idea whether it is the raucous screaming women or the banquet-of-plenty seating arrangements or perhaps it's the harshness of the spotlights but she feels alone, bobbing in a sea of strangeness.

The lights dim at that moment and the women's screams build to a crescendoed frenzy of anticipation. Melusine had thought the decibel level had been extreme before!

A cocky blonde master of ceremonies struts onstage and speaks quickly and incomprehensibly, eliciting further hysteria from the crowd. Melusine gathers that he has divided the room into two halves, pitting the two sides against one another in a shouting match.

Hemmed in, she is trapped. She cannot leave even if she wants to.

Just as Melusine is wondering if the show itself will ever get started, a disco beat sounds a throbbing bass and the first Apollo Boy runs out onto the stage. Melusine thinks he looks like he belongs on the cover of a Harlequin romance novel; his hair is long, brown and curly and he has a soulful gaze. In fact, he is quite unblinking as he faces the crowd. He gyrates his hips, his cutaway cowboy chaps emphasizing that he sports a generously endowed package.

The women scream and whistle and pound the tables with their fists. The divorcees and the bachelorettes have declared a ceasefire and are united in their appreciation of the Spanish cowboy who has snapped off his vest and chaps and is straddling a chair; one foot on the chair back, the other on the seat. He tips the chair forward and swan dives from the stage onto the nearest table. He slides down the length of the table, scattering drinks as he clears his way. When he gets to the far end, he stands and gyrates his crotch, pulling his pale blue thong this way and that.

Even from where she sits, Melusine can see that his buttocks are rock hard and jelly bean shiny. Women grab at him, clawing and reaching. The Apollo Boy, clearly more a man, never loses his smile, flashing his ultra-bright pearly whites as he twists this way and that. He makes his way back to the stage, bestowing hugs and kisses along the way. He bounces back up onto the stage and takes a bow next to the MC, and his chest is heaving with exertion. The women scream and pound their applause.

Next up is a Michael Jackson impersonator who moonwalks and quick-steps. His socks are glaring patches of snowy whiteness against the backdrop of the dark stage.

"Take it off, take it off," the women chant, a soccer match war cry. Although Melusine has no understanding, she knows what they are saying.

Soon stripped to his thong, Apollo Michael calls for a volunteer and a conservative woman in her fifties is hefted up to the stage, aided by the MC and her eager friends.

She lies down on the stage floor, her long polyester frock seemingly incongruous and her expression perplexed, but she's trying hard to look enthused. Then again, Melusine tells herself, this could be entirely her own projection of the woman's reaction, maybe the woman's having the time of her life. Because certainly, Melusine is not.

Apollo Michael lowers himself splitsville close to the woman's face, his crotch inches from her mouth. She lies supine, with her arms stiffly alongside her body; she's a very still, very wide-eyed corpse. Melusine wonders what would happen if Apollo lost his balance and plopped downwards; would he smother the woman with his balls and penis? That would make for a story back at the woman's workplace. Melusine's mind is wandering; she is not concentrating. But the Apollo Boy does not fall, he stays like that, balanced and suspended for ages as the frenzy grows while all the time, the woman lies motionless.

Apollo Michael finally elevates his legs into a handstand, flips backwards and stands, and he helps the woman to her feet. The woman is all smiles, clearly relieved that her part in the show is over. They hug and the woman is helped offstage to loud applause, clutching the free calendar that the MC has given her as a prize for her endeavors.

Melusine wonders if the next act will be more arousing. Because to this point, the boys, okay, men, have been more like sleazy gymnasts than erotic dancers. She takes a long swallow of her drink and wishes that she'd ordered two on the way in.

The MC seems to be talking for ages. He's gathered three women onstage: a stout well-endowed middle-aged woman, a skinny blonde in her twenties, and a plump black woman with neatly coiffed hair. There's a lot of screaming from the crowd but Melusine has no idea as to what's going on.

The MC hands the microphone to the skinny blonde who

startles Melusine by screeching out a high-pitched orgasm with her eyes closed and her lips close to fellating the microphone.

She grins and hands the microphone to the black woman who responds with a groaning orgasm while she rubs her hands all over the MC's body.

The third woman's orgasm is a series of *oh gods* that culminate in a piercing catlike yowl.

The crowd is wild, pounding the tables, whistling and stamping their feet. The three women take their free calendars and are helped off the stage.

Melusine finishes the last of her drink. She is about to get up and force her way to the door when the next act kicks in: a gigantic blonde man with a huge shaggy mop of hair struts centre stage. He has bigger shoulders than Melusine had imagined possible on a human and he flexes like a bat-winged bodybuilder. He immediately jumps off the stage and heads for Melusine's table. She is glad she is seated at the very far end. Meanwhile the divorcees and the bachelorettes nearly have seizures of delight. The blonde hunk sashays and flexes his way down the length of the table, stopping a couple of feet away from Melusine.

He is glistening and tanned; a man sculpted from butterscotch and steel. He drops to his knees and crawls forward on the table and Melusine is treated to an up close and personal view of his cleanly waxed butt crack. She can smell baby oil and antiperspirant and when he turns to face her, she sees that he is far from a boy and that the effort of his exertions are costing him dearly.

She catches his eye for the briefest of seconds and is reminded of a caged lion she had seen at the zoo when Jonas was a boy. Big blonde Apollo makes his way back to the stage but not before Melusine sees the deep scratches across his thighs where the women have clawed at him.

She has had enough.

All of a sudden she can take it no longer and she pushes

her chair back and shoves a pathway to the door. She fights through the screaming women and is relieved when she finally reaches the door and pulls it open.

She stands outside the theatre door, her chest heaving, the whoops and yells muffled and distant behind her. Her heart is pounding hard and there's a ringing in her ears. She tries to catch her breath and wonders if she's having a panic attack although she's never experienced one before.

She feels disappointed and furious. The show was a rip-off, there was nothing sensual about it whatsoever, it had not even amounted to a cheap thrill; it was irritating and boring.

She is wired and angry and she stalks off down the Strip, taking every girly card on offer, and again feeling that hot arousal. Why does she get aroused from the cards and not from the show? Once again she's ashamed of herself. She's a feminist, she's always believed that, and yet here she is, feeling sexually aroused by women who are working in the sex trade, surely the most demeaning means of survival.

Why am I aroused by them? Do I envy them? What could I possibly envy? Oh, I hate this, I hate feeling; it was better when I felt nothing at all.

The crowd on the Strip grows bigger. Melusine is hungry and thirsty. She stops on a whim to buy a large drink in a big plastic bottle shaped like the Eiffel Tower, choosing it over a soccer ball, gallon jug, and gigantic bong.

"Tequila or rum?" the bartender asks. She figures out his question and she points to the rum; she'll have a pina colada. The man then says a whole lot of other things and Melusine just nods and pushes money at him. He hands her the change and the drink.

The alcohol is raw and strong and she downs a good third of it without even pausing. There is ice cream mixed in it too and she thinks it's all quite delicious, particularly the bits that are neat rum. Soon she cannot feel the pain in her feet from all her walking and the night-lights host multiple haloes and the whole world moves in a motion blur. She tells herself to take it easy with the drink but she doesn't want to. She takes large sips and it is nearly all gone by the time she gets back to her hotel. She is quite drunk and has to concentrate on getting through the security gate.

She leans on the wall beside the elevator, steadying herself.

In her drunken confusion, she goes to the wrong floor. She stabs the key card into the door repeatedly, hating Hans for his prediction having come true. She cannot face going back down to the lobby and she curses Hans for not being in the room to help her. She is determined to make the card work, and she will not give up, cursing loudly in German, as if that might help.

She is bent over the keyhole, her nose inches from the door handle when the door abruptly opens and a man looks down at her. "You're not Hans," she says stupidly, standing up awkwardly and leaning against the wall with one hand. To her surprise, the man answers her in German.

"No, I'm not Hans. What room are you looking for?" he asks and his manner is kind.

She tells him. He laughs and points to his room number. She is on the wrong floor. She is aware that she is disheveled and clutching her empty Eiffel Tower bottle.

"I'm so sorry," she says, "and this time of night too."

The man tells her he doesn't mind. She can see he's looking at her appraisingly, and he is attractive, and for a moment she thinks about walking into his room and shedding her clothes in an act of brazen declaration.

Then she thinks the only thing that would come of all of that, would be her falling asleep on his sofa. She straightens up and thanks the man again.

"If you ever need a midnight friend to chat to," he calls after her, grinning, "you know where to find me."

Melusine turns to him and smiles, grateful for the joke. She goes back to her room and wonders where Hans is and what he is up to. She considers the possibility of Hans being a secret gambler, which would explain his reluctance at her joining him on the trip but right now, she does not care about him and she is just glad to be alone.

She has a long hot shower and climbs into bed naked, enjoying the feeling of the cool and silky sheets against her body. She thinks about giving Kurt the dildo another try but she cannot be bothered. She feels horribly sober and thinks it felt much nicer when the rum was potent in her blood. She decides she'll have another pina colada for breakfast — she should have checked what time they start serving them.

She lies in bed, thinking back to her teenage years when she would rush home from school while her parents were still at work, and soak for hours in a bubble bath and masturbate until she was wrinkled and the bath water was cold, and she was blissfully at peace. Boys had been far less interesting to her than her fantasies about abstract love and she had been content to harbor a crush on her beloved author and poet Ingeborg Bachmann, reading her work, memorizing her words and letting them be the voice of her longing.

For some reason she could never explain to herself or dare approach with anyone, not even her best friend Ana, Melusine had always felt that she did not fit in. She did not fit among the unquestioning people who went from day to day seamlessly doing whatever was required of them while she stood to the side of her own life, a restless ghostlike voyeur, mimicking the actions of others; her movements fragments of seconds behind but faking things quickly enough so that no one ever saw the disparity.

Melusine had wondered if her distanced view of life stemmed from being the only child of two elderly parents but when she was introduced to the works of Ingeborg Bachmann, esteemed post-war German-language poet and author, she realized it wasn't that but that reasons didn't matter anyway — the only thing that mattered was that she no longer felt alone. Ingeborg, with her dark Sylvia Plath-like observations, put voice to every flotsam anxiety; she was solidarity personified.

It was as if Ingeborg had written for an audience of one; written love letters to Melusine by way of poetry and prose. Words that found ways to express the separation between her and the rest of the world, even though Ingeborg herself ultimately felt that she had failed words, and that words had failed her.

Melusine carried Ingeborg's books with her, merging her writer heroine with the unnamed protagonist in *Malina*, Ich, and melding the two into one über-friend who saw the foolishness of sex-crazed pimply school kids and the general meaninglessness of everything.

Melusine was a virgin when she married Hans. She was twenty-three. It had been a matter of determined Catholic principle on her part; she had been a stalwart churchgoer because it was important to her mother, and Hans had encouraged her sexual abstinence, supporting her purity and purpose.

On their wedding night, Hans had turned to her. "I hope you don't mind," he said, "but I purchased this to help you, it being your first time."

'It' was a tube of lubricating gel and she had been both insulted and relieved. "Thank you," she had said, but he used too much and it was hard for her to feel anything other than the cool snake-like slithering of his narrow cock.

And the sex did not change in tone, personality or modus operandi in the years that followed: Thursday nights, he would lean over to his nightstand, fish out the tube of jelly, lube her up and pump away in silence until he achieved orgasm. Melusine would lie there, unmoving, her eyes open and her hands resting lightly on his shoulders. When he was done, he would wipe himself off with a hand towel he had placed next to the bed, pull up his pajama bottoms and go to sleep while she would slip out of bed and go and wash up, hating the cold sticky gel and semen running down her legs.

Melusine would return to bed and, as her husband slept,

she'd run her hands down her legs, her beautiful legs that
Hans never seemed to notice or simply took for granted and
she often wondered if other husbands bothered to take off
their pajamas while making love to their wives. She has never
felt Hans's bare chest on hers and for that she now feels glad.
These days, after so many years, her spontaneous desires having
faded, his pale, cool, hairless flesh seems distasteful to her, and
the intimacy of skin embarrassing.

Melusine's best friend Ana had sighed over the injustice of
Melusine's leggy beauty. Ana was chunky and stocky but her
face was that of an angel while Melusine felt herself to be
plain at best.

She and Ana had known each other since they were toddlers,
and had been inseparable apart from a brief period when Ana
had watched Melusine leave school early to hang out with the
speed freak druggie girls.

One day at school, Ana broached the subject and asked
Melusine, "and so? What's it like? Speed, I mean?"

*"It is an orgy of the wind, the lust of mountains where a
pious star loses its way, collides and dissolves into dust."*

"You're quoting from that stupid poetry book again, aren't
you? Come on, Melu, I mean it, tell me the appeal."

Melusine paused. "It's incredible. I never knew I could feel
that alive. I cannot describe it to you. It's like every single
nerve-ending is ignited by crystal diamonds and washed clean
with the sharpness of glass and I feel like I could shatter and
fly through the universe and I am invincible."

Ana looked at her. "How long are you going to do this for?
It seems to be becoming a habit."

Melusine shrugged. "I'm not sure. I don't know."

"Your parents," Ana said, and those two small words carried volumes of meaning. "It would kill them if you really go
down this road, Melu, you know that. You were their miracle
when they thought they could never have children. Not like
my parents who had five kids and can hardly remember our

names or who's who."

Melusine laughed. "Your parents know every single thing about every one of you," she said.

Ana had paused. "How do you do it, do you take a pill, snort a powder, what? I've always wondered."

"The first few times I took pills," Melusine said, "but the last two times, I injected."

Ana was shocked. "But how did you know how much to use or how to do it?"

"Marthe showed me. She was very nice, very gentle. It felt quite erotic actually, her shooting me up. Like I would imagine lovemaking."

"So now you're a lesbian?"

Melusine blushed. "No, Ana. I'm just saying it felt good, it was very erotic, the intimacy of it."

"Marthe's a manipulative bitch. I'm telling you. You think she's your friend but she's not. If you stop going to her drug parties, she'll drop you like a stone."

"They aren't drug parties," Melusine objected, knowing that they were.

"Melu, get a grip, okay? Marthe's going to end up a scabby junkie. You think she's so cool but imagine her a couple of years from now. No teeth, bad skin, you've seen what happens. Your whole life will be ruined."

"I don't want to talk about it, you're bugging me big time, Ana. Back off."

Ana let it go. "Let's go clubbing tonight then? Dress up like Cyndi Lauper and go dancing."

"Clubbing? The community centre spins a disco ball above a basketball court, we all wear fingerless lace gloves and put food colouring in our hair. Yeah, right, big time party."

Ana got angry. "Fine. So go hang out with your druggie friends, see if I care."

Melusine watched her friend march off. She couldn't tell Ana that she was struggling with life and the seeming pointlessness of it all. Only Ingeborg seemed to understand.

I am cut off from myself and from everything else.

Melusine returned to Marthe that night but the thrill had been diluted by Ana's bleak prognosis. Melusine felt slightly removed from it all and even Marthe's sensual touch seemed cooler, more rushed and impersonal.

"You know you can do this yourself," Marthe said, her tone slightly sharp. "And I can hook you up with a guy. He's got lots of stuff, he'll keep you happy forever."

Melusine, enjoying the crystalline surge of godlike power, was not listening to Marthe. She ran out into the night and she ran and ran, into the forest, with the leaves slapping at her face and the smell of loam strong in her nostrils and her ears throbbing with the loud drumbeat of her pounding heart. The blackness was thick and the night was full of sounds. She ran until she could run no longer and then she lay under a tree, feeling the worms crawling in the earth beneath her and the insects burrowing in the leaves and she herself was a glowing prism of light; a star burning in a frenzy while the trees stretched and yawned and grew and the leaves groaned as they flexed green fingers.

She lay there in the dirt until the euphoria faded and the buzz-glow dimmed and it was just her, Melusine, tired and dirty; cold and horribly awake, exhausted and far from home.

She had lost her shoes and she limped home, arriving to find her mother brewing coffee.

"Long party?" her mother asked.

"Communing with nature."

"Is this communing going to be a regular occurrence?"

Melusine gulped a large swallow of scalding coffee and took a slice of toast that her mother was about to eat. "No, Mami," she said. "I'm done communing."

The tension fell away from her mother's shoulders. "Good then. And clean your room, it's a terrible mess." She turned away so that Melusine could not see her cry.

Later that day, Melusine told Ana she was done experimenting and Ana hit her hard on the arm with a punch she'd learned from her brothers.

"Ow! What did you do that for?"

"For freaking me out. We were all worried. You've been messing around with that stuff for ages, you think we didn't know? You're like a sister to me, Melu, and you drive me crazy but I love you."

"I'm sorry," Melusine said, although she wasn't. "But it's water under the bridge now, okay? Let's never talk about it again."

Melusine went on to study philosophy and German literature while Ana focused on selecting her future husband and Marthe ignored Melusine with lip-curled disdain. But Melusine no longer cared and years later Ana proved right; Marthe dropped out, lost her youth, her teeth, and most of her brain cells. Melusine came across her panhandling, gave her ten dollars and was grateful for having dodged that bullet.

And now decades later, lying in her bed in Las Vegas, Melusine questions if her longing for grinding sex is like her once-upon-a-time craving for amphetamines; it had come out of nowhere and was threatening to dislodge everything she knew and stood for.

She had recently reread Ingeborg's complicated novel *Malina,* the first in a planned series of three novels on styles of dying and how patriarchal society murders women in seemingly invisible ways. In *Malina,* the protagonist's lover tells her: "Your problem is you don't have anything that needs you to be there!"

Melusine feels as if she has nothing that needs her to be anywhere at all. She decides that she needs to get out of Las Vegas for a day. Get out into the desert, see the Grand Canyon. Get a grip.

She swallows half a sleeping pill, happy to have a plan.

4.

THE NEXT MORNING she wakes to find Hans lying beside her, his hands folded behind his head, his eyes wide open. Melusine is glad she's hidden Kurt, the giant black dildo, as well as her ticket stub to The Apollo Boys.

"I love Vegas," she says to Hans as they dress and get ready to go down to breakfast and she is surprised; she really does love it though it is aggravating her volcanic emotional disruptions.

Hans looks surprised. "I really thought you'd hate it," he says. "All the chaos. Vegas is humanity at its chaotic worst."

"But it's a glittering chaos," she says. "*Eine glitzernde chaos.* Hans, can you book that show *Zumanity* for me? It's too hard for me to try to explain to the concierge. And I want to go to the Skywalk at the Grand Canyon — and you need to talk to the concierge before you go, because I want to go today. So you can't leave before she gets here, okay?"

Hans looks at her. "You want to see *Zumanity*? Of all the Cirque du Soleil shows, that's the one you want? It's like a glamourized strip show. Why don't you go and see Celine Dion? Or Donny and Marie? Or one of the other Cirque shows?"

"Are you crazy? Donny and Marie? Give me a break. Hans, for once, just do what I want, and book my shows, okay?"

They stare at each other and she tries to recall a time when she found him endearing, funny and astute. He has not changed. He still brings her flowers and thoughtfully-wrapped first editions of obscure German novels that he hunted down for her, but she is suddenly aware that he's lost in his own world of pain and she is too preoccupied by her issues to be able to ask him what is going on. She wonders if he too has been triggered into an emotional wasteland by the empty chair at the kitchen table, a chair that, previously filled, used to unite them as a family at dinner. Has the departure of their son brought home anew the terrible loss that Hans had suffered in his late teens?

He straightens his tie. "I swear Melusine, I have no idea right now who you are. I know your parents' death is still recent and Jonas has left home, so you have a lot of empty nest syndrome going on but still..."

"Right now, Hans," she says, "I couldn't agree with you more. I don't know who I am either. Maybe I'm not coping so well with Jonas's departure, or my parents' death. And I agree, it doesn't help that Jonas is seeing some gothic Cinderella who's so far removed from all the girls he used to date, the ones that I understood. But whatever, let me go and see my shows and just enjoy my holiday, okay?"

He nods, wishing only to be away from her. "I'll book the Grand Canyon tour for you after we've had breakfast. I'm sure you'll be able to go today. And I'll be back in time to take you out for dinner tonight too, so that's your day taken care of. By the way, I phoned and Mimi's fine."

She looks at him uncomprehendingly. Oh, right, the dog.

"That's good," she says, absently.

5.

AN HOUR LATER, Melusine is waiting outside the hotel for the tour bus to take her to the Grand Canyon. She's drinking a cup of coffee. The hotel offers free Starbucks coffee 24-seven and she admits she enjoys it although she misses her good German coffee that delivers caffeine with such vehement potency. She looks at her watch. She wonders if the tour bus missed her hotel or if it left already and Hans got the details wrong. She sits forward on the wrought-iron bench, admiring the wild pink oleander flowers, the vibrant green grass and the cobalt sky, and loving the postcard vividness of Las Vegas even in the daytime.

A man carrying a large camera pushes his way through the front door and stops to light a cigarette with an old-fashioned Zippo. To her discomfit, it's the man from the second floor, the one whose door she'd repeatedly tried to get into when she was drunk and exhausted. She hopes, foolishly, that he won't remember the incident, or her.

He stands next to her, smoking his cigarette, in no hurry to leave.

Melusine carefully avoids making eye contact. He was witness to her at a time when she was distraught and undone and she feels embarrassed. She notices again that he's good-looking, although he carries too much weight. He's got curly brown hair with a reddish tinge, a square head, a strong jaw and a pug-shaped nose. He looks like he could have been a rugby player at university. She blushes and stares at her feet, hating herself for her thoughts, how obsessed she is with men and their bodies and the various related desires thereof.

"The grass is fake," the man says in German and he grins at her. He's got deep dimples when he smiles and a cleft in his chin.

She looks up at him. She is surprised that he is offering so mundane an avenue of conversation when all she can think about is what his cock would feel like. It seems she is obsessed with this too; what a man's hardware would look like, how it would feel in her hand and oh, dear god, what it would taste like. She has never held Hans's cock or taken it in her mouth, and now, as she cannot help but think of it, she is filled with a vision of a limp Chinese noodle, flaccid, narrow and pale. Poor Hans, he has done nothing to deserve her vitriol. Or has he? Did all husbands have the same sex with their wives for over twenty years and expect that to be good enough? Maybe they did. She has no way of knowing and no one to ask. She supposes she could ask Ana, but that would be too revealing, far too humiliating. Ana has always let her know that she enjoys a great sex life with Dirk, although she had told Melusine that when Dirk mentioned he would like them to join the swingers in the neighbourhood, just for one night you understand, to see if she'd like it, she had fixed him with an icy stare and shut that idea down. For good.

"And he'd better not be getting any on the side either," she had told Melusine. "And if he does, he'd better make sure that I never find out about it because if I do, I'll boil his balls for breakfast and feed them to the dog. And he knows it. Isn't it enough that I dress up like a nurse and wear those latex boots that really hurt my feet? I mean I'm all for a bit of fun and I don't mind trying new things and he knows that, but I don't share and I told him that before we got married."

Nurse's uniform? Latex boots? Melusine had changed the subject. She had wondered though, where one would find things like that, in their small town. But then she reasoned that Dirk did a lot of work with high-end vehicles in Frankfurt and he most likely shopped there.

"Yes, it's plastic grass," the man continues, distracting her. "I guess it's because it's the desert. It's too hard to keep the real stuff watered and lush and green and they want everything in Vegas to look perfect. Disneyland for adults is what they want, with everything nice and bright and shiny."

He sits down on the bench next to her. "Do you mind?" he asks, sitting down as he does so, so what can she say? She nods, meaning she doesn't mind, or if she does, that it's too late anyway.

"Well even if it's fake, it looks good," she says and the man laughs.

"That's Vegas, isn't that right? Doesn't matter how fake it is, so long as it looks good. It's all about looking good. If you don't look good, don't bother showing up."

"I've seen lots of people here who don't look good," she says. "Lots of women mainly; out of shape, wearing clothes twenty years too young for them and with suntans that are just horrible. But they look so happy, running around in their evening gowns as if they're about to attend some glittering ball for the middle class — you know, big drinks in hand, more feather boas than I've seen in years, and bad cleavage."

She stops, having no idea where that came from and thinking it an entirely inappropriate utterance.

But the man just laughs. "Bad cleavage?" he asks. "From a male perspective, I'm not sure such a thing exists. But I know what you mean. And that's the beauty of Vegas; you can pretend for five minutes that you're a movie star about to get laid by the hottest thing out there, and you're young again and randy as all hell and life's one big party."

She wants to tell him that she never had that youth but she remains quiet and looks at her watch.

"What are your plans for the day?" he asks.

"Going on a tour to the Skywalk," she says, "if the bus ever gets there that is. I think my husband booked the wrong one or something."

"I'm going on that one too." The man looks amused. "Imagine that. Don't worry, the bus will be here soon."

Melusine is not happy that the man is coming on the trip. She wants to be alone with her fantasies, alone with her longing. She doesn't want a real life distraction butting in.

But she tries to be polite and she smiles.

"Great," she says, "we can enjoy the spectacular scenery together." But she looks away.

The man stretches his legs out in front of him. "Don't worry," he says, "I won't get in your headspace. I need some time to myself anyway. And forgive me for confiding in you — a total stranger — but I really need to tell someone or I'll go crazy. A few months ago, my wife lost our fifth baby, another miscarriage, and this one was in her second trimester. We thought everything was going to be fine. The nursery was ready and we had named the baby, it was a little girl. It was terrible." He looks away. "Thank god I was invited to do some work here in Vegas. Don't get me wrong, I'm totally cut up about it too, but I don't know what to do with her grief. I don't have any answers. She looks to me for answers. She looks to me and all I can see is that she's begging me to fix this; fix it, her eyes say, but I can't. I'm worried it's the end of us. And I love her."

Melusine turns to him, taken aback by his revelations, thinking it odd he would confide that much in her, a total stranger. She wonders if it's the fact that they are both German that has him assuming such familiarity. Nevertheless she is moved by his sincerity.

"Oh, I'm very sorry," she says. "I can't imagine that kind of loss. Poor you. And your poor wife."

The man nods. He folds his arms across his chest. "I had this trip planned long before and I guess I could have cancelled but I didn't. I didn't want to. And she knew that too.

She watched me packing and I knew she was thinking that I could have cancelled but what could I do? What good would I do by staying?" He sighs.

"How old is your wife?"

"She's only thirty-six. But I don't think there will be any children now. We can't even try again. It's too much for her. Too much for me. Funny, we always took it so for granted, that having babies would be so easy, so natural. That we'd have to take precautions to not let it happen too soon and now it's the opposite; now it would take a miracle for it to come true. And I never realized how long a month can be, all that waiting. And then, once the baby is conceived, there is every single long day of worrying until finally the worst nightmare happens again and again and again and then you have nothing."

Melusine has no idea what to say. "I'm sorry," she repeats and she stands up and throws away her empty coffee cup.

She thinks this man is far more eloquent than any she has ever known and again, she wonders at how much he has shared with her so soon. She tells herself that perhaps it is just because they are in Las Vegas where everything is strangely unreal; a no-man's land where honest emotions can rise up and voice themselves without any regard for place or propriety.

The bus arrives and they hand their tickets to the driver and climb inside. They are the only people on the bus.

"Thank you for listening," the man says once they're seated. "I needed to get that off my chest. Were we ever introduced?" he asks.

She smiles. "I don't think we were. I'm Melusine."

"Such a beautiful name. Is it French? I'm Gunther."

"Yes, it's French. I had a great-aunt Melusine who died before I was born. And, according to myth, my name means I'm a fairy whose lower body turns into a snake every Saturday."

"Good thing today's not Saturday," Gunther comments. "That'd be tough to explain even in Vegas."

She laughs. She is sitting next to the window, gazing out at the Strip. The bus driver makes an announcement that Melusine does not understand.

"He says even though it'll take a little longer, he's driving us down the Strip so we can see the sights and also so he can pick up the other passengers from the various hotels," Gunther translates for her.

Melusine nods.

"It must be odd," Gunther says, "to not understand anything."

"In a way it's nice. Well," she smiles and elaborates, "it's not so nice when you're lost in a hotel like I was, or anything like that, but I'm certain I'm seeing Vegas in a way no-one else might. Or perhaps not. Maybe I make too much of things. Perhaps I am just like any foreigner in a land where they don't speak the language."

But she knows she isn't telling the truth. Not being able to speak English has changed things for her.

"It's like I have more freedom because I don't understand what's being said. If I can't understand the rules, I can't be expected to follow them, can I?"

Gunther frowns though she has been making a joke. A sort of joke.

"They say what happens in Vegas stays in Vegas so I guess no one will hold you accountable for following the rules one way or the other." He seems disapproving of what she had said but she has no idea why. She tells herself she does not care and she puts on her sunglasses and stares out the window. The Strip is mostly empty, and she likes to see it this way, wide open, without the pulsating nighttime crowds.

Gunther holds his camera carefully with one hand and looks straight ahead. They are seated at the front of the bus.

The bus stops at half a dozen hotels and soon there are no empty seats left. The driver turns on the air conditioning and Melusine shivers, having preferred the natural warmth of before.

She has brought a small cardigan with her as well as her floppy sunhat and her purse is laden with sunscreen, a bottle of water and a bar of dark chocolate. She was excited when she made her purchases at the hotel store; that mundane collection of goods belied the sense of wild freedom she was feeling. She was going out into the desert; she was going to see the Grand Canyon.

The bus nears the Stratosphere tower and stops at a traffic light. Melusine sees a sex-toy novelty store to her left; the windows are covered with thick black plastic with a curvy wave to it as if the sheet of blackness had been badly fitted and buckled in the sunlight. But of course, the wave is intentional, just like everything else in Vegas; it's planned to catch the neon night-lights and mirror them, turning the shabby houses of filth into glittering palaces of beckoning delight.

The parking lot in front of the sex store is home to a strange assortment of artwork, although Melusine doubts it can even be called art — a raggedy Marilyn Monroe mannequin with thick black tape across her mouth is strapped to a battered mechanical bull who tosses her in a circular motion; the old bull is bucking with the enthusiasm of a retired circus clown.

Another worn-out fashion mannequin in full bondage gear is tied to one of a pair of playground swings. Sitting next to her, on the accompanying swing, is a small Latino child kicking herself higher and higher, unaware of the strangeness of her playground companions. Melusine looks around for the child's mother and sees a man on a cell phone who must be the girl's father; he's stocky and blunt and he glances at the child now and then.

Gunther watches Melusine.

"Freaky, no?" he says. "The kid's got no idea where she is. Look at the sign right above her head: *Nude Dancers, All Day.*"

Melusine nods and watches the girl who's swinging happily. Melusine makes a note of the store's name, thinking that she might come back later — perhaps they'll have something better than Kurt the ever-erect über impotent dildo to help her relieve her pent-up frustrations.

She watches a grungy teenage couple stop and exchange a deep-tongued kiss and she is furious with herself; she should never have let her youth leave without having experienced the normal illicit adolescent lusts. She should have been promiscuous, and she should have kissed drunken boys at parties and been drunk herself. She should have fallen into flowerbeds and other kids' parents' bedrooms and been felt up without even knowing anything about her nameless partner other than how good he tasted at that moment. She should have tasted cocks and semen and sweat, and her own juices. She has no idea what another's skin feels like, or even, stupidly, the different shapes of men's backs. She wishes she'd drawn men to her naked body, and caressed them and delighted in their differences, delighted in her pleasure of them.

But that is all gone, and it is too late. She has never had oral sex in her life and she is certain that except for moments by her own hand, she has never had an orgasm.

She wants to weep with loss and anger. She is forty-three years old and it is too late.

She looks out the window and bites her lip, hard.

They have passed through the Strip and the bus has turned onto the freeway.

Melusine is lost in her own thoughts.

I just want it for a bit. Or, I just want a bit of it. Please, don't let it be too late. In the darkness no one will know that I'm too old. In the darkness no one will say that it's too late. I don't feel old but oh, dear god, am I? What's wrong with me?

She sighs, tired. Morals, desires; it's all so tiring.

The bus travels for hours through the arid burro countryside, with the sky a flawless blue dome above. Next to her, Gunther is equally disinclined to talk. He gazes ahead or closes his eyes to doze. Melusine is sure the other couples on the bus think that they too are husband and wife. She looks down at Gunther's hands as he sleeps, noting the careful grip he keeps on his camera. His hands are strong, finely-sculpted and tanned.

Once again she thinks of Hans; his hands are pale and he has thin narrow bony fingers; fingers bleached by washing with antiseptic, fingers that change lenses to measure prescriptions and make fine adjustments.

Hans, whose hands fluttered like disturbed moths around their baby when he was born; hands that disappointingly failed to settle and caress.

And Melusine had been further disappointed when Hans's air of diffident parental reserve failed to disappear as their son grew older.

Hans had, in the most polite of ways, refused to even hold Jonas as a baby, saying that he was too nervous he'd hurt him. When Jonas was three months old and in his crib, Hans had once held the boy's tiny foot briefly and Melusine had exhaled a gust of relieved air, believing that the worst was over and that a threshold had been crossed. But the action had not heralded the emotional breakthrough that she had thought or hoped for.

Throughout the years, Hans continued to project teacherly rather than fatherly affection and Melusine had feared that her son would suffer lasting damage from his father's steady distance. Not that Hans was disinterested in Jonas — he was deeply interested in him and he dedicated much of his time to focusing on projects that they could do together; showing him how to fly kites, teaching him photography and taking a keen interest in his homework and even attending his soccer matches. But as much as Hans could be present in body and scholarly mind, his heart and love were inaccessible.

Melusine often wondered how he would have been had their child been a girl. She thought that he would have been very different. She'd suggested that they try for a second baby but Hans remarked that the world was already full of enough children and that one was exactly the correct amount of child.

Exactly the correct amount of child? Melusine had despised him at that moment, and then understood the awful consequence of allowing such a feeling to linger, so she chose to call him sensible and thoughtful instead.

"Your father is the most thoughtful man I know," she'd remark frequently throughout the years to Jonas, her constant companion when he was young. "Unlike most people who just blunder through life, your father thinks consequentially." Jonas would nod and pick at her pastry dough or peer into a mixing bowl.

Jonas was a serious little boy but exuberant, full of fun and joyful with his mother, while carefully respectful and distant with his father. He participated in Hans's projects with an almost indiscernible impatience, as if he understood that his father was trying his best and he was too polite to tell him outright that he was failing.

As a teenager, Jonas became increasingly less tolerant towards his father, and he went through a difficult period where he was downright rude to Hans. Then his anger morphed into depression and he spent a lot of time in bed, sleeping. Just when Melusine was despairing, Jonas discovered, almost by accident, that girls liked him, and being on the receiving end of their crushes cheered him up again.

His period of dating cheerleaders lasted for about two years and then he got bored of them and discovered the pothead boys instead, giving Melusine a whole new avenue of concern.

Jonas moved out of home when he started university and he had been gone for just over six months when Melusine's parents died in rapid succession. He attended both of their funerals, crying with Melusine and holding her hand, while Hans hovered, concerned but incapable of empathy, despite his ongoing pain at the devastating loss of his own sister when he was a young man. Melusine had felt bitter; surely he of all people could understand loss. And perhaps he could understand but he could not open his heart to her, or let her share his own unresolved grief, and Melusine took this to be a deliberate slight; she was filled with a bitter fury that found its way into her baking, and even her signature specialties carried a sourness she couldn't eradicate, which was why she'd prepared no more than a simple Apple Walnut Bundt cake at recent dinner parties — an offering far beneath her usual high standards.

Thinking about all of this now, she hopes she'll be able to get over her anger soon so that she might return to baking; the one creative outlet that had literally and figuratively fed her soul. She missed it, and she missed being with Jonas while she baked; he'd sit and chat for hours or do his homework or help her.

"Do you have any children?" Gunther asks her suddenly, startling her by apparently reading her mind.

"Yes. One. A boy."

Jonas feels light-years away and she chokes, swallowing down how much she misses him. "I had him when I was young although at that time it just seemed like that's what you did; you left school, got married, had a child. Although I did go to university in between, to study German Literature and Fine Art. That's where I met Hans; he was studying optometry, and we met because I was lost in the wrong cafeteria."

Gunther laughs. "I can imagine! So what is he like, your son?"

She thinks. "Self-reliant. Protective of his mother. Kind. And of course very handsome and intelligent and all the rest."

Gunther grins. "How old is he?"

"He's eighteen, nearly nineteen. He's studying engineering at university although I get the feeling he might switch to law. I had him when I was twenty-five. I'm forty-three," she says, "and I've been married for twenty one years. There, you have all the mathematical statistics of my life."

"I'm thirty-six, same age as my wife," Gunther says.

"Thirty-six feels like so long ago," Melusine muses.

"Just seven years."

"A lot can change in seven years," Melusine tells him. "Or nothing much at all which can amount to a lot, too."

She decides to change the subject. "That's a huge camera,"

she says. "Do you take pictures professionally?"

"Yes, I shoot fashion for a catalogue in London. Which is where my wife and I live. I went there after graduation, wanting to get in with the famous, or shall I say infamous, fashion crowd. I never did that but I've managed to earn a healthy living and I do my own photography on the side. I've won a lot of awards for my fine art."

"Are you trying to impress me?" She hears her voice flirting with him and she suddenly feels confused.

He smiles at her and she notices for the first time that one of his front teeth is slightly chipped and she finds this sexy. She looks down and blushes.

"Is it working?" he asks. "Because, if it's working then yes, I'm trying to impress you."

The bus pulls into their destination, and saves Melusine from answering. She cranes her head forward. "Oh, my god," she says, "look over there."

She is pointing at the Grand Canyon and it's magnificent, breathtaking. She cannot wait to get off the bus. "You're coming on the Skywalk too?" she asks Gunther, who nods.

They are led through an information area to a ticket centre with lockers where they leave their shoes and Gunther's camera, and they slip on hospital booties with large brown and beige polka dots.

"Ruins the atmosphere somewhat," Gunther observes. "Ladies and Gentlemen, your colonoscopies will begin shortly..."

Melusine smiles. "It's to protect the glass, I suppose. I do presume this thing is safe?"

"The Skywalk? Rock solid. I read that you can land seventy-one planes on it and have more than seven hundred people on it and it wouldn't budge."

"Reassuring," Melusine says and they step out.

"I must admit it's much smaller than I thought it would be. I thought it would jut out over the Canyon a lot more. This is really just a little glass circle."

"Yes, but the view's incredible," Melusine says, peering over the edge and grinning back at him. "It's elemental, raw, wild. Look, there's the Eagle Rock that it's all named after. It does look like an Eagle spreading its wings."

"Or Christ on the cross," Gunther says and she squints, trying to see it as he does.

"But look," she points to the side, "at those people right on the edge of the Canyon. Surely that's very dangerous? They have all these precautions about not scratching the glass but there's not even a little piece of rope to stop people from going too close to the edge."

Gunther looks over to where she is pointing.

"I bet I could get some very good pictures from there," he says.

"Just don't fall off," Melusine says.

"You'd care would you?" he replies and Melusine's stomach flips at the way he is smiling and she feels like a teenager on a school outing. She cannot think of a smart reply so she does not say anything and looks down through the glass floor.

"Let me take a picture of you lovely couple," one of the hovering photographers says. "Put your arms around each other and move just a little to the right. That way I can get the Eagle in."

They do as he says, and Melusine, tucked under Gunther's arm and close to him, is aware of his heat, the tang of his perspiration mixed with cologne and deodorant and the fabric softener of his shirts. She is self-conscious about her unwashed hair, and she is glad she's wearing her sunhat. She also wishes she was wearing something more fashionable — he said he's a fashion photographer and here she is, wearing a floral frock made from a polyester cotton blend so it won't wrinkle. She tells herself that she does not care what Gunther thinks and she moves away from him slightly. But the photographer is not finished and Gunther pulls her back to him and grins at the camera.

"Not used to being on this side of the lens," he says. "Make sure your polarizer is turned to maximum," he instructs the boy.

"Got it," the kid says back. "Okay, now lie on the glass floor."

"I'm not lying on the floor," Melusine says as she steps away.

Gunther shrugs at the photographer and follows Melusine.

"The Skywalk is smaller than I thought it would be too," she says. "Not much to do really once you've walked slowly around and looked down a lot. I'm ready to go and explore that dangerous-looking edge, and I want to visit the Indian Village and go to Guano Point and the other lookout."

Gunther, leaning over the railing, looks at her. "I'll catch up with you then," he says, "go ahead."

She is instantly disappointed but she nods in agreement and rushes out the doorway, throwing her booties in the bin provided and then instantly retrieving them as a souvenir. She walks through the gift shop and one of the girls on the computers calls her over and chatters, pointing at the screen. Melusine peers at the monitor and there she is, and she looks perfect with Gunther. They seem like the ideal couple, happy and relaxed.

Goes to show you never can tell.

She shrugs at the girl, turns and pushes her way out into the hot sunshine. She misses Gunther and wonders what to do next.

She takes the bus to the Guano point and the view is so spectacular it makes her want to cry. She buys a coffee and sits on top of a rock, watching the ravens swoop for scraps of junk food. She gazes at the people around her; they are scrambling and chattering and taking pictures of each other and laughing and she feels unpleasantly invisible.

She stares vacuously at the river far below, it looks to be a mere trickle on the Canyon bed.

"You look very philosophical," Gunther says, appearing next to her and sitting down. "I bought a hamburger, you want half?"

She is flooded with happiness. "I'd love half," she says, "as long as that won't leave you hungry?"

He shakes his head. "This place is fantastic, even better than the Skywalk if you ask me. I love it. Did you go to the Indian village yet?"

She shakes her head, her mouth full.

"Me neither. We'll go after this. Let's climb this mountain of rocks, right to the top."

He is as excited as a kid.

"I don't really have the right shoes on," she apologizes. "You go. I'll applaud your daring from the safety of solid ground."

He nods and finishes his hamburger. Melusine watches his figure grow tiny as he climbs the rocks and stops and waves at her from time to time. She shades her eyes and waves back.

Later, once he has come down, laughing and breathing hard, they explore the village and crawl into a healing tent together. The walls are made of strong logs and there's the aromatic smell of wood smoke.

"Maybe if I say a prayer in here, then my wife will be healed," Gunther says. "But I doubt it. I think we're broken, she and I."

To her surprise, he starts to cry and she holds him, his camera in between them, jutting into her breastbone. She strokes his head and he cries like a child.

"I can't fix it," he says. "I don't think anything can fix it."

He finally stops crying and she digs in her purse for a Kleenex. She hands it to him and he blows his nose loudly, leaving a speck of tissue on his chin. She wants to brush it off but that would seem overly familiar despite the rawness of the moment they have just shared.

"Sorry," he says.

"Don't be," she replies.

A young boy pokes his head into the tent. "You guys making out?" he asks in English and Gunther laughs.

"Nope. We're just leaving, it's all yours."

He explains what the boy said and Melusine admits to herself that she wishes they had been making out. They walk outside and Gunther points to a tiny antelope squirrel that is sitting up on its hind legs watching them. Drums sound from the village enclave and the sun is lower in the sky; it is early afternoon and Melusine wishes the day would never end.

Gunther buys them each an ice cream and they sit on the edge of the Canyon. He teases her because she licks the melting bottom of the ice cream first to stop it from running down the cone, while he eats from the top. He eats quickly while she savours every mouthful.

When they are finished, he leans back and puts one arm behind her. He does not touch her but she can feel his arm encircling the area behind her back. She is filled with a craving to kiss him and taste the salt of his sweat along with the sweet remnants of the ice cream, but she stares fixedly ahead.

He looks at his watch and turns towards the bus. "We'd better get going," he says, "I can see the rest of the group are already lining up. I'm sure we've lost our good seats near the front."

She stands up with a sigh. "Goodbye, Eagle," she says and on impulse she stoops to pick up a small pebble.

"I'm taking it home for good luck," she says to Gunther.

"What if it brings bad luck?" he asks.

"Then I will post it back to the Canyon." She looks at the pebble. "Pebble," she asks, "do you wish to accompany me back to Germany?" She holds the stone to her ear. "It says it always dreamed of being a jetsetter," she reports to Gunther, who grins.

"We'd better hurry up or your pebble will miss the bus," he says, and they run towards the driver who is waving at them.

They find seats at the back and Melusine once again sits next to the window while Gunther stretches his legs into the aisle. She falls into a dreamlike state, hardly thinking, and it seems as if they arrive back at the Strip much too soon.

The neon signs have just begun to come alive, more iridescent than ever against the electric blue sky. They pass through the Fremont area, the oldest part of Las Vegas.

"Would you like to have dinner with me?" Gunther asks.

She shakes her head. She needs time alone. Time to savour her day with him.

"I can't. My husband's taking me out for dinner."

"I do have a suggestion for tomorrow. I'd love to see the Valley of Fire; it's a National State Park, the one with all those red rocks. It's about an hour and a half outside of town. I could rent a car tomorrow and we could go?"

She is uncertain, alarmed at the thought of being alone with him. What if she behaves foolishly, out in the middle of nowhere? It is not him she doubts, it's herself.

"You're perfectly safe with me," he adds. "I just thought it would be nice. I could get the car first thing in the morning and we could set off around ten. What do you say? Come on, it will be an adventure. Our own private adventure."

"Yes," she's hesitant but she agrees. "Okay, sure."

He grins. "I'll meet you at the front of the hotel at ten a.m. If I'm late, it's because the car rental place is busy, so don't leave, okay? Don't leave until at least eleven."

"You want me to wait for an hour?" She is smiling.

"I want to make sure you'll be there," he says.

"I'll be there."

The bus drops them off at their hotel and Melusine is suddenly very tired.

They take the elevator up to the second floor and Gunther steps out. "Enjoy your evening," he says.

"Wait," she calls after him, holding the door open. "What will you do tonight?"

He shrugs. "Watch TV, read, have a shower. I'm not having any girls over if that's what you're thinking."

She blushes beet red. The elevator beeps, objecting to being held open for so long.

"I don't care if you have a thousand girls in your room," she says, "I was just worried you would be bored or lonely."

"I'll most probably sort through my photos of the day and get a pizza," he says and he grins at her. "See you tomorrow."

He tips a mock cap and waves.

She closes the elevator door and goes up to her floor. She imagines him below her and she leans over the balcony and peers down. To her surprise and embarrassment, he is there, craning his head to look up at her.

They both burst out laughing.

"See you tomorrow," Melusine says and she steps away from the railing.

She is still laughing when she opens the door and finds Hans sprawled out on the sofa, his hands behind his head, watching TV.

6.

"YOU LOOK VERY HAPPY," he says. "You had a good day?"

"Very good," she says, startled to see him, her laughter extinguished. "I thought you'd still be at the conference."

"Nope, wrapped things up for the night. I said I'd take you out for dinner and here I am."

The last thing in the world she wants is to be with Hans. "I'd love that," she says, her eyes turned slightly away from his. "I'll go and take a shower and get ready."

"Take your time. No rush."

She stands motionless under the shower, trying to adjust her mindset in order to have a wifely dinner with her husband.

She dries herself and finds a clean dress. Despite all her ablutions, she can still smell Gunther — his cigarettes, his sweat and his cologne. She can see his casual grin, and the way his eyes crinkled when he smiled and how he cocked a single eyebrow when he was thinking. And how strong and warm and beautifully solid he felt as she held him while he cried.

"I'm thinking we go to Jimmy Buffet's Margaritaville," Hans says when Melusine sits down next to him, and she is astonished.

"Of all the places," she says, "I never thought you'd choose that one." But she is smiling and her tone is affectionate.

"I'll get us a pitcher of margaritas," Hans is expansive, "and we'll misbehave so much that not even Jonas would recognize us in a lineup."

"Sounds good to me," Melusine says, wishing that Hans wasn't so pale and anemic compared to Gunther. She decides to tell Hans about her planned trip to the Valley of Fire and get it off her chest.

"I booked a tour to see the Valley of Fire tomorrow," she says, "can I still go or do you need me?"

"You booked it? How?"

"There's a man in our hotel who speaks English and German," she says, amazed at the smoothness of her lies. "He booked it for me. But do you need me for anything?"

"The only thing I want or need, is for you to go and have a great time," Hans says and she breathes a sigh of relief.

She grabs her purse. "I'm ready."

They leave and Melusine is worried that Gunther will see her leaving with Hans. Then she remembers that she'd told him she was dining with her husband and so it isn't anything he doesn't already know. She glances at the second floor but it's deserted.

She and Hans walk down the Strip to the restaurant.

"They disgust me," Hans growls, of the card-snapping men and women. "And women too, women selling other women. They should all be ashamed."

It would not do to tell Hans that she finds the pictures erotic and arousing.

Then she stops suddenly, recalling with shame and horror why he feels the way he does.

"Oh, Hans," she said, taking him by the arm. "It's because of Kateri, isn't it?"

"No," he says shortly. "Okay, well yes, I suppose so. It's still so hard not knowing where she is, even after all these years."

Hans's younger sister, Kateri, disappeared inexplicably one day when she was fourteen. Hans was seventeen at the time.

Despite exhaustive investigations, no trace of Kateri had ever been found and, even some twenty-eight years later, the loss of his sister is no easier for Hans to bear. When Melusine met Hans at university, Kateri had been missing for three years. He still held a small vigil for her every Tuesday — the day of her disappearance — and Melusine knows he's never stopped hoping to learn the truth about what happened.

She looks at him now, as he discards the cards in anger, and she has no idea the degree to which Kateri has always been a part of their life; a third wheel on the bicycle of their marriage.

She also has no idea what Hans is really doing in Las Vegas.

7.

THERE IS NO optometry conference in Las Vegas, there never was. It was all a ruse. Hans's work colleagues had little interest in his area of lens study and simply said they would cover his appointments, no problem.

He was initially concerned that Melusine would discover his lie but to his relief, she got caught up in the excitement of Las Vegas and hardly seems to notice that he is not around much. He thinks she is behaving rather oddly but he is convinced it is simply due to Jonas's leaving home and her parents' death.

He is relieved to put her on a bus to go and see the Grand Canyon, a request that seemed far healthier than her wish to see *Zumanity*, which was most out of character with her generally sexually-incurious nature.

Throughout the years of his marriage, Hans has often felt that what others considered to be a sterling example of a successful life was, in fact, no more than the high maintenance of an ultimate fraud.

Each evening, arriving home and pulling into the driveway, he was plagued by the unpleasant expectation that Melusine would greet him at the front door, raining pots and pans down upon his head, and shrieking like a banshee all the while that he had ruined her life. Because he had. She might not know it on a conscious level, but he knew it. He had had no right to court her — or marry her.

Hans's life had stopped like a smashed clock on the seventh

of June in the summer of his eighteenth year. He was seventeen and Kateri was fourteen.

The worst of it was that he could still remember her beauty as clearly as if he had been with her only moments before. She was the luminous and radiant star around which the planet of his life revolved. Her pale milky skin, her large light-blue eyes, and her long soft white-blonde hair that was as fine as silk, her full and luscious lips, pouting but never petulant. Her forehead, like his, was broad and smooth and her ears were tiny shells.

He studied her beauty for hours after school, when it was just the two of them. During the heady days of summer they would be up in the tree house their father had built for them, and there, under the great canopied tree, with only the whispering leaves for company, they would lie on the mattress, face-to-face, their noses almost touching and he'd talk about his dreams and stroke her long fine hair.

Hans dreamed they would go on adventures together; wild journeys to Africa and the Amazon and to the far northern regions of China and India where he'd find jewels and treasures and she'd be his splendid companion and his radiant bride.

"Hush, Hans," she would say while the light danced above them, dappling dancing polka dots of green and gold, "you know we're not supposed to talk like that, about you and me. And besides, you'll be a fine adventurer without me. I don't know what my dreams are yet but one day I will. And you'll be a great conqueror of worlds, I know you will."

"Kateri," he would persist, "tell me your dreams, I know you know what they are. I know you know everything. You just won't say. Why not? Don't you trust me? You know you can trust me with anything, you know that."

"Fine. In my dreams, I'm alone," she would say. "Alone in a white world with falling snow and it's so quiet and there're no voices except for the beating of my heart."

He never liked it when she talked like that and he wouldn't

listen, trying to persuade her to see things his way instead, and to want nothing more than to walk with him on his envisaged path of glory.

They would lie there until their mother would call them in for supper. "What do you two do up there all day?" she would ask and Hans would shrug.

"We talk," he would say and Kateri would give him a secret smile and lower her gaze.

In winter, they would escape to his room where she lay on his bed, her head on his pillow, and he held her feet in his hands and rubbed them, keeping them warm.

"You have the most beautiful feet," he would say. "You are the most beautiful girl in the whole world."

He still cannot recall with any clarity the day she vanished. He recalls only the process of becoming conscious at the end of that day, coming to, while his mother wept and cried and his father sat still like a statue, frozen in shock and horror.

Hans summons his memories of Kateri's disappearance as a man might recall suffering a bad blow to the head or having to swim through a dark tunnel filled with dank water to reach the light on the other side. And, when he surfaced and his mind cleared, he knew that Kateri was gone but there were gaps in his memory; he had lost time he couldn't find.

His friends told him that he had been with them at the time of her disappearance and he was perplexed. "Why wasn't I with her?" he asked. "Why did I leave her all alone? I can't believe I did that. I never leave her alone."

"I think she was meeting some friends from school," Phillip, his best friend had told him.

"What friends?" Hans was agitated. "She doesn't have any friends apart from me." But Phillip could not add anything more.

The police immediately looked to lay the blame on their father and they cast doubt and suspicion upon him to the point where Hans could no longer look him in the eye.

The only other lead was that Kateri had been seen talking

to a young girl on a street corner; a girl with a white bonnet who was collecting charitable donations for a group of gypsies she travelled with.

"They took her," Hans insisted to the police. "The gypsies took her. Why aren't you questioning them instead of my father?"

The police kommissar said they had investigated the group and had even searched their caravans from top to bottom.

"But they're hiding her," Hans said, "hiding her until they leave. She's a jewel, she's perfection; of course, they think they must have her. Do you have someone watching them?"

The kommissar confirmed that they did.

Hans found out where the gypsies were camping and he knocked on every caravan door, begging them to give him back his sister. The gypsies were patient and kind, and explained that they belonged to the Oracle of the Sun and would never harm a soul.

"You want her to be your queen," Hans shouted, sounding mad even to himself. "You want her but you must give her back, you must give her back to me."

The gypsies looked at him sadly. "We'll pray for the return of your sister," they said.

Hans knew they were lying; he was sure they were holding Kateri prisoner.

"Then let me come and live with you," he challenged. "Let me join you. That way I'll know for sure that you don't have her."

"You don't belong with us," they replied. "You haven't been called."

"Convenient answer," Hans answered harshly. "Well, I'm not leaving, you'll have to have me thrown out."

And they did.

The police kommissar took him home. "It won't do your mother any good to lose two children," he said. "Buck up and be a man, won't you? We still think it was your father. We just need to break him."

Hans looked at him in horror. "I can't believe that my father could have done this," he said but the slightest hint of doubt had crept into his voice and the police kommissar looked at him.

"My father could never have done this," Hans said again, but this time it sounded like a question.

When he got home he sat down at the kitchen table with his parents. "Papa," he said, "why do they think it's you?"

His mother looked down at her hands and his father was silent.

"Oh," his mother said. "For heaven's sake, Helmut, tell him. Or I will."

His father said nothing.

"I was fourteen when your father took me from my home," his mother said. "But times were different then. Life was different then. There was nothing wrong with it. But now they're using that to say that your father has a thing for fourteen-year-old girls."

Hans looked at his father. His father's expression was pleading, asking for forgiveness and some tiny modicum of understanding and kindness.

Hans shot to his feet. "You're sick, both of you," he shouted. "Maybe she ran away. Maybe she saw you both for who you really are and she ran away."

He rushed up to his room and lay on his bed, crying.

When he woke the next day, exhausted by his grief, his father was gone.

"He'll send money," his mother said, without expression. "No matter what you think, he's a good man and I love him. I went with him when I was fourteen because I loved him then and I love him now. I could never doubt him. Tell me, do you honestly believe your father could kill your sister?"

Hans just looked at her. "I don't know what to believe any more."

"Hans," she entreated him, "you and I are all that's left of our family. And maybe one day your father will return and who knows, your sister too. But in the meantime, it's only you and me."

The rest of her family — her parents, her brother, his wife and their two children had all died in a fire on the farm — something had gone wrong with the wiring and the farmhouse had burnt down while they were sleeping, before any of them could wake and escape.

"Hans," his mother appealed to him again, "you are my son."

But he was silent and he left to go to the tree house where he stayed for two days.

When he climbed down, it seemed he had resolved the greatest of his loss and pain.

He returned to school. He studied hard. He was politely respectful to his mother. He never enquired about his father. And he learned to laugh again with his peers; he learned to present the façade of a happy popular heroic leader, full of bold tales and bright ideas.

And when Melusine first saw him, she having wandered into the wrong cafeteria in the wrong building on campus, the thing she noticed most about him was that he was laughing. He was a beautiful blond god and he was laughing with his head thrown back, with a group of admirers gathered around.

Needing to bask in the rays of his glory, she forced her way into the centre of the group, to ask that laughing blond god where the Arts and Letters club was, and he took her by the arm and showed her personally.

And before they reached their destination, he'd asked her out for dinner and after that night, they were inseparable.

She saw instantly that he could be the sun to light her darkness.

Your eyes, which administer heaven, I can only speak of darkness.

Ingeborg knew. And Melusine did not want to end up like Ingeborg, dead at forty-seven, alone, her life snuffed out by suicide or accident, the truth had never been proven. Melusine thought that if she could only stand in the glowing light of Han's sun, that she would be able to navigate the bleak journey of life without disaster. Ingeborg had been vocal about marriage smothering the female voice, but Melusine felt certain that it would save her.

Hans told Melusine about Kateri on their first date. Reaching across the table to grab his hand, she said she admired him for being able to pick up the pieces of his life and carry on.

Hans had shrugged. "What else could I do?" he asked her and then he told her he had gotten them a couple of sought-after tickets to an obscure art show that she had mentioned she wanted to see. And back then, at university, Hans's optimism had not been forced. He had felt happy. He liked his chosen career and he felt certain that he would enjoy a happy and contented life with Melusine, with the perfect family at his side.

But it was not to be and he knew that he was to blame for this failure, him and his dark secret. He had hidden from himself the real reason for his secret addictive needs, convincing himself that he simply needed a good marriage and a fulfilling career in order to stop needing to satisfy that hunger, the hunger that forced him to cut off his breath daily while he masturbated and orgasmed to the blackness of hypoxia, losing consciousness for a perfect moment, and in that perfect moment, joining his beloved Kateri.

He could laugh with others and appear fully functioning and joyous, even mad-capped and enviable as long as he had his private time with Kateri. He had assumed, wrongly, that Melusine would take her place and that he would no longer have the need for secrets.

He was ashamed of his wedding night. He could only perform the most perfunctory of acts. Fortunately for him, Melusine had known no other. And then, soon into their marriage, something happened that he had never intended at all; he found release by rubbing his wife's feet in the same way he had rubbed Kateri's, and soon he needed that nearly as much as he needed the erotic asphyxiation.

Yes, he had ruined Melusine's life. He was guilty as charged. Except that the poor woman had no idea — although he knew that even she had noticed the steady decline in his emotional well-being, as the reality of juggling the discordant aspects of his life took their toll.

"You never laugh any more," she said to him with increasing and irritating frequency. "When we met, you were always laughing. It was one of the things I loved about you the most."

How could he possibly answer that?

"So then, give me a reason to laugh," he would reply, knowing that it was a cruel thing to say and no real answer at all.

"You see, it's not so simple, is it?" he would say in response to her accusing silence and he would have to leave because the sadness in her eyes was too much for him to bear. He was guilty but incapable of explaining, and all he could do was take the mantle of his self-hatred and leave her feeling perplexed and hurt.

He had recently participated in an online class reunion and he had been transfixed by the collection of photographs that catalogued the loss of his youth. Even to his own eye, what was left of his wheat-gold hair had turned an unpleasant grayish white, and he was much thinner, bony, and his very skin seemed thinner, like brittle paper vulnerable to rip and tear.

He recognized, in the photographs, a familiar gesture; the way he would flick the mop of thick hair back from his eyes with a toss of his head, and he knew that while he still affected the gesture, there was no longer a reason for it. His robust good health and glowing beauty had been replaced by skeletal pallor and he bore the fluorescent stain of a marked man.

And he knew what it was that had leached the life from his blood, and from his bones, and it wasn't the lack of sunshine and it wasn't work. It was his addiction, his craving.

If only he could find Kateri. Just for a minute, a fleeting minute. He needed to ask her if she was all right. He needed to ask her where she was. He needed to ask her if she forgave him for leaving her alone that day and he needed her help so that he could carry on with his life. Because, this way, he was dying.

And that was why he had come to Las Vegas. To the Plaza hotel at the Fremont, which was hosting the biggest psychic fair in the world. He had figured, hoped, that he could get an answer there, he had to.

He had been extremely upset when Melusine insisted on joining him for the trip. Why did she feel the need to assert herself now, of all times? He felt it was most inconsiderate of her. Perhaps she had thought the trip would be a catalyst to rekindling their love, or be some kind of second honeymoon, not that they'd had much of a first. After he had proposed, he had talked of going to India or China and he had even mentioned Africa, but when it came to booking the tickets, he had suggested they wait for a few months and enjoy the wedding festivities with their out-of-town friends and relatives and then have their honeymoon later. She had been disappointed, wanting to be romantically whisked off away to be alone with him, and in any case, she did not have any friends or relatives from out of town to look forward to seeing; she had grown up in the university town where they had met. But he had persuaded her and later, she never mentioned the lost adventures of their missing honeymoon.

And so, while Melusine is off admiring the marvels of the Grand Canyon, Hans is lying on his bed at the Plaza. He can hardly bring himself to leave his room, as much as he wants to ask the psychics for counsel. All he wants to do is stop the breathing and find orgasm, again and again. He is in a dangerous place and he knows it.

He can picture his wife on her tour. He knows she will be amazed by the spectacular beauty of the wildly eroded desert because, although she would not think this of herself, it's her nature to embrace new things with enthusiasm, and he wishes he was the right man to be at her side.

He thinks of her, with her boyish long-legged beauty; if he were there, no doubt he would be the envy of every man. And her smile — Melusine has a smile to stop traffic, she has no idea. Her mouth is small and full and she is slightly buck-toothed, with the one top front tooth crossing the other ever so slightly. He still finds her smile wonderful after all these years; it is shy and inviting, slightly unsure, and he knows that if he were any kind of normal man, he would not be able to stop kissing her. He can see that which he would desire if he were not so damaged, but his damage is like an unbreakable glass wall imprisoning him from being the man he could and should have been.

He knows that Melusine believes herself to be a plain woman. He knows that. But she is lovely, with a perfect body and slender graceful hands, and her shy smile, and her almond-shaped eyes; cat's eyes, sleepy and sensual. He even loves her neat cap of dark curly hair. He never thought he could love a woman with short dark curly hair but he does. And he loves her upturned nose that is slightly too long and a fraction too sharp at the end but perfect nevertheless.

And when he learned of her vow to remain a virgin until her wedding night, he was further encouraged that she was the right partner for him. Her breasts were bigger than he would have liked but she was not keen to show them off, which suited him fine. He tried to avoid ever seeing her naked or even in her underwear, preferring her to remain clothed, which allowed him to fashion her with Kateri's body, albeit an older Kateri.

He hopes that he has managed to satisfy her adequately throughout the years. It has become easier with Viagra, but he has been afraid to try too much by way of departure from his customary routine in case of humiliating results. In the early days of his marriage, he found that he performed better if he held his breath and he did this repeatedly with effective result, hoping that she never noticed his silence.

He is lying in his room in The Plaza and he forces himself to get to his feet. He must get going. He is here to save himself, save his marriage and save his life. After seeing the shocking photographs at the reunion, he had worked out a plan to save himself, a plan that Melusine had unknowingly tried to interrupt by coming on the trip, and he blamed her for his inability to put his plan into action until now. But it is the third day since they arrived and he has to get going.

He needs to see the psychics, and then he needs to get some sunshine and he also needs to put some meat on his bones. He needs to stop masturbating and focus on the task at hand.

He had booked a room at the Desert Rose Resort for Melusine at the other end of the Strip, hoping that she would believe his explanations of a demanding conference schedule and that he would be able to carry on with his itinerary uninterrupted. And she had obliged. Now, it was up to him.

He gets up and forces himself to go down to the conference hall and begin his search.

8.

AND, COME END OF DAY, Hans is even less enthusiastic to see his wife than she is to see him. While Melusine enjoyed a wonderful day exploring the Grand Canyon with Gunther, Hans was dissatisfied. As far as he could see, the whole psychic setup was a sham, a carnival of practiced shysters preying on the lonely and the desperate who had no other place to turn.

He had forced himself to go into the main conference center where they had set up shop and that is exactly what it was: shop. They were selling lies and empty promises, offering fool's gold and maps to rainbows' end. He could see right through them.

He questioned them and they offered to light candles of healing to balance his chakras, they offered to look into crystal balls and read cards. Stuff and nonsense.

He wanted to give up but he had only seen a third of them and he told himself there was still hope. There had to be hope.

But later he returned to his room in anger. He tightened the noose with fury, punishing himself and seeking a black orgasm, a treat for all his hard work for having to suffer those fools.

But he could not orgasm, his penis was tired and unwilling and he was betrayed by even that. He prepared himself to meet Melusine, even making up a few anecdotal stories about his day should she ask. He wants to get back to the hotel before she does, and have a shower. He is mindful of making the pretense of a single hotel believable.

He is irritable as he takes a cab back.

He lets himself into the room which looks untouched. House-keeping has made the bed and the entire area is neat and tidy. Hans looks around and wonders about his wife. Who is she? Where does she really live, inside her head?

He opens her drawers more out of idle curiosity than any real interest and looks through her t-shirts and sweaters. All very neatly packed.

Next, her underwear; all perfect, matching bras and panties of fine lace. He takes out one of her panties; he is glad she doesn't wear thongs or G-strings, he finds them so ugly. Her underwear is feminine and shapely, cut high on the leg. He sniffs at her underwear, it carries the soft fragrance of hand-washed items.

He wonders what it would feel like to wear a pair of her panties and it's a thought that both horrifies and arouses him. His penis is awake now. He imagines the peach lace rubbing against his soft skin; the fabric would be rough and tantalizingly scratchy. He places the panties carefully back in the drawer

He opens the last drawer and finds her swimsuit and socks. And a giant black dildo.

He is transfixed. Ah, so she does have a secret life. He tries to imagine her with the dildo and he can see her having one orgasm after another, arching her back up in joy as she comes again and again. He is a little disconcerted that she has chosen such a generously endowed model.

Clearly his well-lubricated sexual acts with her have not worked as well as he had hoped.

He looks at his watch and decides he had better get on with his shower. He showers, shaves and gets dressed. Then he sits in the living room reading one of her German magazines, waiting.

And Melusine, when she opens the door, is taken aback to see him there.

Yes, he had said he would take her out for dinner, and they had made a plan. But she was hoping that perhaps he would be too busy or change his mind.

She wants nothing more than to soak in a hot bath and think about her day; think about Gunther and how it had felt to hold him in her arms while he cried. She wants to think about eating ice cream while sitting on a wobbly rock on the edge of the most beautiful canyon in the world. And she wants to think about the day ahead and the possibilities that it might hold.

So she is not in the mood to see her husband and they look at each other — two strangers in a room — two strangers who have lived together for over twenty years and who have raised a son.

"I'll go and take a shower and get ready." Melusine says, breaking the silence.

"Take your time. No rush."

By the time she has done her makeup, she is ready to face the evening. "Where shall we go?" she asks.

"I'm thinking we go to Jimmy Buffet's Margaritaville," Hans says when Melusine sits down next to him, and she is astonished.

"Of all the places," she says, "I never thought you'd choose that one. But yes, that would be fun."

"Shall we take a cab?"

"Let's walk," she says, "we can always cab back. It's such a great night, it's perfect out."

Hans would have preferred to take a cab but he defers to her.

They walk down the Strip and once they get the card-bearing lowlifes out of the way, they begin to enjoy themselves and Melusine marvels at the brightness of the jewel-like neon.

"Let's get lots of neon for our house when we get back," she says and he snorts.

"I just wish we could take some of this sparkle back with us," she says, "some of this shininess."

"Shininess?"

"Yes. Everything shines and glitters here."

"Ah, back to your love for glitter. I never knew that."

"Neither did I," she admits. "Although actually when you

think about my Christmas trees, they've always been very sparkly."

"This is true. I wonder if Jonas will come for Christmas dinner."

"He said he will. He said he might bring Nika. I'm really surprised they are still together."

"She looks like a street punk," Hans says and Melusine agrees.

"We shouldn't judge her on her appearance," Melusine says. "Sure, she looks different to all the other clean-cut girls he dated but if Jonas likes her, she must have something special. We must give her more of a chance. She's an orphan; her parents died when she was just ten. Oh Hans, I do miss my boy."

"I know you do."

"When he was little he loved to help me bake," Melusine says. "But then in his teens he just got so withdrawn. Remember when he was fourteen? He slept all the time. I couldn't get him out of bed."

"And then that long time smoking marijuana."

"Ah, so you know about that then?"

"Of course I do. I hope he's done with all that now."

"Everybody goes through experimental stages," Melusine says and Hans looks at her.

"Everybody?"

She shrugs. "He's a good boy," she says. "I trust him. He'll be fine. We did a good job with him, Hans, we did."

Hans thinks for a moment. "I don't know if I was such a great father," he admits. "Have you ever seen him being spontaneous or having fun or laughing at anything or doing something just for the hell of it? I haven't and I feel as if I should have shown him how but instead, he learned his seriousness from me. I failed him."

She wonders if he is waiting for her to object and say that he was a wonderful father but she cannot find words that will ring true. She also wants to tell him that Jonas is a very upbeat boy, only not when his father is around.

Fortunately they reach the restaurant.

"I'm going to have a huge jug of margaritas," Hans says.

She smiles at him. "Does that mean I have to get my own jug or can I have some of yours?"

"You can have some of mine," he says and he flashes her a grin she has not seen in a while and he tosses invisible hair out of his eyes.

He places their order and they study the menu.

The waitress returns quickly and places the enormous pitcher on their table and Hans pours the drinks.

They both down a few glasses quickly and soon the food is unimportant. They order hamburgers and she and Hans giggle at everything and the world seems silly and harmless and the night is endless and there is not a single adult responsibility in sight.

A show starts in the restaurant and a young woman dives into a huge floor-to-ceiling margarita-shaped glass and pole-dances in and out of the water.

Watching a nearly naked girl with her husband at her side excites Melusine and she feels optimistic about the evening. "This is such fun," she says and her skin is flushed and she has a healthy colour from the sunshine of day.

Hans leans towards her and kisses her lightly on the brow. "Yes," he says, "it really is."

They eat dinner and finish the jug of margaritas and Hans asks Melusine if they should get another one.

"Hmm, no, I'll have a cocktail, instead of dessert. Something sweet."

They order a final round and wait.

The water-girl pole-dancing show has gone on three times since they've been there and each time Melusine finds herself sitting closer to Hans, with her hand on his leg, or caressing his back. She has never been this forward with him. She is bordering on downright promiscuity.

But he does not object and he leans towards her and he looks young again in her eyes, powerful, popular and sexy just like he did when she met him.

They take a cab back to the Desert Rose Resort and Melusine lets her skirt ride high up her thighs and she encourages Hans to caress her, even teasing his fingers to the edge of her panties.

Hans makes sure he dry swallows a Viagra on the way when Melusine isn't looking.

They arrive at the hotel and clumsily find their way to the room and their bed, shedding clothes along the way.

Melusine is running her hands over Hans's body, thinking oh, he feels so thin, and his skin is cold, so paper-thin and dry. She is reminded of the finest of her phyllo pastries; baked, they're almost powdery — so breakable and brittle.

Once again Gunther creeps into her mind and she can taste a decadent profiterole; the thick luxurious pastry exploding in her mouth with rich Bavarian cream and real chocolate drizzle. She forces thoughts of Gunther and pastries away and is startled by the realization that this is the first time she has seen her husband naked. He has always been so fastidious, going about his washroom routines in private, even shaving behind closed doors.

She explores his body and he is long, lean and hairless. She is groaning with desire and even he is moaning out loud with the sweet joy of discovery.

He runs his hands over her legs, gripping her buttocks hard and he feels for her breasts. But no! Her breasts are too large, much too large. Kateri would never have had such large breasts, such sexual breasts, such womanly mammaries. These breasts have suckled and fed; they are no longer pure.

No! He cannot think about his sister now as this will lead to certain catastrophe and he stops touching Melusine's breasts and returns to the safer area of her smooth flat stomach, not letting his thoughts stray.

Melusine can wait no longer. She lies down on the bed and pulls him on top of her.

His penis is hard and engorged and she grasps it but Hans once again thinks of his sister and how she would never have done so unseemly a thing as to clutch a man's penis with such unbecoming hunger and he feels himself shrinking.

He quickly forces himself inside Melusine but it is too late, he is losing his erection.

In desperation, he holds his breath; he goes silent but she is still making too much noise.

He wants to tell her that it's better when it's quiet, that it's better when it's dark and you fall back into that place where you become one with your orgasm and nothing else matters, nothing else exists.

Before either of them knows what's happening, he has one hand around her neck and the other across her mouth. He cuts off her air, his hand big enough to cover her mouth and her nose. And he is pushing down on her neck harder and harder and he is getting harder again, and he closes his eyes and pumps himself inside her and he is about to come when he feels a blow to the side of his head that sends a ringing in his ears and flashes a blinding light behind his eyeballs.

He falls off the side of the bed and both he and Melusine lie dead still, both of them quietly horrified.

The room is dark except for the eerie pink light reflecting from the Tropicana hotel across the way like a muslin curtain of Turkish Delight.

Hans gets up and crawls towards his clothes.

Melusine lies there naked, unmoving. Her eyes are huge, frightened.

He does not look at her.

He buttons his shirt and zips up his fly. He sits down on a chair and pulls on his socks, then his shoes. She hears his shoelaces snapping against the leather as he ties his laces tightly, precisely. She realizes the familiarity of this sound, of Hans snapping his laces, getting the knot and bow just so. He stands.

Every sound is so loud in the booming silence of everything

they cannot say. He picks up his jacket and leaves without a backward glance.

She hears the door close, not exactly quietly, and she sits up.

She has no idea what happened except that her husband tried to strangle her while they were having sex. Does he hate her that much that he wants to kill her? Does he wish that she were dead?

She gets off the bed and runs a deep hot bath, sitting on the edge while the water fills the tub. She bites her lip and frowns.

She does not know what to think.

9.

THE NEXT DAY, Melusine tries to put the night with Hans behind her while she waits for Gunther.

She is glad, in the morning, to see that her neck is unbruised, although her skin and larynx feel tender.

She tries to make sense of what happened. She recalls a passage from *Malina*, in which Ich talks about the throttle marks on her neck but at the time she had read it, Melusine had thought the woman was referring to the stranglehold of doomed love that had her by the throat, but perhaps it had been some practice of lovemaking with which she was unfamiliar.

Melusine thinks about Ich's instant love for Ivan, her married lover, and how she, Melusine, had always found the story unconvincing; what woman would fall in love so wildly with a man, and so quickly? Unbelievable! And yet, here she is waiting for Gunther, sitting on the same bench as the previous morning, looking at the same pink oleander flowers, at the same very green, very fake grass, and at the vivid cobalt sky; it all looks the same but everything has changed.

Her heart is beating like a schoolgirl's and her armpits are sweaty. Good thing she had doubled up on her deodorant. And she had selected her underwear with care, feeling foolish and excited at the same time. She is wearing the shortest dress in her collection to show off her legs to their best advantage and she chose her sexiest sandals, dubious footwear given that they were going to explore rocks in the desert.

In her excitement, she skipped breakfast and her stomach makes loud gurgling sounds and she tries to hush it by breathing deeply and slowly. She checks her watch and she wonders if she should go inside and grab a coffee but what if she misses Gunther?

Her thoughts drift and she cannot help but wonder where Hans went. She had thought he would come back eventually but he did not. She had also thought perhaps, that as a good wife, she should have waited for him in the room all day but she could not do it.

Instead, she showered as carefully as if she were going on a date and she even put on the slightest trace of make-up. Not so much that Gunther would notice, well, hopefully not, but just enough to increase her allure.

Increase her allure. She mocks herself, sitting there, waiting, with her sweaty armpits and her dry mouth and her tumbling noisy stomach.

She tucks her hands under her thighs and leans forward, lost in thought. She hears a car horn and she looks up and sees Gunther waving from a nondescript white rental sedan.

"Cool car," she says, opening the door.

"I would've got you a Mustang, but they were all gone. Did you have breakfast?"

She shakes her head and makes up an excuse. "No. I didn't even get a coffee. I was going to but there were too many people."

"I didn't have anything either. We can stop off somewhere and get ourselves some pancakes or something."

"Sounds lovely," Melusine says politely, but she couldn't care less about eating. She's wondering if she is attracted to Gunther simply because of her confused emotions and she asks herself if she would have been attracted to anybody who had come along? Or was it specifically him that she was attracted to? And was she really attracted to him or just attracted to the idea of attraction? All at once, she feels exhausted.

Gunther gets them onto the highway. His window is open and the air is blowing in noisily. "We'll find somewhere to eat along the way," he shouts. She nods and suddenly feels a wave of claustrophobia; she wants out, out of the car. She cannot be here, trapped with this stranger, going off into the middle of nowhere. She eyes the door-handle of the car and thinks of leaping out but car's moving too fast. She tells herself that she can run away from him as soon they stop for breakfast; she can get a cab back to the hotel regardless of the cost. She stares at Gunther wild-eyed through her sunglasses but he doesn't notice, he is trying to find a radio station that will work.

"Static, country and western, eighties pop," he says, finally giving up. "Melusine, you're very quiet. Are you okay?"

"Fine. Yes, I'm good, just tired I suppose. I had an odd evening last night with my husband. I think he might be having a nervous breakdown."

Gunther laughs. "Aren't we all? What did he do?"

She shakes her head. She cannot tell him. "Nothing specific, it was just a general thing really. Very general. Funny, I look at my son. He thinks life is so straightforward and for him, at eighteen, it is. And yet, for us, the older we get, the more complicated it gets. Why did we think it would get easier?"

"Blame the fairytales," Gunther says. "They all stopped with 'and they lived happily ever-after.' No one ever told us what that would look like. We weren't armed."

She smiles for the first time that day, a real smile. "You're very right. They didn't. Maybe they should have ended their stories with 'and they all lived on and on and on, fighting battles, going to war, getting married, getting divorced, losing their fortunes, growing old and finally dying.' But who would have wanted to read that? That's just depressing."

"Yes, but those aren't the only possible endings. They could also have said they had children and grandchildren, feasts and celebrations, increased their fortunes, won wars and loved until the grave while having fantastic sex along the way."

Melusine thinks about her own inherent lack of optimism and how her gloom had gone quiet during the years of Jonas's upbringing, gloom that had recently elbowed its way back into her life. She was three years away from the age when Ingeborg had died and although she could not really imagine wanting to die, she sometimes felt as if life itself was a death sentence of sorts.

Before Jonas was born, she had spoken to a doctor, wanting to know if she was suffering from depression but she left the appointment convinced that she was just more philosophically aware than most people, and more given to profound, darker thoughts.

She looks at Gunther. She does not want to let herself get in the way of their day and she resolves to be more cheerful.

"Are you okay without the air con?" he asks. "I know it's hot but I hate the tin can cold of air con but if the heat's too much for you, just say so."

"I'm fine, don't worry," she looks around. "We're going to be hard-pressed to find any kind of food places, it's like we're in the middle of nowhere."

There are brown hills on either side of the highway and not a road or town in sight.

Gunther groans and Melusine leans toward him. "I hope you have gas," she says.

"Comes with a full tank," he replies, sounding discouraged by the lack of pancake houses en route.

They drive for half an hour and Gunther spots a road.

"I'm taking it," he says, swinging to the right. "We must find food."

She laughs. "You have no idea where this goes. It could get us more lost than ever."

"We're pioneers," he says, "unstoppable explorers, driven forward, or in this case, west, by our hunger. Our hunger, not for land but for pancakes and fried eggs and oh, I'm so goddamned hungry."

"You're making it worse by talking about it."

"You're right. So did Hans go to his conference this morning?" He asks the question casually and Melusine wonders how to lie about the fact that Hans did not come home at all.

"As a matter of fact, we argued and he rushed out of the room around two a.m. and didn't return."

He turns to look at her. "He didn't come back?"

She shakes her head. "He didn't come back. I know what you're thinking, that maybe I should have stayed at the hotel to wait for him, or maybe put out a missing person's report but I didn't think I could."

"I didn't say anything," Gunther says and he scratches his head. "It's not like there's a shortage of hotels. He must have stayed elsewhere."

"I guess I should have gone to the conference centre and tried to find him this morning," she says and Gunther looks at her in alarm.

"No." He's emphatic. "There're too many conferences and you'd never find him."

The previous night, out of idle curiosity and keen to see if there was any mention of Melusine's husband, Gunther had googled all the current conferences in Vegas and optometry was not listed. But he does not want to tell Melusine that. "Listen Melu, people do crazy things in Vegas, but I'm sure he's fine."

"Fine but doing crazy things? Besides, Hans doesn't do crazy, he never has." Her stomach flutters at his casual and intimate shortening of her name but she doesn't mention it. She hopes he'll say it again.

"Everybody does crazy," Gunther says. "That's another thing the fairy tales don't tell you. Everybody does crazy but only the kind that makes sense to them and no one else. Oh my god, look, there's a McDonald's! In the middle of nowhere too."

"Well, it might once have been a McDonald's," Melusine says. "It looks like it's been closed forever."

Gunther looks ready to weep at this news. He pulls up close

to the building and sees that it is true; the McDonald's has been shut for a while. It is an old place, without the signature golden arch logo. It has two single, curved arches, one on either side of the restaurant, and the whole setup is like an old-fashioned gas station from the fifties. It is heavily boarded-up and in a bad state of disrepair.

"Look at that sign. Burgers were fifteen cents," Gunther says with reverence.

He leans back and closes his eyes. Then he sits up straight. "Melusine, can we take a moment to explore? You never know what photographs I could get here."

"Fine by me. I'd love to stretch my legs. We've been driving for nearly two hours."

"Are you serious? I hope I haven't got us lost. I'm not great with maps," he says, and she smiles.

"Now you tell me!" She gets out the car and stretches, arches her back and yawns. "This fresh air feels great. And I love this insane heat."

Gunther, meanwhile, is loosening a board across a window. He tugs, gets the window open and peers inside.

"This is fantastic!" He runs back for his camera bag. "It's falling apart, it's a McDonald's after the apocalypse, when there's nothing left and the bomb's gone off and everybody's dead and they find this retro time capsule..."

"I'd hardly call McDonald's retro," she laughs.

"Wait 'til you see inside this one. Hang on, I'll go first and help you in."

"Let me get my purse," Melusine says and he grins at her.

"Sure," he says, teasing her. "And I'll lock the car while we're at it. Melu, we're out in the middle of nowhere, who's going to steal anything?"

She shrugs. "Okay, I'm ready, let's go inside."

They climb in and their eyes take a moment to adjust to the dim light. Gunther sees that a few of the wooden boards are coming loose at the far end of the room and he pulls them off, allowing the sunlight to stream in, which illuminates an old-fashioned counter with all kinds of equipment for making milkshakes and fries.

"They actually made all this stuff from scratch," Gunther says, awed. "Melu, do you have any idea what all this stuff would be worth on eBay?"

She shrugs and dusts off a stool. "It's very cool, I'll give it that," she says. "It is a time capsule, you were right. But I wonder who built it out here in the middle of nowhere?"

Gunther sets up his tripod. He adjusts his camera, changes the settings, flips switches and grunts with concentration while muttering to himself. He has apparently forgotten his hunger.

Melusine gets up to explore behind the counter. She leans forward and says in a sexy voice, "And what can I get for you, young man?"

He turns to her and grins. "You," he says, "just you. Be the cherry on top of my sundae. Hey, Melu, don't move, not a millimeter, not a hair, you look incredible there. The light is catching you just right."

He makes more adjustments, takes a few shots and then stops. "Do you have any red lipstick?" he asks. "And hair gel?"

She roots through her purse. "I have lipstick, yes," she says, "but I've never used hair gel in my life."

"Put a lot of lipstick on," Gunther says, "so your lips look really dark."

He looks at her critically after she's done. "Wait," he says, "I want images of you applying the lipstick."

She does it again.

He cannot help but think that her somewhat old-fashioned dress fits the look of the place and he seats her at a table and has her mime the lipstick action again, with her looking into a small compact mirror and crossing her legs to one side; fifties poster girl look. The sunlight is a diagonal beam behind her, throwing her features into stark relief. He moves her to face into the direct sunlight and she squints at him.

"It's very hard to keep my eyes open like this," she says. But she is enjoying his attention.

"Do you trust me?" he asks and she looks at him with suspicion.

"To a degree, I suppose," she says and he grins.

"Fair enough. I just want to do something with your hair, with homemade hair gel, the spit-in-hand variety. Will you indulge me?"

She agrees. He spits into his hands, rubs them together and tousles her hair. She leans into his hands slightly as he rubs and he works the curls into spikes. It is the first time he has touched her and she is very still, hoping this might lead to something more but he is all work, adjusting her hair and tucking a small strand behind her ear and her skin tingles, she feels electric.

He studies her. "Yes, that works, take a look."

She gets up and goes over to look at herself in the mirror behind the counter. The mirror is dust-speckled and rust-stained and she catches more of a shadow of herself than her real reflection.

"That's incredible," he says, "do not move." He shoots her reflection until he's satisfied he got the shot.

"Uh," he says, "you want to have some more fun? Take it one step further?"

"Oh goodness Gunther, don't tell me you want me naked? That's such a cliché."

"I was thinking of you in your underwear," he grins, "but naked would be fantastic, you'll get no objections from me. Unless of course you're wearing granny panties up to your waist and an industrial bra that my great-aunties would favour and you're too embarrassed to show me?"

She gives him a filthy look and eases her dress over her head. "My underwear," she says, her voice muffled by cloth, "is always topnotch Victoria's Secret, my one indulgence in life, if you must know. Just promise me," she says and her head pops back up through her dress, "that no one will ever see these except us."

"You have my word."

But then she quickly smooths her dress back down and blushes.

"What?" he asks, "you changed your mind?"

"Uh, well, I just thought of something. About the nakedness…"

"You've got your period?"

She flushes. She is not used to discussing things like that, not even with Hans; they've never mentioned bodily functions except in the vaguest of terms.

"I do not. But I don't believe in shaving, the way women do these days. I won't bikini wax or Brazilian wax. I'm proud of my hair. But I know it's really not the fashion, in terms of your expectations."

"Melu, I expect nothing except to be constantly, pleasantly surprised by you. Armpits unshaven too?"

She nods.

He is incredibly aroused at the thought but does not want to let her know. He hides his erection behind his tripod and motions for her to take her dress off.

She has always been very proud of her body and she watches Gunther's reaction, not disappointed by his obvious appreciation. Her long legs, narrow hips, tiny waist and full large breasts. Her skin tone is flawless and he tells her so.

"And my underwear meets your approval?"

"It's very sexy, Melusine. Let's take some pictures like this and then get you naked."

He sets her up in various poses and she is an instinctive model, holding a pose, folding into the shot, and merging with his ideas.

"Okay, I'm ready for naked if you are," he says and she looks shy.

He positions her in the sunlight. "Now," he says, "wait until I tell you and then slowly, very slowly, start to undo your bra and then take off your panties. When you slip your panties off, look at me, not down at the floor."

She nods.

"Ready," he says and she begins to unclasp her bra, looking down and then at him. She slips off her panties and stands naked before him.

"Melusine, you are utterly spectacular. You take my breath away."

She is delighted. The entire scene is like nothing she ever imagined, but it all feels perfectly natural.

"I want to shoot you from above. Come and lie here, if you're okay with lying on the floor? It's just dust really..."

"It's fine."

This photo-shoot feels like a dream. She is the centre of his attention and she would not be anywhere else, doing anything else.

He stands on a bench above her and from her vantage point she can see up his untucked shirt. He has a generous belly and she thinks about the ripped and toned Apollo Boys. Gunther is not quite what she'd thought she was after. If, in fact, she's after him at all. She tells herself that she may not even be interested in him, in that way.

The poses get more and more graphic and Melusine doesn't question him. She offers suggestions, experiments with angles.

"You're so feminine and so strong," he says. "You're like a goddess."

They finally run out of ideas and Melusine is tired. She feels as if she has run a thousand miles and her body is aching. She had thought too, that he would have made a move on her by now, and seduced her, and the fact that he has not, makes her irritable. She stands up, puts her hands on her lower back and stretches. "That was hard work," she says.

She knows she had told herself earlier that she was not interested in him sexually, but that had been when she was assuming he was interested in her. She admits now that she had thought he was doing all this in order to seduce her and since he has not, she is becoming increasingly bad-tempered. She looks over at him.

He is standing with his hands on his hips, looking this way and that to see if he has missed any opportunities for another shot. His cock is causing his trousers to stick out at a right angle like a gigantic tent pole but he does not seem aware of it.

"Is that erection because of me or because you're turned on by the art we just created?" Her tone is accusatory.

"I don't rationalize my erections," he replies calmly, turning to her. "If I did, they might go away and I'd like them to stay."

She scowls at him, feeling betrayed, and stupid for it. She walks over to where her underwear has been left on the floor and she pulls it on roughly.

He watches her in silence.

Then she pulls on her dress, furious.

Taking his cue from her, he dismantles his tripod and sets about putting his equipment away.

She hates herself because she's ruined the moment between them and she feels close to tears.

"Melusine," he says gently and she looks at him, her eyes shining too brightly, "you fascinate me."

She tries to laugh, tries to take this consolation prize. It is clear he has no real interest in her. Her hair is still spiky with his spit and she hasn't wiped off the lipstick. She sits on the bench, waiting for him to tell her when they will leave. She looks around and her truculence leaves her as she watches the sunlight sliding in through the nailed-up boards and suddenly she feels magical again in this lost place.

He walks up to her and holds out his hand. She takes it and he pulls her to her feet. He yanks her close and puts her hand on his cock. He is rock hard through his trousers and he whispers to her, "no pictures now, are there?"

She does not move her hand and she leans in to him but he pulls back.

"I don't think you know what you want, Melusine," he says.

"How can I know?" she asks. "This is unchartered territory."

He shrugs. "And, in mapping it so meticulously, you'll lose all joy in the scenery." He turns and walks across the room and climbs out the window.

But she stays for a moment.

I'm a cartographer, not a hedonist. I can't change who I am.

She climbs out the window and joins him.

"What's the time?" she asks and he looks at his watch and laughs.

"After two p.m."

"My goodness. Do we still have time to go the State Park?"

He sighs. "Probably not. I guess I ruined this day for us."

She grabs his arm. "No. You didn't. I did. I'm sorry."

He puts his arm around her. "How about we both stop blaming ourselves, okay? And maybe we should know this, that nothing either one of us does with each other is either right or wrong. It just is."

With that she turns to him and wraps her arms around his neck. She kisses him, thinking that he won't kiss her back, and when he does, she is startled and joyful.

He pulls away for a moment. "You want to try this again?" he says and she nods.

They climb back in the window and he leads her over to the sunlit area and pulls the dress over her head, pulls off her underwear while she undresses him, unzipping and unbuttoning him.

"So extraordinary," he says, and he sucks on each of her breasts in turn, sucks hard.

She grasps his cock. "Can you make love to me first and then seduce me later?" she asks and he laughs, murmuring that he can do just that.

He fucks her while she leans across the bench, while she lies on the floor, dirt digging into her back; he fucks her while she sits on the bench with her legs spread wide. She opens herself to him and she pulls him toward her and she tastes every sensation she thought she would never have. Her lipstick is smeared and then gone, maybe it's on his cock, his mouth, his neck, his ear lobes, his face.

He finally rolls over and lies on the floor, his chest heaving, his cock flaccid, reduced and wet.

"Melusine," he says. "I'm done. For now, anyway."

She's lying next to him and she laughs. "Don't worry. Me too."

They're silent for a while and then Melusine suddenly sits up. "I," she says, "am starving. I've never been this hungry in all my life."

He gets up and pulls on his shirt. Ravenous though she is, watching him dress makes her sad and he sees the shadow cross her face.

"More later," he says, and he grins at her. "Don't you doubt that. Time to leave the Love Shack, baby. Come on."

He holds out his hand. "Let's go and try to find some food, okay?" They climb into the sedan and drive off.

Melusine has no thoughts. The hot sunshine, the man next to her, the hunger in her belly, and the stickiness on her thighs all render her timeless, painless. She never knew it was possible to be so void and yet so full.

Gunther is driving at high speed down the road they had come, pursuing his path, not returning to the highway.

She sees something in the distance. "Oh my god, it's a shop!" Buffalo Bill's, in the middle of nowhere.

"We look a bit ragged," she says, pulling down her visor and examining herself in the mirror.

"Who cares?" Gunther asks, and he pulls up the car in a cloud of dust.

They buy two bags of food: sandwiches, chips, chocolate, pop. A feast.

They sit outside in the dusty picnic area and eat without manners. "This is the most delicious thing I've ever eaten," Melusine says of her pre-packed egg salad sandwich. "And this Coke is superb."

Gunther grunts in agreement, his mouth full. Melusine wishes she had a camera so she could capture him. She closes her eyes. *Let me never forget this moment, ever.*

He looks at her. "Wait," he says. "Time for a picture of us together like this."

She nods.

He sets up the camera and puts it on the self-timer. They sit close together, grinning without reserve, the remnants of their food around them. The camera clicks.

The sun sinks lower and the shadows become longer and the Joshua trees darken. The mountains to the one side turn black, while the others, in the spotlight of the western setting sun, glow a fiery red.

"What a place," Gunther marvels. He looks at her. "I have an admission to make," he says and her stomach grows hard and cold and the food she has eaten roils greasily.

"I don't have any work scheduled in Vegas," he says. "I cancelled it after the baby died but I never told my wife and then when things got worse between us, all I wanted was some time to myself, all I wanted to do was come and get drunk for a week and so I told her I was still booked."

She takes his hand. "That's understandable, don't you think?"

"I just couldn't stand it, Melu. I couldn't do anything. It was my sperm that her body was rejecting and I saw that in her eyes every time she looked at me. I had failed her. Five times. I was the one to cause five unspeakable tragedies from which we'll never recover. It's my fault. And I wanted oblivion and I thought this was the one place to come where I could get that, where I could just disappear for five days and not have to feel the weight of all that pain.

"And I was so drunk," he says, "that night you thought your door was mine. It was my second night. And being drunk wasn't really working. I was drunk but I couldn't forget. And then the next morning, after you were at my door, I saw you while I was eating my breakfast, you were waiting for your husband to book your tours and I followed you to the Skywalk."

He looks at her. "That's my admission. Are you angry with me?" he asks.

She shakes her head. "I couldn't be, not even if I tried." A thought occurs to her. "You leave the day after tomorrow?"

He nods. "In the morning, yes."

For a while they say nothing.

He takes her hand and they sit there in the dirt outside Buffalo Bill's convenience store.

"What would you like to do later?" he asks.

"I never want to wash again," she says seriously and he laughs. "I don't," she says. "I want to keep the glorious stickiness of our day on me forever."

"Okay, so showering isn't on the agenda," he says. "How about we go and hang out for a bit in the Fremont area in old Vegas? Watch the neon signs come alive. They have a light show that's apparently spectacular. Then we can take the car back and maybe have dinner somewhere?"

She doesn't care. She could sit on this piece of concrete forever with her feet in the sand.

"Sure," she says, shading her eyes from the sun. "Sounds great. Look, not a cloud in the sky. Amazing."

He pulls her to her feet. "Let's head out on the highway," he says, "looking for adventure and whatever comes our way..."

He starts singing *Born to Be Wild* and she hums along. They get back in the sedan and turn back the way they came.

At one point, Gunther pulls over on the lonely stretch of road.

"Are we running out of gas?" she asks.

"You're very anxious about our gas situation," he says. "We're fine. I just thought it might be nice to make love to you again, unless you have any objections."

"None whatsoever," she says, laughing, and he slides his fingers under her dress and pulls down her panties, while she turns to him and kisses him deeply, unbuttoning his shirt.

It is amazing, she thinks, how they manage to do this so

perfectly, as if they have choreographed it, their movements perfectly aligned.

He pushes her seat all the way back and she tears off her dress and bra and pulls him on top of her. Her left foot is anchored on the steering wheel and she raises her hips to him, holding onto his back. The sunshine is hot on her hands and their bodies are slick with sweat and they come together and he lies on top of her, not moving.

"Too heavy?" he asks.

"No, you're perfect."

"We're going to get stuck like this you know," he says, "when all our bodily juices dry."

"Superglue," she says, sleepily.

He rolls off her gently and pulls on his shirt. She grabs her dress and pulls it over her head, stuffing her bra into her purse. She retrieves her panties from the floor of the car and tugs them on.

They turn to grin at each other.

"I'm thirsty," she says and he finds a leftover bottle of Sprite that is hot but tastes just fine.

They head back to Las Vegas and she watches the sun dropping low behind the mountains. The Joshua trees are now black silhouettes, backlit by a hellfire glow.

"Where are the stars?" she asks anxiously, craning to look.

"They're still there," he reassures her. "Just not visible yet. They'll arrive, give them time."

Just before they near Las Vegas, a blood red moon appears in the sky, as large as a grapefruit and Melusine sees one star, just one, before the city lights obscure all else. She makes a wish.

They park near the Fremont and she smooths down her dress with her hands and laughs.

"I can't imagine how I look," she says.

"You look more beautiful than I can describe," Gunther tells her. "Wait. I must lock my camera in the trunk, this area doesn't look all that safe."

She waits for him and they walk down through the Fremont, ambling, window shopping, chatting.

They stop at the far end, down near The Plaza hotel.

"That's where Frank Sinatra used to perform," he tells her.

"Does it still work?" she asks, dreamily.

"Do you mean does it still operate as a hotel? Yes, I believe it does," he says.

She is leaning back against him, and they are listening to some techno music while the strippers on a bar counter dance out of time, swinging their hips from side to side like a school chorus without meaning.

Gunther stands behind Melusine, his hands around her waist and he leans down and whispers in her ear. She runs her hand up behind his head and tilts her face back. She is smiling and her eyes are closed and she does not see Hans who is standing half a dozen steps away.

10.

HANS CANNOT BELIEVE what he is seeing. He stares at his wife, seeing her the way he left her the previous night; lying on her back, her legs still spread wide, her breasts flopping outwards and that big bushy cunt shouting all kinds of hatred at him, her eyes wide open in horror.

He hates her pubic hair. He has asked her a thousand times to shave it, trim it, shape it but she will not, she refuses, most uncharacteristically for she usually acquiesces to his requests. He wants her pure and childlike, surely she can understand that?

He knows his thoughts are crazy, he knows he should be thinking about Melusine's infidelity, and the man with her, not about her ridiculous pelt of pubic hair.

He looks over at her again, and then he doubles over as if he has been punched and vomit rises in his throat.

He sees her as he left her; she was shocked and horrified by his assault and now, here she is, laughing with a complete stranger, a stranger who has his hand up her dress.

How did this happen? And when did this happen?

He stares at the man. He recognizes him now; he saw him at breakfast a day or so ago, and after breakfast, the man had waited behind him in line, waiting to see the chatty concierge, the one on the diet, who was drinking ten calorie blue Gatorade and telling everyone how bad it tasted.

The man had met his wife on the trip. The trip that Hans had pictured her innocently enjoying.

But how had things evolved from that trip to this?

Hans had seen her only last night; it was only last night that they had tried to make exciting love with terrible consequence.

And now today, this very afternoon, here she was, having an affair.

He could not understand it at all. It didn't make any sense whatsoever. Melusine was a good woman, a good wife.

The shock. The betrayal. Her happiness, her freedom and her all too apparent joy.

He tries to think back. Could Melusine have known the man even as they stood in line but managed to hide it from him?

He did not believe it was possible. No, she could not have known him then.

But what was going on with her? He recalls the big black dildo in the bottom drawer and his wife's insistence that he book *Zumanity* for her. Perhaps he did not know her as well as he thought he did.

He looks at the man who is shorter than him and stockier. He carries quite the belly too and Hans notes this with satisfaction. Then he remembers that the man is fucking his wife and there really is not too much to feel satisfied about.

That man, inside Melusine. Inside Melusine's hairy bush. He cannot bear to think about it.

His thoughts whir in crazy circles.

The man is whispering in Melusine's ear and whatever it is that he has to say, she is loving it.

Hans turns to a potted plant nearby and throws up what is left of his lunch; the lunch that is rancid in his mouth, vile with digestive fluids and poisoning his mouth with a bitter aftertaste.

He heaves and retches, oblivious to passersby, none of whom stop to ask him if he is all right.

When he looks up again, Melusine and the man have vanished.

He is tempted to run after them but he asks himself what that would achieve.

Nothing.

Besides, he has a second appointment with Juditha Estima, the Intuit of the Ascended Masters who specializes in past life therapy and he has faith that she can find Kateri. Juditha will find the key to unlock the mystery of Kateri's disappearance.

And he is glad Melusine has gone because he hates her now, hates her with all his heart. He never wants to see her again. She is defiled, soiled; she has proven herself to be the worst kind of liar.

He tries to push her from his thoughts but he does wonder if she will be there, waiting for him as if nothing happened, come the end of their trip.

But he is not even sure if he cares.

He has a little time before he needs to meet the psychic and he decides to go and phone his son and see how Mimi is faring.

At least, he thinks, viciously, he can always rely on the loyalty of his dog.

11.

MELUSINE AND GUNTHER soon tire of the Fremont. "It's too late to take our passion wagon back now," he says, unlocking the car door. "I'll take it back tomorrow. But I wouldn't mind going back to the hotel and lying down for a while. I hope you won't think me a lesser man for it, but I'm tired out. You tired me out, lady."

She laughs and reaches for her seat belt. "Yes, I could certainly have a nap too." Then she stops, with the belt pulled halfway across her. "Can I come back to your room with you? I don't want to go to mine."

"Of course you can. Won't Hans be worried though?"

She shrugs. "I doubt it."

She thinks for a moment. "Can I tell you something?"

"Anything. And I'm not just saying that."

She hesitates. "It's very awkward really. But I just don't know what to think…"

He takes the keys out of the ignition, turns to her and strokes her hair.

"You can tell me anything," he says.

"I think Hans may have tried to strangle me last night while we were making love — oh, I shouldn't be telling you this … it's entirely inappropriate…"

"Just tell me. He's your husband, what did you think? That I thought you were celibate? Tell me what happened."

"He covered my mouth and my nose and I couldn't breathe

which seemed to excite him. He also had his hand on my throat and it really hurt. I hit him hard across the head and he fell on the floor." She looks away. "Why would he do that?"

Gunther takes her hand. "A lot of men think that holding a woman by the throat is very erotic. It must tie into some kind of fantasy he has. He's never done anything like that before?"

She shakes her head. "No. He is usually very conservative and straightforward about it all, to put it bluntly." A thought occurs to her. "He's also incredibly silent and maybe he was trying to shut me up because I was making too much noise. We'd both had a lot to drink and I..." She blushed a dark red. "And I was thinking about how it had felt to hold you in that tent and I'm sorry because there I was, aroused at a time when you had been so upset, I was thinking about you and trying not to of course and I was being much more enthusiastic than I usually am. And maybe he didn't like that."

"You were thinking about me! Melu, I couldn't stop thinking about you either. I don't know what to say about Hans except that Vegas does weird things to people. I'm sure he just got carried away. Did it feel abusive to you?"

She shakes her head again. "No, it was more like he was getting off on it as if I wasn't even there, it was like I was some kind of sex prop or something." She shrugs. "Let's not talk about it any more. Okay?"

He looks at her and puts his hand on her knee. "Absolutely."

"But thank you for listening."

They drive up through the Strip and pass the novelty store with the curved black windows and the bucking bronco with the mannequin strapped to it. Melusine is relieved to see that the little girl isn't there. The day, the whole Las Vegas experience, is so surreal that nothing would surprise her. The tawdry storefront sparkles with the reflection of the city lights and even the 'nude strippers daily' sign doesn't look as worn and dirty.

Melusine thinks that Vegas forgives all sins at night.

They pass the row of wedding chapels, come up to the Stratosphere, followed by Circus Circus with its giant neon clown. They drive up towards the Wynn and past the now-familiar sights of Treasure Island, the Bellagio, Paris, The Venetian, Harrah's and the Pink Flamingo.

They stop at the traffic lights next to the Excalibur and Melusine thinks back to her cravings and wild longings. She looks at the man next to her, thinking that she'd never have figured him to be her fix. Her unlikely suitor looks exhausted while she feels high, crazy and free like she did when she used speed; she's all-powerful and her energy is electric and without end. She had only said she was tired because she wants to lie down beside him and be with him.

They turn towards Hooters and into the resort parking lot.

She wonders for a moment if they will bump into Hans at the hotel but she thinks it is unlikely. She feels as if her husband is a million miles away.

They take the elevator up to the second floor and Gunther opens the door to his room.

The place is littered with old pizza boxes, beer bottles, vodka bottles and orange juice cartons. The remnants of Chinese take-out sit on the counter along with crumpled napkins and half-empty coffee cups.

"Housekeeping doesn't do the kitchen area," he explains, unnecessarily.

He leads her through to the bedroom, where his open suitcase is on the floor, spilling clothes. The bed is perfectly made and he immediately falls on it, kicking off his shoes and making groaning noises of happiness.

Melusine pulls the bedding out from its strong tucking on her side of the bed and rearranges the pillows. Then she lies down next to him on top of the coverlet, not sure whether he wants her to touch him. Perhaps he just wants to sleep. Maybe he is not the cuddling kind. God knows she is not, not usually. He solves her dilemma by turning towards her and pulling her close, tucking her in to him.

He strokes her head and her hair and she closes her eyes and soon falls asleep with her hand resting on his waist.

When she wakes, it is because she needs to go to the toilet. She fumbles her way in the dark, trying to be soundless, embarrassed by the ordinariness of her bodily needs. He stays sound asleep, oblivious.

She is wide-awake though. She lies down again. He snores now and then, and turns over. She feels restless but doesn't want to leave.

She looks at the clock, it's two a.m. It's always two a.m., she thinks. The universal hour of insomniac torment.

Despite her earlier avowals to Gunther about never washing off the dust and passion of their day, she is longing to have a deep hot bath and get into some clean clothes.

She wonders what to do. She cannot leave because then she will not be able to get back in to the room without waking him. But she cannot stay either. She stands up quietly. They forgot to draw the curtains and the pink lights from the Tropicana hotel shine brightly into their room along with the beam from the pyramidal Luxor.

She picks her way through the debris of the living room and sees that he left the key card on the table when they came in. She takes it and lets herself out, padding down the corridor to the elevator.

She stands outside the door to her room, reluctant to open it. Will Hans be there? What on earth will she say to him if he is?

She inserts her card quietly and the green light flashes. She turns the handle and slowly pushes the door open.

But it is quiet inside. She goes in and turns on the lights. It is exactly like it was when she left. It does not look as if Hans has returned to the room either, not since he rushed out into the night, to god knows where.

She is not worried about him. She is increasingly convinced that there is something going on with him, the truth of which she might never know. She is beginning to wonder if he has had some agenda for this trip all along, and that while he tried to accommodate her being there with him, it had not worked out. She shrugs. She is just glad he's not there.

She runs a hot bath and luxuriates in it, marveling at her body and the pleasures she has enjoyed. She soaps herself gently, wishing she had a better quality soap than the small cheap bar from the hotel.

She washes her hair, sorrowful to lose the touch of Gunther's hands, but she wants to be clean and fresh.

She dries herself and rubs lotion on her legs, her breasts and her arms.

How wonderful to be appreciated. All these years without being caressed. Oh arms, legs, how did you survive, all this time?

She puts on bright yellow underwear and a new dress and leaves the room. She cannot wait to be back with Gunter and the elevator seems frustratingly slow.

She inserts his key card and is relieved when the door opens.

She thinks he is fast asleep but when she lies down next to him, he pulls her close, almost grabbing her.

He burrows into her neck, turning her body so he can spoon into her back and he rubs her thighs, her buttocks and her stomach.

"You smell nice," he says and he yawns. "What's the time?"

"Five a.m."

"I'm going to have a shower," he says. "You smell too good, I have to catch up with you. You stay right there."

"I'm going to get under the covers," Melusine says and she strips her dress over her head. She hears Gunther give a sound of appreciation that makes her laugh with joy.

"You undo me, Melu, you undo me. I hope the underwear's also coming off?"

"Of course," she says primly and steps out of her panties and unclasps her bra.

"Magnificent. Good god, your breasts, Melu. I love your breasts. And your legs and all the rest."

He is sporting a gigantic erection, his cock is dark and his balls are full and heavy and she longs to lick them and take them in her mouth.

He sees what she is thinking. "Let me get him all cleaned up first and then we can have more fun."

She nods and slides under the covers. The sheets are deliciously soft and clean and the bed is heavenly. She doesn't mean to but she falls asleep, a dreamless, beautiful sleep.

She wakes later to find him gone. She sits up and her heart is pounding quickly, it's too quiet. Where is he?

He has left her a note. Oh, right, he had to take the car back. She looks at the clock. She has no idea when he left.

She dresses and leaves him a note. *Meet me at the swimming pool.* She leaves the note half-sticking out from under the door and goes back to her room to get her swimsuit.

Gunther had explained, when she had told him about her odd non-conversation with the man in the elevator who had pointed to her breasts, that the towels for swimming were kept in the drawers under the television set. She pulls out a blue and white striped towel and smiles, thinking back to that day, and how the world had been so different. She had been so alone then.

Poolside, she is far from alone but again she's the only one swimming — the others find the water far too cold. She dives in and swims the length of the pool underwater. She swims a few laps and then goes over to the heated round spa pool and turns on the jets.

She sits on the concrete step with the water up to her chin, surveying her world. It is a beautiful world, with a view of the crystal-clear kidney-shaped swimming pool, a large palm tree, the stucco resort and a heavenly blue sky. But it is not the view that makes her world beautiful and she knows it. It's the prospect of her lover returning, and it's the knowledge that her starved limbs and heart will be loved and fulfilled. There is the certainty of love in her future.

She thinks of Ingeborg's Ich in *Malina*, and Ich's desperate, all-consuming love for Ivan.

I'm sorry. I judged you, Ich. I didn't understand. And now I have this man. Can I say that I'm in love with him after so short a time? Certainly I cannot wait for his return. I ask only that he be at my side. And Ingeborg, your work was so focused on how women repeatedly fall victim to Bluebeards, fascists and colonizers and are smothered and destroyed by the patriarchal society as much in marriage as by murder. So I ask myself, what am I doing with this man? Ach, I think too much!

She sees him coming; he opens the tall wrought-iron gate and looks around for her.

She waves him over, banishing the ghosts of Ingeborg and Ich and their ill-fated lives and forsaken loves. While she shares their philosophical angst, she does not want to share their fate but does she have a choice?

He dips his foot in the spa tub. "Wow, it's hot."

"It's nice after the big pool," Melusine says, "go and try it. The others won't go in but I did."

He walks over to the pool and wades down the steps. She can tell he thinks it's too cold but he won't admit it. He swims a quick lap and then joins her in the hot tub, laughing.

"Yes," he says, "this is quite delicious now."

He sits close to her and slips his hand inside her thigh. She rubs him; his arm, his shoulder and his back. She is trying to memorize every freckle on his body. But there are a lot of them.

"You've got a lot of freckles," she says and he agrees.

"Hated them when I was a kid," he says. "There's a lot of red to my hair and there was more when I was younger. So freckles come with the territory."

"Were you a hell-raiser as a child?" she asks and he nods.

"Pretty much. Always breaking windows with soccer balls, or breaking bones, or coming home covered in bruises and scrapes. But I never really got into anything bad like drugs or stuff like that. You?"

She thinks about her love of speed and amphetamines and her narrow escape from that way of life.

"Nothing to talk about," she says. "I fulfilled my parent's wishes of a successful and happy life and that's important to me."

He laughs. "I far exceeded my parents' expectations. But I think they set the bar pretty low. And now they're not going to be happy because I can't see me and my wife staying together and they love her."

"Do they live in London too?"

"Yes. In the same neighbourhood."

"Have you thought about adopting?" she asks. "Or having the baby carried by a surrogate? If you've got the money, there're all kinds of options, these days."

He thinks for a moment. "We never thought of a surrogate. But that would make my wife feel like she failed."

Melusine is impatient. "If she's not willing to try to move on, then you can't help her. If she's only got one expectation of a perfect result, then she's doomed both of you and you can't help that. One needs to be flexible in life. Things more often than not don't turn out the way we hoped or planned." She realizes that's she's trying to give herself advice in case things do not work out between her and Hans after Vegas. She wonders if she will be able to take her own advice with the kind of grace she's glibly advocating.

"It sounds very simple when you say it like that."

"It is." Melusine insists. "What if you go back to your wife and say look, yes, we've suffered terrible tragedies, there's no escaping that. These are our options; stay stuck in our grief, or try to make a change. I've heard that adopting can be very fulfilling. You just need to change your mindset — or hers, if you can."

He is quiet for a moment. "I don't even know if I want children. If they're yours, you just deal with it, it's like they come with the package of marriage and so forth. But if you have to order them on the side, to put it in crass terms, well, it makes you think about what you really want from life and from marriage."

"And what do you want?" she asks. "You've got a good job as well as your creative photography. Is that enough?"

"I don't know the answer to that question. I don't. You're right. When you put it like that, my life sounds quite barren."

"I didn't mean it like that," she is quick to correct him. "I was just asking."

"It's okay. It's all stuff I need to think about."

She nuzzles his neck. "You taste like chlorine now," she says and he nods and kisses her.

"So do you. Considering that we only have the rest of today and one more night together, do you have any ideas what we should do? I don't."

"I'd like to pretend we have more time than that. Let's do that. Let's pretend we've got all the time in the world. What would we do then?"

He rubs her neck and thinks. "We'd plan where to have lunch. Then we'd think about taking in a show and where to have supper. Then we'd watch the pirate show down at Treasure Island and the volcano at the Mirage and then we'd walk the Strip and buy large drinks in plastic beakers shaped like bongs and I'd stand by impatiently while you shopped for trinkets and knick-knacks. And then, finally, inebriated, we'd come back home and I'd fuck the panties off you, or you'd fuck the living daylights out of me and then we'd go to sleep. That's what we'd do, if we had all the time in the world."

She grins. "Let's do that, shall we?"

He pulls her close. "Why don't we go and have a shower together first and wash all this chlorine off and play it by ear? How does that sound?"

She agrees and they get out of the spa pool that had stopped whirling a while back.

Back in his room, he fixes the *Sweet Dreams, Do Not Dis-*

turb sign on the door and takes her into the bathroom. He pulls the shower curtain closed, adjusts the water and climbs in, holding his hand out to her.

Her hair is soon wet and water runs down her face, and her arms are around his neck and her eyes are closed. He is soaping her back, her buttocks, her breasts. She faces him and he cannot stop his hands from exploring her body. His fingers dip into the curves behind her knees, his thumbs speak to the muscles and ligaments of her calves. He cups her breasts, one at a time, holding their sweet heaviness in his hands. Her nipples are taut and she is so hot for him and she wants him right then but he makes her wait. With his cock pushing against her, and the water running down their bodies, he slips his finger inside her and she comes again and again. Then he turns her to face the wall, and he spreads her legs the width of the bath and bends her over. He pushes himself inside her and despite her orgasms, the water has made her dry but he feels so good, so immense.

Melusine is glad he can't see her face. Pleasure has contorted her features and she's relieved to have privacy. She lets go with abandon, matching his thrusts and he soon comes inside her and she sees blinding colours of exploding lights behind her eyeballs.

He turns off the shower and they step out and dry each other clumsily, leaving large wet patches.

"Let's lie down for a bit," Gunther says and she nods.

He closes the heavy drapes and the room becomes as night. It's not yet noon.

She moves towards him under the covers, and they lie chest to chest and the sensation of his skin, and his hair, and his heat — and the realization of the oncoming loss of it all — fills her with tears and she can't stop herself; she cries rivers before she can disguise what's happening or even turn away.

He holds her and she cries harder.

"I know," he says. "I know."

She cries herself out and gets up to blow her nose.

"Well," she says. "I guess it's too late for me to play it cool."

"You don't have to play it at all, Melusine. You know what I wish?" he asks her.

"What?"

"I wish we were the couple on the Skywalk, the one the photographer saw. I wish that was our lives."

But it's not and he doesn't have to say it.

"We should go shopping," he says unexpectedly and she gapes at him.

"Yep, retail therapy. Always makes everything better. Let's go and spend some money, okay? We'll have fun and it'll be stuff that will always be ours, yours and mine."

She laughs. "My face is too swollen to go out."

"Sunglasses. No one will care anyway."

They get dressed and walk down the Strip, holding hands.

"Expensive stuff or cheap stuff?" she asks. "I can't afford expensive stuff."

"Me neither. I haven't exactly lived a budget-conscious life. Cheap it is. There isn't a cheap store in Vegas that doesn't have our name on it. But I wish I could buy you Prada. You're very Prada, Melusine."

She strikes a fashion pose and he reaches for his camera. Melusine carries on strutting her stuff and she realizes that she's having fun for the first time in years; her own fun, and not just the joy of watching Jonas discover the world. This is her moment, hers.

They carry on down the Strip and buy crazy sunglasses, fridge magnets, shot glasses, mouse pads. Melusine buys earrings and a huge pink piggy bank that she tells Gunther is actually a wishing well.

"What will you wish for?"

"You know I can't tell you," she teases him. "But here, you may have the honour of making the first wish."

He drops a dime into the piggy bank with his eyes shut tight and then she does the same, holding her breath.

Please let something happen in my life. Let me do something that means something, something real. And keep this man in my life. I know that's two wishes but everyone's allowed to push their luck in Vegas.

Every item they buy is ablaze with *Welcome to Las Vegas* or scantily clad showgirls. They spend hours perusing clothing, backpacks, hip flasks. Seems like there is nothing in the world that does not have a Las Vegas logo on it.

They walk down to the Sugar Factory and Gunther buys her a *Sweet All Over* tote bag and a large red velvet cupcake that they share messily, trying to eat from it at the same time and ending up with frosting everywhere.

Back on the Strip, he buys her a bracelet with blue glass beads and a necklace with her name spelt out in diamanté block letters that the shop girl strings on a leather cord.

They walk for hours, and Gunther translates some of the t-shirt slogans for her; *sorry boys, I eat pussy* and *you say bitch like it's a bad thing* and *young cunts are all the same.*

"And even I can understand that one," Melusine says, pointing, "*fuck you, fuck fucking fuck you.* I guess they just couldn't fit another fuck on it."

They pass a crazy girl playing the concertina, her teeth bared in a horrible facsimile of a smile and they come across some dreadlocked hippy teenagers selling roses made from palm fronds and they end up at the Venetian, watching the gondoliers floating around.

"How will we stay in touch?" Gunther asks suddenly. He's drinking a beer and he passes it to her.

She takes a long swallow and nearly finishes it. "Gosh, I was thirsty, I didn't realize. Um, I don't know, Gunther. Don't you think the question really should be whether we stay in touch at all?"

He looks crushed and her heart lifts. She was testing him.

"Ah, come on," she says. "You know I didn't mean that. I'd like to mean it but I can't."

He is relieved.

"I don't want to email," she says. "It would seem so...,"

"...so glassy, cold, flat and impersonal," Gunther finishes her thought.

"Exactly. And email and those things, they're not communicating in a real way. You adopt a persona that isn't quite you, even if you don't mean to. And after you and I have had all this," she sweeps her hand around, "I can't bear to think of us being trapped on a Skype screen, looking all contorted, and trying to pretend like it feels good to be talking to a computer. It would make you feel even further away from me."

"I've got an idea, we can write letters to each other! Do things the old-fashioned way."

Melusine is taken aback; that was going to be her suggestion. "How odd that you should say that. I had that idea too. My favourite poet and her married lover wrote letters to each other for years but I must point out that their relationship ended in madness and death."

He laughs. "Gotta love a happy ending. And who was she, your favourite poet? It's a pity I'm only beginning to get to know you now and it's nearly time for us to leave each other."

"Her name was Ingeborg Bachmann and her lover was also a poet, Paul Celan. He committed suicide by jumping into the Seine and she died from a lit cigarette that set her apartment on fire in Rome. They're not sure whether her death was an accident or not."

"She sounds very Sylvia Plath," Gunther comments and Melusine is further surprised.

"She was. But how do you know about Sylvia Plath anyway?"

"A girl I had a thing for at university was in love with Plath and I was so into this girl that I even read *The Bell Jar*. I wouldn't say I enjoyed it but I could appreciate the prose."

Melusine feels a flash of jealousy towards this ghost girlfriend from Gunther's past and the effort he had gone to. "I had a big crush on Ingeborg when I was a girl. I learned a lot of her poems off by heart. I often feel as if she sums up how I feel much better than I can." She closes her eyes:

When someone departs he must throw his hat,
filled with the mussels he spent the summer
gathering, in the sea
and sail off with his hair in the wind

She regrets saying the poem out loud, thinking that she has revealed too much.

"That's beautiful. But even though we're sailing off in different directions, Melu, don't think this is the end of us, okay?"

She bites her lip. "But how will we post things? You can't send things to my house. Hans will see. Or Jonas might see. And I can't ask my best friend because she abhors affairs. Oh god, Gunther, was this an affair?"

"This was just us. And whatever it was, or is, I thank god for it. I guess sending you things at work is out of the question too. Here's a suggestion." He encircles her and kisses her neck as he speaks. Melusine wonders at her own daring with these public displays of affection but she figures the odds of Hans seeing her are slim to none.

"Not to change the subject," he says, "but I've been meaning to ask you something but you keep distracting me." He brushes his hand lightly over the curve of her breast to emphasize his point. "You studied literature at university which means you must have studied English at school — how come you don't understand a word of it?"

She grins, proudly. "Stupid guttural language. I did the minimum and then forgot it all as fast as I could. Which is easy if you don't use it. German is so lyrical and lovely and Ingeborg convinced me of that too:

I with the German language
this cloud about me

that I keep as a house
drive through all languages.

"Ingeborg didn't need English, so why would I? But back to you and me. I like the idea of this posting thing but I just don't know how it will work."

"Get a post office box," he says. "And when you've got it, email me the address, just email me once. I'll give you my email address. Don't write anything else, not hello or a message or your name or anything because then I will feel like I have to reply and I agree, no virtual anything. Because this, what we have, will always be real."

She nods, resting her forehead on his chest.

And then, out of nowhere, she wants him gone already. She cannot bear the thought of saying goodbye and she wishes their parting was over so that she could be alone to mourn her loss and nurse her memories. But, equally and immediately, she knows she is wishing away time that she will long for later.

"Why am I always two people at the same time?"

Gunther doesn't seem startled by the question. He runs his thumb down her cheekbone and caresses her lips.

"I've got no idea. But it makes you doubly intriguing. Come on you, and you, it's time for supper. We're going up the Stratosphere to have dinner and drinks and watch the world turn. How does that sound?"

"Sounds great. But we may have to cab it, my feet are killing me from all this walking."

"A cab it shall be."

Up at the Stratosphere, he studies a wine list. "Red or white?"

"White!" she knows she replies too emphatically and he gives her a glance.

She picks up her menu, seeing typography with no meaning. She wants to tell him she will miss him but she does not think he wants to hear it; she fears it will drive him away. But, she asks herself, is she confusing him with Ivan from *Malina*, or with Ingeborg's Paul? She looks at him. He is talking to the waiter and pointing at the wine list.

"So, Melu," he says, handing the wine list to the waiter and turning to her, "I have to go back and sort out my life. What about you? If you could change just one thing about your life when you get back, what would it be?"

She is flummoxed by the bluntness of this question. She had been grappling with her own inner conversation, she is not ready for this new tack.

"Um? I don't know. I'd like to try to do something creative. I used to want to do so many things. I might take a course at the university or something, I don't know." The question depresses her. As if taking a course at university will give her life meaning. But she can't think of anything that will.

The wine arrives and while it's being poured, she thinks about her dreams as a girl.

She takes a large swallow of her wine. "This is delicious. Fruity, clean. I don't know, Gunther. It's been so long since I even had any dreams of my own. My dreams have been for my child for as long as I can remember. Or I tried to make my parents' dream for my life come true. But if you ask me what my dreams are, my own dreams, I can't answer that."

He puts his arm around her shoulders. "Maybe this discussion will get your subconscious thinking. I know I hardly know you but I feel as if you are capable of doing anything." He rubs her shoulders and buries his head in her neck and she feels her groin tighten. The slightest touch and her body wakens.

"And you? Do you know what you'll do?"

He shakes his head. "I just walked through my life to this point, not unhappily, not until now anyway, and I never thought about things one way or the other. I wasn't suffering from an absence of dreams or a death of a dream. Sometimes you only realize you had a dream in the first place once it's gone. Such a cliché but it's true."

"A family?"

He sighs. "A family. Enough about that. Let's order some food or we'll be drunk in no time."

The first bottle of wine is already gone and the sun sets and the lights below them explode the Strip into a river of molten jewels; they sit as close to one another as they can and try to pretend that time is not passing.

When they get back to Gunther's room, Melusine feels quite ill from the rich food and wine. She props herself upright on the bed, supported by pillows while Gunther crashes beside her, snoring loudly. She watches him. She cannot close her eyes because when she does, the room spins — although she notices that she must close her eyes from time to time because the clock radio tells her that she dozes. In this way, she keeps vigil until the early hours of the morning and then she makes the decision to leave. She leans down and kisses Gunther, rubbing her nose lightly on his cheek, and inhaling the scent of him deep into her lungs. She whispers a poem to him:

Mouth, that spent the night in my mouth,
Eye that guarded my own,
Hand —
and those eyes that drilled through me!
Mouth, which spoke the sentence,
Hand, which executed me!

"Will you be Paul to my Ingeborg?" she whispers. "Ivan to Ich? My future broken heart — or didn't we mean that much to each other at all?"

Then she slips off the bed and puts on her shoes. She quietly gathers her purse and her bags of purchases and eases the door open. She pauses for a moment before closing it behind her. The sound of the door clicking shut delivers a blow to her belly that is staggering. Her body is a leaden cargo of concrete sorrow and she pushes herself forward, hardly able to breathe. For her, the Vegas holiday is over.

12.

THINGS HAD NOT GONE WELL the first day Hans forced himself to go down to the psychics. The stadium-sized hall was filled with what seemed like hundreds of psychics, clairvoyants, mediums and card readers, and each of them was accessorized with statues, charts, effigies, ornaments, charms, jewelry, oils, crystals, feathers, dreamcatchers, ointments, potions, talismans, symbols and water fountains.

Strange sounds filled the air; and it was a different kind of music, and Hans stopped at one table, mesmerized by a man who was stroking a large crystal bowl. The melody was like nothing Hans had ever heard; it was a keening wail, as if the crystal was weeping with him and for him.

"What you're hearing is the music of Celestial Sound Vibrations," the man said, looking up. "It's the energy of the universe, the fundamental core energy that creates life and lives in crystals in the form of fossilized water. Our bodies are crystalline too, in their structure, and that's why the noise you hear affects you like it does — all your tissues and cells feel the energy and respond."

Hans was skeptical. Healing by the sound of a bowl being stroked? But he found it hard to leave.

"I'm doing a show tonight," the man said, and he handed Hans a leaflet. "In one of the rooms to the side here. Come along. You don't have to do anything, just lie there and listen. Your body will do the rest."

Hans took a pamphlet.

"If you can't make the show, you can always buy the CD," the man called after him and Hans thought that he might.

Apart from the man and his bowl, Hans did not find anyone that showed the slightest potential to help him and he left the hall discouraged, to take Melusine out to dinner. He passed Jimmy Buffett's Margaritaville on the way back to the Desert Rose Resort, and the only thing he had wanted in life at that moment was to be one of those normal couples going out to dinner and drinking too much and then going home to make love.

And he tried his best and failed at his worst.

The following morning, after that terrible night with Melusine, Hans ventured back into the hall. He headed towards the crystal bowl man and it was then that he saw her: the Reverend Juditha Estima. He liked her immediately for the comparable normalcy of her name; he had walked past countless variations of Sunshine Eden's, Celestial Seraphina's, Trinity del Luna's, Countess Sophia's and even one Nevaeh, which was heaven, spelled backwards. It was a relief to find Juditha and the peaceful sanctuary of her tent.

Most of the other psychics at the convention were seated behind tables without any privacy and Hans had not enjoyed the flea market feeling of pawing through their wares while speaking to them.

But, with her tent, Juditha had a very different set-up.

Apart from a warm honeyed glow emanating from a large Himalayan salt crystal light, the tent was dark and there was the quiet murmur of a water fountain and the subtle soothing scent of magnolia and jasmine. Hans stepped inside, closed his eyes and inhaled the fragrant air.

"What you're smelling," the Reverend said and her voice was as gentle and pure as the quiet bubbling water, "is essence of peony, in a fragrance called *Healing Petals of Peony*. This essence will help lift you out of your ego-bound state of pain and assist you in moving to a place where you can connect with love, and find the truth that wishes to speak from the realms of your soul."

Hans did not hear a word she said. He knew that she was talking and that sounds were coming out of her perfect mouth but her beauty and serenity mesmerized him and he suddenly became aware that she was looking at him as if expecting an answer to a question.

"Sorry," he said, feeling stupid, "what did you say?"

"Would you like to make an appointment to see me later? Because I'm busy until late this evening. Would it work for you, if we met at seven p.m.? I'm sorry it has to be so late. What's your name? I'm Juditha."

"I'm Hans," he said. "Please, let me take you out to dinner," he blurted out, "even psychics have to eat, don't they?"

She laughed and the sound made Hans think of blossoms falling from a cherry tree.

"I'm having strangely poetic thoughts," he said, "your powers, or whatever they are, must be very strong."

She laughed again. "I'm an intuit, a healer. And I sense that you're in a lot of pain. I sense you're in need of something more than most, so I accept your invitation to dinner. That way I can get to know you better, and you can explain in an unhurried fashion what it is you think you need and I'll have the opportunity to hear what it is your soul's really trying to tell me."

She looked at her watch. "I tell you what, take a seat, I have a few minutes before my next consultation. Let me get you a cup of tea and I'll tell you who I am and what I do, in order to give you some background information before we meet later. You never know, you might decide that I'm not the one for you but I feel a strong connection to you already."

"Yes, me too," Hans said and he sat down.

"Jasmine honey tea," she handed him a cup. "With almond flavouring, no caffeine, all natural."

Juditha explained that she was an ordained minister, a qualified hypnotherapist, a crystal therapist, a verified life psychic, a certified paranormal investigator, a certified tarot card reader and a certified intuit. She had been a guest speaker on talk radio shows and had written for magazines. That she was also a member of the Witches of the Healing Cauldron, Hans chose to ignore. She was a third generation advisor and spiritual reader; she'd also studied Druid therapy and was certified in past life regression therapy.

"Karma," she said. "First off, know this. There is no good or bad karma. Karma just is."

Hans nodded.

"However," she continued, "karma does assert a basic law; that for every action there is an equal and corresponding action or reaction and it is our willingness to make a choice, to move beyond karma and reclaim our power to choose a course of action that aligns us with our Source."

He nodded again. He had no idea what she was talking about.

"But how will this help me get in touch with my sister?" he asked. "That's all I want. My sister disappeared when I was seventeen and she was fourteen and I must find her. I've tried to do everything in my power to enjoy my life, and move on but I'm tormented every second and it's only getting worse. I must find her. Can you help me?"

She nodded. "We'll need to dismantle the brittle shell of the ego," she said, "and then we'll be able to explore your karma and that will lead us to your sister. What is her name?"

"Kateri."

"Kateri," she spoke the name carefully. "Well, Hans, karma is always providing us with opportunities to become more receptive to the higher vibrations of love and compassion and that's how we'll find her. Often, we feel like we are being punished…"

Hans nodded vigorously and she continued.

"…but the true purpose of karma is to teach, not to punish.

Karma intervenes to put us back on the path of our life-lesson which is to learn love, compassion, tolerance and forgiveness."

She leaned forward and held his hands in hers. Her skin was cool and calming. Her touch made him feel as if a healing light was coursing through his body, identifying all the inflamed areas of pain and cooling them, while her energy washed his psyche clean like a mother stroking a child's fevered brow.

He exhaled slowly and tried to maintain the control of interviewing her. "But I still don't see," he said, closing his eyes, "how this will help me find Kateri."

She pulled away and he felt the aching loneliness of his now-empty hands. "It's a matter of cumulative lifetimes. I know it's hard to take it all in. It's complicated, I've been studying this for over thirty years..."

"You must have been very young when you started," Hans said and she nodded.

"Yes, I was. Anyway, I've been studying this for over thirty years and I know I'm asking a lot of you here."

"I just want to find my sister. I don't even have to understand. I just need you to find her for me."

She smiled. "I wish it was that easy, Hans. But together, we'll make a plan to try. I promise you that."

They agreed to meet for dinner and continue the session and Hans left the tent in a daze.

Although he had only known Juditha for so short a time, he felt as if he had reconnected with a dear friend that he had not seen in a while. His body was humming as if he had had a wonderful massage and he felt emotionally light and free.

He had thought he would make straight for his darkened room and seek comfort with his ligature but he didn't feel the need and instead, he found himself at the swimming pool, lying on a deck chair and soaking up the sun.

At that point, he was not thinking about Melusine at all and the memory of their night had faded from his mind entirely.

He enjoyed a hearty lunch and returned to the pool.

And then, an hour before he was due to meet Juditha for dinner, he decided to go for a walk and it was then that he saw Melusine with the man.

He had watched in stupefied horror, turning away to throw up in a nearby pot-plant and when he looked up both Melusine and the man were gone. He went back to his room to brush his teeth and then he went to meet Juditha. His stomach was roiling with acid and his mind was aflame with thoughts of hatred and loathing for his wife.

He sought a darkened area near the rear of the restaurant and waited.

13.

"**I** JUST WANT TO FIND MY SISTER," he says to Juditha. He still cannot believe what he had seen earlier — his wife with another man.

He and Juditha are sitting in a curved dark alcove near the back, and they are both drinking mineral water. Juditha is dressed in flowing white robes and her dark hair is spilling in long wavy curls over her shoulders. Her green eyes are clear and bright, and looking at her, Hans thinks she is one of the most flawlessly beautiful women he has ever seen.

"And find her we shall," Juditha says. "But first I need to understand more about you. Start at the beginning. Tell me your earliest memories as a child. Start there."

Hans is startled. "I can't remember anything," he says and she takes his hand in hers.

"Yes," she says, "you can. Just relax. This isn't an exam. You can't fail. Close your eyes and think of anything and talk to me as it happens, describe it out loud. It doesn't have to make any sense to you. Just tell me what you see, what you feel."

Hans closes his eyes. He can feel his sister's feet in his hands, the unfathomable softness of her skin and the birdlike delicacy of her tiny bones. He casts his mind back further; he's sitting in the back of the car with his sister, they are on a family road-trip and their father is playing eye-spy. Then Hans is even younger, and again, they are all in the car, coming home from a dinner and he and Kateri are wearing the red downy jackets that Hans is so proud of and he sees that when they pass under the yellow street lights, that the jacket becomes a strange mustard colour. He points this out to his father who tells him he is right and that none of our senses can be relied upon, for is the jacket red or is it really mustard? Hans is frightened. He wants it to be red; always red, red under any and all lights.

His voice is a murmur in his ears, he is hardly aware that he is talking. He travels further back in time and he and Kateri are hunting for Easter Eggs and even then, she is so beautiful.

Back even more and he has no self-awareness apart from a vague hum and his father comes home and gives him a beautiful toy and tells him that he has a baby sister. Hans takes the toy and loves the sister he has not yet seen.

"I remember being wrapped in a towel by a babysitter," he says, in a low voice to Juditha. "She wrapped me tightly, very tightly and I loved it. My arms were pinned inside the towel. And when she put me to bed, I wanted to be tucked in very tightly, as tightly as she could; tighter, tighter, tighter, I'd say."

"Anything else?" Juditha's voice is soft and light and she's still holding his hand.

He tries not to force his thoughts, but simply wander back down the road of his life.

"My mother," he said, "and my uncle, yes, it was my uncle, they were in the bathtub together, with me … my mother, and her brother, and he was washing her back, and she was washing me and there we were, the three of us, sitting in a train for a while, in a row, my mother washing me, and her brother washing her. We sat there until the water got cold. I remember the water getting cold and we were all wrinkled. I was very cold."

"That's excellent, Hans," Juditha says, warmly, and he is proud of himself but then he is slapped in the face by the recollection of his current shame and he snatches his hand back.

"My wife's having an affair," he spits out suddenly and Juditha is startled.

"We came here together and now, she's sleeping with another man. A fat man too. She's ruined now, ruined. She's dirty, ruined. I came here to find you, I didn't want her to come with me but she did and now look what she's done."

Juditha stands up and he is frightened and sorry; it was going so well and now he has driven her away.

"Please forgive me," he says. "You're right to leave. I cannot be helped. It's no good."

She smiles. "Nonsense. I just thought we might go somewhere more conducive to talking, that's all. We'll go up to my room, I have a healing area there. We'll get comfortable and continue with our work."

Tears of relief fill his eyes and his chest burns.

"Thank you," he says. "I thought the things I said sent you away."

"We've been brought together by the universe Hans, and by you and me. We both manifested this, our meeting. We have a purpose together, a goal, and there are many choices that we can make during this encounter. We can choose to learn the lessons of karma or we can make further mistakes. It's all up to us."

"What do you mean, we manifested this?" he asks, getting up.

"That our being here is in alignment with our soul's true purpose. We met outside of ourselves in the realm of pure love; the realm in which our truest selves reside, the realm in which we are all one — one in love and one with love. We've made this happen, Hans."

He hopes she won't talk in circles like this the whole night.

They leave the bar and reach her room and she opens the door to reveal the magic that she has worked in transforming the generic hotel room into an oasis of fragrant comfort. It is decorated in the same manner as her tent and is dark, soothing and fragrant.

"Lie down," Juditha says. "Take your shoes off. Get completely comfortable."

He does as she says and she covers him with a light blanket. He feels utterly joyful and as safe as a child in a warm maternal embrace.

"Before we talk about the specifics of your sister," she says, "and don't worry, we will get to that soon, but before we do, I want to explain some things to you, so you'll have a context of awareness. I've already explained about karma but what's even more important is that you become aware that we're not humans trying to have a spiritual experience in this world; we're spiritual beings having a human experience and that is a fundamental and essential difference."

Hans finds her voice so soothing that he can hardly concentrate on what she saying and perhaps she senses this.

"Hans," she says, "let me make you some tea and then we'll carry on."

He sits up and watches her move gracefully around the kitchenette.

He takes a drink of the tea that she gives him and he feels instantly more awake.

"So fine, we're spiritual beings," he says. "Look, Juditha, don't get me wrong, that's great but I'm not a spiritual person and forgive me for that, but all I want to do is find Kateri."

She's implacable. "We're all spiritual. It's not a choice, it simply is."

He has noticed that she is very big on this 'it simply is' stuff, and he just nods. He does not want to get argumentative about the wrong things and he listens as she carries on talking.

"When we choose to have this human experience, it comes with much joy and many treasures. However, as humans, we also come into this world in an individual sense; we all come with an ego and this ego is very self-protective and wishes to keep us separate from our soulful selves and it fears the loss of itself by the immersion or acceptance of the soul-self.

"So there's a great battle between the ego and the soul and because the soul won't fight for a place in the same way that the ego does — the soul simply is — the ego generally wins and most humans live their lives with no idea that there is anything else to be except ego-driven and ego-bound.

"Hans," she says now, "the point of all of this is that in order for us to find Kateri, I'm going to need to do some work with your ego."

He is alarmed and she sees this.

"You're in too much pain, Hans," she says, "for me to be able to channel Kateri, do you understand? Before we can find her, we need to help you find your way back to your inner loving self, the self who views the ego with kindness, compassion and acceptance. First we see the ego, then we forgive the ego. Then we can align our hearts with our true energy, and Hans, all that energy, all that life energy is love. Love is the life-blood of the universe. Right now your ego is a gigantic wall that's standing between you and your finding peace with Kateri. We need to become friends with the ego and thereby dismantle its power and then you'll find what you're looking for."

Hans sighs. "Juditha, honestly, this all sounds very tiring. I just want to find my sister. I don't know if I can do this. I'm so tired. I've got issues I can't even tell you about..."

"You mean your sexual addiction," she says and he nearly drops the teacup and his pale skin flushes scarlet.

"How did you know?"

"Of course I know, Hans, of course. I'm an intuit, I know these things. But the universe loves you, Hans, it loves everything about you, even your addictive needs because they come from a place of pain, a place that is crying out for love. In a way, Hans, your addiction is a gift from the universe, because it's like a sign that something is in need of your attention. Be grateful for the gift, for it will bring self-knowledge and with self-knowledge comes love and forgiveness."

Love and forgiveness. He swallows hard and looks down.

"Listen," he says quietly, "I'm a disgusting man. I lost my way. I loved my sister too much and my wife not enough. And now they are both lost to me and it's my fault, with both of them."

"You haven't lost your wife, Hans. You manifested her affair with this man because it's what you needed right now. You can't blame her. You brought this situation into your life."

This makes Hans angry. "I did not make this affair happen," he says and his mouth is grim. "Don't be stupid. That's just a stupid thing to say." He does not care that he is being rude to her.

She is unmoved by his anger. "Every action in life, every encounter, every person, every single thing; all of it is manifested by our soul-selves because the soul wants to evolve and develop and grow. Your soul, which is you, makes these things happen in order for growth to occur. But the ego fears this evolution and does everything it can to stop the healing.

"For example, take your situation with your wife. You wanted to come on this trip alone. You couldn't accommodate her needs. Also, perhaps you wanted to see how you would feel if she had an affair. Perhaps you've felt unworthy of her love all along and you wanted to prove this to be true. I can't know exactly why your soul called out for this lesson but it did. And now, you are torn. One the one hand your ego is calling for hatred, vengeance, and bitterness. But the soul, which is love, wants to forgive. You feel that you failed your wife and that's why she's having the affair, don't you? And you hate yourself."

"Yes!" Hans cries out.

"Forgive yourself, Hans. Say 'I forgive myself for my wife's affair. It wasn't her fault. It wasn't my fault, I wish to learn compassion and tolerance with this lesson'."

Hans puts down his teacup and opens his mouth but the words won't come out. "I can't." A sense of great weariness fills him, along with a great rage that drains him. "Listen Juditha, thank you but I can see this isn't for me. All these things you're talking about, I'm sorry but they're just not me, and I can't do it." He puts on his shoes and stands up and she also rises to her feet.

"Hans, I understand that all of this feels wrong and new and very frightening. I do know. If, tomorrow, you wish to continue, you know where I am and I'd very much like to help you, please, know that. You're a good man, a man in a tremendous amount of pain and I'm here for you if you'll let me be."

He nods. He cannot look at her. All he wants is to be away from her.

He is more tired than he can ever remember being.

"Before you go," she says, "one more thing. A world of love does exist, Hans. And it's waiting for you and it will wait as long as you need it to. It's not going anywhere."

"Yes, good," he says and he rushes towards the door and out into the hallway.

He feels so foolish, so stupid, so incredibly vulnerable. He feels ashamed, as if he has some dirty secret to hide and he just wants to pretend that the meeting with Juditha never happened.

He goes back down to the bar and then changes his mind. He does not want to go where they met. He heads out into the night; the Fremont's in full swing and Hans goes into the nearest bar and orders a bottle of red wine, mindless of the vintage. He settles down to drink, watching the passersby. He does not think about Melusine; his mind is spinning with his conversation with Juditha.

He is disappointed. He does not want to lie on a couch and talk about his childhood. God knows there's enough crap there to keep a convention of analysts in business for decades but he isn't interested in that. He is a ghost in the stage production of his own life and he has no interest in playing a lead role; he has already accepted that. But even his ghost-self needs some release from all the chains that bind him.

He laughs silently. Ghosts and chains. He is thinking like a crazy person.

He drinks the bottle of wine steadily, and soon it's gone. He switches to brandy and, to his surprise, he finds that he is missing Juditha. He is sorry he rushed out of her room.

She was kind and soothing and he enjoyed being around her, even if she was making no sense to him and asking him to do impossible things. *Forgive himself.* What a cliché. Be at one with his soul. He laughs out loud. What a crock of shit that is. Dismantle the ego. Couldn't she think of anything more original? He decides to go back to his room and carry on drinking there. He is unsteady on his feet and he picks his way slowly back to his hotel.

Once he is inside his room, he sheds his clothes and opens the second bottle of wine that he bought from the bar before he left. He stands in front of the mirror, naked, drinking from the bottle. "What a piece of work is a man," he says, "how pathetic, how fundamentally useless."

He sits down on the bed with a thump. He suddenly, bird's eye view, sees himself in the car with his family; he is a small boy in his red bomber jacket, snuggling next to Kateri and he is worrying, under those passing lights, about the colours being unreliable. Where has the red gone?

He feels the full weight of his childish anxiety and he feels a rush of love and sadness for the boy that he was and he wants to tell the boy that everything will be fine.

But it will not be fine. It never was and it never will be.

He reaches for his ligature and fumbles for his penis. But he falls asleep before he can do anything and he wakes the next morning feeling hungover and alone. He is deserted; there's no one who can help him, no one who can understand.

He looks at himself in the mirror, his eyes are bloodshot and his thinning hair is sticking up in all directions. He drags himself up to the swimming pool so he does not have to be alone. He falls into a doze and when he wakes, he knows he is going back to see Juditha.

He goes back to the room, has a shower and puts on a suit. He wants to look in control.

He passes the man with the crystal bowls in the convention

centre and the man gives him another leaflet for a different show.

"Come tonight," the man urges him and Hans says he'll try.

Juditha is standing outside her tent. She senses his approach and smiles, clearly glad to see him. He's gratified that she cares, and a warmth fills his belly.

She is with a client who is talking non-stop and she signals for Hans to wait.

He sits down outside her tent and watches the surrounding vendors. One of them lights a stick of incense and the smell wafts close to Hans, making his nose feel itchy.

The talkative woman finally leaves and Juditha motions Hans to come inside the tent with her. She closes the tent opening and as soon as they are seated, she takes his hands in hers.

"I'm so very glad to see you," she says, "you have no idea."

He smiles at her. "Can we start over again?"

She nods. "I'm free now for half an hour."

"Hans," she says, "I'm sorry I rushed you last night. I overwhelmed you."

"No. I was wrong. I can't expect results unless I do some work too and help you. I was just hoping it would be easier."

They both laugh. "Yes," Juditha agrees, "easier is always nicer. But not realistic. So tell me about her, Hans. Tell me about Kateri. Every single thing you can remember, leave nothing out and also, tell me as much as you can about the day she disappeared."

"I don't remember much about that day. It's all such a blur. But I'll tell you everything I can."

He tells her the truth about Kateri; how he loved her, not as a brother but as a lover. How he wanted to be with Kateri all of his life, and have adventures with her and there would be no world beyond the two of them. He describes Kateri's beauty and her ethereal poetic nature. He tells Juditha everything he can remember, about Kateri's clothes, the books she read, and the way her room was decorated.

And the tree house, the precious tree house.

He describes their hometown in detail, the school that he and Kateri attended, the playing fields, the stores where they bought their groceries, the movie theatre and the skating rink. He describes how he left the town as soon as he could and never returned except once, online, for a class reunion that showed him how far he had fallen into the abyss of addiction and loneliness.

And then he backtracks and tells her about the day Kateri vanished but the details are sketchy. "I just can't remember," he slaps his knee with frustration. "I could never remember. It drives me crazy."

He tells her about the police investigation and the departure of his father, and how he had not so much suspected his father as been out of his mind with grief and rage.

"I never saw my father again. I never wanted to. That thing about him marrying my mother when she was fourteen turned my stomach, and I could never look at him again. Which was hypocritical of me if you think about how I felt about Kateri. Maybe I hated him for being able to do what I couldn't. Anyway, I never spoke to him again and my mother died while I was at university and so I don't have any family left, unless you count Melusine and Jonas."

"And you can't recall what you did or where you were, the day Kateri vanished?"

He shakes his head.

Juditha looks at her watch. "I've got an idea that might help. But I have to go now, to luncheon with a friend but are you keen to continue tonight?"

"Yes. The more we do the better. Juditha, we need to discuss money, that old thing."

She names an hourly figure which, in another time and place, he would have found exorbitant but he happily agrees.

"We're going to need to talk every day, once you get back to Germany. We're going to work together on this, Hans and I'm going to help you. No matter how long it takes, and Hans, you need to know, it won't be a quick thing. Because as you've gathered, I can't simply look into a crystal ball or read some tea leaves and tell you where Kateri is or how she's doing and anybody here who claims to be able to do that is a charlatan, believe me."

He agrees with enthusiasm. "You wouldn't believe some of the people I've spoken to here," he says and is about to elaborate when she interrupts him.

"Be that as it may," she says, and Hans feels reprimanded, as if he'd been caught in school, passing a crude drawing of the teacher.

"The idea I had for later is this but you may find it alarming."

He sits up straighter.

"I'd like to hypnotize you tonight. I'll record the entire session so you can hear everything. I believe there may be things that you do recall but they're hidden so deep that you don't even know they're there."

He readily agrees. He had considered this option before but he had had no idea how to find a reputable hypnotherapist and it had gone no further.

He leaves the tent, feeling calm and centred. He goes over to chat to the crystal bowl man and buys a copy of the *Celestial Sound Vibrations* CD.

Then he has lunch and returns to the pool to soak up the sunshine, eager to see Juditha again. He feels excited and hopeful.

14.

LATER THAT NIGHT, he is once again lying on her sofa
with his shoes off and his eyes closed. The air is filled
with the fragrance of flower essences.

She hypnotizes him and he wakes an hour later.

"So," he says, sitting up, keen to hear good news, "did I say
anything new?"

She shakes her head. "I'm sorry Hans. I thought it would
work but there wasn't anything."

He is very disappointed. "I'm sorry too," he says.

"We'll just keep trying with one thing and another. We'll
pursue every avenue we can." She thinks for a moment. "Hans,
do you have any items of Kateri's clothing with you? I know
it's most unlikely that you would, but even just a picture of
her? Or of your family perhaps?"

He swallows his disappointment and nods. "Yes, I brought
lots of things. I can go and get them now."

"No hurry. We've done enough work for one night. Let's
resume tomorrow, how does that sound?"

"But I have to leave in the morning. I'll get them for you now."

He rushes up to his room and retrieves a treasured lock of
Kateri's hair, a picture of the family when Hans was about
fourteen, and a blouse that Kateri had loved.

He gets back to Juditha and gives her the items and she
handles them with reverence.

"Don't worry, Hans," she says, "I'll look after these with

great care. They might be the key that will help us open the door to her whereabouts."

"Juditha, you have no idea how grateful I am that we've met. And I'll try to do the things you need me to. I can't do all that love and forgiveness stuff but I'll do my best to do whatever you need."

"You may find," she takes his hands in hers, "that love, peace and forgiveness follow as a consequence of our work. You don't have to do anything, Hans, you just have to be. This may be the hardest thing for you to believe but every single thing is exactly as it should be right now."

And he believes her because at that moment, it feels that way to him too. They make arrangements to begin their daily sessions when he returns to Germany and Juditha hugs Hans lightly.

She is very slender under her loose clothing, almost bony and he wants to stay within her embrace for longer but she pulls away. "Juditha," he says, "I've never asked you. Where do you live?"

She laughs. "Cleveland, Ohio. Not the most glamorous place in the world."

"And do you have family?"

"I've got a sister. And funnily enough Hans, I have family in Germany too. But they live in Berlin."

"You could come to Germany and see them and visit me," Hans speaks like a child, filled with enthusiasm. He cannot bear to think that he might never see her again.

"That's a wonderful idea. Who knows, it may even happen."

"I'm worried that when I leave this room, you'll vanish. I'm afraid that all of this has been a magical trick, just like the red of my jacket that disappeared under the yellow light."

"But the red was always there," she reminds him, "it only looked different for a little while. And when you leave here, your world will look lonely for a bit too but we'll soon be talking again and it'll be just like it is now, with you and me together."

He smiles.

"Oh, and Hans, before you go, I wanted to say this. Try to forgive your wife. Remember, like it or not, you were responsible for her infidelity too. Try to see her as a woman who needed love and it came to her at a time when you could not be there for her."

"If she is still my wife…" He is bitter. "Who knows? Maybe she ran off with that fellow."

"Of course, she's still your wife, Hans. She's like the red coat too; her being with that other man was an impermanent change. You and she have a life, a real life. Vegas isn't real life."

He shrugs. "I'll try. But right now, I don't care about her at all. I don't care if I never see her again."

"That's your hurt ego talking, Hans. Try to reach out from a place of love and compassion for her actions. I know you can. Losing her would cause you a great deal of pain. Go now, sleep and rest. You've done a lot of work tonight and you're very tired. It's hard to think straight when you're tired. All I'm saying is be careful, don't throw away your jacket because a passing light caused you to doubt it."

"I'm getting sick of that jacket," he grumbles, "let's stop talking about it, okay?"

But he does see what she is trying to tell him. "I'll do my best," he assures her and he makes to leave.

"I'm always here for you, Hans," she says, knowing what he is thinking; that she too will vanish. "You have my word."

He tries to smile and he leaves.

He feels utterly spent. It is as if the past few days were a hallucination or a troubled dream. He has difficulty making sense of anything.

He has a hot shower when he gets back to his room and falls into bed. His sleep is filled with strange visions and he tosses and turns, waking and lying there, thinking. He finally falls into a restless doze and when he wakes, he is ravenous.

He eats a generous breakfast and has a swim in the pool. He begins to think about Melusine and he suddenly worries that she will not be at the hotel upon his return.

He had thought that he no longer cared about her and he is surprised to find that he does.

He does not believe Juditha when she says they will keep in touch; he feels as if she is lost to him and he cannot imagine losing Melusine too.

He rushes back to his room, packs and checks out. Then he takes a cab to the Desert Rose Resort. She is not there and he has no way of knowing where she is. She has been shopping, and there are bags of trinkets and souvenirs everywhere. He is glad to see these signs of normalcy and he settles down to wait for her.

15.

MELUSINE OPENS THE DOOR and sees Hans sitting on the sofa. He has his feet up on the table and is flicking through the TV channels. While she tries to sort through her emotions, she thinks, with some surprise, that he is still a good-looking man. And even though it has only been a couple of days since she has seen him, he has gained a little weight, enough to have filled him out somewhat and his colour looks healthier. There is an awkward silence.

"Hello," Melusine says, and her voice sounds strained. "So the conference went well in the end?"

"Yes, thank you," Hans is formal. "It was fine. A lot of work but we managed to have a few outdoor lunches and such. As you can see, I, like you, got a bit of a tan."

"I'm glad it went well," she says and they look at each other.

Hans knows the ball is in his court to make things right. He cannot lose her. And while he cannot view her with the tolerance and forgiveness that Juditha thinks he can and should, he can smooth out the surface tensions and get things back to some kind of normal. "I'm sorry I left you alone so much," he says. "I got caught up in things. I was busier than I thought I'd be. I'm sorry."

They both know this is a lie.

You were gone for two nights. No one is that busy.

She also knows it is a lie that he is sorry. He has never been sorry for anything.

She looks down at the floor. "Don't worry," she says, "I kept myself entertained."

I'm sure you did, with another man's cock in your mouth.

Bile rises in his throat and he swallows hard. "That's good," he says.

He knows he needs to say something about the dreadful night after their dinner at Margaritaville. "About what happened," he says, and he gestures towards the bedroom. "I have no idea where that came from. I'd had too much to drink. It was crazy. I'm sorry for that, Melusine." He gives a lopsided smile. "Vegas can make a man do strange things."

She tries to reciprocate with as much of a smile as she can. "It's fine. I'd had a lot to drink too; I really don't remember much."

He nods.

"I guess I should pack up all this stuff," she waves a hand at the bags.

"I'm already packed," he says, "but don't worry, you've got lots of time, we only have to leave in four hours."

"In which case, if you don't mind, I'll pack and have a small nap. Vegas is fun but it does take a lot out of you."

I'm sure it does. Fucking a strange man for two days straight, yes, that would tire anybody out.

"Excellent idea," he says. "I'll join you."

She packs her suitcase while he goes back to flicking through the TV channels. She does not know what to do with the giant black dildo. She cannot leave it, what if the hotel staff were to find it and then try to contact Hans: *Hello Sir, you left a giant black dildo behind, would you like that forwarded to you?*

She is being silly; hotels would never go to that amount of effort. Particularly in Vegas where she is sure a plethora of sex toys were left stranded as their owners flew back to resume their straitlaced lives.

But she cannot leave it because she knows Hans will check

the room thoroughly; he will check each drawer and closet and under the bed.

So she packs the dildo along with her clothes and her trinkets. She leaves the trinkets in their bags because she cannot bear to look at each item; the memories of Gunther are too strong and she is afraid she will cry. She caresses the bracelet and necklace that he gave her; she has not taken them off.

She finishes packing and she closes the blinds and sets the alarm and lies down on the bed.

Hans comes in and lies down next to her. He is sure he can smell the man on her skin and his nostrils flare in disgust.

He closes his eyes and pretends that she is Kateri and he reaches for her hand.

She jerks in surprise; Hans has never been given to gestures of affection.

She squeezes his hand back, as if telling him that everything is all right and while neither of them wants to keep holding on, they do not know how to let go without offending the other.

And in truth, Melusine is relieved that Hans has returned.

She had been walking the Strip that morning, thinking. She has built a life with Hans, a friendship, a family, a home of togetherness.

And now that Gunther is gone, she needs Hans.

She has realized that there are wells of darkness in her husband that she will never understand, or even want to know, but she cannot lose him because that would mean losing too much.

They lie in the air-conditioned darkness of the hotel room, neither of them sleeping, both of them wide-awake, waiting to leave.

Two
the loan of borrowed time

16.

THEY RETURN to Germany and as the smell of Europe fills Melusine's nostrils, her eyes sting with the loss of brash sunlight and the primary colours she has left behind. Europe smells nothing like Vegas; Germany is cobblestones steeped in history and damp.

Standing in a grocery store on the way home from the airport, she even finds her favourite aromas offensive — the freshly ground coffee beans, spicy sausages and German bread.

Vegas was air-conditioned, lacquered and gelled. Who knew I preferred plastic and enamel to hand-painted carpentry? And I miss the sunshine so bright I had to close my eyes. I miss the vivid gashes of colour.

Opening the door to their home, she feels as if she is stepping inside a second-hand clothing store; it is dark, low-ceilinged, musty. She has never noticed the smell before.

"Needs airing."

Hans shrugs and Melusine opens all the windows, which Hans immediately closes.

"Don't be ridiculous, Melusine, you'll let in the damp. Let's make a sandwich and go to bed. We can unpack in the morning."

Melusine slices rye bread and makes him a sandwich. She is not hungry.

I can't eat. I miss him so much. How did it happen that we even met? And why?

"How was Vegas?" Ana wants to know and Melusine shrugs.

"Fine."

"Fine? That's all you have to say? Fine? Did something happen there that you're not telling me? You seem upset about something. What's going on?"

"Nothing's going on. Here, I bought you a gift."

She hands Ana the shot glasses with the crude genitals and Ana howls with delight. Melusine is glad to have distracted her; she can hardly talk, her heart is broken, and it is all she can do to keep up her end of the conversation, words feel like stones in her mouth.

You made consonants constant again, and comprehensible. You unlocked vowels to their full resounding, to let words come over my lips once more. Oh Ich, you said it best. And now Gunther, you are gone from me and my words are once again imprisoned, silenced. Oh, Gunther.

She says his name a thousand times a day. She cannot believe she cannot see him; the separation feels unnatural, an aberration.

17.

IN THE WEEKS that follow their arrival back home, it is as if Hans and Melusine have agreed to give each other a wide berth and they hardly see one another.

Melusine sets up a shrine in her study; all her trinkets from Las Vegas are neatly arranged and each dollar store item is a treasure.

She rents a post office box in the nearby town of Dornburge and she emails the address to Gunther, typing only that: the address.

And then she waits.

Why doesn't he write? Why?

She is an automaton, obsessed by his silence. She uncharacteristically avoids her son who is perplexed by her aloofness.

"I'm just busy, Jonas. I've got to catch up on a whole bunch of things," she lies. "We will make a plan soon. How are things with you and Nika?"

"Nika's awesome. She's the best thing that ever happened to me. Um, actually, we've moved into an apartment together, I know you might think it's too soon but it feels right. Mami, are you sure you're okay? You don't sound like yourself."

I'm not myself. My self has been banished to purgatory, to wait.

Meanwhile, Hans phones Juditha as soon as he can and she sounds delighted to hear from him and he is beyond relieved that she is where she said she would be. *She is true to her word.*

Juditha had given him a telephone number that she told him only he had access to, an unlisted number.

"You can understand that I have to guard my privacy very carefully, Hans. I am trusting you not to give this number to anybody. I've had a number of instances in which people weren't happy with my findings and I have felt in real danger. Or sometimes family members don't understand what it is I do and they get angry. So now I take every precaution to be as invisible as possible. Unfortunately, I can't just give people the easy solutions they are looking for..." Her voice trails off and Hans feels for her.

"I won't tell anybody a thing," he says. He schedules an hour every day in his calendar, establishing a set time for their calls.

"How are you?" she asks. "How are things with you and your wife?"

"Fine," he says, and he begins to ask her a question about Kateri when she interrupts him.

"No, Hans. There's only one rule between us and that is that you always have to tell me the truth. My love for you is unconditional; your actions and thoughts cannot change that. I love you fundamentally and I always will. So let's try that again. How are you? How are things with your wife?"

She loves him. Hans lets those beautiful words sink into his heart like ink on parchment.

"I hate her," he says simply, of Melusine. "I'm trying to keep things somewhat normal but she's ruined for me. She's been with another man and I can't forgive her."

"Forgiveness is already there, Hans. If you lower your ego wall, you will find that forgiveness is waiting for you on the other side."

Hans isn't interested in talking about Melusine. "Have you made any progress with Kateri?"

"I've done a series of meditations. You've only been gone for two days, Hans. Remember, I told you that this is going to take a lot of time."

She is billing him for each meditation in addition to the phone calls and he calculates that this entire enterprise could end up with a hefty price tag. But he does not care.

He sighs.

"Tell me about your life," Juditha says. "All of it will help me, and while we develop our contact with Kateri, I'd like you to work on trying to experience more joy in your day. By seeking joy, you will be addressing karma and bringing Kateri closer to you."

Hans gives a snort. "Joy. Ridiculous concept."

"I understand that it may seem incomprehensible now but joy will come. Tell me about your day. Describe it."

Hans is not used to talking about himself. He starts hesitantly and before he knows it, their hour is up.

"You see, Hans, was that so bad?"

Hans rather enjoyed talking and having Juditha listen.

"It was tolerable," he tells her and he knows that she is smiling.

"We'll talk tomorrow then," she says. "And until then, seek joy, Hans, and even if you can't seek it, try not to drive it away, if it seeks to find you."

18.

LIFE SETTLES INTO A ROUTINE. Hans works longer hours in order to avoid his wife, while she hurries off to Dornburge as soon as she finishes work.

The long dark month of November arrives and Melusine returns each night from her fruitless trips to the post office box and she sits in her study, staring at her trinkets and wondering if she will ever hear from Gunther. Each day without word feels like a dozen years and she is exhausted.

At night she eats dinner alone in front of the television with Mimi for company and for the first time, she is grateful for the dog's warm companionship.

"Oh Mimi," she says, "I miss him so much. Why hasn't he written? Will I ever hear from him again?"

And Mimi buries her head in Melusine's lap, nuzzling her, comforting her.

One bleak Friday evening, she has nearly given up. Resigned to the prospect of an empty box, she opens the tiny metal door and is stunned to see a large manila envelope folded into a curve. She snatches it and examines it, yes, it's from him.

Her heart is pounding; she can feel it high up in her throat, almost choking her and she breaks out in a sweat.

Thank God. I thought I would go mad.

She leans against the wall of letterboxes. It is as if she's been holding her breath and she lets it out, hugging herself, almost doubled over.

She locks the box and returns to her car.

She sits inside and opens the envelope.

She pulls out a letter and with it, the picture of her and Gunther on the Skywalk.

Her hand flies to her heart. He bought the picture. That's why he wanted her to go ahead to Guano Point without him. She studies the photograph greedily then she leans back in her seat and closes her eyes, holding the photograph close to her chest.

Again she exhales a prayer to a god she did not know she believed in; *thank you, thank you.* She repeats this like a mantra until she finally accepts that the photograph is not a figment of her imagination.

She reads the letter.

Melu, my dear, I miss you. I can't say I have any idea what our friendship is going to be but I can only be honest with you, and in my honesty, I need to tell you that I miss you.

Things are not good with me and my wife. She's so hurt. And she hates me for having gone to Vegas.

I've got no idea what to do. My life feels like a terrible trap right now and I can't make it better no matter how much I want to. I'm chained to this misery.

I'm sorry. I don't mean to be such a downer. I hope you like the photo. I got one for myself too. It was a perfect day. Being with you was perfect.

Anyway, that's all I have to say right now. I hope you won't be put off by this letter of self-pity and that you'll write to me.

How are you? I haven't even asked. I trust you know you can tell me everything.

Your friend,
Gunther.

Melusine lowers the letter and stares out the window of her car, not seeing a thing. She's thrilled that he misses her but she's disappointed that he keeps emphasizing the friendship aspect of things. Were they not lovers first? There was nothing in the letter that alluded to their passion.

You're being ridiculous. Stop thinking like a stupid schoolgirl. What were you expecting?

More than this. Or, something different. *I don't know what I thought.*

Her relief at having heard from him settles into a new kind of discomfort by all the things he has not said.

She studies his letter. He's written to her on a blank sheet of plain white photocopy paper, and his writing is a large scrawl; a mix of upper and lower case letters, and he used a black fine-liner ink pen.

She thinks it looks very artistic, very Matisse.

She drives back to her town and goes into the stationary store near the university. Choosing the right paper is as exciting as choosing her underwear the day she'd known she was going to see him.

While she prepares supper, she thinks of things to write about. Hans is home at a decent hour for once and she is surprised to see him.

They finish supper and she gets up to clear the table and wash the dishes.

He comes into the kitchen after her. "Melusine," he says, "a long day standing?"

Which is their signal for a foot rub.

She is startled, taken aback. "But my feet need attention," she says, "all that walking in Vegas. I haven't had time to get them soft and smooth. You won't be happy."

"I'm sure they're just fine. You can fix them tomorrow. Tonight I will rub them as they are. Leave the dishes until the morning and go and give your feet a wash. I'll put on the music and get things ready."

"Fine." She is not enthusiastic. She wants to write to Gunther. She consoles herself with the thought that she can figure out what to say in her letter while her feet are being rubbed.

She goes to wash while Hans sinks into the sofa and waits for her.

Hans has had an odd day. His life feels out of control.

His daily call with Juditha had unsettled him for reasons he could not pinpoint. They had not discussed anything out of the ordinary, but after he put the phone down, he had felt utterly discombobulated.

"I'm coming down with a migraine," he told his office assistant. "How many appointments do we have this afternoon?" She consulted the book. "Three."

"Can you cancel them, move them to tomorrow?" Hans has never done this in his life and she gives him a strange look.

"I'm sure I can," she said.

She made the calls and he got her to turn on the answering machine and then he sent her home for the day. The other partners were all out of town and he could hardly wait to hustle her out the door.

"I'll close everything up," he said, "see you tomorrow."

Then he locked himself inside his office, took off his tie and used it to masturbate, achieving an intense orgasm and a successful blackout.

He lay back on his big office chair, feeling cleansed and satiated.

He dozed, woke and did it again. Although he could not achieve orgasm the second time, he once again fell into that soothing blanket of darkness and when he came to, his penis felt raw; his actions had been too rough and even his neck felt bruised from the assault.

He was humiliated by the craven hunger that had led him to the unprofessionalism of closing his work place. He was ashamed. He knew he was out of control.

Hans had used the office on previous occasions for his sex acts but always after hours, long after everyone had left. He had never closed up for the day and he knows it cannot happen again. And now, while he waits for Melusine to wash her feet, he vows that it will never happen again.

He needs to resume his former routine of rubbing her feet and pretending it is Kateri he is touching. Then he must have sex with his wife because it did serve to release some of his tensions.

He wonders what it was about the conversation with Juditha that had triggered such increased craving for intense self-abuse.

He decides he will tell Juditha what happened, because she will know what to do.

19.

THE FOLLOWING DAY, Melusine leaves her colleagues at lunchtime and goes to a café to write to Gunther. The foot rub of the previous night had gone on for much longer than it usually did and to her dismayed surprise, it had led to sex.

As she lay there, with her silent husband thrusting back and forth inside her, she felt a repulsion she was careful not to show. Compared to Gunther's healthy robust appetites, everything Hans did seemed weird and strange. And what was with his silence? Melusine, observing, noticed that Hans held his breath the entire time he made love to her; his eyes were fixed shut and his face turned an angry purple.

When he was done, he cleaned himself off as he always did, rolled over and went to sleep.

Melusine had a hot shower and she scrubbed her body, feeling as if she had failed to take care of herself; she had allowed herself to be violated. But what else could she have done? She could not very well refuse to have sex with her husband or tell him that she could no longer stomach his touch.

After her shower, she made a cup of tea and decided to wait until the next day to write to Gunther. And now, pen poised over paper, a coffee in front of her, she has no idea what to say.

A part of her is angry at the friendship aspect of things that his letter had seemed to dwell upon but she reasons with herself, what had she been expecting?

She puts down her pen and looks around. The café is warm and welcoming and filled with people chatting or typing on laptops or reading newspapers. Melusine wishes she could stay there all afternoon and not have to go back to the library. She picks up her pen. She doesn't have anything of interest to tell Gunther and she is afraid she'll bore him.

Dear Gunther,

She chews her pen. Is 'dear' too much? She studies his now-familiar letter that he began with "Melu, my dear…" She decides to be bold and stick with the affectionate salutation.

Dear Gunther, I was glad to get your letter.

Ach, too pathetic. She crumples up the piece of paper and tries again.

Dear Gunther, I miss you. You were frank, I shall be too. I miss you. It's gray here and cold but it's November, what else can I expect? I am worried you will find me and my life very boring. It is boring.

I am sorry to hear about you and your wife. Things are strained between me and Hans — it feels awkward, as if there are a thousand unspoken angers wishing to make themselves heard.

Thank you for the photograph, by the way. Yes, it was a perfect day. Vegas feels like a Technicolor dream that's fading by the moment but in the same breath, I can still recall your every freckle. Forgive me if I am being too forward.

Writing letters feels very odd! I am going to sign off now and post this before I decide it's no good and that I must rewrite it again and again.

She gets stuck on the closing. Should she sign off *love, Melu* or *Fondly, Melusine,* or *your friend, Melu…* she's uncertain. She drinks the last of her coffee and chews on her pen.

Your friend, Melu.

She seals the letter and posts it before she can change her mind.

Meanwhile, Hans manages to get through his day until he can phone Juditha at noon and he tells her what happened. He tells her everything and he is wild with anxiety.

"I lost total control," he says. "I closed the whole office. I can't do things like that. What's going on? It was something you said — I know it was. I felt like I was out of my mind."

"Hans," Juditha replies calmly, "I know this will be very hard for you to understand but what happened is a wonderful sign of healing. When the soul begins to emerge and is acknowledged, then the ego panics and throws every spanner it can into the works to disrupt the healing process. That chaos you were feeling is an excellent sign that we're making headway and that things are happening."

"Well, you're right about one thing. I don't understand. And I can't have it happen again. I may have to stop with this, Juditha. Yesterday was very frightening. I'm just fortunate my colleagues are still away and hopefully the receptionist won't tell them when they get back."

"If it happens again, you must just take a moment for yourself; lock your office door and phone me and we'll work through the anxiety attack together and you'll be fine. Hans, I really want you to start meditating every day. Just for ten minutes okay? No more than that. Can you do that? Ten minutes."

"I don't think meditation's going to cut it. I think I need anti-anxiety medication." He's never had this thought before, as he had previously been able to rely on himself to be strong.

She thinks for a moment. "I don't think you do. Anyway, they can be very dangerous and can lead to suicidal impulses and all kinds of things. Hans, I really need you to calm down. I told you this wouldn't be easy; you're embarking on a very difficult journey, a journey that most people wouldn't have the courage to do. But you do have the courage and that marks you as a person who deserves special rewards in life and you will get them. How do you feel right at this moment? Describe the sensations in your body."

"I'm finding it hard to breathe. I feel like my vision is distorted and it feels like the floor is moving away from me in all different directions. I feel like I can't focus my eyes and my heart is beating much too fast."

"Hmm, perhaps you should see a doctor. Those are classic signs of a panic attack. But, first let's try something else. Close your eyes. Now, Hans, you're in control. Take a deep breath. Hold it in. Now exhale."

She takes him through various breathing exercises and he starts to feel slightly better.

"Are you eating properly?" she asks, and he admits he has been eating poorly.

"Well, that's very irresponsible of you, Hans. In order for us to do this, we need your body to be nourished. Your body relies on the chemicals in food in order to operate properly. You're putting our work in jeopardy if you don't eat correctly. I want you to promise me you'll eat three healthy meals a day even if you have to force them down, can you promise me that?"

Hans makes a noncommittal noise.

"If you can't do this, Hans, then we will have to terminate our work. I'm doing my best here to really help you but you need to lower your walls of resistance."

"Fine," Hans is surly. "Meditate for ten minutes, breathe like you showed me and eat right. Anything else?"

"Yes. Go for a half an hour walk every single day. Morning or night, whenever you can but you must get outside and get some exercise and fresh air."

"Okay. Enough about me, any progress on Kateri?"

"Yes. I sensed her while I was in a meditative state last night. I was going to tell you but it was more important that we talk about you."

Hans is filled with excitement. He sits up. "What did she say?"

"She didn't say anything. I didn't see her or talk to her, it doesn't work like that, but I sensed her for a moment and then she was gone. These things take a long time."

"You're telling me." He is angry. "Long is an understatement."

"I know how hard this is for you," she says with great patience, "I really do. Now, back to our quest to find joy in your life. Where will you find joy in your world today?"

"It will be very hard to fit joy in, what with all the eating, breathing, meditating and walking that I have to do." Hans knows he sounds like a sulky child and he cannot help laughing and she joins him.

"There you go, Hans. Was that so hard?"

They end the call and he feels better. He does his breathing exercises for a while and then he unlocks his door to admit his next patient.

20.

NOVEMBER PASSES. Melusine gets letters from Gunther two to three times a week and they fall into an easy communication. It is clear from his replies that her letters mean a great deal to him and she feels reassured that she is important to him.

His letters are the focal point of her world; she feels like an addict always in need of more, more.

Hans is eating well and following Juditha's regime and he does feel better. Stronger, fitter, more mentally alert. He enjoys his long walks with Mimi and wonders why he has not done this before.

Kateri has not made any further contact but Juditha is confident that she will, and she continues to work on it and she and Hans talk daily except on weekends.

Melusine asks Hans if they can try sex without the lubrication and although he is hesitant, he obliges and it is much more enjoyable for her this way. This makes Hans feel more confident and their relationship improves although Hans has to work hard to push Melusine's infidelity to the back of his mind.

Jonas pops in for a visit and observes that his parents are treating each other with considered wariness, as if they are each carrying something unwanted and yet fragile for the other. He is puzzled; something has changed but he has no clue as to what it is.

He also notices that Melusine is less enthused by decorations and Christmas festivities and he does not like that.

He mentions it to her and she shrugs. "You're all grown up now," she says, "it's not worth me doing it for just me and your father. You're hardly ever home."

"I'll do the tree with you then, Mami," he says gruffly and she is surprised and pleased.

"Okay," she says, "that will be fun."

Hans returns home to find them knee-deep in tinsel and ornaments, with the fresh smell of pine filling the room.

"Well, this is nice," he says. "Can I help?"

Both Melusine and Jonas laugh. The one time he tried to help, he nearly toppled the entire tree.

"No thanks, Papa," Jonas says. "Your job is to buy gifts and put them under the tree once we're done."

"Will you be here for Christmas dinner?" Hans asks.

"Yes, and Nika's also coming for sure."

Hans thinks that Nika, with her anger and her face full of piercings and studs, makes a Russian warlord seem like the Easter bunny.

"Great," Hans says, flatly. "Try to get her to lose some of the anger, okay? Just for the night. Tell her she has to pretend to like life just for one evening, if she can do that."

To his surprise, his son laughs again. "She's a lot less angry than you think, Papa," he says. "She's very shy, that's all. I'm looking forward to Christmas Eve. We'll listen to *Stille Nacht* and it will be wonderful like always."

"I had no idea you even noticed our traditions," Melusine says, "never mind liked them."

Jonas shrugs. "Being away from home makes you see a lot of things. You appreciate things more. Also, like I've told you, Nika's an orphan. Makes me realize how lucky I've been with you two."

"We're the blessed ones, my sweet boy," Melusine says, "to have you. Now, any ideas what kind of gift I can buy for Nika?"

"I'm going to take Mimi for her walk," Hans interrupts them and Melusine waves a hand at him.

"Dunno, Mami. She's not like an ordinary girl. It's hard to say. She loves reading. Maybe buy her a gift card from a bookstore."

"She reads?" Melusine is surprised.

"She reads every single thing she can lay her hands on," Jonas says. "Our apartment is full of books. She loves German literature the best, novellas by German woman authors. She says she's going to write a book one day and so she is studying them. Oh, and she loves your precious Ingeborg too. I laughed when I found that out, let me tell you."

Melusine beams. "She loves Ingeborg Bachmann? That's wonderful! Goodness, I really misjudged her. I'm sorry."

"Well, she does look very aggressive and she hardly said a word when you met her. Hey, Papa looks a bit better these days, doesn't he? I'm glad. Before you went to Vegas, he was like a skeleton, and so deathly pale. I'm glad he's happier."

"Me too," Melusine says. "Now let's plan our Christmas feast. Tell me all the things you want."

"Bavarian Crème and lots and lots of cookies, especially the *lebkuchen* ones, the gingerbread ones."

Melusine hugs him, delighted to have his company.

"Fine but we need some real food too," she tells him and he shrugs.

"I'll leave that up to you. I must go, I'm taking Nika to the Christmas market, can I bring you anything?"

"Yes," she says, "an Advent wreath would be nice, if you see a good one. If not, don't worry, I'll make one."

He grins, gives her the thumbs up and leaves.

Later, she settles down to write to Gunther.

Jonas was here! He wants to have a real Christmas! Oh Gunther, I feel so happy. I felt as if I had lost him. His girlfriend, Nika, sounds much more interesting than I gave her credit for; she too loves Ingeborg Bachmann!

I want to share a secret ... it's not really a secret except that you're the only person I'm going to tell — I'm going to write a novella. I've an idea that I can't get rid of and so I'm going to give it a try, why not?

She seals the letter and begins to plan her story; it's the tale of two women, Yvonne and Isolde. She is not sure where the idea came from although she vaguely recalls having seen an unlikely couple kissing when she went into Frankfurt for a library conference.

A tall thin woman in a grey business suit was holding hands with an extraordinarily pretty younger woman who was casually dressed, and as Melusine watched, the older woman drew the girl in for a deep kiss, pulling the girl close to her with obvious hunger.

Yvonne and Isolde.

And Melusine finds that once she starts writing, she cannot stop.

Hans notices her pounding away on her antiquated computer and asks what she's up to. She tells him she is writing a book and to her surprise, he is very supportive. "I always thought you'd be a very good writer," he says. "What's it about?"

She cannot tell him. "I'm trying to write an existential story. A sort of plotless fiction piece with obscure internal narrative."

"Ah. I have no idea what you mean by that but I wish you good luck." And they both laugh.

He looks at her and feels guilty about his secret life with Juditha but then he remembers Melusine's infidelity and his guilt vanishes. He still has to work very hard at not lashing out at her for what happened but he does not want to risk destroying their fragile peace. Once again, he pushes thoughts of her affair to the back of his mind.

He is disappointed because Juditha does not seem to be making much progress with finding Kateri and she is costing him a fortune. He has decided, without telling her, to give her a time limit; she's got until March to deliver the goods.

Melusine looks at her husband as he leaves her study, and she marvels at the duplicity of their life. She is certain he's riddled with secrets while she has her lockbox carefully stored under a pile of old shoes in her closet; a box filled with letters and photographs of her taken by Gunther, for he has sent more. She had not noticed him taking so many pictures of her. She thinks about McDonald's, and the photos he took of her naked, which she has not yet seen.

She goes back to her novel, fascinated to find out what happens next. Her thoughts are flowing faster than her fingers can type and it is as if she is the last to know the plot thread; the characters have come to life and taken occupancy of her brain.

Isolde is narrow and bony, an accountant by day and hash smoker by night. With opiates her only companion, she watches endless documentaries, marveling at the oddities and braveries of ordinary people. She has long since given up on love or even friendship; she is a spinster at thirty and she sometimes repeats the word out loud while she lies on the sofa, holding the hash deep in her lungs; *alte Junger*, spinster...

There's Yvonne, in her twenties, smooth skinned and voluptuous, her colouring from her Jamaican mother and her fine-boned features from her French father who moved the family to Germany when she was a baby.

The two women work in the same office; Isolde in finance, while Yvonne delivers the mail and empties the recycling and garbage bins.

Yvonne, who leans in too close to Isolde, and Isolde, who soon regards Yvonne's visits as the highlight of her day.

One day Isolde decides to take the stairs instead of the elevator to deliver some paperwork.

She pushes open the heavy door and bumps right into Yvonne who is staring out the stairwell window.

"I wish I was out there," Yvonne says to Isolde, as if they had been in the middle of a conversation, despite the fact that they've never spoken to each other before. "I hate working. It's like I'm in prison."

"It's real life," Isolde says. "How else do we pay the bills?"

Yvonne shrugs.

Isolde moves to pass Yvonne but the younger woman blocks her way.

"Do you think I visit your desk too often?" she asks and Isolde does not know what to say.

"I like to see you," she replies.

Yvonne laughs. "Sometimes when I lean over to give you a letter, I want to grab your hand and put it down my shirt. Does that shock you?"

Isolde realizes that her heart feels like a trapped bird in her chest. She pats her chest, to soothe it.

"Yes," she says. "But I am a boring old spinster, easily shocked."

Yvonne looks at her. "I don't think you're boring or old at all," she says and Isolde looks at her full soft mouth and perfect small teeth and she wishes that Yvonne would kiss her.

She leans in slightly but Yvonne pulls back.

"See you here tomorrow, same time?" Yvonne asks and Isolde nods.

She wants Yvonne to touch her and she knows that Yvonne knows this also. Yvonne seems to take pity on her, and she runs a finger up Isolde's arm, sending chills and heat simultaneously through the other woman's body.

Yvonne leaves the stairwell and Isolde stares after her for a long time.

Melusine looks up from her typing. She is amazed to see that she is in her study and not in the stairwell with the two women. She looks at her watch; it is close to midnight and time for bed.

21.

A COUPLE OF WEEKS LATER it is Christmas Eve and Melusine is checking the smoked ham and sausages and putting a big dish of potato salad on the table.

She is flushed with happiness. A wonderful Christmas present had arrived from Gunther; a copy of *Herzzeit Briefwechsel, Correspondence,* a book with all the documents, letters, postcards and telegrams between Ingeborg Bachmann and Paul Celan.

I had a look through, couldn't resist. Looks like depressing stuff, Melu — remember, we're not them! But I thought you'd like it. Happy Christmas.

She hopes, when he says that they are not like Ingeborg and Paul, that he is referring to their descent in madness, despair and death, and not the fact that their love was so compelling. But, she reasons with herself, he would not have sent her such a thoughtful gift if he did not care about her — and he even read it to know what she reads.

"We'll have the best Christmas ever," she says to Hans who looks up from his wine selection and agrees.

Melusine studies the table with a worried frown. "I made a lot of vegetables for Nika," she says, "and I hope there's enough for her."

"There's enough for an army," Hans says. "There they are, at the door. I'll get it."

They all fall into easy happy chatter and settle down to open the gifts before dinner.

"We know that gifts should come after dinner," Melusine says to Nika, "but Jonas switched things up years ago."

"I was so excited to get to my presents that I couldn't concentrate on the food," Jonas admits, grinning. "So it just made more sense to open them first. Here, Mami, this is for you, from Nika and me."

Melusine unwraps the gift and her hand flies to her heart. She is speechless.

"Do you like it?" Nika is anxious.

"I love it!" Melusine gives the girl a big hug and grabs Jonas. They too have bought her a copy of *Herzzeit Briefwechsel*.

"I had a look through," Nika says, "I hope you don't mind, I couldn't resist."

Melusine has an inward chuckle at the echo of Gunther's words. "Of course I don't mind," she said. "What did you think?"

"So much pain. If being a genius means you have be in that much pain, I'll pass."

Hans has bought Melusine a brand new computer, a shiny new laptop. "I'll configure it for you," he says, "you can't write a book on that old piece of rubbish of yours."

She is delighted.

Nika is amazed. "You're writing a book? So am I."

The two fall into a passionate discussion but Melusine is uneasy; she cannot tell Nika the truth about her subject matter because her novel has evolved even further, with a dark plot she had no idea she was capable of writing.

Isolde and Yvonne are now having a full-blown affair, meeting each day in the stairwell to make frenzied love. Yvonne tells Isolde that she wears her tiny mini skirts especially for her and more often than not, Yvonne is without panties. But Yvonne is complicated; she has a young son and a boyfriend, the father of her child who wants to marry her.

"He is a crazy jealous man," Yvonne says. "I worry that if I try to leave him, he'll hunt me down. He's that crazy. I live in fear all the time. If I'm late coming home, even five minutes, he gets so violent, I can't tell you."

"Come away with me then," Isolde says, rubbing Yvonne's buttocks, her fingers slipping into the smooth soft crack and lingering in the warmth of the girl's most private place. She draws Yvonne close and kisses her neck and bites her ear. Isolde has become adventurous; she is bold and takes the lead.

"Come with me," Isolde says again, "we'll go to Berlin. We'll take Ralf with us. I'll take care of both of you. I won't let him find us." Ralf is Yvonne's son.

Yvonne pulls away. "He'll find us. He'll bring us back. I will never escape." Her voice is small. "He's evil, Isolde, I'm telling you, evil. You've never met anyone like him. He seems so normal but he's not, he's dangerous. You have no idea how often I feel as if my life is in danger."

Isolde has heard Yvonne say this dozens of times before. "So then all the more reason to leave with me," she says but Yvonne shakes her head and her large eyes fill with tears.

At the supper table, and loading a plate of food for Jonas, Melusine forces her attention away from Isolde and Yvonne and back to what Nika is saying.

"We can read each other's work if you like," Nika says. "I find that helps me a lot."

"I'm a bit stuck right now," Melusine lies, "but maybe this new computer will help me. Here you go, Jonas, this should do, for round one anyway."

They all laugh and Jonas nods enthusiastically. The food is delicious and Melusine is relieved that since their return from Vegas her baking has returned to its former perfection.

Later, she slices her version of Beigli, the Hungarian poppy seed pastry; she has added extra raisins and a touch of rum.

She looks around, marveling at how life can seem so perfect, while the knot in her stomach spoke a different truth.

"Let me get a photograph of you and Nika," Jonas tells her and Melusine hugs the girl close, glad when Nika relaxes into her embrace. Melusine is startled by how tiny Nika is; her shoulders are narrow and bony and she is short enough to fit underneath Melusine's arm. Melusine feels a rush of protective warmth towards the girl.

"Now, family photograph, with the self-timer."

"I'll get Mimi from the kitchen," Hans says, "she must be in the picture too."

As Melusine smiles into the camera, with her feet puddled in discarded ribbons and torn gift wrap, she thinks about Gunther and she misses him so badly that it is hard to hold back the tears. She tries to be grateful for all the good in her life and she tells herself that she has so much to be grateful for: a husband, a son who loves her, and a wonderful home. But her heart craves the man she loves, a man who feels a million miles away.

And when New Year's Eve comes, she stands next to Hans and Ana and Dirk and a host of others at a party, and she feels a premonition of doom; nothing good will come of this next year, of that she is certain.

She disappears into the kitchen and is followed by Ana.

"You okay?" Ana asks.

Melusine nods, holding herself tall, and then without warning she folds into Ana's arms and cries.

Ana is startled. Her friend has never done this, not in all the years they have known each other.

Melusine is much bigger than Ana and she bends over awkwardly, crying, with Ana stroking her back and murmuring hushing sounds.

"*Ach,* it's just New Year getting to me," Melusine says, and she straightens up and blows her nose loudly.

Ana looks at her. "It never did before."

Melusine shrugs. "As one gets older, different things make you sad."

She wonders how Gunther is. In his last letter, he had said that he had made the decision; he could not stay with his wife any longer and he was applying for jobs in Australia and New York.

She hopes he will go to New York — Australia is so far way. Much further than London, and she cannot bear to think about it.

"Sorry to be a party pooper," she says with a watery smile. "I'm fine, let's get back to the others."

"Let me fix your face first." Ana pulls a make-up bag out of her purse.

"You and Hans okay?" she asks casually.

"Never better, why?"

"Nothing, just asking. He looks good. Just asking."

They change the subject and return to the party where no one has noticed their absence and when midnight comes, they raise their glasses high and drink to the New Year but Melusine cannot help but think harder days are coming. *The loan of borrowed time will be due on the horizon...*

22.

IT IS NOT LONG before things start to go wrong. One cold day in early January, Melusine is hunting through Hans's desk for the warranty for her new computer; she needs the serial number to register some software that she has purchased.

She roots through all the drawers to find the warranty, finding the bank statement from their trip to Vegas instead, with a sum for the Desert Rose Motel.

And, in addition, a close-to-equal sum for the Plaza Hotel.

And a huge sum of money to Healing Lives Ministries.

Melusine is dumbfounded. She stares at the statements for a long time. Then, using Hans's computer, she logs onto their shared bank account and checks the recent activity.

She sees that a horrifying sum is being paid each month to Healing Lives Ministries by cheque; the same monthly sum ever since their return from Las Vegas.

She has no idea what to think. The first thing she does is try to find Healing Lives Ministries on the Internet but she cannot find anything. She sits back in the chair, feeling as if the axis of her world has tilted and everything is about to slide irrevocably off the table of her life. She holds onto the edge of the desk, as if that will help.

A thought occurs to her and she does an online search for all the conventions that were held in Vegas when she and Hans were there. There were 153. She carefully scrolls down through each of the listings and there was not an optometrist's convention in sight. There is, however, an International Certified Psychic Convention that was held at the Plaza Hotel.

Melusine chews hard on her lip. Hans and psychics? It does not compute; he's a man of science. But he is also a man who's never recovered from the loss of his sister. Perhaps he went to see the psychics to try to find Kateri? She can see how that would make some kind of sense.

She goes through all the drawers again, trying to find something to explain Healing Lives Ministries but she comes up empty. She searches his computer but cannot find anything.

She is still sitting at his desk when he comes home.

"Hello!" he calls out. "I finally found a bottle of great wine that I've been trying to hunt down for ages. It's very rare! You're going to love it. Where are you?"

"In the study," she answers. "Wait, I'm coming now."

She finds him in the kitchen, opening his wine.

"I see dinner isn't ready," he says, "but we can have a glass now anyway. I've been reading about this wine for a while and now I've found it!" He is happy, oblivious to her quietness.

She sits down at the big wooden kitchen table where Jonas did his homework and where she arranged her ingredients and pots and pans for the meals she had prepared over the years. She looks at her husband who is holding the glass to his nose; his eyes are closed and he is smiling.

"Why did you pay the bill for the Plaza Hotel in Vegas?" she asks flatly and his eyes fly open and his jaw drops. But he recovers quickly.

"For Bill," he says smoothly. He had this lie prepared, in case, and just as well he did. Bill is a fellow optometrist who often attends their dinner parties.

She shakes her head. "No you didn't. Because there wasn't an optometrists convention in Vegas that month. There were 153 conventions but not one for optometry."

"For god's sake Melusine, have you gone mad? Of course there was a convention. You've lost your mind, woman."

He leaves the kitchen and she follows him into the living room. "You went there to find Kateri." She confronts him and he blanches. "You booked the Plaza Hotel because there was a convention of psychics there and then, when I said I wanted to come along, you booked the Desert Rose Resort at the other end of the Strip to keep me out of the way. Admit it, Hans."

His face is deathly pale and his skin appears to be pasted to the bony outline of his skull. He stands up and throws the glass of wine at the wall.

Yes, and then you didn't miss the opportunity to get fucked by some other man, did you, Melusine, did you?

He wants to shout at her but he doesn't say a thing, he just stares at her. Melusine is startled by his violence and for a moment they both watch the red wine drip down the wall like blood.

"And," she says, continuing, "you've spent a fortune on some Healing Lives Ministries — a fortune."

"What I spend my money on is none of your goddamned business," he spits out at her.

"It's our money, Hans. Yours and mine. How would you feel if I did that? If I lied to you like that? If I used our money like that?"

He comes up close to her and she can see the red veins in his eyeballs. His nostrils are flaring and he's breathing in small sharp gasps. "Like you've never lied, Melusine? Never? Tell me that. Tell me that my precious wife, go on. Tell me a lie right now."

She backs away. This is not what she expected. Does he know about her and Gunther? But how can he know? She sits down. "Listen," she says calmly, "let's talk about this. I was just very hurt that you never told me. Why did you think you couldn't tell me?"

He goes back to the kitchen and pours himself another glass of wine. He returns and sits down. "Because," he says, "it was a crazy thing to do. But I had to do it. I was losing my mind. I had to try this thing. But what would you have said, Melusine? Honestly?"

He, like her, does not want to open up the can of worms that is Gunther.

"Fine, so I would have said you were crazy and wasting our money and being foolish. I would have said that. But Hans, so much money? And I see it's still going on, every single month; you're paying this person, or this place. How long do you plan to carry on doing this?"

He swallows half the wine in the glass. "As long as it takes," he says shortly. "And you can accept it or you can leave."

"Leave? I'm not going anywhere and I've got a piece of advice for you. Tell me when you're done with this craziness and we'll resume our marriage, all right? And remember one thing, the house is in my name. And I'm going to go to the bank tomorrow and make sure I'm not culpable for any of your debts. You've lost your mind and you're going to lose all your savings too. I can't believe you're being this stupid, this gullible. The man I married would never have bought into such *bullshit*."

She shouts the last word as loudly as she can. "Imagine what Jonas would say if he knew? Or your business partners? Everyone will think you've been taken for a ride."

He looks at her calmly. "You, and everyone else, can think whatever you want, Melusine. This is my life and I'm finally doing what I want with it."

"Yes, well, good luck with that," Melusine says and she marches out of the room.

Her heart is beating so strongly she feels sick and there is a ringing in her ears. She goes to her study and sits down. What on earth to do next? She wishes she could tell someone but her pride stops her. She is too embarrassed to tell Ana that her respected and intellectual husband has fallen prey to some cult who have led him to believe they will help him find his sister.

She buries her head in her hands. What a mess. She has been so stupid to think that their make-believe marriage could work.

Back in the living room, Hans reclines in his chair, drinking wine and looking at the stain on the wallpaper.

He feels very serene, removed from all anxiety and it is a wonderful feeling.

He wonders how Melusine will clean the wall. He is sure she will find a way. She likes things to look perfect on the surface. Then he chides himself for the thought since that was the very reason he married her; so she would make his life look perfect.

He thinks back to his conversation with Juditha earlier that day. She had, in a recent dream, sensed Kateri again. She had asked Hans if he could send more of Kateri's items to her, as the connection was getting stronger — she could sense it. He is overjoyed at the thought. His lost sister is returning to him, so what does he care for an unfaithful wife?

He finishes the bottle of wine and falls asleep in his chair.

Melusine, moving her items from their bedroom to Jonas's old room, is puzzled by her husband's lack of concern over the state of their marriage. This cult must have more of a hold over him than she had thought. The Hans of the old days would have reassured her and told her that his crazy dalliance was over and that he had things in control. But the Hans of the old days would never have lied, and he would never have sought out a psychic.

She is also concerned by his aggressive attack on her, telling her that she lied. What did he know, and how did he know it? She wishes Gunther were near and that she could talk to him. He has accepted a job in New York and he has already left his wife. He has a whole new life, a life in which she has no real role except that of a pen pal.

She tries to work on her novel. The story has evolved to the point where Yvonne is trying to convince Isolde to help her kill her boyfriend.

"I can get you a gun, no problem. We live in a bad area, lots of gangs. Then all you have to do is wait for him, I'll show you the exact way he comes home, he always comes home the same way. There's a building you can hide in; I'm telling you no one will see you. And I'll make sure the gun has a silencer, I know people Isolde, I'm telling you, we can do this."

"It'd be me doing it, not you. There's no 'we' if I kill a man. And I still don't understand why we can't just leave and go to Berlin. Honestly, Yvonne, you're being crazy."

They are stuck in an impasse; they still meet daily in the stairwell but their passion has turned to rows, they argue about their future. Yvonne is sulky and then tremulous. Isolde is at her wits end.

"I can't go on like this," Yvonne says. "I'm going to run away from both of you. You're just like him. You both want to keep me trapped like an animal in a cage."

Isolde is desperate. "But I can make you happy," she says, "he can't. You know he can't."

Yvonne buttons her blouse closed. Her breasts are straining at the fabric and she sees Isolde eyeing her with hunger.

"You can't have everything without giving me something," Yvonne says. "Think about it. I'm only asking for one thing. One thing."

She leaves Isolde in the stairwell and Isolde leans her forehead against the smooth concrete wall. She has no idea what to do next.

Melusine looks away from her computer. She is distracted; she can feel Hans's anger through the walls. She can feel Isolde's longing and Yvonne's frustrated fury.

It seems as if everything is falling apart for everyone.

23.

WHEN JONAS COMES TO VISIT in mid-February, he finds his parents living in separate bedrooms and he is upset to see that his father's brief spell of good health has vanished; Hans is gaunt, thin and pre-occupied.

"What on earth happened?" Jonas whispers to Melusine. They are in the kitchen and Hans is lying in his chair with a bottle of wine next to him and Mimi asleep at his feet.

Melusine frowns and thinks about what to tell him. Jonas is her son and he is still only a child and she cannot tell him the whole brutal truth. It would not be fair to burden him.

"It's very complicated," she says. "Your father's struggling right now. It seems he hasn't come to terms with losing Kateri and it's wreaking havoc with our lives. I'm sorry, my sweet boy, I really am. I can only imagine how upsetting this is for you. Trust me, it is for me also. I have always been able to rely on your father but right now, the man I married, the man who fathered you, well, I've got no idea where he is."

Jonas is nonplussed. "Do you want me to talk to him?" he asks and Melusine shakes her head.

"But Aunt Kateri disappeared what, twenty five years ago?"

"I know, Jonas. Perhaps it's getting harder for your father as he gets older, not easier. I don't know why."

Her face crumples and she turns away, not wanting to let her son see her cry. She gathers her composure.

"Let's get out of the house, she says. "Let's go for supper, you and me. You can tell me how things are with Nika."

His face breaks into a smile. "She's great. Yes, good idea, Mami, let's go out. Nika asks after you too, she said you must tell me how your book's coming along."

"Ah, not well," Melusine says, thinking that she is adding yet another layer of lies to the family's deceptions. She is close to completing her first draft. The work is simply called *Yvonne and Isolde*.

One evening, after a particularly nasty row in the stairwell, Isolde follows Yvonne home and sees her with her boyfriend and her son and it is clear that Yvonne lied; her boyfriend worships the ground she walks on. And what is most devastating of all is that Yvonne looks happy to be with him; she is hanging onto his arm while he carries the boy, and Isolde's heart is slashed by every one of Yvonne's smiling glances.

She had lied. Yvonne had lied. But why? Why would she say she wanted her boyfriend killed when she was so happy with him? And what if Isolde had agreed to do it?

Isolde follows the family and when they reach a small park, she makes sure that she is in Yvonne's line of sight. But Yvonne, when she catches sight of her, seems no more taken aback or surprised than if Isolde is a regular in the area. After an initial glance, in which it was perfectly clear that she has seen Isolde, Yvonne behaves as if the other woman is quite invisible.

Isolde feels as if she has fallen down a rabbit hole. She cannot believe what is happening. What is Yvonne playing at? Can this be the same person that Isolde had met in the stairwell for close to six months, the same person who has let Isolde explore every crease and fold and curve and scar of her body, the same person who arched her back against the cold stairs while Isolde made her come again and again, her tongue buried in Yvonne's salty wet hotness, her tongue sucking and licking and nibbling Yvonne's pointy little clitoris.

Yvonne, who now turns laughingly to her boyfriend, as if Isolde does not exist at all.

Melusine wondered what Isolde would do next. Would she confront Yvonne the following day? Would she get drunk and high that night and go on a week's bender, phoning in sick? Would she think about harming Yvonne; shouting at her and demanding an explanation?

But Isolde, stricken, does none of those things. She is utterly calm. Frozen and nearly numb with calm. She goes home. She has a bath and climbs into bed, swallowing a couple of sleeping pills.

The following day she gets dressed and goes into work earlier than usual. She needs to be in control of her tiny world, now more than ever.

She does not acknowledge Yvonne when she comes to deliver the mail. She does not meet her eye when she empties the trash. Isolde's heart feels strangled and frightened and it is hard to breathe, but she knows that if she can just make it through one day without weakening, that she will be fine.

She meets Yvonne in the stairwell. Sweat is running down her armpits to the waistband of her trousers. "Why? Just tell me why? You owe me that much, Yvonne. You wanted me to kill a man. Kill him! Please, just explain."

Yvonne shrugs. "He's got lots of money and I'd get it all. It's true, he's not a bad guy, not really but I just want more. If I had money, I could get on with my life. I was meant to be a star, not do jobs like this. I only took this job because I was so bored I was going crazy. I don't even need the money; he takes care of me. He doesn't understand why I want to do this. He doesn't understand anything about me."

"And for that you wanted me to kill a man?" Isolde is incredulous. "Because you're bored and you wanted money and a shot at fame. What exactly do you think you're so talented at apart from being a seductress? Did you ever even feel anything for me? Don't bother to answer that. It doesn't matter."

Isolde wraps her arms around herself. "You," she says

evenly, "will leave. And I don't just mean for the day. Do you understand me?"

Yvonne nods and she starts to say something but Isolde holds up her hand and speaks quietly.

"Lies come out of your mouth like toads. You could have broken my heart but I've seen you for what you are. Leave and don't come back."

Yvonne nods again and leaves the stairwell. Isolde worries for a split second that she will run after the girl and grab her and kiss her and apologize and tell her that she will do anything to make her stay.

But she doesn't. She goes back to her desk and puts her head in her hands.

The novella ends there and Melusine feels as if she has been left hanging. She wants to know what happens to Isolde; does she find love or does she go back to lying on her sofa in the small hours of the morning, smoking hash and watching documentaries about other people's lives?

Melusine had, on a whim, printed out the manuscript and sent it to Gunther.

It's just a first draft, of the first thing I've ever written. I know you're so busy, only read it if you want to, only if you've got time.

"How is Nika's writing going?" she asks, wrenching her thoughts away from Isolde and what Gunther might think of the whole thing, and Jonas looks glum.

"She keeps getting rejected by publishers and agents," he says. "It's getting hard for her to keep her faith. I tell her that she's very young and anyway, it's a number's game; that she has to just keep on trying but she's a bit down in the dumps about it. She's even thinking of packing it in and becoming a nurse instead."

"That's quite a big switch," Melusine says. "Perhaps she should give herself more time and then see?"

He shakes his head. "I don't know. The thing is, Mami, if

we're ever going to get married and have children, she'll need to be able to earn a living and being a writer or even a journalist isn't financially the best bet."

Melusine ruffles her son's hair. "Finances, marriage and babies? Aren't you a bit young for all of that?"

By now they are seated in a McDonald's that never fails to remind Melusine of Gunther and the photographs he took that day. She wonders what happened to those images. She reminds herself to ask Gunther in her next letter.

Jonas looks stubborn. "We're just talking about it. Okay, so my first year at university was a washout but I learned what I really want to be."

"And that is?"

"A lawyer. I'm going to switch my major next semester, I've already talked to all the professors about carrying over the credits that I can."

"Jonas! I'm so proud of you," Melusine says, grinning. "What an impressive young man you are. You know, not so long ago I was worried you would turn into a pothead and not do anything with your life."

He blushes. "Ah, so you knew about that?"

Melusine laughs. "It was hard to miss. I just hoped you'd grow out of it and you did."

"Maybe Papa will grow out of whatever he's going through," Jonas says, taking a large bite of his hamburger. "I guess we should be very grateful he's not out buying sports cars and having young mistresses."

Melusine thinks about the money draining out of their account and into Healing Lives Ministries and she thinks she would have preferred a sports car. "I've got no idea what to think," she says. "It's like he's a ghost of the man I knew."

They finish eating and say goodbye. Melusine watches Jonas walk towards the bus stop and she is grateful that at least his life is turning out well. Her husband might be falling apart but her son is rallying.

She sighs and starts the car. She turns towards Dornburge to see if there is anything from Gunther. She has a feeling in her gut that he is seeing a woman in New York and she dreads having him confirm it. She thinks he must have been with other women since Vegas but she has held out the crazy hope that if there were to be any new significant other in his life, that the role would be filled by her. Although how that would work out, practically speaking, she has no idea.

She opens the post office box with trepidation and finds a bulky envelope but she does not open it. She puts it in her handbag and drives home to find that Hans has passed out in his chair, his wine bottle empty next to him.

She has noticed that his previously expensive and rare wines have made way for greater numbers of a cheaper variety. He is drinking much more than she has ever known him to but she cannot say anything to him; he's unreachable.

She knows he is still paying Healing Lives Ministries a hefty monthly fee and she wonders if this is why he is cutting back on his expensive wines or if he simply wants to drink more.

She goes to her room and shuts the door.

She opens the letter from Gunther and half a dozen black and white photographs fall out.

Certain that these are images of his new lover, Melusine lets them fall to the floor and she unfolds the letter. She's convinced that he's writing to tell her about his new love and her stomach feels as painful as if she's swallowed shards of glass. She closes her eyes for a moment, wanting to put off the bad news.

His handwriting, as ever, is bold and wild and his pen digs deep into the paper.

She reads the letter.

I have great news! Well, I think it's great. You might be very angry with me, Melu and if you are, I understand. I do. Remember the shoot we did? Here's the thing, the Museum of Modern Art in New York wants to give me a solo show! Solo!

She bends down and picks the images up off the floor. The

prints are all of her; they are the photographs he took in the old McDonald's and she looks incredible, so vital, so alive.

Melusine laughs out loud. She is now an international nude model. The thought fills her with glee and she wonders how she will explain this to Jonas.

I'm so sorry I didn't tell you. I so badly wanted to make my mark with this work. It's the best stuff I've ever done and I was so afraid you'd say no to my submitting it and I gave you my word that no one would ever see these except for you and me. But when I saw them, I realized how great they were and so I did a very wrong thing and I apologize. It was selfish of me. Can you forgive me, Melu? And if you do give us the go ahead, will you come to New York to the opening with me? Please say you will. And if you don't want these to be shown, just let me know, it's completely up to you. I'll be happy just knowing they loved my work enough to want to show it. Of course, showing it would be fantastic!

PS: I got your manuscript yesterday, I can't wait to read it! Thank you for sharing it with me. I'll read it as soon as I can.

PS#2: Please forgive me, Melu.

Forgive him? Once again he is the sunshine in a dark time of her life.

She writes back immediately. *There is nothing to forgive. Oh, how I wish I could be there for the opening. But things are such a mess here. Hans is getting worse by the day.*

She has already told Gunther about the cult and how Hans is spending all the money he can on them, and she told him about their now-separate bedrooms and Gunther's response was sympathy but not surprise.

She continues with her letter. *I don't know what's going to happen with Hans. I feel like it's going to end badly but I don't know how. He ends up drunk most evenings, and he is skin and bone, he's so thin. I've got no idea how he's even coping at work. When I met him, he was so golden. And now, he's turned to ash.*

Oh Gunther, I'm so happy for you about the gallery. I'm happy for me too! Of course you must show them, use my letter as approval if they want to see it in writing.

She seals the envelope and gets ready for bed. She is filled with a warm joy. There is no other woman — yet. There is no other lover — yet. She is the one who has taken him to New York; she is the one going with him to New York even if not in person. She will always have that place in his life and he, in hers.

She turns off her light and goes to sleep.

24.

HANS WAKES from his intoxicated slumber and stumbles to the bathroom. He fumbles with his penis and stands swaying, waiting for the urine to flow.

He holds his sad member in one hand and clutches his already-aching head with the other.

He cannot stop the dreams. They come to him every night and he cannot escape them.

Juditha is no help. She insists every day that Kateri is coming closer and closer and that the dreams mean that her presence is being made stronger. Juditha is certain that Kateri is alive and well and that it is only a matter of time before they know where she is.

But Hans knows otherwise.

Since Melusine moved out of their bedroom and he could no longer make love to her or rub her feet, or lie in bed with her and pretend he is next to Kateri, he has been bereft and increasingly broken.

Lying there, in their large bed, alone, he has grown afraid of the darkness and afraid of the memories that assail him. And no matter how much he drinks, the visions are getting stronger and stronger, like poltergeists wanting to take possession of his brain.

He has implored Juditha to help him. Her repeated reply is for him to trust her and for him to get healthy again. She says he must mend things with his wife and that he must stop drinking.

Well, he cannot fix the problems between him and Melusine and he told Juditha that in their most recent phone call earlier that day.

"She thinks you're taking all our money," he said thickly. "She hates you."

"She doesn't even know me," Juditha said. "How can she hate me? Hans, you've never actually given her details about me, have you?"

"Of course not. She only knows of a setup called Healing Lives Ministries. She's tried to trace you, trust me, she has but she can't find a thing."

"Good." Juditha sounds relieved. "Hans, why don't you get a new bank account from which to pay me and tell her you've ended it with me? I don't believe in lying but you're getting ill from all this and I'm just trying to help you."

"I cannot get another bank account Juditha, because I do not have any money left. All I have is the money I earn every month and you are taking all of that. And she knows it. And she would know whether it was our joint account or one of my own."

"I'm working very hard for what you pay me, Hans," Juditha says and she sounds indignant and upset. "I spend all my time on you. Meditating, doing exercises with the clothing, reaching out to the Higher Masters. It's the most intense work I've ever done with anyone. And it's very exhausting. I'm not saying I don't want to do it, of course I do, it's my calling but please, don't think it's easy."

"Easy or not Juditha," he says tiredly, "I'm nearly out of money. I can't go on much longer."

"Can't you take out a second mortgage on your house?"

"No, I can't. The house and all assets are in Melusine's name." He thinks for a moment. "I can sell my car. Yes, I can do that. But Juditha, you must listen to me. You must take my dreams seriously. I keep telling you about them but you won't hear me. Please, hear me. I need your help now."

"You dream that Kateri is dead. But you've been dreaming that for years, Hans. That's not new."

"But Juditha, I don't just dream that she's dead. I keep telling you, I dream that I killed her, that I was the one who killed her." His voice is a shriek and he doesn't care if the outer office receptionist hears him.

"I killed her," he says again. "I killed her. The dream comes to me every night. It has been coming slowly but increasingly since Melusine left me. I cannot stand to be alone in that bed at night. I know I am drinking too much but it is the only way to try to shut out that terrible image that won't leave me alone."

"But Hans, I now know that Kateri is alive. I keep telling you that. What's happening is that the reality of your being able to really see your sister in this lifetime is unsettling all the notions of her death that you've come to accept. Your brain and your heart can't accept this living Kateri because it means a huge change and your ego doesn't want anything to change. Your ego finds comfort in your established hunger for missing Kateri. And you need to accept that it's the fear of change that's driving all these demons to haunt you in the night. The demons are manifestations of your ego's banshee protest because it's so afraid of your becoming whole and healed."

"No," Hans is adamant. "I killed her. I know I did. I see it every night. At first the dreams only hinted at it but in the last few nights, I see how it happened. We were in the tree house and we were lying down, with our bodies close together like always. And I wanted that moment to last forever. I loved her too much to lose her to the next moment, because in that next moment lay the possibility that she would leave me. Because I knew that she would leave me sooner or later. So I put my hands on her throat and I kissed her while she died; I pressed my face right up against hers while I strangled her. I smothered her mouth with mine and I crushed her neck."

"And then what happened, Hans?" Juditha is pragmatic.

"What did you do with her body? And how is it that they never found her?"

"I haven't seen that part yet," Hans says. "All I have seen, in slow developments every night, is me, killing her. I'm a monster. A monster."

"When was the last time you masturbated?"

"This morning of course. But it's getting harder to orgasm. I can't concentrate because all I can feel is my sister's dying tongue against mine while I killed her."

"And when last did you make love to Melusine?"

He thinks hard. "Um, just before she found out there was no conference. Actually the sex between us had been improving a bit. But then she moved to Jonas's room."

"And her feet? When last did you rub her feet?" Juditha knows all about Hans's continued connection to his sister via Melusine's feet.

He utters a sob. "It was the same time. I'm all alone, Juditha. All I have is my empty bed and my dead sister. I can't bear to go to sleep at night. Why do you think I'm drinking so much? I have to."

"No you don't, Hans," Juditha says. "Oh Hans, what am I going to do with you? Listen, you're an addict; addicted to the foot rubs and to the sexual release of masturbation. And now it's like you're in withdrawal and you equate the loss of your wife to the loss of your sister. Don't you remember, you told me about what happened in Vegas when you were making love to Melusine and she thought you tried to strangle her? And now you're taking that image, of you making love to your wife, with your hands around her neck and you're transposing it onto your sister because you're filled with grief and loss at having driven Melusine away. Can't you see that?"

"No. You're wrong. I tried to strangle Melusine because I once strangled my sister and now that's how I achieve sexual and emotional satisfaction," Hans says in a flat voice. "You've got it completely the wrong way around, Juditha."

"But your sister's alive," Juditha insists, and she sounds almost desperate. "Come on, Hans. We're so nearly there. Don't give up now. Don't do this now. Please."

"I'm trying not to give up," Hans says, with his eyes closed. "But I can't escape the truth."

"It's not the truth. Oh, Hans. You're worrying me. I feel like you're in such a dark place."

Hans thinks she has no idea. He wonders if he should tell her about his latest, other, problem. But they're nearly out of time. He'll have to save it for their next conversation.

She senses something. "Hans, what else? Tell me. We can talk for longer this time, please Hans, tell me, what else is going on?"

He hesitates. "I ... well you know I do the eye exams for the school kids?"

She immediately senses what is coming. "Yes, I do. What happened?"

"Nothing. Yet. It's just that when I'm alone in the room with the girls, the fourteen-year-old girls, and it's dark and they're reading the letters off the wall, well, all I want to do is touch their feet. I just want to hold their soft naked feet, just for a moment."

"Dear god," Juditha says. "Hans, this is going to get you into real trouble. Do you hear me? The nightmares are just your mind playing tricks on you because you've lost your wife but this, wanting to touch young girls' feet, Hans, that's sexual abuse. Listen, Hans you need to take a leave of absence from work. And then you need to find a doctor. Tell him you're suffering from exhaustion and that you need some rest and help."

"Yes, right, and then who'll pay your bills, Juditha? Don't tell me you'll take me on pro-bono."

"I couldn't afford to do as much work with you as I am doing now, but I would never abandon you, never."

"Isn't that what they all say? And yet look, out the door they all walk. And you will too."

There's silence on the other end of the phone.

"Hans," Juditha says very softly. "You're in deep trouble. Forgive me for not having seen this sooner. The war on your soul is overtaking everything. Your ego is running rampant like a vigilante who would die rather than surrender. I'm very frightened for you. Please, we've known each other for a good amount of time, enough that you should trust me. And we've done deep work together. You must stop drinking and you must find help."

He is quiet. "Okay," he says. "Okay."

She is relieved. "Fine then. I'll talk to you once you've seen your doctor. Call him now and call me tomorrow at the usual time. Oh, Hans. I'm sorry. I should have been more aware of the toll this was taking on you."

Hans is suddenly very tired of talking to her. All he wants to do is sleep.

"I must go," he says. "Our time is up. Goodbye, Juditha, I'll call you tomorrow."

He hangs up the phone and goes out into the receptionist's office. "I've got another migraine," he says. "I must go home. Please cancel all my appointments. I'm very sorry."

"You should see a doctor," the receptionist says. "Forgive me for saying this, but you look terrible. Shall I phone and make an appointment for you?"

Hans sinks down into a chair. "My head hurts too much to think," he says. "I don't want to see a doctor. I'm just going to go home."

"Let me drive you," she offers but Hans shakes his head.

"The other partners won't like that," he says, "and you know that. They're already angry with me because my patient list is down. The only people I see these days are the school kids. I know I haven't been pulling my weight but I'm not well. I wouldn't be surprised if they kick me out soon."

"Don't say things like that," the receptionist says reproachfully, "they're very fond of you, we all are. They're worried about you too, if you must know. You've lost so much weight and your skin's a bad colour and you have these terrible head-aches. Let me drive you to the doctor."

But once again, Hans refuses her help. He gets to his feet and fumbles for his keys.

"I'll be better tomorrow," he says. And he is sure that he will be, because he has had an idea that he is certain will help. He is going to get his own kind of medicine.

25.

HANS WALKS SLOWLY out of the office and gets into his car. He drives to the poorest part of town, a seedy area filled with rundown motels that offer rooms by the hour.

He parks his car and looks around. He has never picked up a prostitute before and has no idea how to go about it. But he does not have to wait or wonder for long.

A woman in her early thirties comes up to him; she is wearing battered brown cowboy boots, an ill-fitting denim mini-skirt and an unbuttoned purple satin blouse that reveals a lacy orange bra.

"You looking for company?" she asks.

"Yes, but you're too old." Hans is brusque. "I want someone about fourteen."

The woman gives a phlegmy laugh. "You're gonna get yourself into trouble, honey, talking like that. I think what you meant to say was you'd like a girl who looks about fourteen. Don't want to get caught for rape, now do you?"

He nods. "So, do you know anyone who looks about fourteen?"

"Yes. Go into that hotel there on the corner, tell them Rosalind is fixing you up and ask for Room 215. Got it?"

Hans heads over the hotel and does what she says.

He takes the stairs to the second floor, not trusting the elevator. The place smells of tired unwashed folk who have been down on their luck for a while; it is as if he has fallen into a bin of unsorted clothes at the Salvation Army.

He opens the door to the room and sits down on the edge of the bed. The room is as stale and musty as the hallway and there is the added hint of bug spray and cheap furniture polish, although he is at a loss to see what would warrant polishing. He thinks that he should feel nervous but he does not really feel anything at all.

There is a knock at the door and a girl comes in and Hans is instantly disappointed. Apart from being the right age, she couldn't be more different to Kateri; she has short black hair with crimson streaks and dozens of piercings. She reminds him of Nika.

"No," he says, "you're all wrong. I'm sorry but I need a pale blonde girl your age with no piercings, no thick make-up and no tattoos. I want a clean girl."

The girl shrugs and vanishes.

Hans looks at his watch. He is not sure what to do. Should he go downstairs and find Rosalind or will the gothic girl give her the message?

He decides to wait for a bit.

Fifteen minutes later a new girl sticks her head around the door. She is younger, platinum blonde and skinny and from the looks of it; she has just given her face a scrubbing and she is not wearing any jewelry.

"Good." Hans nods and waves her in. "Much better. Come in. Would you mind washing your feet for me?"

The girl goes into the bathroom without comment and washes her feet in the basin.

Then she comes back and starts to undress.

"No, no, keep your clothes on. Sit on the bed, like so, a little propped up."

He gets her organized and then he sits on the bed, cross-legged and takes her feet in his hands.

She does not say anything.

Hans tries very hard. He closes his eyes and tries to pretend that the girl is Kateri but he cannot. The room's putrid funk is too strong and more importantly, the girl's feet feel all wrong; they are callused, cracked and hard, particularly around her heels — and she has strange toes, with the second toe much longer than her big toe and all her toes splay out slightly.

"For such a pretty girl, you've got very ugly feet," Hans says accusingly after a while, when he realizes this exercise is in vain. "Let's try something else. Lie down, I'll show you how."

He positions her and then he lies down next to her, with his forehead almost touching hers.

He closes his eyes.

But the girl smells wrong wrong wrong and Hans is angry. Despite her efforts to clean herself off, he can smell the remnants of her cheap make-up and he feels nauseous. This was such a good idea and it should have worked.

He sighs.

He experimentally puts one hand on the girl's throat and the other on her mouth and his penis quivers slightly but again, nothing works.

Hans wants to weep. "Look," he says, sitting up, "you are wrong and I can't fix it." He pays her. "Go. Just leave me alone."

She takes the money, slips on her shoes and leaves. She has not said one word throughout their encounter.

Hans looks around the dingy room. He knows he was rude to the girl but he does not care. It was her fault. He thinks about her nasty feet and shudders. He gets up to wash his hands, running the water to scalding and rubbing his hands for a long time.

Unsure what to do next, he looks at his watch. He does not want to go home yet but he does not want to stay in the room. He goes downstairs and out into the wintry sunshine. He sees a park bench across the street and he goes over and sits down. The sunshine feels good on his skin and in that moment, he is happy; happy and free. Free from his work and his wife and his worries. The only way his life could be any better at that moment would be if he had a glass of red wine.

He looks up and sees a liquor store in his direct line of vision. Thinking that he might as well get stocked up for the evening, he goes in and buys four bottles of the cheapest red wine he can find. He has long since decided that he would rather have more of a cheaper brand than less of a favourite.

Then, without having made any conscious decision to do such a thing, he goes to a nearby convenience store and buys a bottle of cranberry juice. He empties the juice into a concrete planter full of dead leaves and pigeon crud and then he quickly decants half a bottle of wine into the juice bottle.

He returns to the bench and sits in the fading sunshine, drinking contentedly. The mid-February temperatures are only slightly above freezing but Hans does not feel the cold.

He wonders what to do about Juditha. It is clear that she will not carry on unless he can pay her and the only asset he has left is his car. He thinks about borrowing from Jonas, borrowing from the college fund that he set up for him. But he cannot figure out a way to do it without Melusine finding out.

Come evening, he is drunk and he staggers over to his car. He drives home with extra care and immediately makes for his easy chair.

Melusine arrives shortly after him, and soon after that, his son drops by for a visit. He ignores them both and lies in his chair, wondering if he will be drunk enough by bedtime to be able to have just one good night's sleep. He thinks that perhaps he should sleep in his chair and avoid the bedroom entirely. Yes, that might help.

26.

THE NEXT DAY, Melusine wakes and dresses for work. She walks through the living room and sees that Hans is still in his chair, fast asleep. He has been there all night. She shakes him. He stinks of cheap wine and rancid sweat. "Hans! Wake up. My god, look at you. Smell you. Go and take a hot shower and use a lot of mouthwash. You stink of booze. You really need to get a grip, Hans."

He opens one eye and wishes she would shut up. He eases himself upright. His head is pounding but he feels better. He is delighted to notice that he did not dream about murdering Kateri. He gets up clumsily and heads toward the bathroom.

"What a great job Healing Lives Ministries is doing," Melusine shouts after him. "Tell them thanks, from me. Good god, Hans. I'm leaving. Good luck with your day."

He closes the bathroom door and stands in the shower. He feels numb, removed from reality.

He dries himself and shaves, nicking himself in a few places that won't stop bleeding. He sticks bits of tissue paper onto the cuts and goes into the bedroom to get dressed.

But even being in there for such a short time is bad for him; he sees Kateri with her eyes bulging as he squeezes the life out of her and he tastes her tongue as she forces it into his mouth with a deathly kiss.

He retches, grabs his clothes and runs out to the living room to get dressed.

His hands are shaking as he fixes his tie. He cannot stop seeing Kateri and her eyes turning bloodshot as her veins burst from the pressure.

He scurries into the kitchen and opens the last bottle of wine. He downs two full mugs and feels slightly better.

He locks the house and gets into his car. On the way to the office, he stops at a convenience store and buys a variety of breath mints.

He rushes past the receptionist who is asking him how his head feels and if his headache has cleared. "I'm fine," he shouts over his shoulder, closing his office door behind him.

He sits behind his desk with his head in his hands. He wishes he was sitting on the bench in the sunshine with his wine.

There's a knock at the door and the receptionist shows a young girl in. "This is Hilde," she says, her hand on the girl's back, "from the school. She's here for her eye exam. Are you okay? Do you want me to ask one of the others to do it?"

"I told you, I'm fine," he says sharply. "Come in, Hilde. Take a seat in the big black chair. Don't be nervous."

Hilde does as he says. She's a gangly girl in her early teens, with a high forehead and a sharp, pointed chin. She is looking at him with alarm for no reason he can pinpoint.

"I'll be outside if you need me," the receptionist says to Hilde and she leaves, closing the door behind her.

"Don't be nervous," Hans says, "this won't hurt. Have you had an eye exam before?"

"No," Hilde says in a small voice. "I never needed one till now."

"Don't worry. I'm just going to ask you which letters look better to you and you have to answer as quickly as you can, don't think too much, just answer, all right?"

Hilde nods and clasps her hands tightly together.

Hans begins the test. He stands close to her, adjusting the various lenses. Unable to help himself, he glances down at her feet; she is wearing black school shoes with the laces neatly tied.

He moves the equipment to one side. "Hilde," he says, conversationally, "if you like, you can take your shoes off. Lots of people find it very helpful; they can concentrate better. Would you like to try that?"

"No," Hilde says in her small voice.

"Oh, come on," Hans says. "It's very important that you are nice and relaxed so that your brain can send you a clear message about which letters are the brightest and the sharpest. Take your shoes off."

The last sentence comes out as a command and Hilde unties her laces and slips off her shoes and Hans repositions the equipment in front of her.

"How old are you?" Hans asks.

"I'm thirteen. Nearly fourteen."

Hans nods. "Good. Okay, now let's try again." He clicks a few lenses into place and asks her which letters are the sharpest.

He has an erection and he is sweating and he recalls that he forgot to put on any antiperspirant and he knows that last night's alcohol is seeping through his pores.

"I tell you what, Hilda," he says and his voice is hoarse, "I'm going to touch each foot, one at a time, and then you must tell me if this makes you see better or worse. Can you do that?"

"Yes," she says meekly.

"Very good. All right, so now, with me touching your right foot do you see the letters better or worse?"

"The same."

"They can't be the same. Let's try again."

He does this for a while, and then he tries her left foot.

Hilde shakes her head. "There's no difference."

Hans pretends to think for a moment. "Aha. I know why. It's because you still have your socks on. Take them off and we'll try again."

Hilde obligingly pulls off her socks.

Hans rubs her right foot. It is slightly sweaty and it is soft and tiny in his hand.

Her foot is perfect. She is perfect. The sparrow-like bones, the softly rounded heel, the silky smooth virgin purity of her skin.

"I can still see the same," Hilde offers.

"I'm going to try the left one," Hans says and he caresses the left foot.

"No, it's still the same," Hilde insists and she sounds a little impatient.

Then Hans does something unspeakable. He darts down, puts her foot in his mouth and quickly snakes his tongue in between her toes, and he sucks, hard.

Hilde sits bolt upright and screams. Her long piercing cry has the receptionist bursting into the room within seconds.

"What on earth's going on?" she asks, out of breath.

"He licked my toes," Hilde shouts hysterically, unable to move; she is still wedged in by the heavy equipment. "He put my foot in his mouth and he used his tongue!" She starts to wail in earnest, her face crumpled.

The receptionist rushes toward the girl and Hans steps aside and sits down heavily in his chair.

His mind is an absolute blank.

"He told me it would help me see the test better," the girl sobs. "First I just had to take my shoes off and then my socks and he rubbed me and then he put my foot in his mouth and he used his tongue!" She wails the last word and sobs even more hysterically.

The receptionist moves the equipment to the side and puts her arm around the girl. "Come on. Come with me."

She glances at Hans as she leads the girl away but he is bent forward, studying his hands.

He is considering his options.

It is safe to say that his career is over. And the same, no doubt, can be said for his marriage.

And, since he is out of funds, Juditha is also out of the picture. But what would she say to him now, if he were talking to her? He thinks that apart from instructing him to stop drinking and dreaming murderous thoughts, she would tell him to find joy in his day.

Hans gets up and collects his car keys. He walks past his colleagues who are all huddled around the hysterical girl.

"You'll pay for this," one of his former best friends shouts. "She's the same age as my daughter, you sick pervert."

But Hans hardly hears him. He gets into his car and starts the engine. Then he backs up, makes a perfect turn and heads out to find his joy.

Three
*war is no longer declared
but rather continued*

27.

WHEN HANS DOES NOT come home that night, Melusine is both concerned and angry. She is sure that a part of him is trying to provoke her but she does not know what sought-after response he is looking for, and she thinks that perhaps he does not know himself.

She stays awake all night, sitting in the kitchen and worrying. She goes to work the next morning, exhausted and silent.

The second night of his absence sees her frightened. It is cold outside and she has no idea where he could be. She wonders if she should call Jonas, or the police. Or Hans's colleagues. Or Ana and Dirk. But again, she does nothing, choosing with her stubborn pride to believe instead that he is on a bender; one that will punish her sufficiently and see him work all this nonsense out of his system.

On the third day, she calls in sick and stays at home and that night, she phones Jonas who immediately gets in his car and comes over.

"He'd never leave Mimi for this long," he says to Melusine. They are both standing in the kitchen, looking out the window as if they expect Hans's car to pull into the driveway at any moment.

"Previously he wouldn't, you're right," Melusine agrees, "but everything's changed now. Oh, Jonas. Do you think we should call the police?"

He chews his lip. "Yes. I'll call."

Neither of them can believe this is happening and the conversation with the *polizeikommissar* feels surreal.

"Perhaps he's gone on a business trip that he forgot to mention," the officer suggests to Jonas. "Have you spoken to his colleagues?"

Jonas relays this to Melusine and she shakes her head, no. The police officer asks for a description of Hans and Jonas hands the phone to Melusine.

"He's about six foot two, he has blonde hair, a very high forehead. He's thin and he would have been dressed in a suit and tie. Um, I can't think of anything else."

"Does he have seizures or take any medication?"

"No, he's just a normal guy." She wonders if she should say anything about Hans's drinking but decides against it.

"Give his colleagues a call first thing in the morning. And now that we have the car license and a description, I'll put out a call for our guys to be on the lookout. You should also phone the hospitals. And try not to worry too much. These things are usually nothing more than a man needing to let off some steam. If you don't have any luck, then come in tomorrow and we'll file a missing person's report."

Melusine and Jonas phone all the hospitals in the town and the surrounding areas but Hans has not been admitted to any of them. They do not know whether to feel relieved or further concerned.

They stay up all night talking and waiting, once again hoping that Hans will simply come home.

Melusine finally tells Jonas about the Healing Lives Ministries and he is immediately convinced that they are involved in Hans's disappearance. Jonas insists they must tell the police about them and Melusine says they will, in the morning.

The next morning, they decide to go straight to Hans's workplace; they're unable to sit still any longer and feel the need to start searching physically.

They are silent as they drive to Hans's office. They have not been there often as Hans discouraged what he referred to as unprofessional familial relationships during working hours. He had made a point of asking them to never even phone him there.

They pull into the parking lot and see that Hans's allocated spot is empty. Jonas nevertheless chooses to park elsewhere, as if leaving his father's place untouched might somehow forestall disaster.

"I'm coming in with you," he says when he sees that his mother is about to tell him to wait in the car. "I'm not a baby. Whatever's happened, I need to know."

"I'm sure that nothing's happened," Melusine says but her words ring false to both of them.

They climb the concrete steps to the front door and a buzzer sounds as they enter.

The receptionist, who knows Melusine from Christmas parties, takes one look at them and pales.

"Frau Meier, please sit down, let me call Herr Hinkle for you." She rushes away from them as fast as she can.

"That doesn't bode well," Jonas comments and Melusine takes his hand, more for her own comfort than his.

"Melu!" Bill is overly hearty. "And Jonas, look at you, all grown up. Listen, why don't both of you come with me? We can talk in private."

Melusine and Jonas exchange a glance. So there is something to talk about. Something bad.

They follow Bill to his office and sit down. Bill closes the door behind them.

"Don't sugar-coat it, Bill," Melusine says bluntly. "Just tell us what's going on."

Bill nods. "Let me ask you first, when last did you see Hans?"

"Monday night. And frankly, he wasn't doing too well."

"My dear, I can tell you now that however badly he was doing on Monday night, he fared far worse on Tuesday," Bill says and he leans his chin on the tips of his steepled fingers.

"Cut the crap, Bill, and get to the point," Melusine says and she can see that her son is taken-aback by her rudeness but she's scared now.

"Okay. He sexually abused a schoolgirl while doing an eye exam."

"What?" Melusine and Jonas both shout the word at the same time and then start voicing violent objections.

"Papa would never do that, never," Jonas insists, close to tears.

"What happened, Bill? And I do mean exactly."

"He managed to coerce a thirteen-year-old schoolgirl into taking her socks and shoes off during an eye exam by telling her it would help him test her eyes better. Then he rubbed her feet, put her foot in his mouth and sucked on her toes."

Jonas cannot believe what he is hearing. He looks to his mother, needing her to deny it and prove the impossibility of the allegation. But she doesn't.

"Her feet?" Melusine whispers. "Oh, dear god. And then what happened Bill?"

Bill scratches his head. "You know I hate to be telling you this," he says. "The girl screamed her head off when he sucked her toes and Gretchen ran in to find her crying and Hans kneeling there, holding her foot. Gretchen took the girl out and Hans just sat there. He didn't say anything. He didn't do anything. Gretchen said he had a strangely blank expression, like he wasn't thinking or feeling anything at all. We took the girl into another office and immediately notified the school. The headmaster rushed over, along with the school physician."

"And then what?" Melusine can hardly form the words.

"We were all attending to the girl, waiting for the headmaster and the doctor, and next thing I look up and Hans just strolls out, he just saunters past us, as if he's going out to buy a coffee or something, like this terrible thing never happened. I saw him get into his car and we haven't seen him since."

"Is the school going to press charges against him?" Melusine asks. "And her parents? What's going to happen?"

Bill shakes his head. "I'm not sure. It also depends on Hans, if he offers an apology or something maybe ... but none of us has seen him. But Melu, I don't think Hans has been well for quite some months now, to tell you the truth. He's been losing clients and can hardly seem to concentrate at work. He locks himself in his office for long periods of time and talks on the phone..."

"Do you have the number of who he calls?" Melusine is fierce.

"He wasn't having an affair, Melu, don't worry," Bill rushes to reassure her but she cuts him off.

"Of course he wasn't. He was phoning some person from the Healing Lives Ministries, a psychic he met in Vegas, some fraud who's going to help him find his sister."

"What?" This time it's Bill who is astounded.

"It's hard to explain," Melusine says. "Bill, is there any way at all that you can get the number he called?"

Bill picks up his phone and explains to Gretchen what they're after.

"Here," Gretchen says, arriving with a scrap of paper. "But I tried it yesterday and it just rings. I tried to find out who the number belongs to, but I couldn't find anything."

"You did all that? Why?" Melusine asks.

"Because I thought they might know where he is. I was worried too but I didn't want to phone him or you at home. I was worried," Gretchen says again and she blushes. "I care for him a lot, Frau Meier. I've worked for him for years."

"Let's try the number again," Bill says, and he dials. "Yes, Gretchen's right, it just rings." They couldn't know that Juditha had told Hans she would only answer the phone at their appointed time, so she would know it was him calling. "So what do we do now?"

"We've called the police," Melusine says. "And we're going there now to file a missing person report and we'll try to find him and we'll let you know what happens."

"Melusine," Bill looks embarrassed. "Obviously we care about Hans but this was very bad for our little firm. We've worked so hard to build a good reputation and it was a big coup, getting the school contract. And now ... you know I love Hans like a brother but if it comes to us being sued..."

"I understand, Bill," Melusine says and she stands up. "But right now, all I want to do is find him. We'll deal with everything else later. Come on, Jonas, let's go. Listen, Bill, let me know right away if you hear from him. Oh, that poor schoolgirl."

"You should be saying your poor husband," Gretchen says loudly. "I felt so sorry for him. He was getting sicker every day, thinner and thinner too. And you should have heard the noises coming out of his office sometimes, when he was alone in there. It's like the devil possessed his soul and was torturing him. You should have done something!"

"That's enough, Gretchen," Bill says and he too stands. "I apologize on behalf of Gretchen, Melusine."

"I'm not sorry," Gretchen insists. "He's a good man. As his wife, you should have done something. I tried to help him but he wouldn't let me. And his headaches, he was in such pain."

"What headaches?" Melusine is baffled.

"Exactly!" Gretchen is triumphant. "You didn't even know. You didn't care."

"I did care," Melusine says quietly. "Not that it's any of your business."

"Ladies!" Bill interjects, his hands outstretched in an appeasing motion. "We all cared. But Hans could be impossible. Don't you think I tried too? I could also see that he wasn't okay but he wouldn't talk to me. There wasn't anything we could do. But we all cared."

He gives a meaningful glance to Gretchen who turns and walks out the room.

"I'll let you know what we find," Melusine says and she puts her arm around Jonas who has been very quiet.

They walk out through the office and down into the parking lot. "You drive, Mami," Jonas says. "I'm too upset. Maybe the police can get a hold of whoever's at the end of that phone number. It's the cult's fault — I'm telling you, they drove Papa crazy."

"Yes, good idea, maybe the police will be able to get to the bottom of it," Melusine says.

They buckle up and Melusine eases into the morning traffic.

"I can't believe Papa bought into that crock of psychic shit," Jonas exclaims and they're both so upset that Melusine doesn't think to correct his language which she otherwise would have done.

"I know," she says. "Oh, Jonas. I don't know what to say."

They drive to the police station in silence and when they get there, they find there has been a development.

The officer behind the desk pulls out a file. "A man answering to your husband's description has been seen downtown with a bunch of homeless guys; regulars that we keep an eye on."

"We'll go there now," Melusine tells the police officer who looks uneasy.

"Everyone's out on call," he says, "I don't have anyone to go with you right now. Do you mind waiting?"

"We must go now," Melusine insists and Jonas agrees.

"Just be careful and if it does turn out to be him be sure to call us immediately, okay?"

Melusine says that she will and she and Jonas rush out to the car and Melusine drives; her face is pale and her hands grip the steering wheel tightly.

"Okay, we're here," Jonas says. "There's a parking spot over there, Mami."

They park and sit for a moment, unwilling to have their worst suspicions confirmed, and it is then that Melusine sees him. "Oh, Jonas, oh, dear god, there he is, oh, look..." Melusine's voice breaks and her breath is coming in harsh gasps. "Look, Jonas, there on the bench. He looks just like a homeless person. How could this have happened? There were signs he wasn't coping, but this?"

"I know," Jonas says and his voice is distant, and shocked and it's as if she is hearing her son through a tunnel. "I know, Mami. It's like he just snapped."

"I guess neither of us had any idea how much it had been building inside him," Melusine says.

They both just sit there, looking at the eroded husk of a man that was once Hans Meier.

"I'm going to talk to him," Melusine says, eventually.

"I'm coming with you."

They get out the car and walk across to Hans, watching his face closely as they move into his line of sight but his expression doesn't change. He looks at them with the same casual disinterest he would two strangers.

"Hans?" Melusine is gentle. "What are you doing here?"

He gives a snorting laugh. "Drinking my cup of joy. She told me that my authentic soul would lead me to my joy and it has. I've abandoned my ego, left it far behind, that tiring old coat. Yes, I left it and I'm glad."

"Has he gone mad, Mami?" Jonas asks and Hans snorts again.

"Mad? I'm the sanest of the mad people I know and everybody's quite crazy in this world. But not everybody did what I did. I can't live with it anymore, not in our bedroom anyway. She keeps finding me there. She won't leave me alone, and it's all my fault, it's all my fault."

"What's he talking about?" Jonas asks. He and Melusine are seated on either side of Hans.

"Kateri," Melusine says and Hans nods. He has not shaved since Monday and he scratches at his bristle. His fingernails are already dirty. Melusine wonders where his gloves are, and his hat. She wants to ask him but she does not want to interrupt him.

"Kateri. My blood. Her blood. I loved her too much, too wrongly. She lives in the bedroom and she comes to me at night, she's dead and her eyes are filled with blood, the blood that I put there. And I can't tell her I'm sorry because I can't find her.

She was supposed to find her but she didn't. She kept saying Kateri is coming; that she's alive and she's coming and she did come but she's dead and I can't sleep lying down anymore."

"Oh, Hans. We need to take you to a doctor, you need help, we can get you help. You didn't kill Kateri. It's all just been too much for you. Come on, let Jonas and me take you home."

"No!" Hans shouts and jumps to his feet. "They'll make me lie down. I can't lie down. I'm telling you, I killed her and she won't let me say sorry. When I lie down, she comes, and she won't leave me alone. I won't lie down again, ever!"

He backs away.

"No, no, Papa, don't go," Jonas calls out to him, pleadingly. "We promise, no doctors, and we won't take you home, okay? We just want to talk to you. Please, Papa, don't leave us, please."

Jonas gives Melusine a warning look. *If we startle him, he'll run away forever and we'll never find him.*

She nods.

"Jonas is right, Hans," she says soothingly. "Please, come back, please. We won't make you lie down, we promise."

Hans inches back towards them but he doesn't sit down.

"Hans, where have you been sleeping?" Melusine asks cautiously.

"I sit up," Hans says, proudly. "I sit all night and I can sleep in the day if I sit up. But I can't sleep at night. She finds me at night but not if I sleep during the day but I can't lie down."

She looks at him. He's wearing his long thick winter coat over a grimy sweater she has never seen before but at least he is protected from the cold. "And what are you eating?"

"Not hungry, not hungry. Anyway, there's lots of food. Too much food. Too much everything. I don't want anything anymore. Things things things. She told me, find your joy, your authentic joy and I did. I did."

"Do you still talk to her?" Melusine asks in a carefully pleasant and even tone.

Hans shakes his head. "She wanted more money. I don't have

any money. Well, some, I sold my car. She wanted me to use that to pay her but enough talking. She was wrong anyway, Kateri is dead and I killed her."

"You sold your car? Where's the money?" Melusine asks and Hans looks furtive.

"I won't say. It's for my joy. My daily joy. I don't need my daily bread but I need my daily joy."

A bunch of indigent men come up to Hans.

"We're going to the Mission for the lunchtime sandwich," one of them says, and he is missing most of his teeth. "You coming?"

Hans's face lights up. "Yes, I'm coming. These are my friends," he says to Melusine and Jonas. "That's Kristian. This is my home. We are going to get our sandwich. Thank you for the visit. Don't worry about me. I'm fine as long as I don't lie down."

He rushes after the men who have started toward the Mission without him, none of them willing to give up getting their place in line.

Melusine is stunned. "Jonas," she says, eventually, "are you okay?"

"Not really, Mami," he replies quietly, picking at a splinter on the wooden bench. AW. Someone carved their initials into the bench and Jonas picks at it. He wonders who AW is. Thinking about that is easier than thinking about his father.

"No. Me neither. I'm going to get Dr. Glott to come and take a look at him." Glott is their family doctor.

"Good idea. Let's call him now. You phone him while I call the police and let them know we found Papa."

They make their calls and wait for the doctor to arrive.

"Uh, I should mention that he has been drinking more than usual," Melusine starts to explain to the physician when he arrives and then she stops short. Jonas puts his arm around her.

"Tell him everything, Mami, tell him the whole story."

Melusine starts with the trip to Las Vegas and the deception with the two hotels, and she tells him about the Healing Lives

Ministries and Hans's increased drinking and finally, his assault on the schoolgirl. She leaves out his strange attack on her that night in Las Vegas.

The doctor shakes his head. "Poor man. This might be delayed grief at having lost his sister. Jonas is all grown up and left home — that in itself could have triggered this. There are any number of factors. I hate to use the cliché of mid-life crisis but it could be that, coupled with increased drinking that has led to a nervous breakdown. Certainly aided and abetted by this New Age place. I just wish Hans had come to see me when he started to feel out of control. I could have helped him and stopped things from disintegrating to this degree. Perhaps it's not as bad as you suspect, perhaps..."

"Look," Jonas interrupts him, "there he is, there's Papa."

Hans and his group are returning to the park, and Hans is animated, waving his hands about.

The doctor looks to where Jonas is pointing and his face pales. "That's Hans? I wouldn't have recognized him."

"Whatever you do, don't frighten him," Jonas says. "We don't want him running off somewhere where we can't find him. It's more important that we know where he is."

Melusine and Jonas join the doctor who is heading towards Hans as carefully as he would an easily startled animal.

Hans eyes the approaching doctor with disinterest. He is drinking from a plastic bottle with a grape juice label.

"Hans?" The doctor holds his hands out in front of him, a placatory gesture. "It's me, Glott. Come on, man, you know me. What's going on here?"

Hans backs away and the group of men form a protective circle around him.

The doctor edges closer. "Come on, Hans, we've known each other for ages. You can trust me. You know you can trust me. Come on, let me help you."

As one, the group of men sidle off to the far edge of the park with Hans cocooned in the middle.

"Are the police going to arrest him for what he did to that schoolgirl? Because if they do, I can try to get him into a psych ward for evaluation, get him onto some meds and get him cleaned up. But I can see that he isn't going to come with us voluntarily."

"I don't know what the girl or her family or the school are going to do," Melusine says. The evening sun is setting and she is suddenly exhausted. She sits down on Hans's bench. "I don't know what we should do either."

"For now, you should go home, both of you. I'm going to the police station to see what they have to say and I know the woman who runs the Mission, I'll talk to her as well and get all the information I can. All we can do is keep him as safe as possible until we can try to get him some help. Both of you, go home and get some rest. At least we know where he is and what he's up to. Here's my cellphone number in case you need me."

Jonas stands up and offers Melusine his hand.

"Come on, Mami, let's get out of here. I tell you one thing, the school can't sue him. He's gone crazy. And Dr. Glott's right, we'll find a way to get him checked into a hospital. We'll get this all sorted out. We'll have Papa back to normal in no time."

They walk back to the car. Jonas looks at his watch. "I have to meet up with Nika in an hour. Let me drive you home. Are you all right, Mami?"

"Yes, I'm fine," Melusine says distantly. She is still trying to process what has happened. "Dr. Glott is right. We'll get him into a hospital. I'd better call work too, they think I've got the flu." She feels as if she is rambling, her thoughts are scrambled, fluttering.

They drive home in silence.

Jonas pulls into the driveway and they sit there for a while then he hands her the keys. "I'll call you later," he says. He reaches over and gives her a hug.

"Will you be alright tonight? Do you want Nika and me to come back and stay here with you? We can."

Melusine appreciates the offer but she would prefer to be alone and have some time to think about things. She pats his knee. "I'm fine my sweet boy, fine. You go home to Nika. I'll see you tomorrow. We'll figure all this out, okay? Try not to worry."

She waves goodbye to Jonas and unlocks the front door. As soon as she is inside, the enormity of what has happened hits her. Her husband has gone mad. Her intelligent, handsome, funny husband has gone mad. He sucked the toes of a hapless schoolgirl and turned into a homeless drunk and all in an inexcusably short period of time. It seems improbable and yet, there it is.

Melusine sinks down into a chair beside the big wooden table. She catches sight of one of her copies of *Herzzeit Brief-wechsel* and she makes a ragged sound — a mocking laugh. How romantic madness seemed when it was contained to the artistic worlds of Ingeborg and Paul. Death by suicide, preceded by years of breakdowns; how intriguing the fragile mind had been. Not so intriguing or lovely when it happened to a member of your family.

"I imagined you suffering a movie star madness," she says out loud to Ingeborg. "And I apologize. I imagined teenaged drama but acted out in an adult fashion, in other words with a solid substrate of rational control. But there's no control, I see that now."

She does not feel foolish, conversing with a dead poet; she feels reassured, comforted. "And Paul, I'm sorry I romanticized your suffering too. What pain you must have endured, pain that finally defeated you. Madness is not a vacation from the boring self, it's a descent into hell and the boring self seems like an idyllic heaven from which one is barred. I thought madness was heroic but really, it's just tragic."

The darkness of the night seems menacing and Melusine wants to get up and close the curtains but she feels too tired to move.

"And now my husband has gone mad. I know I betrayed

him by falling in love with Gunther but Hans had already left me and perhaps I sensed that. Not that I'm trying to excuse myself, I'm not."

She crosses her arms and stares out into space. "We'll sort all this out. We will." She gets up and closes the curtains and pours a drink of water. She dials the doctor's telephone number; she cannot wait until the morning.

"According to the police, the girl is not going to press charges." Glott is blunt and to the point. "This is not a good thing even though it might appear that way. Because without her statement, the police cannot arrest Hans and unless they arrest him, we can't get him into a hospital. It's clear he won't be coming voluntarily."

"Why won't the girl press charges? I would have thought her family would insist?"

"They don't want to put the girl under any kind of stress. Further stress, should I say. Melusine, you should be warned, the tabloid newspapers are all over this. That woman from Hans's office, the receptionist…"

"Gretchen."

"Yes, her. She told them everything she knows. Someone at the school, one of the teachers said something to alert the media's interest and the newspaper called Gretchen and she told them the whole story."

Melusine is cold, her legs feel rubbery and she shrinks against the wall. "How do you know this?"

"The police told me because the paper called them to ask if the girl's going to press charges since no one from the family would talk to them. Not easy to keep a thing like this under wraps in a town our size."

"That's just great. Just when I thought it couldn't get any worse. But you're right, the main thing is how can we help Hans now?"

She can almost feel the doctor's shrug down the line. "Not much really unless Hans does something that'll land him in jail. I also spoke to Ellen, she runs the Mission and she said she'll keep an eye on him. I gave her both your and Jonas's telephone numbers."

"Thank you Dr. Glott." Melusine is exhausted. "I'll go and see her tomorrow. Thank you for everything you've done."

"Haven't done anything." The doctor is gruff. "Wish I'd had the chance to treat him sooner. Let's keep in touch, alright?"

Melusine agrees and replaces the receiver.

"Oh, Hans," she says, looking through the kitchen to the living room at his empty chair. "I really don't know what to think. Or feel. I guess I should have known something was wrong after that night in Vegas but I just couldn't deal with it. You've always been so dependable. Why? Why, after all these years, did you come undone now? I don't understand."

She knows she should call Bill and her boss and Ana but she cannot bear to talk about it yet. They'll know soon enough anyway and she can deal with it then. The silence in the house feels ominous and Melusine has no idea what to do with herself.

She feels as if the house is alive, as if it is breathing and watching her to see if she will break too. And if she does break, it will have won and she too will be driven out into the night.

She shakes herself. These are stupid thoughts. She is a rational woman, Hans is the crazy one.

She forces herself to enter what was their bedroom and she tries to make herself lie down on the bed, to exorcise the tormented energy of Hans and his demons but she can't bring herself to do it.

She tells herself that it is just a bed, that she slept there for over twenty years but the bed — unmade, rumpled, sweat-stained — is the pit of Hans's hell and she can feel the horror of his pain. She leaves the room and closes the door. She feels as if the room is the devil's lair and again, she feels the living pulse of the house and she reminds herself that it's only her poor startled heart that's beating too fast.

She walks through to the living room and she sees the ghost

of Hans as he lay on his chair only days before, guzzling cheap red wine to stop the evil spirit from approaching.

She looks at the wine stain on the wall. She never cleaned it; she wanted it to be a stain of reproach; a visible symbol that would bring Hans to his knees and restore his sanity. It mocks her now, that hurled splash of anger.

Melusine turns on her heel, grabs her handbag and leaves the house. She gets into her car and drives to a hotel at the edge of town. She sits on her bed and phones the police who do not tell her anything she has not already heard from Glott. Then she phones Bill.

"I can't tell you how sorry I am that Gretchen ran her mouth off to the newspaper. She's been reprimanded, let's put it that way. I don't know what she was thinking."

Melusine shakes her head. "She made things a lot worse. So, the girl's family are not pressing charges?"

"No, and I'm glad to say that there will be no charges, not to Hans or to our little business. I'm relieved about that, Melu, I can't say I'm not. And the school says that they'll continue the contract, so that's good too."

"Bill ... didn't you see anything? About Hans's deteriorating. Didn't you notice anything? I know I'm the one who really should have seen it coming, but didn't you notice anything?"

Bill hesitates. "There were odd things but nothing I could confront him about. He locked himself in his office regularly, said he had a conference call and he didn't tell us anything more and we didn't ask. Gretchen was the most observant; the rest of us guys didn't pay it much mind. We all have stuff to deal with, wives, kids, money. If Hans seemed distracted, we just figured it was the usual."

"I should have noticed. I'm the one. Oh, Bill, I'm sorry about all of this."

"Melusine! It's not your fault! If there's anything I can do, you let me know, okay?"

"Okay. Thanks Bill."

Next on the list is Ana. Melusine sighs. While she loves her friend, she is too tired for drama. She picks up the receiver and then changes her mind and calls her boss instead. She figures it is better if Ana reads about it in the newspaper first and lets off some steam before she talks to her.

"Take as much time as you need," her boss says when Melusine explains the situation as sparsely as she can.

"Uh, there's one more thing..." Melusine hesitates. "The newspapers have picked up the story so it's going to be everywhere."

"Thanks for the heads-up," the woman says, "and don't worry. You have our full support. This is a tragedy, Hans was, is, a very fine man."

Melusine thanks her and says she will take the following day and then she calls Jonas to see how he is doing and tell him where she is.

"Good thinking, Mami, going to a hotel. So there's no way of getting Papa to a hospital? What are we supposed to do now?"

"I don't know. I'll talk to the woman at the Mission tomorrow and tell you what she says."

"I tell you, Mami, what makes me so angry is this Healing Lives place. I'm going to find them if it's the last thing I do. They're to blame, they should be held accountable."

"I've tried to find them, Jonas, believe me, I've tried. The number is unlisted and they cashed the cheques your father sent so there's no trail to follow and there's nothing about them online either." Melusine takes a deep breath. "Jonas, I want you to listen to me, really listen. The police know about the Healing Lives Ministries now, let's leave it with them, please. I want you to enjoy your life with Nika and not go off chasing lost causes. Your father never got over the loss of his sister. It stunted his emotional growth, it stunted his whole life, and now look what's happened."

"But..."

"No buts. Please. Promise me you won't let this thing with

your father do the same thing to you. Promise me you will do all the things we were talking about the other day — law school and marriage and babies." Her chest is tight and she finds it hard to breathe. Her jaw hurts and there's a ringing in her ears. "Promise me, Jonas, promise me."

"Okay, Mami," he says, with obvious reluctance, "but only if you promise to do the same. Papa's a good man but he never let you spread your wings and fly, so you promise me that in return that you'll do some of the things in this life that you really want to, okay?"

"We've got a deal," Melusine says, exhaling loudly.

"Mami," Jonas says, "it's not that I don't love Papa. I really do love him. But I just can't cry. I feel like I should cry but I can't. Why is that?"

"I don't know, Jonas. Me too. Maybe we're still in shock. I want you to get some rest now. I'm going to have a long hot bath and then go to bed. It's been an exhausting few days. We'll talk later, my sweet boy."

"One more thing, Mami. Nika asked me to tell you something, wait, what was it? Nika?"

Nika comes to the phone. "*I step, a bundle of goodness and godliness that must make good this devilry that has happened.* And we will, Melu, we will make good of this, all of us together."

"Ah, my dear, I was thinking it was more a case of *war is no longer declared but continued. The outrageous has become the everyday.* But I'm more than willing to accede to your quote instead."

She hands the phone back to Jonas who manages a laugh. "Whoever thought I'd have two of you quoting Ingeborg at me?"

"There's no escape!" Melusine summons a wan smile. "Goodnight then, we'll talk tomorrow." Melusine orders a hamburger from room service and sits down on the bed, waiting.

She wonders if she should sell the house. She tells herself that it is Jonas's childhood home with many good memories but still, she cannot imagine going back. The tall red-shingled, gabled house with yellow climbing roses in the summertime was her home too, but now it is a mocking place, dark and cold.

Her food arrives and she wolfs down half of it then suddenly feels sick and rushes to the washroom to throw up. She splashes her face with cold water and looks at herself in the mirror. She is haggard and grey, with lines etched deeply in her face. She turns away and runs a bath, the water so hot it stings her skin and she wants to scrub herself but lacks the energy.

Steaming and lobster red, she wraps herself in a towel and climbs into bed, the humid heat a comfort. She thinks about Hans, out in the freezing night, without his gloves, hat or scarf.

She balances the hotel stationery on her lap and begins to write to Gunther.

I feel as if this is my fault. I should have seen this coming. In all fairness, I couldn't have known the fallout would be this bad, how could I know? But still ... I should have stopped this from happening.

She wishes she could tell Gunther that she longs to see him again and that it would be wonderful for him to be by her side during this terrible time. Then she reminds herself that this is her lover she is talking about; it would hardly be appropriate. She shakes her head. Never mind Hans, it's not like she is keeping her own house in order either.

I never got the chance to thank you for what you said about my manuscript, I'm very happy you liked it. I made some of the changes you suggested and sent it off to a publisher. Funny how long ago that seems; it's a lifetime ago. Maybe if I hadn't been so preoccupied by my writing I would have been able to help Hans. Ach, I know that's not really true. We can only help others if they want us to, isn't that so?

She puts the letter on the bedside table, turns off the light and rolls over on her side, encased in her warm cocoon and falling into an unconscious sleep.

28.

AS SOON AS MELUSINE WAKES, she dresses and drives down to the park. She quickly spots Hans; he is with the same group of men as the previous day and he already has a bottle in hand. She sits watching him for an hour or so and when they leave, she follows them as they head towards the Mission.

The Mission is housed in a community hall adjoining a gothic old church with a single ornate turret filthied by time.

Melusine makes her way to the hall entrance, threading through the scattered group of men and women who are wandering in and out, leaving and returning. None of them seem to notice her.

The hall is clean and bright and the linoleum floor is polished but the smell of sour unwashed bodies, acrid bleach and strong coffee mingle, and Melusine breathes through her mouth. There are long folding tables with plastic yellow table cloths and stainless steel serviette holders.

She stands at the back of the hall and watches Hans line up for a sandwich. He shakes his head at the offer of a glass of milk or orange juice. He sits down at one of the tables and chews his food with enthusiasm, talking loudly and waving his hands. If he notices Melusine, he hides it well. It seems to her as if he is enjoying himself, he is the centre of attention, holding court and laughing.

As soon as they have eaten, the men file past and even though

Melusine is in clear view, Hans does not appear to see her.

"Can I help you?" A skinny birdlike woman in her sixties appears at Melusine's side.

Melusine startles and she turns to the woman.

"The man in the tan trousers ... the new one..."

"Hans?"

"You know his name?"

"Of course. Kristian, one of the more lucid fellows in the group told me. How can I help you?"

The skinny woman is dressed in a navy floral frock with bright yellow flowers and a beige cardigan and her glasses hang low off a beaded chain. She looks quizzically at Melusine.

"I'm his wife." Melusine cannot think what to say next.

"And I'm Sister Mary Anne. Come on, let's go where we can talk." The woman takes Melusine by the arm and leads her to an office. She seats Melusine on a sofa and sits down beside her. "Can I get you a coffee?"

Melusine shakes her head. There is something motherly about this skinny straightforward woman and Melusine feels tears welling up in her throat, threatening to choke her. Her eyes fill and before she can take control, her face is splashed with tears.

The woman is silent; she hands over a box of Kleenex and waits.

"I just don't know what happened!" To her chagrin, Melusine is keening in a way she has not cried since her parents died. And, having opened the floodgates now, she cannot seem to close them.

"I don't know what happened," she says again. "One minute we were a normal family, a family ... sure, we had faults and problems, all families do but we were happy...." This sets her off again, a thin wailing sound that comes from her gut and winds around and out through her heart, and again the woman just nods and waits.

"I failed everybody!" Melusine manages to say, "my poor sweet boy, my marriage..."

She slowly begins to calm down, and she hugs her arms around her sides.

"These things just happen, dear." The woman is imperturbable and yet not unsympathetic.

"These things don't just happen to *us*!" Melusine blows her nose loudly as if to emphasize her point.

The woman shrugs her bony shoulders and smiles for the first time. "I'm sorry, dear, they do. And when they do, all we can do is manage the situation to the best of our abilities. From our side, we'll feed Hans and keep an eye on him and offer him counsel if he seems open to it and that's all we can do."

"Do any of them ever ... get normal again?"

The woman sighs and pats Melusine on the knee. "Not usually. If they show any signs of wanting to rejoin the real world, then of course we help them and we get in touch with their families. Hans is pretty far gone which is surprising in a sense, considering that last week he had a job and a home. But there's a breaking point for all of us and this must have been building inside him for quite some time."

"It must have been on his mind for a while but it all really started going wrong in October when we went to Vegas and Hans attended a psychic fair. They destroyed him," Melusine says and the woman smiles again and Melusine notices that she has large, horsy teeth.

"What happened in Vegas followed you home instead of staying there," the sister said. "We have a fellow mission out there in the desert. I hear lots of horror stories."

"The psychic responsible for this mess works for the Healing Lives Ministries and if you have contacts there, maybe you can help me find whoever Hans was seeing at the fair?" Melusine is hopeful but the woman shakes her head.

"We're nuns, dear, not detectives. And besides, if you ask me, you're looking for a needle in a haystack. I understand you want to know what happened but the odds aren't in your favour. You're better off trying to move forward."

"But just from a practical point of view I don't know how I can live with it. How can I be alright in my warm safe home when it's freezing out there and I can't bear to think of him out there in the cold, sleeping in the park. He'll die of exposure, he's not used to that kind of thing. For goodness sake, Hans never even liked camping!" She feels foolish for blurting out the last and Sister Mary Anne pats her hand.

"They find places when it's cold and the police turn a blind eye as long as they don't get up to any mischief and they seem to know which lines not to cross. We used to have beds here but the funding got pulled. But don't worry, they find shelter in abandoned houses and some of them even have shacks down in the old tunnels behind the train station. And your husband has made friends. He'll be alright, dear, hard as that might be to believe."

Melusine nods. Her face feels hot and swollen and she presses the palms of her hands to her eyes. She takes a deep breath. "To think I once thought madness was a romantic and poetic notion." She sits up straighter. "Sister Mary Anne, you're right. I need to deal with this situation as best I can and do the best I can for my son. And that's exactly what I'll do. Thank you for listening."

They stand and Melusine feels foolish. "It will all be fine," she says, knowing the lie as she says it.

The woman shows her out and Melusine stands blinking in the winter sunlight. She gets into her car and drives across town to the bank; she wants to find out what happened to the money Hans got from selling his car.

The bank teller clicks through several files. "Yes, here it is, he set up a savings account. He's got a bank card. I'm not sure what you can do about it, it all looks to be above board."

"I don't want to do anything, I just wanted to find out. If he ever needs any money, don't tell him but phone me, okay?" She is not sure why she says this; is she saying she is prepared to fund her husband's indigent life? She shakes her head, having no idea. She checks the time on her cellphone, and she notices five missed calls from Ana. That can wait. She calls Jonas and tells him about her conversation with the nun.

He gives a loud sigh. "I didn't get a wink of sleep. I didn't go to classes today, I just needed to think. Mami, I don't want to sound defeatist but I don't think there's anything we can do except keep an eye on him."

"Jonas," Melusine says and then her voice catches in her throat.

"What Mami? Are you okay?"

"I'm so sorry. I'm so sorry you have to go through this my sweet boy."

"Mami!" Jonas is stern. "You've got nothing to be sorry for. This was no more your fault than mine, okay? We loved Papa, we did. We still do. Have you seen Auntie Ana yet by the way? She's phoned me like four times today, looking for you."

"Yes, she called me too. I'd better phone her." Melusine takes a deep breath.

"Better yet, go over there."

Melusine sighs. "I can't, not yet."

But once again Jonas is firm. "Go and get it over with, Mami. You drive there and I'll phone Auntie Ana and tell her to tone down the drama. You might want to prepare yourself for something else, too. Dr. Glott was right, the newspapers are full of it and it's not pretty."

"Yes, I'll have to see what they said. Fine, I'm bravely setting off to see my best friend and carry the load of her excitement and drama."

"And her love."

"Yes, and her love."

And when Melusine climbs out of the car and sees Ana waiting for her, all she sees on her friend's face is love and worry. Melusine hugs her tight and together they go into the house.

29.

B Y THE END of the following day, the whole town is familiar with the story. The national newspapers pick up the schoolgirl incident and run it in detail, and Kateri's disappearance and investigation are thrashed through once again, featuring a large grainy black and white picture of the girl when she was fourteen.

Melusine stays at the hotel for a week. She cannot face going home but eventually she has to.

She does not sell the house. Primarily because no one wants it. No one from the town anyway and there are no newcomers to the area. Her house is worthless.

"Forget about selling it," the real estate guy says, his pomaded hair the wrong blonde and ridiculous. "I'm not even going to put it on the market, I'd be flooded with nosy people with no intention of buying but just wanting to see the house of horror."

"House of horror?"

He looks at her. "House of Toe Sucker?"

She shudders. "Okay, house of horror. I get your point."

She goes to a café where she's arranged to meet Jonas.

"I don't know what to do," she says.

They both think in silence.

"We could pack up everything of Papa's," Jonas says, "and we can throw out some of the furniture or put it into storage with Papa's stuff. Then you, me and Nika can repaint the house and make it like new. We can do that, Mami, what do you think? That way you don't have to live with it but if Papa ever comes back, all his stuff will be there for him."

"I love it," she says and she starts sorting things into various piles the minute she gets home.

And she wonders, as she packs up Hans's belongings, if he will ever return. She searches for clues for the Healing Lives Ministries but comes up empty. She searches on Hans's computer again and does not find a single thing there either.

The only thing she finds in his desk drawer is a leaflet from the psychic convention for a show called Celestial Sound Vibrations and she puts it aside, thinking that she will contact them; they might have seen who Hans was talking to.

She finds a box filled with family photographs from Hans's childhood and she studies the people in the pictures, wondering about Kateri and marveling at the girl's power.

She also finds two boxes filled with Kateri's old diaries, books and toiletries. It looks like Hans has kept every single item that his sister left behind.

And even though she knows that he would have done it a thousand times before, she roots through the contents, looking to see if she can find a clue that somehow, miraculously, the others might have missed; some clue that will explain Kateri's disappearance.

But she does not find anything. She does not even get a real sense of the girl; Kateri seems fey. And while she knows that Hans thought her ethereal, Melusine, meeting her for the first time through the remnants of her belongings, finds her boneless, insubstantial and distant. Melusine tells herself that she is being unfair to the girl but she thinks back to her own possessions at fourteen; her books were diverse and interesting and her trinkets spoke volumes about her passions: art, music and science. She packs up Kateri's things and prepares them for storage.

She comes across a picture of herself and Hans on their wedding day and she feels a terrible sadness for her naiveté;

there was no way she could have known. There was Hans, confident and assured while she looked hesitant but then again, she thinks, that was just her way of smiling to hide her crooked front tooth.

She does not want to feel anger towards Hans. She sees him as a tragic, unheroic man who cannot be compared to Ingeborg's Paul who was tragic and yet still heroic — Hans is more the tragedy of pathos. And she does feel sorry for him until she comes across a picture of Hans teaching Jonas to fly a kite. Hans is explaining something and it is not the image of him that moves Melusine to rage, it is Jonas's stoic little figure standing to attention as his father demonstrates the correct maneuver.

He wasn't even six years old! Why couldn't you just have loved him? Because you couldn't love anybody except your stupid, perfect sister. Oh, I hate you, Hans, I do.

She knows this is not true but she says it out loud as she stuffs the photographs into a box. She keeps the pictures of her parents and Jonas, and puts all the others away.

Nika and Jonas repaint the inside of the house, along with a bunch of Nika's friends who work at high speed in exchange for generous orders of pizza. Melusine finds painting to be unexpectedly exhausting and she is delighted to buy them as much pizza as they want.

She and Jonas had argued over colour. Melusine had chosen what she called her 'Vegas palette'; the rich cinnamon of the desert sand for the kitchen, the vibrant red of the rocks bathed in the glowing evening sun for the living room, the bright yellow of the noonday sun for the hallway and study and the deep cobalt blue of the clear sky for the main bedroom and bathrooms.

"It will look like a circus," Jonas objected. "No one has a house like that."

They were in a speciality paint store in Frankfurt, having made a day's trip as Melusine knew that none of the local stores would have the exact tones she had in mind.

"All the more reason that your mom should," Nika said, leaning on the counter and playing with swatches. "I love the idea. You'll see, Jonas, you'll love it in the end too."

And he does.

"It's great," he says when they are finished painting and he is slumped down on the sofa. "Okay, Mami, I was wrong."

Melusine further surprises Jonas, Nika and Ana by ordering a huge aerial photograph of Las Vegas, taken at night, with the Strip ablaze with lights and glittering with colour. She has the photograph framed with a thick gold border and the oversized art hangs centrepiece in the living room, covering the place that Hans once stained with his glass of wine.

"Could you get a picture any bigger?" Ana asks.

"Actually, no," Melusine says and she grins. "I was happy there, Ana. I loved it."

She tells Gunther about the photograph when she writes to him but his response seems somewhat distant, although she wonders if she is imagining things. She is worried she is losing him too, along with her marriage and all the other things she could rely on in her life. Gunther has been sympathetic about Hans, and while she knows that is the most she could expect from him, she cannot help wishing that he had been willing, or able to do more.

She is reminded of the periods of silence in the correspondence between Ingeborg Bachmann and Paul Celan and then she tells herself they are not Ingeborg and Paul; Gunther has made it clear he has no use for romanticizing tragedy and she herself is too sensible for poetic madness.

But even though Gunther is no Paul, she wonders if he is uneasy by what he might perceive as her increased need for him by the changed circumstances of her life.

She wants to tell him that she is no Ich, the tragic heroine of *Malina*. At the end of *Malina*, the woman disappears into a crack in the wall and the reader is left wondering whether she ever existed at all.

I exist, Melusine wants to tell Gunther. *I no longer doubt my worth or my existence. You have nothing to fear. I will not leach you dry by my need nor will I let what I feel for you smother me.*

In *Malina,* Ivan, Ich's lover tells her that without a game their relationship will not work and she tells him she does not want to play any kind of game.

Melusine wonders if, like Ivan, Gunther wants her to be less accessible, to be remote.

Melusine knows that she cannot tell Gunther what he means to her and once again "whereof one cannot speak, thereof one must be silent."

Ingeborg had written to Paul: "I love you and I do not want to love you, it is too much and too difficult..." and Melusine understands. It is too tormenting but she has no choice; she cannot *un*love him.

Melusine decorates the main bedroom with large pictures of the Nevada desert at sunset and she forces herself to start sleeping in the big queensize bed again and after a few tough nights, it is almost as if the bad stuff never happened.

Her need for sexual release has been dormant for quite some time and she wonders if it is gone forever, banished by the destruction of Hans's madness. Her writing has also gone quiet, or maybe, she thinks, she simply does not have anything else to say. *Yvonne and Isolde* had been a sexual release of sorts too and now all her creative and sexual fires have been extinguished.

She strokes her body as she waits to fall asleep and although she finds the gesture soothing, it is as if her body has lost all power of passion.

A few nights later, she fishes Kurt the big black dildo out of the shoebox at the back of her study closet and looks at him, holding him at eye level. "What do you think, big man? You want to try again?" But she is not stirred to lust; there is not even a flicker. She does however appreciate his phallic beauty, and thinks that his sensual sculpted gleam is marred only by the ugliness of the dangling white electrical cord. She finds a pair of garden clippers, cuts off the cord and puts him on the bedside table.

"So much has happened since we first met," she tells him, and she lies down on the bed and folds her hands behind her head. She wishes she didn't feel so sad.

Mimi sticks her nose around the door, pads into the room and jumps on the bed. She has never done this before.

Melusine turns to the dog and wraps her arms around Mimi's kind furry warmth. "Good dog," she says, "good dog."

30

MELUSINE VISITS HANS at the park every day and on the days when she cannot make it, Jonas goes. And when Nika's in the area, she stops by for a while. He sometimes remembers who they are but other times, not.

He is triumphant about his success at staying awake during the night and napping while sitting upright on his bench during the day. He tells everyone loudly that he killed his sister but they all chalk it up to the ravings of a broken mind.

But Melusine is not so sure and once things have settled down, she has the chance to think about it more and do some investigating of her own.

She takes a day off work and drives to the nearby town of Erfurt where Hans grew up. She goes to the police station, identifies herself and asks the police officer behind the desk if she can talk to someone about a twenty-five-year old case. She gives all the details she can and the man disappears. To her surprise, she does not have to wait for long before he reappears with another man who is holding a file.

"This is Herr Kommissar Klein," the desk officer says, "he can help you."

The police commissioner smiles and shakes her hand. "Follow me." Klein takes her to a comfortable lounge area at the back of the police station.

"Let's look through this together. Your main purpose, I gather, is to try to ascertain whether your husband could have killed his sister as he is now claiming he did, although, your husband is now sadly indigent and also an alcoholic and therefore his testimony is, in all likelihood, the ravings of a distressed lunatic?"

"That would sum it up, yes," Melusine says. The brutal succinctness of his speech leaves her feeling slightly dizzy and she forces herself to concentrate. Klein gives her a look.

"I'm going to get you a coffee," he says. "This would be stressful for anyone."

He comes back with a large mug of coffee and a few snacks from the vending machine.

"I insist," he says and she nods and takes a bar of chocolate; she has been so preoccupied about the visit that she hasn't eaten all day. But she puts the chocolate aside, anxious to get on with things.

She figures the police commissioner is in his early fifties; he is a tall and good-looking barrel-chested man with clear blue eyes and an army-cut hairstyle. Something about him reminds her of Gunther but she pushes that thought away.

"Where were we?" He picks up the file again. "Well, you're not alone in wondering if your husband did in fact kill his sister. I got a call from your police department the day after he started telling the whole world that he's the one responsible for her death. The newspapers called too. It was a really big national story, in case you didn't notice."

"I noticed," Melusine says drily. "I noticed."

"We hoped that the media attention might help, that it might jog somebody's memory or something, but nothing new came to light. The Senior Police Commissioner from Frankfurt even called me to see if there had been any new developments and everybody asks the same question: is there any chance that he could have done it?"

"And?"

"It says here that your husband's friends at the time swear that he was with them when she was killed. However, since we don't know that she was actually killed, that puts their statement in some doubt."

"Perhaps they just mean when she vanished?"

"Yes, but no one has a time for that either. A woman walking her dog thinks she saw the girl talking to a gypsy who was panhandling but she can't be sure. It's as if this girl was a ghost. The notes clearly indicate that no trace was ever found of her body or her belongings. She truly vanished. And as for other suspects, well, the father looked good for it. He'd taken his wife from her hometown when she was only fourteen, so detectives at the time put two and two together and got fourteen. And then the father ran away, which never looks good. After all, why run if you're innocent?"

"Perhaps he didn't want to be charged with a twenty-year-old rape and abduction?"

"*Ach,* I doubt it would have come to that. And if your daughter was taken, wouldn't you want to stick around and see that the perpetrators were found and have your kid brought back home?"

"I agree, I'd never run," she says. "So even though they could never prove it, they thought the father did it?"

"All the statements point that way. I'm sorry I can't be more helpful. The parents are both dead now and the house they lived in was torn down to build an apartment block."

Melusine thanks the commissioner but she feels frustrated. Hans both could and could not have done it.

And what about his dreams?

The last time she saw Hans, he was almost rational.

"Tell me about her coming to you at night," she had said. "And don't worry Hans, it's daytime now, she can't get to you. But can you tell me why you think you killed her? You always said you couldn't remember that day at all."

"The Reverend helped me." This is how he has taken to referring to the psychic from the Healing Lives Ministries — The Reverend. "She helped me. First we had to break down

my ego so that my truest self could shine through. I needed to
be stripped bare. And then, when I was my truest self, I tried
to strangle a girl. I tried to kill her too and she was only kind
and she loved me and I tried to kill her."

"What girl, Hans?"

He looked furtive and scratched his beard. Melusine thought
she would never get used to seeing her formerly clean-shaven
husband so thoroughly hirsute. "I paid her. I tried to kill them
all. Even my wife. I tried to kill my wife too."

"By strangling her?"

He looked away.

"My wife was dirty," he said, turning his gaze to stare down
at the ground. "But I tried to kill her before she was dirty. And
then she came to me, Kateri did, and she asked me, why did
you kill me when you loved me?"

Melusine was struck dumb by his assertion that she was
dirty. What did he know about Gunther? He has referred to
it before; her lies. It is clear he knows something. But he was
right, he had tried to throttle her before she'd had sex with
Gunther. But she had been with Gunther earlier that day, and
she had been so happy — didn't that constitute as much by
way of infidelity as sex?

"I don't think you killed Kateri," she said. "What did you
do with her body then? They never found her body."

"She's in the tree," Hans said. "She's in the tree."

Melusine remembered him talking about the treehouse where
he and Kateri would lie for hours and talk.

Before she takes leave of the police commissioner, she asks
him about the tree house and he consults his notes.

"They were all over the tree, looking for evidence, of course
they were. But there wasn't anything."

"Is the tree still there?"

Klein shrugs. "I'll take you there myself if you like."

They drive for half an hour but both the tree and the tree
house are gone.

Melusine stands with Commissioner Klein at the place where Hans once lived and she is angry. She wants some answers; having to live with this incertitude is not fair.

"May I ask you something else? I've asked our police officers but they say it's not possible — I found a pamphlet that Hans got from the psychic fair, for Celestial Sound Vibrations. Is there a way you could contact them and ask them who Hans might have been talking to? Or look at the security cameras? Surely there must be a way that more policing can be done to find the Healing Lives Ministries? They're the ones responsible, not for Kateri I know, but they are accountable for Hans."

"You know how things get so neatly wrapped up in movies?" Klein asks. "It's very rarely like that in real life. You should know that. Your husband was victim to a tragedy and now you and your son are too. There are no answers. There's just putting one foot in front of the other, day by day."

Melusine looks at him but she does not say anything.

He sighs and pulls a card out of his pocket. "Email me all the details on the pamphlet. I can tell you now that the security cameras will be a dead end, it was too long ago, but I'll see what I can do about following up with this other thing."

"Thank you," she says, and she shakes his hand again. "For your time and your kindness and coffee and everything. Here's me, putting one foot in front of the other."

Melusine flips through the radio stations on the way home, trying to find some music but she feels haunted by uncertainty and the dismal facelessness of lives ruined.

31.

SUMMER PASSES and autumn arrives. Melusine spends a lot of time with Nika and Jonas who are regulars for dinner.

Melusine watches as Nika takes napkins out of the decorated wooden sideboard and folds them into ornate fans that she tucks into the water glasses. It always amuses Melusine and this time is no different.

"It looks pretty," Nika says, grinning as she catches sight of Melusine watching her but then both of them fall sombre. "*Ach*, Melu, I know. Hans is in a bad way. He didn't even recognize me today."

Melusine nods. "I went by to give him his coat for the cooler weather and he looked at it as if he had no idea what it was."

Jonas comes back from his run, and pulls off a sweaty t-shirt. "I'll just have a quick shower," he says. "You guys talking about Papa? It's weird how we're all living with this, this, which would have been out of the question not so long ago. And look, we all just get on with things."

Yes, Melusine agrees silently, we get on with things. She stirs the sauce for the pasta and wonders if she should share the news she received earlier that day.

A letter had come for her in the post, not from Gunther but from the publishers who had reviewed her novel.

Good news, we love it! We're looking at a spring launch which gives us lots of time. We'll call you to finalize the contract. Also, do you have a follow-up novel? If so, send it along!

But Melusine has not written anything since she submitted the manuscript. She had hoped that Isolde would return to her and continue with the tale of her life but there was nothing. The book itself feels alien to her; she can hardly remember the intricacies of the story and she is amazed to think that such a sensual outpouring had come from her.

Melusine feels as if her entire life has gone quiet and numb. She feels like a clockwork doll, moving carefully and mechanically. When she hears about her book, she tells herself that she should feel joyful but she simply feels accepting. She accepts the good things in her life, like her book, and her brightly painted house and she accepts the bad, like Hans, and how much she still misses Gunther.

Later at the supper table, she tries to summon the energy to tell Jonas and Nika about the book but she does not have the energy to explain the whole thing, and certainly not the energy to pretend to be happy. She knows that Nika would be delighted and she is not up to being a mirror to Nika's joy. It is easier to be quiet. And Jonas, how would he feel, with his father a crazy streetperson and his mother the author of an erotic novel?

No, she thinks, moving her pasta around on her plate, it's better that she remain silent.

"Are you okay, Mami?" Jonas is watching her and she puts down her fork and sighs.

She cannot tell them that she feels like she is waiting, waiting for the next bad thing to happen; she is watchful, and she is waiting.

She pushes her plate away.

"*Each half-baked feeling that passes by me...*" she stops but Nika continues.

"*I have registered for a life sentence with you that cannot be carried out.*"

Jonas looks confused. "I know it's Ingeborg but what does it mean?"

Nika takes Melusine's hand. "It only feels like a life sentence now. Joy will return Melu, and we will be cheerful again, we will."

Melusine summons a smile. "You're right. And meanwhile there is always baking; I've made you your favourite plum cake for dessert."

Jonas jumps up with enthusiasm. "Enough real food! I'll clear these plates away."

Four
at the end is the beginning
of daydreams

32.

IN EARLY OCTOBER, Melusine arrives at work. She parks and lets herself into the library, startled to find the main door unlocked. She is usually the first one there.

In the early days of Hans's defection to the anarchical indigents, Melusine was regarded by the townspeople as a curiosity and the library staff welcomed a host of visitors they had not seen in a long time, and perhaps had never seen. But eventually, the townsfolk accepted the situation and Melusine was left in relative privacy.

She is surprised, today, to find her boss and a member of the board of directors waiting for her. "Did I forget about a meeting?" she asks and they look at each other and shake their heads.

"No, Melusine, you did not."

She makes to join them and pull up a chair.

"Uh, no, you don't need to sit," the director says. "In fact really, you should stand."

"I beg your pardon?"

"As well you should," the director continues. "Beg our pardon, I mean. I have no idea how you thought you could do this. I'm astounded, Melusine Meier. And your parents, such good people. I knew them, did you know that? I used to have my pictures framed in their store. Your father had such a great eye for the perfect frame to bring out the beauty in a painting. One would think, Melusine, that you, given your upbringing, would know art from vulgarity, would you not?"

"I have no idea what you're talking about," Melusine says, baffled.

"And you even studied fine art, did you not? What I have no idea about, madam, is how you thought you could do this and just carry on — do this and get away with it."

"Do what? Please explain. Again, I've got no idea what you are talking about."

The director looks at Melusine's boss and they both nod. The director pulls an art catalogue out of her briefcase and opens it.

There, as a double page spread is one of the images that Melusine is so proud of; one of the images that Gunther had taken. There she is, in all her naked glory, with her generous untrimmed bush wild and curly for all the world to see, her eyes wanton and her lips dark, wet and parted.

Melusine grips the table and her knees buckle. It's not what you think, she wants to say. But she doesn't say anything.

"That these images are part of an exhibit in the Museum of Modern Art in New York means nothing," the director says. She is a bony woman in her late fifties, and she is thin but she has an unfortunate array of unsightly fleshy chins, all of which jiggle when she speaks. "You are one of many respected curators in this, our library, in this, our small town. How do you think parents will feel, having this image of you in their minds when you interact with their children? Did you really think you could remain part of our hallowed institution after exposing yourself like this to the whole world? Honestly, Melusine, I've got no idea what you were thinking and it doesn't even matter. You can't continue working here. You're fired, with immediate effect. We don't need more of a reason than this and we certainly don't need three letters of warning. This catalogue is more than enough reason to let you go. You're not the kind of person we want around our children. We should have known there was something fundamentally wrong in your home after what your husband did to that schoolgirl and everybody knows that he killed his sister because they were lovers. What astounds me is that your son appears to be relatively normal, but he's young, there is still time."

This last comment enrages Melusine and she swells with fighting spirit. She stands tall, and towers over the seated director.

"Director," she says, "firstly, you have my sympathies that you're such a dried-up old carcass of a woman that no one would ever wish to photograph you like this. You'll never be the muse or subject of beauty in one of the world's most respected museums. But I will. And you never had children because your womb is as barren as your mind and as dead as your soul. And if you ever so much as hint that there's anything wrong with my precious boy, you will not withstand the fire of my wrath. Fine, I'll leave the library, I'll leave this 'hallowed institution' as you put it. But remember this, not one word about my boy, ever. Do you understand me?"

She is angrier than she has ever been in her life and she is gratified to see the director go pale.

Melusine turns to leave. "Oh, and one last thing. You say you have no idea how I could do this? I did this for *me*. I did this for *fun*. I did this out of the sheer joy of being alive. And I did it because it made me happy."

She leans down, amused to see the director tilt backwards in her chair with a look of fright on her face and she grabs the catalogue and walks out without a backward glance.

33.

A COUPLE OF HOURS LATER, she is sitting at Ana's kitchen table, sobbing inconsolably. "Jonas," she wails.

"Melu," Ana says, "don't get me wrong but your life certainly turned out to be more interesting than I, or anybody else ever thought it would."

"Jonas," Melusine wails again.

"Oh, stop that. Although why you didn't have a Brazilian wax before taking these pictures is beyond me. I'm going to call Jonas now."

She dials a number. "Jonas? Auntie Ana here. Can you come over? No, your Mami is fine. A little upset but fine. No, it's not your Papa, I'll explain when you get here. Okay, see you now."

"He's on his way," she says unnecessarily to Melusine, who wishes her face was not so swollen; her eyes are nearly closed from crying.

They wait and they finally hear a car pull up. Jonas rushes in. "Mami? Are you all right? What's wrong? Do you have cancer? Did Papa die?" He hurls questions at both the women.

"Oh, Jonas," Melusine wails, "I've done something that you'll hate me for. I just wanted to do something for me. I'm sorry."

"What are you talking about? Auntie Ana, what's she talking about?"

Ana wordlessly hands him the catalogue. He does not understand until Ana turns to the pages that have the images of Melusine.

Jonas sinks down into a chair and stares at the photographs.

"Mami?" He looks at her quizzically and then a gigantic grin spreads across his face. He leans back in his chair and flips through the catalogue, smiling.

"Mami, you thought I'd be upset? These are great! I'm so proud of you. Nika's going to love them. Who took the pictures?"

"A man I met in Vegas. He could speak German. Your father had disappeared to find Kateri with the psychics and he left me all alone. But this man became my friend ... and..."

Jonas pats her hand. "I don't need all the details." He grins. "You might say that everything I need to know is right here in front of me."

"I thought you'd hate me," Melusine says. "Ana, I need a brandy now. My nerves were shot," she says to Jonas.

"She's been crying like a banshee for hours," Ana confirms, pouring a large shot of brandy for each of them. "She couldn't bring herself to tell you. I had to phone you."

"Nika's going to love these," he says again, "I can't wait to show her. I'm so proud of you, Mami."

Melusine sighs. "Ah well, Jonas, I think I'm about to disappoint you now. The library fired me today because of these pictures. I've lost my job."

Jonas gapes at her. "They can't do that. We'll sue them, Mami, that's what we'll do, we'll sue them. I'll get all my professors involved and we'll nail them."

She shakes her head. "No, please, don't do that. I know you're upset, and I am too. But then these images will be flashed everywhere and not only that, the whole toe sucking fiasco will be dredged up again, and everybody will rush around taking pictures again of Hans on his bench and he'll get all frightened. No, Jonas, we have to leave this one be."

"But it makes me so angry," he says and his face crumples into a scowl.

"I know, me too. And I'm very proud of these images, I am. I'll never regret doing them but by the same token, I don't want them in every tabloid newspaper, we've had more than enough of that. Don't you agree?"

He shakes his head. "Yes, but it's just not fair."

Melusine remembers something else. "Ana, I forgot, I must tell you both about something else too. But before I do, you should top up our glasses."

The two of them look at her. "I can't imagine what's coming next," Ana says drily to Jonas, "can you?"

He shakes his head.

Just then, Dirk, Ana's husband, arrives home. He looks at the three of them drinking brandy at noon and he sees Melusine's swollen face. "I guess whatever happened you'd better give me a shot too," he says to Ana and hands her a glass. He takes his jacket off and puts it on the back of a chair.

Dirk still looks like the boxer he was in his youth and he has always been supportive of Melusine and was particularly protective when Hans derailed so spectacularly. Dirk had been the one to keep nosy reporters at bay and despite the fact that he had never much liked Hans, thinking him pretentious and snobbish, he nevertheless checked in on him regularly at the park, and kept an eye on things.

"Did you crash your car?" he turns to Jonas who shakes his head indignantly.

"You should know me better than that, Onkel Dirk," he says. "No, this isn't about me. My parents are the ones who get into trouble, not me." He and Dirk share a grin at this.

They have always got on well; Dirk's a high-end mechanic who fixes Mercedes, Audi's and Porsche's and Jonas loves tinkering with cars. He had learned enough from Dirk to be able to buy a cheap second-hand car and fix it up himself.

Jonas looks at his mother. "Can I show him?"

Melusine nods. "The whole world will see soon anyway."

"Just don't go getting too overly appreciative," Ana says and she punches her husband on the arm, hard.

He winces. "Ana! That hurt! What are you talking about?"

Jonas opens the catalogue and pushes it towards Dirk, whose mouth falls open. Ana punches him again but this time he hardly feels it. "Wow, Melu, I had no idea..." he rubs his upper arm absentmindedly.

"You had no idea what?" Ana asks, icily.

"That she modelled..." Dirk says lamely. "These are great. Why are we so sad then?"

"Because," Ana says, closing the catalogue, "first off, Melu thought Jonas would be devastated by these photos and rush from the house in despair never to be seen again. Which, by the way, did not happen, as you can tell. And secondly, and this is why the tears, the library fired her over them."

"They did what?" Dirk is furious. "Bunch of uptight bitches."

Melusine gives a laugh. "I was one of them this morning, Dirk. And anyway, I can see what they're saying ... you can understand their point of view."

"No," he says. "I can't. This is art. This isn't like *Playboy*. This is like Porsche does *Playboy*."

This cracks Jonas up. He swallows half his brandy and looks at his mother. "Ah, but Mami, you were going to tell us something else. Onkel Dirk, moments before you came in, Mami had just said 'but wait, there's more....'"

They all turn and look at Melusine who leans back and sighs. The brandy has brought a red flush to her cheeks and her face is still damp and swollen. She pushes her hair back and it sticks up in wild tufts. Jonas thinks she looks like a stork caught in a storm but decides not to mention it.

"So?" he prods.

"Well," she says, "remember that book I was writing?"

They all nod.

"I finished it."

"And?" prompts Ana.

"And I sent it to a publisher."

"And?" Dirk says, "come on, woman, out with it."

"And they're going to publish it."

244 LISA DE NIKOLITS

The other three erupt into wild applause but Melusine shakes her head. "No, it's not good. It will just be more strange publicity for our family. You see, the book is quite erotic and it has lesbian relationships and drug-taking..."

They stare at her. In silence.

Then Jonas starts to giggle. "Mami," he says, "not only do you take the cake, you take the champagne and the sports cars. You rock!"

Melusine looks at him. "Jonas! You beautiful boy. What did I ever do to deserve you?"

"You're the best mother in the world, that's what. And you know why I was so difficult to Papa all these years? Because I thought he pushed you down and I hated him for that. So I love all of this. I love these pictures and I love your book, whatever it is."

Melusine goes over to hug him and she is crying again and even Ana has tears in her eyes.

"I wish my boys would say things like that to me," she says and Dirk looks at her.

"They do but you're too busy shouting at them to pick up their clothes and put down the toilet seat to hear them."

She pouts. "This place would be a pigsty, if it weren't for me," she says and Dirk grins.

"Nika is going to be so happy about the book, Mami," Jonas says, "I meant to tell you, she's decided to give up writing, for now anyway. She's changing her major from German literature to midwifery. Which means she'll need to take biology and science which she's very good at. And luckily for her, she took some courses in sociology and psychology and she can use those credits."

"She'll be a wonderful midwife," Melusine says. "She's been so great. Our family's had one crisis after another recently and she's been wonderful. She's great with Hans, too."

She looks down at her hands. "I don't know what I'm going to do for a job now. Nika's quite right to be changing fields, there's not much call for German literature students with a masters in librarianship."

"If you'll allow me, I've got an idea," Dirk says, pouring more brandy. "And it may sound like it's coming out of nowhere but I've actually thought about it before. There's this guy who brings his car in...."

"There's always a guy bringing his car in," Ana says, "be more specific."

"...a rich guy with a lot of money to burn. A homo, but a nice one...."

"Thank you Dirk, for elaborating," Ana says. "He's never learned political correctness, has he?" she asks Melusine.

"Political correctness is for wankers," Dirk says. "Ana, stop interrupting me, okay? Good heavens, woman, no wonder I hardly ever talk in this house, it's too difficult, what with the interruptions every two seconds."

"Talk then," Ana says. "For the record I won't interrupt you, except if you say politically objectionable things."

"Ana!" Melusine says. "Let him talk."

Ana pouts again.

"So," Dirk says. "There's this rich fag who gets his car fixed..." he and Ana exchange furious glances but she remains quiet and he grins. "And he's been wanting to start his own coffee shop for a while now. He wants something arty, something different. And now Melu, here you are, model of this photoshoot, author of an erotic novel and you studied all that artistic crap and most importantly, you are the greatest baker in the world."

"What? Better than me?" Ana is affronted.

Dirk laughs. "My angel, she's in a league you can only dream of."

It appears as if this might develop into a war, but Jonas holds up his hand. "Stop it, you two, stop. Onkel Dirk, please carry on."

Dirk leans back on his chair legs with his arms folded.

"You'll fall back," Ana warns, "you know you will. And you'll break the chair."

"Ana! Please!" Melusine is running out of patience. "I need to hear this."

"So this guy," Dirk says again, "has a shitload of money and he's always wanted an arty coffee shop and now here's Melu, perfect for the job. You won't even need to put any money in. I thought of you before for this, but I admit that I thought maybe he'd think you were too conservative. But now, with these pictures, and your book, well, I'm sure he'll love you. You interested?"

"Yes!" Melusine's face glows. "I'm very interested! I've often daydreamed about baking for a living. But it was only that, daydreaming, since I never thought I'd have enough startup money to do it and anyway, my job at the library was a good one and I had no reason to want to leave. Will you talk to him tomorrow?"

"I'll do better than that," Dirk says, getting up and ruffling Ana's hair as he passes, "I'll call him now. He and I go way back. He travels the world a lot of the time, with his pretty little boyfriend who's nearly twenty years younger than him but hell, if you can do it, why not?"

"What, if you can have a lover twenty years your junior or travel the world?" Ana calls after him.

"Both!" he shouts over his shoulder and Ana gives a mock shrug.

"Ana, do you think this could be for real?" Melusine asks.

"Dirk never says anything unless he means it," Ana says. "You know that. He always delivers. Another round?" she asks, holding up the bottle.

Jonas laughs. "Not for me, I'm meeting Nika soon. I'll leave my car here and take the bus. Mami, don't you worry about anything, okay?" He goes over and gives her a hug.

"And me, and me, where's my hug?" Ana says. "Come over for supper soon, okay Jonas?"

"Wild horses couldn't keep me away," Jonas says. "Mami might be the top baker but no one makes sausages like you, Auntie Ana."

Ana beams. Jonas is a little unsteady on his feet as he leaves; between the three of them, they polished off half a bottle of brandy.

Dirk returns and hands her a piece of paper. "Here you go. His name's Dieter and he'll meet you tomorrow at this address. And don't worry, he knows all about Hans."

"Everybody knows about Hans," Ana interrupts. "Sorry Melu, but it's true."

"...and I told him about the catalogue and your book. You've got nothing to hide, so don't think you need to."

"I cannot thank you enough, Dirk." Melusine stands up. "I am going home to sleep. What a crazy, exhausting, exciting day."

"This will work out better for you in the end," Dirk predicts. "Come on, Melu, leave your car here, let me drive you home. Unlike the rest of you drunkards, I only had one glass."

"Don't get any ideas now, just because you've seen my best friend naked," Ana yells after Dirk.

"I've always had ideas," he shouts back, "about you, you silly woman."

He drops Melusine off and she lets herself inside the house, thinking that it feels awfully quiet after all the hilarity and noise at Ana's, and she is happy to see Mimi who greets her with an enthusiastically wagging tail. Melusine scratches the dog's head and wonders if she will always be alone. For a while, after the Hans episode, as she calls it, she had welcomed the solitude but she increasingly wishes that she had more than a pen pal to share her life with. But then again, she reminds herself, she would be a lot worse off without Gunther, as tenuous as their relationship might be.

She writes a detailed update about being fired from the library and she tells him about telling Ana and Jonas about the novel and about Dirk's friend Dieter who might be interested in starting a coffee shop.

What a crazy day! Could it be that this is the start of something really good and life changing? And if so, I have you to thank. Were it not for the pictures, I probably would have stayed at the library for the rest of my life.

She pauses.

I know you've been so busy with your new, exciting life in New York. My life must sound very mundane. At least now, I'll have a little adventure too! As Ingeborg said, 'at an end is the beginning of daydreams...' which feels very fitting right now.

She feels as if she wants to say more but she cannot think what it is. She seals the letter and decides to have a shower for a change instead of a bath, wanting to feel the rainfall of water rushing down her body. She knows she should feel tired and she is, but she is also wired from the excitement of the day.

Standing in the shower reminds her of the time when Gunther made love to her under the fall of hot water and she is startled to feel the sudden urgent pressing of her body's needs. She reaches down; her vulva is hot and full, and her groin is swollen and heavy.

She slips three fingers inside, pushing hard, probing, seeking, finding that spot. She groans, widens her legs, tilts her head back and opens her mouth to the hot spray of water. She braces her leg on the side of the bathtub and works her fingers harder and harder, supporting herself on the wall with her other hand, working those fingers faster and deeper, letting her bladder go and finding her orgasm; hot water, hot liquid, hot explosion behind her eyeballs.

Spent, she sits down in the bathtub and lets the water hit her back, with her arms wrapped around her legs.

She laughs out loud. And decides to take showers more often.

34

D IETER, the prospective café owner, is a sleek pigeon of a man, with tidy salt and pepper hair. He has a strange mustard-coloured suntan and is dressed for a yachting expedition. He and Melusine hit it off immediately and they talk excitedly, with ideas pouring out, one on top of the other.

"So listen, I'm thinking we should feature a selection of French, German and Hungarian pastries. And not just super high-end ones either. People will kill for a perfect *palacsinta* — they look like ordinary crêpes but when they're done right … they're to die for!" He snaps his fingers.

"Exactly," Melusine agrees. "And a good slice of cake makes people happier than I can tell you. Half the time, when we used to have dinner parties, people were waiting for the dessert and the cakes always got the best welcome. Cupcakes are the big thing in America and I tried a few when I was in Vegas and we could offer some of those too although I'd improve the recipes."

Her mind immediately flashes back to the red velvet cupcake that she shared with Gunther outside the Sugar Factory and a lump fills her throat. She cannot believe that she still misses him as much as she does.

"The thing is," she focuses on the conversation with Dieter, "it's real baking that people want. And excellent coffee too. We'll have to have lattes on offer too, that's just expected these days."

Dieter nods. "And tea," he says, "there are entire shops

dedicated just to tea. We could offer those flower ball teas that unfold so beautifully in glass teapots, they're very eye catching. The possibilities are endless!"

"How about I make you some samples of a few pastries? I'm sure you'll want more proof of my expertise than Dirk's recommendation and my assurances. If you don't mind, you could come to my house and I can give you a selection?"

"That would be great! The day after tomorrow? I'll bring my partner although you'll see, he won't eat a single bite! I do the eating for both of us and then I have to work twice as hard to get rid of it too!"

Melusine spends the afternoon shopping and all of the following day baking.

Nika and Jonas arrive for supper to find her covered in a dusting of flour and rushing this way and that.

"Everything's going wrong," she wails, "just when it needs to be perfect."

"That's because I wasn't here," Jonas says. "I'm her good luck charm," he tells Nika who is gathering bowls and spatulas.

"Calm down, Mami. We've got all night to do this. We'll help you. It will be fine."

Melusine sits down and puts her head in her hands. "Why did I even think I could do this? Look at me, collapsing at the first sign of pressure."

"You'll be perfectly fine," Nika says. "Let's make a list...."

By the time Dieter arrives the following day, with Martin, his exquisite and tiny Filipino boyfriend, everything is ready.

"These are heavenly," Dieter exclaims, tasting one pastry after the other.

Melusine beams. "You see, like we said, there's a mix of Hungarian, German and French," and Dieter nods.

"Your selection is perfect," he says and he holds a tiny piece of white chocolate dacquoise cake towards Martin. "Try this, the meringue is nut-flavoured and the buttercream is light as a feather."

"You enjoy it. I'm watching my figure," Martin says languidly, leaning on the kitchen counter. "So that you will. Can't have you running off with some pretty boy, can I?" He offers little else to the conversation until he sees they are stumped about one thing: location.

"I know a place," he says, his voice light and soft. "We can check it out now if you like. A friend of mine was making dolls there but he couldn't pay the rent and no one's taken over the lease yet. It's near the university which means you'll get all the daytime traffic you want and you won't need to be open at night. You can work the breakfast, brunch, lunch and tea time crowds. You'll be non-stop."

"Good thinking," Dieter says. "The ravenously hungry, art-seeking university crowd. Martin, you're a genius."

Martin grins modestly.

"So listen, let's go now," Dieter says, stuffing a piece of Black Forest cake in his mouth and wiping his hands on one of Nika's elaborately folded napkins.

They climb into Dieter's Porsche, with Martin fitting easily into the tiny back seat.

"The only thing that worries me," Melusine says cautiously, reaching for her seat belt and thinking that the car felt awfully low on the road, "is that I've got no idea how many ingredients I'll need to order or things like that. My learning curve is very steep, Dieter, and I worry that I'll be wasting your money. Wouldn't you be better off with someone who knows the business? Yes, I know pastries and coffees, and I know art but I don't know business. Not the baking business anyway; I helped run my parent's picture framing shop but that was different."

She knows she is rambling but she is suddenly terrified of what she is getting herself into.

"You need a partner," Martin says, sticking his head in between the seats. "Dieter, she needs a partner. She shouldn't have to worry about the business side of things."

"You have someone in mind, I take it? I can always hear when you've already got an idea in place," Dieter grumbles.

"Felix," Martin states and Dieter nearly drives them off the road.

Melusine had just started to feel safe in the cocoon of German-engineered leathered luxury but she grips the dashboard and Dieter grins at her.

"I've got it all under control. Felix? Surely you jest, Martin."

"I never jest about Felix."

"Who's Felix?" Melusine asks with some trepidation.

"She, and I use the term loosely you gather, is a friend of Martin's that I tolerate," Dieter says.

"You hardly tolerate her at all," Martin objects, "in fact you're quite rude to her. But I love her and you should respect that. Felix and I have been through a lot together. Life wasn't always Dolce & Gabbana for us as you know, Dieter. And yes, you rescued me and even her too, in the end. You don't have to remind me. I just think Felix would be great."

"What's her, uh, his experience?" Melusine asks.

"It's her," Martin says. "She worked in her old man's bakery from the time she was eight until she was twelve and ran away."

"Then she worked the streets," Dieter says and Martin ignores him.

"She's also worked in lots of coffee shops," he says, and Dieter snorts and again Martin ignores him.

"And she's been a barmaid and she's great with people."

"She's a druggie. I can't trust her."

"She's been clean for nearly six months and you know it," Martin says. "Come on Dieter, give the girl a chance."

"What kind of drugs?" Melusine asks and Martin mutters something evasive.

"Coke, heroin, pot, you name it," Dieter says. "Took me a while to get Martin clean, too. But you were worth it," he says to him, looking in the rear view mirror.

"And so is Felix," Martin says obstinately.

"It does sound like she's got the skills," Melusine says, "but Martin, can she really be trusted? You don't sound sure and I've had enough craziness. You all know about Hans."

They nod.

"Why don't you just meet her?" Martin says. "Melusine, you can talk to her, ask her anything you like, and then you can make the decision."

Melusine looks at Dieter who nods. "If you like her," he says, "then you can have her. But it's on your head, so make a wise choice."

Martin is grinning in the back and he pokes his head between the front seats again. "She's perfect for this," he says to Melusine, "you won't regret it."

But she is not at all sure.

35.

MELUSINE AND DIETER love the location of the store. "So listen," Dieter whispers. "Make sure you do your due diligence on Felix, okay?"

She nods. "Don't worry. I will. I won't make any snap judgements one way or the other — god knows the things people could say about me."

Dieter laughs loudly. "This is true. But you're fantastic and I love you. So listen, Martin and I are off to Spain for two weeks which will give you some time to come up with ideas for the menu and things like that. The look of the store, all that kind of thing. Go to town. I'm going to start paying you a salary immediately. I'll give you the details of my tax person, so phone him and give him all your info, okay?"

Martin returns. He has been walking back and forth, talking on his cellphone. He holds it out to Melusine who looks at it as if she has never seen one before.

"It's Felix," he says, as if that much is obvious. "Talk to her."

Melusine takes the phone cautiously. "Felix? Hello?"

"Melusine?"

"Yes."

"Ah. Hello."

The conversation seems doomed. But then Felix takes charge. "Are you at the store location?"

"Yes."

"I'll be there in half an hour. Can you wait?"

"Yes," Melusine says and she looks at Dieter who shakes his head.

"I can be here," she says again and Martin gives her a thumbs up and bats his eyelashes at Dieter who scowls at him.

"See you shortly," Felix says and she rings off.

"How will I know what she looks like?" Melusine asks Martin, and Dieter laughs loudly, as if that is the funniest thing he's heard.

"You can't miss her. Mel, here's my accountant's card. Phone him later, he'll give you the paper work. Keep a list of any expenses, like magazines or signage tests that you run. Like I say, go to town, have fun and have it all ready when we get back."

He gives her a wink and signals to Martin who is sending a text message. "Him and that phone," he says tolerantly to Melusine. "He's never off it. See you in two weeks. We have to go shopping now. We need to refresh our wardrobe for Spain."

At the word 'shopping', Martin immediately stops texting and rushes up to Dieter and gazes in his eyes. "I love you," he says and Dieter laughs.

"And so you should," he says good naturedly and the two stroll off, with Martin bounding like a lamb and hanging onto Dieter's arm.

Melusine buys herself a coffee in the town square while she waits for Felix. She looks around at the open market vendors who are there each day selling fresh produce despite the weather turning cold. The cobblestones are slick with recent rain and Melusine checks the time on the ornate gold hands of the clock tower. She cannot help but muse over the twists and turns that her life has taken. From Vegas and Gunther and all the happiness and longing he has brought to her life, to Hans's breakdown, to this latest adventure of opening a café; she is amazed by the happenstance that's come her way.

Then she is startled from her reverie.

"Melusine?" she hears a soft melodic voice beside her and she turns.

"Oh Felix," she exclaims, "you're incredibly beautiful."

Felix flutters her extra long false eyelashes and smiles modestly. "You are very beautiful too, Melusine," she says graciously.

Felix is a long-legged colt of a girl with a head of shocking pink hair — she looks like a neon night-clubbing version of a Disney Heidi; her pink hair is even braided.

"To business," Melusine says. "What did Martin tell you about all of this?"

Felix gets serious. "He told me that you're a great artist when it comes to pastries but you need a front office manager to run the store, keep it stocked and be a good little hostess to our guests."

"And can you do it?"

"I'm the best thing for the job since sliced bread," Felix states, matter-of-factly. "Although why I'd ever compare myself to something so mundane as sliced bread I have no idea. I'm a creamy peppermint meringue; so sweet and tart, you'll never want to taste anything else your whole life."

"Meringues are good," Melusine says and she smiles.

"Did you make a list yet?" Felix asks.

"A list of what?"

"Everything. Martin told me that Dieter wants to see a business plan and logo designs and menus when he gets back. And while Dieter may look like an easy-going old guy, trust me, he's not. When it comes to money, he expects return on investment. So we'd better get our sweet little asses moving. Have you got a computer? If not, Martin said we could buy one and expense it."

"No, that's all right, I've got one," Melusine says. "At home."

"And tell me this, what is your favourite coffee shop in town?"

Melusine is taken aback and then she sees why Felix is asking and she starts to list them, along with their specialities.

"Now we have to take all those things and put them into one store — ours. This will be such fun!"

"I'm glad you're enjoying it," Melusine says. "I am totally panicked. It suddenly all seems immense."

"Nonsense," Felix says. "It's a piece of cake, strawberry shortcake to be exact, and now I promise to stop with the bakery analogies. We need to buy big whiteboards and pens and paper and we'll map it all out, we'll put all our ideas down; the good, the bad and the downright insane. Then we'll fine-tune what we've got, input the data onto the computer and see if it all makes sense. It will be fine, I promise you. Can we do this at your home?"

"Yes, sure we can. But wait," Melusine stops and looks at Felix.

"The drugs, right? You want to know about the drugs?"

Melusine nods.

"Fine. And because I want this to work between us, I'm going to tell you everything, okay? And I'm not ashamed to say it's not a pretty story, it just is what it is. Or, was, shall I say. I've done just about every drug I could lay my hands on — and I do mean anything and everything. From the time I was about ten. Obviously I didn't start off taking all that crap, of course not, I sort of eased into it, as one does. My father used to beat me because of what I am and taking drugs made me feel okay — at least I didn't feel like a freak when I was high. So then of course, I wanted more and more and I needed money and I used my pretty little freak body to get what I needed and then my father found out and he threw me out the house."

"And then what happened?"

"I lived on the street, and yes, Melusine, I know about your husband and I've met him. He's a nice guy. Crazy as a March hare but nice. Kind of crazy for you and me to be here now too if you think about it, but there are times I thank god for life's crazy things too. So there I was, living on the street and working it and I met Martin and we started living together. It was never a sexual thing, him and me; we were just good friends. And then he met Dieter one night, at a high-end party, and they got all excited about each other. And Dieter got Martin clean but Martin said it had to be me too or he wouldn't go with Dieter. I didn't come right, not like Martin did, I kept falling off the wagon for about two more years. Finally Martin persuaded Dieter to pay for me to go to rehab one more time and by that time I was so tired of my shitty life, I even wanted to go, I even begged Dieter myself. I said, please, I'll make good on it. And I've been clean for six months now."

"Do you drink?" Melusine wants to know it all.

Felix shakes her head. "Nope. Not a drop. It's all a bit tough for sure. I'm not saying it's easy but I want this more than anything, to be sober. I don't hate myself anymore, I don't hate what I am. Part of rehab was a lot of therapy and I still go to group, twice a week. I'm learning to be okay with all the crap I did. It's not easy being born a freak..."

"You're not a freak," Melusine protests but Felix shakes her head.

"I felt like one. Some days I still do. But I'm learning to be okay with it. I can understand why Dieter is hesitant about involving me, sure, I understand. But can you see how much this means to me? I want so badly to be a success too. I don't care how hard I have to work, Melusine. I'm not afraid of hard work, I never have been. I'm afraid, or I was afraid, of myself. And I'm not, anymore. I've got a lot to offer and you might think I look like Bambi in drag but I've got a sharp business mind, you'll see."

Melusine is not a hundred percent sure whether this impassioned speech is the truth or if she is being hustled, but she decides to put her doubts aside and give Felix a chance.

"All right, consider yourself officially onboard," Melusine says and she takes Felix by the arm. "Let's find an art store and get supplies. And then let's take a cab. We can expense it."

Felix grins. "Melusine," she says, unknowingly echoing Martin's earlier words, "you won't regret this — believing in me. You'll see."

36.

IT DOES NOT TAKE LONG before Felix makes good on her promise and Melusine cannot imagine life without her.

Jonas finds them on the evening of their first meeting, both of them lying on the floor, surrounded by charts with all kinds of annotations, lists and ideas.

"Jonas, meet Felix, my new business partner," Melusine says, "and Felix, meet Jonas, my son."

Jonas gives Felix an appreciative look.

"Jonas has a girlfriend," Melusine says pointedly and Jonas laughs.

"Don't worry, Mami. Hey, haven't I seen you somewhere before?" he asks Felix who blushes.

"I don't think so," she says primly, pulling down her very short skirt. "I doubt we've travelled in the same circles."

Jonas is about to say something else when Melusine interjects.

"Jonas," she says tactfully, "would you like some tea?" She gestures toward the kitchen.

Felix grins. "Don't worry, Melu. Hey, Jonas, pardon my bluntness since we only just met, but I've got the same wedding tackle as you do, only I'm a girl at heart."

Jonas pales. "Thank you for not letting me discover that by putting my hand up your skirt. Not that I would have put my hand up your skirt," he says, quickly casting a look in his mother's direction, "but you know what I mean."

"I do indeed. Been there, heard the screams," Felix says. "I'm going to make tea for us all. Melu, show Jonas our ideas, see what he thinks."

Just then Nika arrives. Jonas introduces her to Felix.

"I know you from somewhere," Nika says frowning, and Jonas agrees.

"I know. Me too. But Felix says not.

"Oh god," Felix says. "Okay, so fine. Food samples. You both liked the chocolate soy cookies that I thought were the grossest things."

"Right! We were hungry that day," Nika is defensive. "I would have eaten cardboard."

"You pretty much did," Felix says, laughing. "And you both came back for thirds."

"You were a food sample person?" Melusine asks.

Felix nods. "My first job on the straight and narrow. Very nearly drove me back to drugs. After the cookies, I peddled soy chicken wings. I phoned my counsellor and said I'd rather be cleaning toilets with my tongue. So she got me a job at the Mission and that's where I met Hans although I didn't know who he was at the time. I just knew him as the guy who needs to sleep sitting upright during the day. Oh, and that he tells everybody constantly that he killed his sister."

"Poor Hans," Melusine says absently. "Felix, we still don't have a name for our café. Any ideas, children?"

"Children!" Jonas and Nika shriek with laughter.

"You must be tired, Mami," Jonas says.

She smiles. "Yes, I am. It's been a lot to take in over the past few days. You lot think about it, and I'll go and make the tea."

"And I need to phone my counsellor," Felix says. "If you don't mind, Melu."

"Of course not, come with me."

They leave and Jonas and Nika poke at the mess on the floor while Jonas whispers the details of Felix's physique.

"But she's a perfect girl," Melusine hears Nika say before Jonas hushes her.

"They should name the coffee shop after Ingeborg Bachmann," Nika says but Jonas objects.

"Café Bachmann? Ingeborg's Café? I don't think so."

"What about a line from her poem?"

"I hate to tell you this but her poems are too depressing."

Melusine comes back into the living room, carrying a tray.

"I think we need something Ingeborg-ish but Jonas disagrees, he says her work is too depressing."

"The idea has potential," Melusine hands Nika a mug. "Let's see what Felix says and if she has any suggestions."

"About what?" Felix comes back into the room and yawns. "I'm so tired. All this excitement has worn me out. Listen to me, me who used to club 'til all hours. I'm an old lady and proud of it. Melu, I've got my meeting tonight, so I can't stay much longer. What do I think about what?"

Nika explains about Ingeborg Bachmann and Felix looks doubtful.

"I can't say until I've read some of her work. Can I borrow a copy of her poems?"

"Won't be hard to find in this house," Jonas jokes and Melusine returns and hands *Darkness Spoken* to Felix, who thanks her.

"I'll try to look tonight. We'll start on a menu, and then the logo and the colour scheme. Shall I meet you back here in the morning?"

"If it's not too much trouble," Melusine says. "Take a cab."

"Enough cabbing," Felix is stern. "I'm the business manager and we don't have any profits yet. I'll take a bus." Then she gives Melusine a quick hug.

"We can give you a ride if you like," Nika says. "Hey, Melu, when does your book come out?"

"We haven't even started on galleys," Melusine replies. "They're a small press, it takes time. And thank god for that because honestly I couldn't do one more thing right now." She waves goodnight and thinks she is so tired that she might sleep in her clothes.

She wishes she had the energy to update Gunther but even that will have to wait. His emotional distance and erratic mood swings seem to have passed and his past few letters have resumed their personal and affectionate tone. After Hans left, Melusine told Gunther to send letters to her house and she no longer has to do the secret drives to the post office box. In a way she misses those drives — the excitement, the nervousness, the anticipation, but it is also much nicer having the letters come straight to her home.

And she is wondering now whether they should start emailing each other, after all, they have established a real relationship which was the main, unspoken goal of the letter writing. It has been close to a year since they met and she wonders if he will remember the date.

In spite of her exhaustion, she scribbles a note to him.

My dear friend, I'm so tired. Plans for the café take flight. We both have such exciting lives now. Do you even remember me, really? I remember you. Every freckle.

She must be tired or she would not be saying things like this; she has not been this personal in a long time.

I do hope to see you again one day. I know though, that you will find love elsewhere, and I understand that. You've been such a great friend to me. Goodness, I'm rambling! I will concentrate; the point of this letter is to suggest that you and I take a bold leap and try some modern technology, what do you say? A bit of email perhaps? It's just that sometimes I long for a more immediate answer or a way to chat to you in a more direct manner. But I don't mean to pressure you. Here's my email address if you agree. And if you don't email, then I know we should just carry on this way. And now I'm going to seal and send this before I say any more. Goodnight. Melu.

She affixes the stamps that she always has at the ready and, tired though she is, she walks down the street to the post box on the corner and mails her letter.

She stands for a moment, looking at the silent houses around her. Warm lights glow behind the closed curtains and she sees the flickering brightness of TV pictures changing rapidly.

The leaves have all fallen, and although the street lights are on, it is dark and there is a sharp wind. The smell of late autumn is strong and Melusine suddenly feels cold and lonely. She pulls her long sweater around her and hurries home.

37

"I FEEL SICK WITH NERVES," Felix says to Melusine who nods and rubs her chest. She has had terrible indigestion for the weeks leading up to the launch of their coffeeshop and she wonders for the dozenth time if she has an ulcer.

They both look around. "It's so beautiful," Melusine says. "What if no one comes? We put all this work into it and Dieter spent so much money, what if no one comes?"

A big sign hangs across the front windows: Welcome to *Cheerful With Music*, A New Coffeeshop, Grand Opening, 11:00 a.m. Come and Try Our Delicious Pastries!

After much discussion, they decided to name the coffee shop with words taken from Ingeborg's poem, *Advertisement*. It had been Felix's idea and the others had not taken much persuading, even Dieter had been loudly in favour.

"Has the right arty feel and makes you want to be there, right? So listen, Felix, not bad, not bad at all."

Now Felix and Melusine look at one another.

"Well," Melusine says briskly, "Rome wasn't built overnight as they say. We'll just open our doors and keep them open and slowly but surely, hopefully, we'll be fine."

She straightens a menu. "I can't help but wish that we'd started with a smaller shop, this place is huge. Looking at it now, I don't think we'll ever be able to fill it."

"It just looks huge now because it's only you and me and we're scared out of our wits," Felix says, gnawing on a finger.

"Great, there's Jonas and Nika. They'll help distract us. How much longer before we open?"

"Half an hour," Melusine says, looking at the brightly painted mosaic and gold-leaf Dali-styled clock on the wall that one of the students had submitted.

Dieter, having liked the colour scheme of Melusine's home, had suggested they create the same bold and vivid interior. Melusine and Felix had asked local art students to submit their work and they chose a dozen paintings that added to the jewel-like brilliance of the décor.

Melusine and Felix had scoured antique stores in Frankfurt, looking for chandeliers and small table lamps, wanting to add a classical feel to the look, and the crystal chandeliers lit up the room with a glittering sparkle.

They had also spent hours selecting the chairs; they had to be inviting and comfortable as they wanted people to feel at home at the café, and the tables had to be the perfect height for both casual conversation and a person working with a laptop.

There are also two deep red leather sofas, with small coffee tables and it all looks cavernous to Melusine now, all those empty tables and chairs and sofas; it will take so many people to fill them all.

They hear Nika and Jonas come in through the back entrance.

"Are you both nervous?" Jonas asks and he takes one look at them and bursts out laughing. "You two! It's going to be fantastic! Nika and I have been putting up posters everywhere, all around the university and Dieter says he is bringing friends; he'll be here soon. Mami, wait, something came for you at the house, do you have a secret admirer?"

Melusine goes blank, she has no idea what he's talking about.

Jonas goes into the back and returns with a gigantic floral arrangement that must have cost a fortune. Huge yellow sun-flowers mix with yellow roses; the bouquet is a burst of bright sunshine and a perfect complement to the café.

"Did Dieter send the flowers?" she asks Jonas, momentarily

distracted from her worry that no one will show up for the café opening.

Jonas shakes his head. "I don't think so. And wouldn't he have sent them here? There's a card for you."

A sudden wild hope fills Melusine's heart and, not wanting to admit it to herself, she holds her breath as she opens the card.

The café will be incredible, because you're always amazing. I wish I could be there to celebrate with you. It's nearly our anniversary, do you remember? I do. I miss you. Good luck Melu, I'm with you in spirit. Gunther.

Melusine closes her eyes for a moment and hugs the card to her chest.

"Who's it from?" Jonas is curious.

"A friend I met in Vegas," Melusine says. "We've kept in touch. My goodness, yes, this arrangement must have cost a fortune." Her face is flushed and she is beaming and the other three look at her curiously.

"It's a good omen," she says, her eyes bright. "Now I know we'll be fine. Okay everybody, put on your aprons and let's get ready."

They grab their aprons embroidered with the *Cheerful With Music* logo and had no sooner tied them when they saw that a large crowd had gathered outside the front door.

"Fifteen minutes early," Melusine said and she made for the door when Felix grabbed her arm and stopped her.

"No, you don't," she said laughing, "they must wait. You'll see, they'll like us even more if they have to wait."

At the exact hour of eleven, they open the doors and are soon flooded with customers who dive into the pastries and coffees.

Seven hours later the crowd finally lets up and Dieter looks around, satisfied. "You're a hit," he tells Melusine and Felix. "You guys did good." He looks at them; they're glowing with happiness and adrenalin.

"Keep up the energy," he laughs, "you've got to do this again tomorrow and every weekday after that. Come on, Martin, we need to pack for our spa weekend in Gstaad. See you all next week! Great job!"

"I'd better get things prepared for tomorrow morning's baking," Melusine says, getting up.

"I kept up with the dishes," Nika says and Melusine gives her a big hug.

"Mami," Jonas says, "did you see that awful journalist was here, the one from *Der Spiegel*? She came all the way from Frankfurt. You'd think they'd leave us alone by now. You can bet the papers will be full of Papa again tomorrow."

"Don't let her get to you, Jonas," Felix advises from behind the cash register. "Wow, we did really well today! I know it was the opening with so much hype but still. Really, Jonas, you can't let them get to you. I know it hurts though."

He nods. "It isn't easy."

And it is not easy for Felix either, the following day when it turns out that she is the main focus of the woman's vitriol. There are a couple of paragraphs about Hans predilection for toes and Melusine's naked photographs, along with a small nod to the café, but the main focus is on Felix and the woman had really done her homework.

"I can't believe this," Felix says, reading the article for the fifth time. "Was she fucking following me around my whole life? Where did she get this stuff? Makes you wonder how many friends I *don't* have, who'd be willing to share all this shit."

Melusine tries to hug her but Felix is resistant; she is angry and hurt. Melusine tries to comfort her, "I wasn't spared either. She dredged up the whole Hans thing again, too."

But Felix is not consoled. "And everybody knows I'm a cross-dresser, you'd think she discovered it all by herself for fuck's sake." She is crying and her makeup is running down her face.

She is standing in the back with Melusine who is keeping an eye on the front. The phone rings and Melusine answers it, speaks for a moment and hands it to Felix.

268 LISA DE NIKOLITS

"I'm going to be out front," Melusine says, and she slips out.

A few moments later Felix appears. She has fixed her makeup and is smiling again.

"That was Dieter," she says unnecessarily to Melusine, "he said fuck the newspaper bitch. That's exactly what he said! He never swears! He was so angry. He even phoned from the airport. He said he was worried this would make me relapse back into drugs. As if!" She's grinning now. "I've never heard Dieter so angry. Okay, Melu, onwards and upwards!"

"Onwards and upwards," Melusine says, a little vaguely but with a smile, her nose close to a yellow rose.

38.

FELIX FINDS a small apartment near the café and she joins Melusine every morning at five a.m. Yawning, they wordlessly go about their work, opening the café at six-thirty a.m., ready for the early birds, and there are a great deal of those.

Gunther had immediately and enthusiastically accepted Melusine's invitation to email and she is loving hearing from him two or three times a day. She brings her laptop to work so she can update him constantly and there is a new intimacy to their chatter; they are flirting more, which brings a spring to Melusine's step and a glow to her face.

Christmas comes and the café is busier than ever with Melusine's Stollen and traditional German cookies selling out every day. She triples her baking shifts and she and Felix hire Emily, a vivacious student from the university, to help out in the front, serving customers.

Dieter watches the baked goods flying out the door as fast as Melusine can make them and he senses a winner on his hands. He tells Melusine that she should think about doing a year-long range of takeout baked goods.

"We'll hire more staff to run the café," he says, waving his hand around expansively.

Melusine and Felix look at one another. They do not mind an extra person for a short period of time but they like it better when it is just the two of them.

On the night of Christmas Eve, Melusine hosts a small feast for Jonas and Nika. They are subdued at the dinner table; Christmas is hard, knowing that Hans is lost to them.

"He was doing so well this time last year," Jonas says and he looks baffled. "He was taking Mimi for walks and looking healthier and laughing and everything."

"I know," Melusine says. "I still don't know what really happened. Yes, he'd always missed Kateri, but we all knew that. But he was normal for all those years and then he just lost it."

"I'm telling you, Mami, it was that Healing cult whatever," Jonas says, helping himself to more smoked ham and potato salad, and Melusine nods.

"It had to be. There's no other explanation."

Out of deference to Hans, they have hardly decorated the house at all, limiting themselves to setting the table with the traditional Christmas napkins and tablecloths.

"The cult place could have been the trigger," Nika says gently, "but maybe if it hadn't been them, it would have been something else. He was so vulnerable that the trigger to his breakdown could have come from anywhere."

Jonas shakes his head. "No, it was them, I know it was. First they brainwashed him to give them all his money and then, when he didn't have any more, they didn't care and it was too late."

"*Ach,* Jonas, I agree with Nika," Melusine says and she thinks about the obsessiveness with which Hans would rub her feet, and about their literally strangled sex life.

"There were lots of things," she says now. "Lots of little signs, it's just that I had no idea. But you know, all we can do is be grateful that we have each other and we'll take the best care of your father that we can."

They had all visited him earlier that afternoon, and taken him a food basket, but he was drunk and manic and had no idea who they were.

"I'll see he gets this," Kristian says, taking the basket. "You know I won't steal it, he's my friend. I doubt he'll eat any of it though but he'll share it like he always does and the rest of us guys thank you."

Jonas thanks him and they all watch Hans who is waving his hands around and talking incessantly to a stoned Jamaican giant with long dreadlocks.

Melusine had invited Felix to their dinner but the now-blonde lass chose to be with her group instead, saying that Christmas brought its own challenges that she wasn't quite ready to handle without her counselor. Felix did not yet trust herself to be the caretaker of the modicum of peace she had rescued out of the ashes of her life.

"I've got an admission to make," Melusine says sheepishly, at the Christmas dinner table, and Jonas looks amused.

"You've written another book, or done another photoshoot?"

She swats him with a napkin. "No, my sweet boy. I was going to bring dessert from the café, right? Something I baked but then we sold out, and there was nothing left... Anyway, here's the thing and it's a bit ironic ... the only thing we have for dessert is store-bought Stollen."

The three of them look at each other and Nika starts giggling. They're soon all howling with laughter and just when it subsides, Jonas pipes up: "If that doesn't just take the cake, Mami," which sets them off again, tears streaming down their cheeks.

Five
a long, long love
has seen its wings grow heavy

39.

ONE MONDAY MORNING in mid-January, Melusine gets in at her usual time to start baking. She lets herself into the coffee shop and does not notice a woman watching her from across the street. The woman is holding a bundled-up baby who is fast asleep.

Felix arrives and starts brewing coffee. She does not notice the woman with the baby either.

The café doors open at six-thirty and the woman watches as a steady crowd floods the café for fresh buns, pastries and coffees. The baby is still asleep.

Things slow down midmorning but still, the woman does not approach the café. The baby has woken up and she has given him a bottle of formula but he is restless and niggly. He likes to be carried when he is awake; walked back and forth for hours.

The woman then leaves and gets on a bus. She travels to the other end of town. The baby is content now, sucking his thumb and grinning at the other passengers. He is a big boy, close to eighteen pounds even though he is only six months old.

The woman gets off the bus and crosses the street, entering a library that faces a small park. She puts one of the baby's blankets on a table near the window and lays him down. She gives him another bottle of formula and then changes his diaper. She dresses him again and absent-mindedly dangles a toy above his head and he coos and smiles while the woman watches the park, waiting for the homeless men to emerge from their cardboard homes and filthy secret doorways where they sleep.

She is rewarded at noon, as a straggly crowd gathers; stretching, yawning and scratching.

She can see them clearly and yes, there he is.

Hans.

She thinks he doesn't look too bad, all things considered, but he is terribly thin and gaunt. She sees, when he takes his cap off to rub his head, that he has lost most of his hair. His skin is windburnt, and raw from washing with cold water and cheap harsh chemicals. There are broken veins in his face, and his nose looks to have been broken. The woman wonders if this was from a fist fight or if he fell when he was drunk.

She watches him reach into a plastic bag and take out a bottle of rotgut wine. He drinks and passes it around. His generous nature has not changed.

The men are preoccupied with their daily task of survival. Feeding the body's addiction comes first, then a mild nod at ablutions, then thoughts on what the Mission is offering that day and plans on how to keep the wine flowing.

Hans appears to be happy. He is laughing and joking with the others, flicking his imaginary hair back from his broad forehead. She is startled to see that he has a full and bushy beard; for some reason, she had imagined that he would still be the fastidious Hans.

He is dressed in an assortment of good quality clothes that once would have fit him well. The woman guesses that they are his own. They are, however, filthy, and caked with layers of dried fluids and substances the nature of which she would prefer not to think about.

In the early afternoon, the woman gathers the baby, gets back on the bus, and returns to the café.

She stands outside for a moment, knowing that she has to go in this time, unless she is willing to spend yet another night in the bus station, the mere thought of which exhausts her.

She pushes her way through the door, holding her son who is sucking his tiny forefinger and leaning his head on her shoulder.

Felix looks up. "Yes?"

The woman hesitates. "I'm looking ... I'm looking for Melusine Meier."

Felix calls over her shoulder, "Melu, someone's here for you."

She looks at the woman wondering who she is. There's something vaguely familiar about her but Felix cannot place what it is.

Melusine comes out of the baking area, wiping her hands on a dishtowel.

"Yes?" she looks at Felix who gestures to the woman.

"She's here to see you."

"Can I help you?" Melusine asks the woman.

The woman holds the baby tightly. He stirs and grabs a handful of her hair with a plump little hand.

"Can I help you?" Melusine asks again. "I don't believe we've met."

The baby looks at Melusine and flashes a gummy little smile. Then he gets shy and headbutts the woman's neck, burying his head on her shoulder. Melusine smiles at the baby, looks enquiringly at the woman and waits.

"I am Kateri," the woman says simply.

For a moment neither Melusine nor Felix say anything.

Felix is, of course, familiar with the story; she knows exactly who Kateri is.

"But you're dead," Felix says, since Melusine seems incapable of speech. "Hans keeps telling everyone that he killed you."

"Well, he's wrong."

"Where have you been? And why are you here now?" Melusine finds her voice.

"It's a long story," the woman says. Her voice is melodic, musical and light. She also speaks very slowly and Melusine wants to shake the whole story out of her.

"I see," Melusine says. She wants to be polite although she

is very shaken. "I suppose you had better take a seat. Felix, can you get some coffee or something? What would you like?" she asks the woman claiming to be Kateri.

"Water is fine. Oh, and this is my son, Tommy."

"Where's his father? Tommy's father?" Felix asks.

Kateri shrugs. "I have no idea. Just some water is fine."

Tommy starts to cry and Kateri mixes him a bottle of formula.

"I suppose he should start eating solids soon," she says vaguely. "But solids are so complicated." She shrugs and feeds the baby who makes contented mewling sounds and smiles at his mother, with the teat of the bottle still in his mouth.

"How can I believe you?" Melusine says. "That you're Kateri. You can't just arrive here and say that you're her. The story's been in the newspapers for well over a year now, you could be anybody."

"But I'm not. I've got proof, you'll see."

Melusine looks at Felix. "I'm going to phone Kommissar Klein. He's the detective from Hans's hometown. He'll know what to do. Can you take care of them?"

Felix says she will and Melusine excuses herself and goes into the back to use the phone. Then she peers around the door at Felix. "Can you also call Jonas on your cell and ask him to come over?"

Felix nods.

Melusine finds the phone number with shaking hands and dials. "Herr Kommissar Klein? This is Melusine Meier. Yes, fine, thank you. Well, actually no, not really, what am I saying? There's a woman here claiming to be Kateri Meier..."

She listens for a few minutes. "Yes," she says. "I can do that. Okay. What do you make of all this?"

She listens again and nods. "Yes. Fine, see you soon."

She goes back into the main area of the café. "Kommissar Klein is on his way. He's going to alert our police here too as well as the Älterer Polizeikommissar in Frankfurt. It's just that this is all very unexpected," she says to the woman who seems unperturbed, while Tommy has finished his bottle of milk and still looks hungry.

"He should eat something more substantial than that," Melusine turns to leave. "I'm going to purée some apples for him. Felix," she says, quietly, "don't let her go anywhere."

"I'm not going to leave," the woman says. "I don't have anywhere to go."

Melusine is in the back when Jonas bursts in with Nika behind him.

"Where is she?" he shouts and Melusine comes out to greet him.

"Don't shout, Jonas. I know, this is very disturbing. The police are on their way."

She has made a small dish of food for Tommy and she picks him up and starts to feed him. He grins up at her and eats messily, giving her his gummy smile and batting her with his little fists.

"I don't know how you can all be so calm," Jonas says. His chest is heaving and his cheeks are flushed. He stares at the woman rudely, leaning forward on his elbow and studying her face.

"We're all in shock, Jonas," Melusine says. "Sit down. Have a latte."

"I don't want a latte." But he sits down.

The door opens and Dieter and Martin rush in. "Where is she?" Dieter asks and Felix points.

"I phoned them too," she explains to Melusine.

"What do we do now?" Dieter asks. "Are the police on their way?"

Melusine tells him that they are. She looks at her watch. "They'll be here in about an hour."

"An hour!" Jonas is agitated. "We can't wait an hour. Where's your proof?" he shouts at the woman who reaches into her large purse.

She pulls out a family photograph and passes it to Jonas who looks ready to weep. "It's Papa," he says to his mother. "But you could have got this from anywhere."

"Like where?" Nika butts in. "Where could she have got it?"

Jonas doesn't answer. "We'll make you take DNA tests," he threatens the woman who doesn't appear worried.

"Surely the person to tell us if this is Kateri would be Hans," Dieter says. "We should fetch him."

"Firstly, Papa doesn't even recognize *me* sometimes," Jonas says. "And he says he killed her. If he killed her, how come she's here?"

"Obviously he didn't kill her," Melusine says.

"Do you believe her then, Mami?"

"Look at her, she does look like your father. Same forehead, mouth, cheekbones, eyes. She's more narrow though. Hans has got quite a round head."

The woman doesn't respond to any of the theories or accusations flowing around her. She gazes into the distance, her eyes unfocused, and her body relaxed in the chair. She hardly seems present but ephemeral, as if she might disappear at any moment.

Melusine burps Tommy, amazed by the immediate and instinctive return of her long-retired mothering skills and Tommy's solid little weight feels very reassuring in her arms.

"It wouldn't mean anything if Hans didn't recognize her," Dieter points out. "Since Hans is crazy."

"Maybe this would make him snap out of it," Jonas is hopeful. "This could be it, this could be the key to his recovery."

They all think about this for a while.

"Shall we try to fetch him?" Dieter asks but Melusine doesn't think this is a good idea.

"He never leaves the park. Never. We'd have to go there."

She looks at the large mosaic clock on the wall. It's just after four p.m. "He'll still be there," she says. "He goes to have supper at the Mission at five. We'd catch him with time to spare."

"How will we all get there?"

"Someone should stay here and wait for the police," Nika says, "I will."

"And I'll take Kateri, Tommy and Jonas," Melusine says. "Dieter will you bring Martin and Felix?"

He agrees and they all stand up including the woman who appears to follow what is being said, even if she does not contribute.

Melusine hands Tommy to Kateri and takes off her apron.

They herd out and get into the cars. Melusine drives off in the lead, with Dieter following.

They pull up near the park and lock the cars.

"I don't know what to expect at all," Felix whispers to Martin who has not said a word since he and Dieter arrived at the café. Martin nods. He looks nervous.

Melusine once again leads the way. She sees her husband standing with a group of men and he is holding court and laughing. She has a flashback to the first day she saw him; it had been much the same, only then he had been shielded by the beauty of youth and unbridled promise. She is aware of this grotesque parallel and the tragic degree to which his misshapen life has gone horribly wrong.

She approaches him cautiously, not wanting to startle him.

"Hans," she says and he doesn't seem to hear her.

"Hans!" she says with more force and the group of men turns to her.

Hans looks perplexed as if he has no idea who this woman is.

"Hans," she says again, "it's me, Melusine. Do you remember me?"

He doesn't answer and his expression remains neutral.

Melusine decides to be blunt, hoping she will shock him into responding.

"I've brought Kateri. Kateri is alive."

Hans shakes his head vehemently. "No, she's dead. I killed her. I kissed her, then I strangled her then I kissed her again."

"And then what?" Melusine can't help asking. "What did

you do then? Because they never found her body, Hans, they never found her body. She can't be dead."

"She's dead. In the tree." He turns back to talk to the men.

"She's here!" Melusine shouts and she grabs the agreeable Tommy from Kateri and motions the woman forward.

Hans looks at the woman almost curiously for a second. "Kateri is dead," he says conversationally. "I killed her, I kissed her. Then I strangled her, then I kissed her again."

"No, Hans," she says gently. "I'm Kateri. I'm alive." She pulls the photograph out of her pocket and shows it to him. "Look, there we are, together with Mami and Papa."

He takes the photograph from her and the sane individuals of the gathered group hold their breath, hoping this will jog the return of Hans-the-normal.

But he just lets the picture drift from his hand and float to the ground and he turns back to the group.

The woman moves closer to him. "Smell me. Come on, Hans, you won't have forgotten. Smell me."

She sidles closer to him and eases herself into him until her head is against his chest. His eyes widen and his nostrils flare — he is not happy at the intimacy of this proximity. She fits under his chin; he is much taller than she is but, standing so close together, it is easy for the others to see the strong family resemblance.

Kateri looks up at Hans. "It's me, it really is me." She burrows her head in his filthy clothing and puts her arms around his waist. "I'm so sorry you suffered so much. I didn't know. I came as soon as I could after I read that you thought you'd killed me. I thought you were happy all these years and that's why I stayed away but when I found out what you thought and that it had driven you mad, I came. I came as soon as I could. I'm so sorry Hans. I never intended to cause you such pain."

Hans stands deadstill. It is hard to know if he can even hear her. He doesn't seem to understand what she is saying and if he does, he doesn't respond at all.

Then he raises his filthy hand and strokes her head. The gentle intimacy of the gesture turns ugly when he grabs a handful of her fine blonde hair and pulls her head away from him so he can study her face but the woman doesn't flinch. He pulls her toward him again and sniffs her hair, and then he holds her away from him once more, handling her as if she were a doll. He shakes her a little and while the homeless men do not move, the rest of the gathered group all crane forward, their senses on high alert.

Which is a good thing because Hans releases the woman's hair and grabs her by the throat. "I killed you and you know it. And now it's not enough for you that I can't lie down, you've decided to haunt me when I'm standing too, even during the day."

He starts to throttle her. None of the homeless men move a muscle; they just watch impassively. Melusine steps quickly to the side, clutching Tommy close to her, while the others jump on Hans and wrestle him to the ground. Even Felix pounds him and Martin delivers a hefty blow to Hans's ear that sees him relinquish Kateri with a jolt.

"Ow," Hans says, rubbing his ear, and he looks bemused. "That hurt."

"Are you all right?" Melusine asks Kateri and she nods although she is holding her neck.

"He really has gone mad," she says wonderingly, as if she too had thought that the shock of him seeing her would jolt him back to reality.

"Or maybe you're not who you say you are," Jonas points out.

"Hans just tried to murder a woman," Dieter says. "None of you seem to care about that. We should have him locked up."

Melusine, Jonas and Kateri, or whoever she is, all turn on him.

"Not a chance," Jonas says.

"It wasn't his fault," Melusine protests.

"I'll deny that anything happened," Kateri murmurs.

Hans is still rubbing his ear and looking confused.

"He's dangerous," Dieter protests, "he's really homicidal, you all saw it."

"Time for supper," one of the homeless men says in a flat voice that's tinged with worry. "Come on, let's go. We're going to miss out and tonight's tuna casserole."

They leave at a brisk pace, focused on getting their share of the tuna casserole, with Hans shielded in the middle of the pack.

"I guess we should go back to the café," Melusine says. "Maybe the police have arrived by now."

Dieter watches the homeless men go. "I'm not happy about this," he says and Martin agrees with him.

They all drive back to the café. Nika is there with the local police while Kommissar Klein has yet to arrive.

"What happened?" Nika asks and Jonas takes her aside to tell her.

Melusine takes Tommy from Kateri who is yawning. Melusine holds the baby on one hip while she digs around in Kateri's big bag, aware that Tommy needs to have his diaper changed. She doesn't find anything in the bag except for dirty bottles, some toys and clean wipes that have dried out. "Kateri," she asks, "where are the supplies for Tommy? Change of clothing, diapers, food?"

Kateri looks bewildered. "All gone?" she answers, her reply a question.

Melusine is furious. "Nika, I need you to go shopping," she says and she scribbles down a list.

"Don't worry, I used to babysit a lot." Nika takes the list. "I know what to get and I'll be quick."

Tommy is snoozing in Melusine's arms. She figures he must have the resilience of a Hummer to be able to withstand Kateri's mothering.

Shortly after Nika leaves, Kommissar Klein arrives.

Felix has made everyone coffee and she passes the mugs around.

"All right, Kateri, I've got some questions for you," Klein

says, once they're all settled. "But first let me explain a few things. I've been cleared to investigate this by the Senior Police Commissioner in Frankfurt, Herr Kommissar Reichardt. Herr Beamte Richter, as some of you might know, is a police officer from the local *polizei* here and he'll be helping me out as we go."

The local cop nods. Jonas recognizes him; he has chatted to him a couple of times when he has gone to see Hans.

"Okay," Klein says, "formalities out of the way, let's get on with things. Kateri, is Tommy your son?"

She looks surprised. "Yes, of course he is."

"And where did you and he come from? Where were you before you came here?"

She frowns in concentration. "We were on a bus and before that we slept in the bus station."

"Which bus station? In which town?"

"Um, I can't remember the name. It was north of here. No, it was west."

"Do you have the ticket stubs?"

She shakes her head.

Klein motions to the young officer. "Search all her pockets, Richter. Search everywhere. Her every belonging. Search the baby too."

"Oh, wait," Melusine objects. "Wait until Nika gets back. I don't want to disturb him twice and I'll look when I change him."

The constable searches while Klein continues to question the frustratingly evasive Kateri. "You're saying you can't remember where you came from. Why did you decide to come now?"

"It was in the newspapers that Hans said he'd killed me. I had to tell him and the whole world that he didn't."

"Let's go back to the day you vanished or the day you were supposed to have died. What happened that day?"

She looks off into the distance. "I ran away."

"Why did you run away? And who did you run away with?"

"I ran away because Hans loved me too much. I never had any peace. And then one day, I was in the town, alone, just for an hour or so and a couple were filling up their car with petrol and they were towing a caravan. I don't know what I was thinking, I wasn't really thinking, but when they weren't looking, I opened the door — it wasn't locked — and I hid inside. And then when they stopped again, I found a place to hide so they wouldn't find me. They didn't find me until three days had passed and by then they didn't know where I had got on. And I didn't tell them. I pretended I couldn't speak."

Everyone is mesmerized by the length and coherence of this tale.

"And then there was nothing they could do except let me stay. I guess they could have dropped me off at a police station but they decided to keep me. We travelled together and stayed in places. Sometimes we stayed for months, sometimes just days."

"But your father was accused of murdering you. He left your mother and disappeared. Hans left your mother. You destroyed your family. Didn't you ever think about that?"

She shakes her head. "No. They loved me too much. I was tired of being loved so much. It was much easier to be with my new parents. They didn't pressure me about anything and besides, they thought I couldn't speak. My life was much more peaceful. They loved me but they never bothered me. They called me Angelika. You should all call me Angelika."

"But," Jonas interjects loudly, "if you were just in town, on a whim, how come you had the photograph with you, of the family? That doesn't make any sense."

"I always carried a picture of my family with me in my schoolbag. My bag had lots of my special things in it. My new parents never knew about my schoolbag. They never knew."

"And where are they now?" Klein asks.

"Dead," she says simply. "There was an accident one day. They both died in the car. The townspeople also thought I couldn't talk. They thought I was the couple's daughter. I went to stay at the church with the pastor and his family until I was old enough to get a job in a grocery store, stocking the shelves. Then I got my own apartment and I've lived in that town all these years. And then one night, fifteen months ago, as I was going home, a man forced himself on me and that's how I got Tommy."

She stops. She looks tired out from the effort of all that talking and her eyes are dark in her pale face.

"That's quite the story," Jonas says. "All the loose ends neatly tied up and not enough details to give us any real proof that you really are Kateri."

The woman stretches out her arm. "Take my blood. Or whatever you need. Prove it."

"That would take months," Jonas grumbles.

"I've got time," the woman looks at him evenly. "Nothing in my life is in a hurry. It never was. I'm not like you people."

"And what do you propose to do while we all wait?" Jonas asks. "Get a job stacking groceries and pretending that you can't speak? Or do you plan to steal my father's money?"

"Hans is a homeless drunk," Kateri says. "He doesn't have any money. I didn't think any further than getting here and making things right with him."

"And it took you a year to get here? The story was everywhere over a year ago. What were you doing all that time?"

"First, I was thinking what to do and then I got pregnant with Tommy. Then I saw it again, the story about Hans. And I remembered I had to come. I told you, I came as soon as I could and I don't do things in a hurry."

"Tell us," Melusine says, "prove what you say you know. How did Hans show his affection to you?"

"We would lie in our treehouse for hours and talk, and he'd rub my feet. I got very tired of having my feet rubbed. He would also brush my hair."

Jonas jumps up. "The psychic!" he shouts and he points at

her. "My father told the psychic all of this and either you are her or she told you all these things."

Kateri looks completely baffled. "What psychic? What are you talking about?"

"Ha!" Jonas is so angry he's nearly spitting. "You spent all of his money. And then you drove him crazy and he had nothing left to give you, so you came here to pretend to be part of the family and rip us off too. Well, it won't work!"

"What psychic?" Dieter asks. "What is Jonas talking about?"

"Hans went to see a psychic in Vegas," Melusine explains. "And she told him she could put him in touch with Kateri. Hans said that he needed to know that Kateri was okay wherever she was. And then, this woman from the Healing Lives Ministries told him that Kateri was coming closer, that she was alive and that he'd see her soon. But he went crazy first; he started dreaming that he'd killed her or he thought he remembered killing her."

Klein looks over at Melusine. "Melusine, I forgot to tell you, I followed up with that pamphlet you gave me ages ago for the Celestial Sound Vibrations, but the man couldn't remember who Hans was talking to. He said he remembered your husband, that he seemed like a nice guy but very troubled but I didn't get anything else out of him. My apologies for not having contacted you to tell you."

"Thank you for trying anyway."

"So first Hans dreamed that he killed her," Dieter says. "And then he tried to kill her today too. Why is everybody forgetting that?"

"What?" Klein turns to him. "What happened?"

"Nothing," Melusine, Jonas and Kateri all chorus.

"We went to the park to see if he remembered her," Melusine explains. "We all hoped that seeing her would heal him. It was stupid, I know. Anyway, he had a bad reaction."

"A bad reaction!" Dieter is seething. "He tried to strangle her and then he strolled off to get his share of tuna casserole."

"She got too close to him," Jonas defends his father. "It was her fault. The drink has fried his brain. It's not his fault."

"I see," Klein says, and Melusine can see he is not happy with the news that Hans attacked his sister. Or the woman pretending to be his sister.

"And what did he say? What did Hans say?" he asks.

"He said I killed you before, I will kill you again now," Dieter said.

"That's because he thought she was a dream, a demon dream," Jonas insists. "He already can't lie down because he dreams that she'll come to him, reminding him of how he killed her. He has to drink through the night and sleep upright during the day. Can you imagine the hell of that? And now, she appears to him, during the day, while he's standing. No wonder he tried to kill her. No, let me correct that, he didn't try to kill her; he tried to kill what he thought was the dream of her."

Klein sighs. "One thing's for sure, this is one gigantic extraordinary mess."

He turns to Kateri. "Does anybody know that you're here?"

She's startled. "I don't know anybody here."

"What about the people from your town?"

"They don't know any of this. They think I can't speak," she reminds him.

"What's the name of the town?"

"I won't say. It's my home. What if I want to go back? They accept me for who I am."

"But the townspeople would be able to verify your story," Klein says, but the woman simply shrugs and just then, Nika arrives back.

Melusine unpacks the supplies and she and Nika change Tommy's diaper, put him in clean clothes and fix him a bottle.

"Fine." Klein turns to Kateri. "So the only people who know you're here are in this room. Now let's all agree among us that we don't want the townspeople or newspapers finding out about this, not until we figure it out ourselves. Nobody's to say anything to anyone. Are we all agreed?"

There is some muttering. Melusine looks around and she stands up. "Please everyone, please let's do this. For Hans's sake, for Jonas's sake, for mine. For this baby. I'm not asking you on behalf of this woman, because I don't know her either. I don't know what to believe about the story she's told us. I don't. But my family, Jonas and me, we've been through hell more than once for this. Please, I'm asking you. It will be hard to keep it a secret but you can. Please."

"You've got my word that I won't say a thing," Nika is the first to speak up.

"And me too," Felix says.

"And me," Martin agrees.

They all turn to Dieter who looks uncomfortable. "Well, I guess the only people I would have wanted to tell are the police and they're here. So I won't say anything, you have my word too."

"And you?" Melusine turns to Kateri. "What about you?"

"I don't have anyone to tell," she says.

"Look," Melusine says. "I've got no reason to trust you. What's to say you won't take it to the papers? Saying here I am, Hans's long-lost sister. If you're looking for a way to milk this, that would work."

"I'm not looking for anything," the woman says. "I keep telling you, I came here to help my brother."

"You can't go near him again," Klein says. "Do you understand that? If you do, and he attacks you, I'll have to arrest him and lock him up. Which I should probably do anyway but I don't have the grounds if none of you will make a statement about what happened this evening. If you really want to help him, stay away from him. Kateri, I'm with Jonas and Melusine, your story doesn't ring true for me. It's too perfect, like bullet-proof glass, you can see through it but you can't penetrate it."

"She's coming to stay with me," Melusine says and Jonas starts to object. "Just until we get this sorted out, Jonas. Look, she didn't have baby clothes or food or anything. I need to know that Tommy's okay."

"Right, the baby trick," Jonas is scathing. "She probably knew enough about you that you wouldn't be able to resist a baby. Papa probably told the psychic that too. And that stuff that she's got, the souvenirs of her life, her so-called 'proof'. I bet it's all stuff that Papa gave the psychic."

Klein sighs again. "We've already established that we cannot find the Healing Lives Ministries; we have already tried every avenue we can to find them. Let's deal with what we've got here."

"If you're taking her home with you, then I'm coming too," Felix tells Melusine. "I'm not having you alone with this stranger. And anyway, let's not forget we've got a café to run. And you," she points a finger at Kateri, "will have to find a way to keep yourself occupied during the day because you're not swanning around Melu's home digging through her stuff."

"I really don't like any of this," Jonas says. "She could steal everything and disappear tomorrow."

Kateri yawns.

"Here's the thing," Klein says. "I've been thinking. I could arrest her. According to the laws of the *Staatsanwaltschaft*, the public prosecutor's office, we can arrest a suspect if there's a risk of flight or if there is a problem identifying a suspect, both of which are applicable here. I can hold her for a day and I will immediately apply for a warrant to detain her for long and I'm certain I'll get it."

"But she hasn't committed a crime?" Officer Richter pipes up.

"She has insofar as she has no real proof of identity and she's claiming to be someone who is officially dead. And if ever I've seen a flight risk, it's her. We can try to keep her locked up until this whole mess is sorted out. I agree with Jonas, I don't want her staying with Melusine. This woman could be anybody and I don't trust her to stick around."

"But what about Tommy?" Melusine clutches him tighter. "You can't lock him up with her, that would be unspeakable for him. Anyway, we don't even know if he's really her baby."

"Of course he's mine," Kateri looks indignant. "Whose else would he be?"

"There are any number of answers to that question," Klein says. "And we owe it to the child to do a maternity test. You have no papers on you, no ID. For all I know, you could have abducted this baby."

Kateri looks bored. "You're all very dramatic. Sometimes life is boringly simple."

"Can I look after Tommy?" Melusine asks. "Please, Herr Kommissar Klein, don't put him in prison with her, or hand him over to social welfare, I couldn't bear that."

"Since you might well be his next of kin, you can look after him," Klein says after a moment, "if Kateri agrees."

"This all sounds very wishy-washy to me," Officer Richter says. "Like we're bending the laws all kind of ways to suit us."

Klein turns to him.

"Here's what we've got," he says. "A homeless woman without any papers. And while Tommy's well-fed and looks relatively healthy, we don't have any proof that he's her baby. We've got a cockamamie story that she's Hans's sister but we've got no real proof of that either. The other concern is this: Hans could suddenly remember that his so-called sister's in town, giving him bad dreams and interferring with his sleep and he might decide to try and find her and strangle her for real."

"Look what you've done," Jonas says accusingly to Kateri. "Thanks a lot. You really thought this through didn't you? And," he turns to Klein, "even if you lock her up, what's to say my father won't return to my mother, and get confused and try to kill her?"

"I hadn't thought of that," Klein admits. "Good point.

Melusine, can you stay with someone else for a while?"

"She can come and stay with me and Martin," Dieter says. "No problem. We've got lots of rooms. And we're heading off on a safari the day after tomorrow for a month. You'll have all the privacy you need," he says to Melusine.

"Not to mention luxury," Felix whispers to Melusine, and she smiles at Dieter who scowls at her.

"There'll be none of that," he grumbles. "I still remember the party you and Martin threw. It took a week and ten thousand dollars to fix."

Martin and Felix share a grin.

"You want me to go to prison while you all think about this, and Melusine will take care of my baby?" Kateri gets up and stretches. "Sure, it'd be a rest for me. I'm very tired."

"The Älterer Polizeikommissar told me he'll support whatever I make, as this is a unique situation," Klein explains to the young constable. "I'll get Kateri to sign the paperwork so it's legal for Melusine to look after Tommy and I'll keep everyone in the loop with any developments."

He looks at Kateri. "Let's go then," he says and Kateri ambles toward the front door.

"Aren't you forgetting something?" Jonas's voice is cold and she turns and looks at him quizzically.

"Your baby? Aren't you going to say goodbye to your baby?"

Kateri strolls back and pats the sleeping Tommy on the head and looks at Jonas. "Happy now? He was asleep. He never even noticed. Let's go already, I'm worn out."

Klein and Kateri leave, along with the young police officer, Richter.

"You married?" they hear Klein ask him on the way out.

"No, thank god."

"Girlfriend? Mother? Sister? Buddies?"

The officer looks confused. "Of course."

"And you're going to tell them what, about tonight?"

Richter's face clears. "Oh, right. Um, that there was a reported theft at the café but after an extensive and time-consuming search, we found the missing equipment?"

Klein laughs. "You'll be a great cop yet."

"Come on, Melusine," Dieter says, "I'm taking you and the young puppy home. Goodnight everyone."

"Mami, be careful," Jonas says. "I'll come by and see you in the morning."

Nika hands over the bag of purchases. "Come on Jonas. You need some serious TLC after today."

They wave and head out the door.

Melusine notices that Felix is looking forlorn.

"You okay, Sweetie?" she says.

"Yes, fine," Felix says but her chin quivers unmistakeably.

Melusine and Martin both turn to Dieter with beseeching looks.

"Oh fine, then," he says brusquely. "You can come too. Just no partying, okay?"

Felix squeals loudly enough to make Tommy stir and then she clamps a hand to her mouth.

"See what I mean," Dieter says, but he says it kindly, "she's already making enough noise to wake the neighbours. Okay, campers, let's hit the road."

Melusine and Felix follow Dieter's Porsche, with Felix sitting in the backseat, buckled up and carefully cradling Tommy.

Once they are at Dieter's, exhaustion hits.

Melusine and Felix bath Tommy together and take turns showering.

Later they are both lying on a vast bed, with Tommy in between them, barricaded by pillows. He wakes up to feed and promptly falls asleep again.

Melusine is wearing a pair of Dieter's pajamas and Felix has joyfully raided Martin's closet.

"I want all of it back," Martin says and Felix grimaces.

"Why would I keep such boy-wear? I'm just enjoying the feeling of silk on my naked skin."

"Such a slut," Martin says. "Goodnight, you two. I'm glad Dieter and I are escaping to a safari soon, this is all too much excitement for me."

"What do you make of it all?" Felix asks Melusine, as they relax on the big bed and Melusine shakes her head.

"I don't have a single clue," she says. "Not one iota of an idea. I do worry though that this will end badly. How can it not? Oh, Felix. I have a feeling of foreboding."

Felix leans over and strokes Melusine's hand. "I know. Me too. Come on, let's put this little fellow into his laundry basket. Only Dieter would have a laundry basket that can double as a Gucci baby's cot." They laugh quietly and deposit Tommy carefully and Melusine sets the alarm clock.

"Try to get some rest," Felix says, kissing Melusine on the cheek. "We'll figure it out in the morning."

40.

I N THE MORNING, they feel none the wiser. If anything, they are more perplexed than ever. They tiptoe out of Dieter's home, carrying Tommy and arrive at the café at the usual time. Melusine starts baking while Felix cleans up the mess from the night before and Tommy sleeps peacefully. As soon as the breakfast rush leaves, Melusine phones Klein who promises her an update later in the day, and he makes good on his word.

"I've sent DNA tests in for Kateri and Hans," Klein tells her at lunchtime. "I'll get young Richter to come by with a pediatrician and get a test from Tommy and give him a once-over too. He's a really cute baby and he seems healthy enough but let's get him checked out. I doubt she's ever taken him to a doctor. I've spoken to all the legal powers that be and the public prosecutor has issued a warrant for us to keep Miss Cuckoo behind bars as long as we need to, until the tests prove things one way or the other. The tests take anywhere from five to seven days, and I've put a rush on things and when I told Kateri that it might take that long, she said that's fine by her. She's spent most of the time sleeping and hasn't asked after her kid once. She's a piece of work, I'll tell you that. But no one down at the station knows who she is or should I say, who she's claiming to be, so don't worry about that."

"You've had a busy morning," Melusine says. "That sounds great. Felix and I will stay at Dieter's until the tests are in. Better safe than sorry."

They ring off and Melusine updates Felix, who visibly relaxes.

"He calls her Miss Cuckoo," Melusine says, laughing.

"He's right," Felix says fervently. "Off her rocker. She is beautiful though, isn't she?"

"Exquisite. Her skin's flawless. She's like Michelle Pfeiffer from twenty years ago. If she's four years younger than Hans, she's forty-three."

"She's so graceful too. Like a ballerina. But she's got that weird look in her eye. Kind of freaky, and it ruins her beauty. She's all lights on and no one's home — a chandelier ready to blow."

"Exactly. What I want to know is how she stays so clean while Tommy was so grimy. And they were staying in a bus station. And yet Kateri or whoever she is, floats in looking like she's just spent the day at a spa."

"Very odd. Do you think she is the psychic?"

"I've got no idea. The DNA will reveal all."

Tommy chooses that moment to wake up from his afternoon nap and he wails and they both rush over to him.

"We need to go toy shopping," Melusine says, and Felix grins.

"As soon as we close here, we'll hit the mall. What fun!"

Meanwhile, content in her cell, the woman called Kateri Angelika lies half asleep. With someone else taking care of her baby, she can float back to the sanctuary of her private fantasy world and as soon as she lies down and closes her eyes, she is surrounded by the dreamy medieval world that she lives in and loves; a world in which she is feted by knights as she rides on horseback through a forest. It is always summertime in her world and there is the sound of laughter and the smell of a feast being prepared. She knows the feast is in her honour; she is being celebrated for her bravery and her beauty and she sits easily astride the big white horse while admirers line her path and curtsy and bow as she passes.

41

DIETER AND MARTIN leave for their safari, dressed to the nines in khaki and white linen. And Melusine and Felix fall more in love with Tommy every day.

The pediatrician comes by and gives him a clean bill of health and he says Tommy's one of the cutest babies he has seen. Tommy gurgles up at him throughout the exam, grinning and cooing. "He's still got some cradle cap under this fine blonde hair and you can see he scratches his face with his sharp little nails. You might want to get him some mitts."

He runs his finger down the strawberry birthmark on Tommy's forehead. "This is a vascular birthmark, but don't worry, it'll fade by the time he's about two years old. He's got one on the back of his neck too."

Tommy chortles with joy when the doctor picks him up and turns him over.

"He's such a wonder," Melusine smiles, "we just love him."

"Easy to see why," the doctor turns the baby onto his back and Tommy gazes at him. "He's got a very interesting stare, doesn't he?" He tickles Tommy's tummy. "You look right at a person, don't you Tommy?"

"Aren't his eyes so beautiful?" Felix asks. "They're most incredible blue and so big and wide-set. He's gorgeous, just gorgeous!"

The pediatrician weighs Tommy and gives them some advice on what to feed him.

"Is he too fat?" Felix asks. "He does seem very big, especially since he's only been having a bottle."

"He's fine," the doctor says. "The weight will fall off him once he starts moving around, don't worry about it. I want to show you some exercises that you need to do with him to start him sitting on his own. Make sure you give him lots of time on his tummy, so he can start working on his crawling."

He shows them.

"I'll probably have to come back," the doctor says. "I need to get Klein to ask the mother if he's had any of his shots."

"My guess is not," Felix says, darkly. "She's really off the planet."

"That's what Klein said. Anyway, I'll ask him to ask her and we'll take it from there. Okay, you handsome boy, that's nearly it for the day and generally, you're in very fine shape. But now, I'm very sorry I'm going to have to take a little blood and this is going to hurt a bit."

He pricks the underside of Tommy's tiny little foot and both Melusine and Felix wince and Tommy lets out a wail.

"Sorry little guy," the doctor says and Melusine grabs the baby up and a minute later Tommy's grinning again.

The doctor says goodbye and Melusine and Felix examine Tommy's foot.

"Surely there's a more humane way to take blood from a baby?" Felix is indignant and Melusine agrees.

"I'll make him some of his favourite avocado and banana mix," Melusine says while Felix cuddles him.

A couple of days later, Klein calls Melusine.

"The pediatrician will have to come back," he says, "Kateri said, when I could get her to focus, that Tommy hasn't had any of his shots yet."

"No surprises there," Melusine says and Klein agrees.

"There's no word on the DNA yet," he says, "but I'm getting a psych evaluation done this afternoon. I'll phone you tomorrow and let you know the results."

Melusine thanks him, hangs up the phone and updates Felix. Then she emails Gunther.

That woman is shocking! She shouldn't be allowed to call herself a mother. She doesn't even ask about Tommy! Oh Gunther ... I'm really worried about what will happen to him. He's the most special boy, I wish you could meet him, you'd see he's no ordinary baby. What if she disappears with him? I couldn't bear that.

She signs off, knowing that Gunther is not too happy about this unexpected turn of events and she wonders if a time will come when she will have to choose between the baby and the man. And if she does, she already knows who she will choose.

42.

"I WANT YOU TO TELL ME, on a scale of one to five, how true a statement is for you," the state psychiatrist tells Kateri who looks bored. "Five means it's very accurate while one means it's very inaccurate. Three means you are in the middle."

Kateri flicks a speck of dust off the sofa. It is time for her evaluation at the psychiatrist's office and she is irritated by the interruption to her rest. She studies the rows of books on the shelves and the ornaments from far-distant lands. Her mind wanders; she is lying on an embroidered rug in the shade of a cool tree with the soothing sound of a nearby waterfall and a woman is stroking her hair and everything is peaceful and lovely...

"Kateri? I need you to concentrate please." The psychiatrist has the audacity to snap his fingers in front of her face and she looks at him, implacable.

"Focus, please, on what I'm asking you. I want you to answer honestly, remember there's no right or wrong, just answer as quickly as you can."

Kateri sighs. The sooner she gets this over with, the sooner she will be left alone again.

"Fine, I'm concentrating."

"*I prefer to do things alone.* On a scale of one to five, how accurate is that for you?"

"The most accurate."

"I have difficulty making decisions without excessive advice and reassurance of others."

She shakes her head. "That one's stupid. I make all my own decisions by myself."

"I strongly dislike being around people who don't appreciate or care for me."

She is baffled. "Everybody cares about me. Everybody loves me. They love me too much. That one's stupid too."

"I have magical thinking or odd beliefs."

"There's nothing odd about my beliefs. What do you mean by magical? People fall under my spell all the time, I can't help that, I wish they didn't. How many more of these stupid questions do you have?"

"There are forty," the psychiatrist says and Kateri sighs again.

"Well then, let's get this over with."

43.

"THE STATE PSYCHIATRIST says she suffers from schizoid personality disorder," Klein tells Melusine.

"Does that mean she's schizophrenic?" Melusine asks, also worried about what that might mean for Tommy, in a number of ways.

"No. I asked him the same question and apparently with this disorder, the person doesn't have hallucinations, delusions or a complete disconnection from reality. His report says, and I quote: *'With this illness, the person is aloof and detached, they avoid social activities that involve intimacy with other people and they don't want any kind of close relationships, not even with family members.'* Which would explain what she said about needing to leave her family because they loved her too much."

"It would also explain her weird lack of details about things," Melusine says. "She just lives in her own head. But Herr Kommissar Klein, this isn't good for Tommy, if she is in fact his mother."

"Melusine," he says, "may I please ask that you call me Jürgen. And no, it's not good for the boy. Let's see what the tests reveal. They'll take another four to five days. And then, if she isn't his mother, we'll have to take it from there. The psychiatrist also said she's very secretive and most likely spends a lot of time in a fantasy world in which she is the heroine. Apparently her condition's quite rare and most schizoids operate well socially while remaining emotionally withdrawn. Kateri's a rather extreme case."

"Jürgen," Melusine tries out the name. "What's the prognosis for getting her help?"

She can almost hear Jürgen shaking his head on the other end of the phone line. "The psychiatrist said she's one of the most inaccessible people he's ever worked with. She's narcissistic, and feels very superior to the rest of us. She also has no real grasp of the consequences of any of her actions. Everything comes second to her living in her own little world. All we can do now is wait for DNA."

"I can't bear to think of Tommy having to live with this woman, I just can't. Thank you for letting me know, Jürgen. Talk to you soon."

"Was that the sexy policeman?" Felix asks when she hangs up the phone. "Have you noticed how he looks at you? Knowing you, you haven't."

Melusine looks up in surprise. "You think he's sexy? Really? I suppose he is."

Felix laughs. "You suppose? Oh, come on. He's so not my type but even I can see it."

"He's very manly," Melusine admits, and she surprises herself by blushing. "He's most likely married though. He just strikes me as a married man."

"He isn't wearing a ring..."

"Which means nothing these days. Most men don't like wearing rings. Funnily though, Hans still wears his. Probably doesn't notice it's there and when he does, he'll sell it for booze."

"I just think you and Mr. Detective would make an interesting couple."

"And I think we have other things on our minds." Melusine ends the conversation and she considers telling Felix about Gunther but something stops her. He has always been her own private secret, her quiet joy. Prior to Kateri's arrival, their correspondence had, increasingly, hinted at getting together, he had even said he would come to Germany, but now that feels like a remote dream to Melusine, with little chance of coming true.

Gunther does not hide how he feels about Tommy particularly when she tells him she hopes to be a part of the baby's life.

You've had your time parenting. Why on earth would you even want that? I don't understand.

I guess I've fallen in love with the little guy, she writes back, and it's true, she's besotted. *I'd be willing to keep Kateri around even if she isn't Kateri, just to be near Tommy.*

That woman sounds dangerous, he immediately fires back. *You wouldn't be able to trust her. You'd come home one day and all your possessions would be gone, and her and Tommy too. She's not to be trusted.*

She knows what he says is true, and now, with Jürgen Klein's words ringing in her ears, she feels even more anxious about how things will turn out.

Thinking about her relationship with Gunther and the inevitable change it faces makes her sad and she turns her thoughts to Felix's love-life instead.

"You're the one who should be thinking about finding love," she scolds, as she's done before. "You're so young, too young to be alone."

"I'm perfectly happy being alone," Felix says calmly. "Happier than I have ever been. I don't need the complications of love. Anyway, where there's sex, there's rarely love, not the lasting kind anyway. No, I'm quite fine." She changes the subject. "When are they going to start working on your book? Feels like they're taking forever."

"The publisher says we should start working on the galleys soon. I'm getting excited. I wonder what suggestions they'll make?"

"I love your book. I don't think they'll change anything."

In the early days of their partnership, Felix had insisted that Melusine give her a copy and she had read it in a single sitting.

"It's going to be a bestseller, I'm telling you now."

Melusine laughs. "Oh, I don't think so. But after all this time, it will be nice to have it in print. We can have the launch party here at the café, what do you think?"

"This place won't be big enough. Dieter will hire a hall or something. He wouldn't miss an opportunity for a big celebration but watch, he'll use it to launch our line of store goods too, we'll end up working our asses off!"

"Quite right." Melusine groans. "Good thing you mentioned that, I can mentally prepare. *Ach*, I shouldn't complain, he's a good and generous man."

"We're making him good money too," Felix says and it's true. "And he's very proud of us. Martin says he tells all his friends about his famous arty café run by his Modern Art nude model, soon-to-be-author, pastry chef and his Bambi drag queen. That's what he calls us!"

They both laugh.

"It's all good," Melusine says and she picks up Tommy. "But what will become of this little fellow? Oh Tommy, you gorgeous edible boy, what will happen to you?"

Tommy gurgles and grins and Jonas arrives at that point and takes Tommy from Melusine. "Mami, this little guy makes me want to have a dozen babies right now."

"And what does Nika say about that?" Felix says, making him a latte.

"She says we have to wait. Any word on what's happening with Mama Loony Tunes?"

Melusine tells him about the psych evaluation, and a worried frown crosses his face. "Hearing that makes me want to grab Tommy and run away," he says.

"Don't even joke about things like that, Jonas. I know, though. I'm worried too."

"Speaking of worried, have you seen Papa lately?"

Melusine shakes her head. "No, actually not since the day in the park. We've been so busy with the café and Tommy that I quite forgot about him to be honest, which I know is awful. Why?"

Jonas shrugs. "He seems much worse. I couldn't get him to make any sense at all today. The whole thing with Kateri really upset him. I asked that guy Kristian, one of the group he hangs out with, if Papa's been sleeping at all and he says not. The guys even sit right next to him, on either side of him, in the middle of the day and he falls asleep but then he wakes up screaming. Even they're worried about him and that's saying something. And he's seeing her even when he's awake. Apparently he stands there, screaming at the air in front of him."

"I should stop by and see him," Melusine says. "You know, apart from our Tommy here, this visit from Kateri has been very destructive." She sighs.

They all look at each other, worried about the baby they fear they will lose, while Tommy gurgles and bats his toys with strong little fists.

44.

A WEEK LATER Melusine is drying her hands on a tea towel and chatting to Tommy, who is practicing sitting up all by himself when, to her surprise, Jürgen Klein walks in and a feeling of dread fills her heart.

"She's going to take him back," she whispers, her hand pressed against her mouth as if not letting the words out would stop the awfulness from coming true. "Oh Jürgen, I know it was stupid of me but I hoped things could stay like this, with Felix and me and Tommy."

She cannot help it, tears well up in her eyes and she starts to cry, burying her face in the tea towel. Next thing, she is sobbing and Jürgen is holding her, talking frantically.

"Melu, listen to me, listen to me, she's gone, she's gone."

She looks at him, her mouth agape. She blows her nose in the tea towel and he takes it from her gently and puts it where she won't be tempted to use it to dry the cutlery.

"What I'm trying to tell you is that she's really *gone*. She convinced one of the officers to let her go outside for some air. And now, since her disappearance, he admitted that he'd done it before but she always came back. He's very red-faced, believe me. And this time she's gone for good. She even left a note. Well, a kind of a note. She's not very coherent. Here, I made a photocopy for you, the note's been filed in evidence. I tell you, Melu, she's a special kind of wingnut. By the way, she really is Tommy's mother."

He hands the note to Melusine.

Melusine, I know the boy will be better with you. I'm not going to come back ever, don't worry. I know I don't feel the things I should. I never have.

"That's it?"

"That's it."

Melusine utters a wild howl and grabs Tommy who, not understanding that a good thing has happened, starts crying at the top of his lungs.

Felix arrives back to find them both wailing, and she immediately assumes the worst and starts bawling too.

"No, no," Jürgen shouts at Felix and he shoves the note at her. She reads it and gives a piercing shriek of joy.

Jürgen takes Tommy from Melusine and calms him down while Melusine and Felix grab each other and waltz around the café, laughing with happiness.

When they finally calm down, Jürgen tells them more. "The Älterer Polizeikommissar and the public prosecutor have put the wheels in motion for the guardianship papers to be filed, so don't worry about that. Everything will be legal and above board. *Ach*, poor little fellow, I hope he doesn't hate her later, for leaving him. Things like this can leave real scars."

"Listen, my real father was a bastard," Felix says. "I wish I'd had two guardian angels like me and Melu when I was young. He'll thank his lucky stars he was rescued from El Cuckoo Burro, let me tell you. You can go through life mourning the crap that happened or you can take the gifts you're given and this little fellow is too much of a happy lad to wallow in self-pity. He's going to be just fine, won't you schnookie?"

"Oh, but wait," Melusine asks "is Kateri or Angelika or whatever her name is, is she Hans's sister?"

She and Felix wait for the answer, staring at Klein. Even Tommy is still and quiet.

"Yes. She's his sister."

"My God," Melusine says, sinking down into a chair.

"Look at all the damage she caused. Yes, so she has schizoid personality disorder so maybe it's not her fault but look at the fallout that one damaged person can cause. Jürgen, I meant to tell you, Jonas said Hans is getting worse. Can you ask Officer Richter to keep an eye on him? Apparently Hans is screaming at invisible ghosts during the day now too. I would hate any more innocent bystanders to be hurt in all of this."

"I'll call him right now," Jürgen says, taking out his phone.

Felix is cooing at Tommy.

"Felix," Melusine says, "I'm sure it's safe for us to leave Dieter's place now, but will you come home with me? Will you stay with Tommy and me? We both need you. Gunther's right, a new baby's a big step at my age and I feel like we're family, you and me."

Felix's face lights up. "Yes! I would love nothing more in the whole world." Then, "Who's Gunther?"

Melusine realizes she's made a slip. "Just a friend, a penpal."

"I didn't even know you were on Facebook," Felix is disapproving, and Melusine laughs.

"I'm not. We just email. Hey, we haven't told Jonas the good news. I must phone him."

"She's really Papa's sister?" Jonas is incredulous. "Wow. How do we know she won't come back?"

"Because it would mean having to do all the things she hates," Melusine is confident. "Family gatherings, communicating, pretending to care. She can't find it within herself to care and she knows she'd be expected to. She can't bear even the tiniest of responsibilities to the point where she can't even handle a conversation. I bet she's gone back to her town where she doesn't even have to speak. She won't want to come back."

"I must tell Nika, she'll be so happy about Tommy. That's great news. So are you going home then?"

"Yes, and Felix is coming to stay with me from now on."

"I'm very glad to hear that. She's family and anyway, you'll need help to look after Tommy although we'll help a lot too.

Nika and I will come over later, we need to celebrate. And you do enough cooking, I'll bring takeout. What do you feel like? Indian? Chinese? Pizza? Anything you like."

"You choose, Jonas, anything is fine. My goodness, I must say, I still feel very shocked by all of this, don't you?"

"Yes, Mami. The worst thing for me was that woman's coldness. She really frightened me. She doesn't care about anything. In a way, she doesn't even care about herself the way other normal people do. She's very beautiful and very crazy. I can't stop seeing her face."

"Time will heal that. It's a cliché but it's true. And having a fantastic little baby to love will help us more than anything. What a gift, what a beautiful gift."

Gunther's emailed response, later, is less than delighted and they get into a furious email argument. *And what about us? Have you thought about that?*

Melusine responds without hesitation. *Gunther, what us? Writing doesn't mean a real relationship, look at Ingeborg and Paul. They wrote to each other all that time and yes, they loved each other but they couldn't live together. While with Tommy, I have the chance to make a real difference to his life.*

Gunther is equally quick. *Oh, for god's sake, Ingeborg and Paul were crazy poets. You really think we should base the future of our relationship on them? Grow up, Melusine. Frankly, that's just stupid.*

This time she takes a deep breath before replying. *Gunther, you mean the world to me. You have, ever since we met. Let's not say things in haste that we don't mean, things that could ruin what we have. I care very deeply for you. You know that. It isn't like I went out and decided to find myself a baby, he came to me. And I can't say I am sorry he did. I love him. But I don't want to lose you.*

There is no reply even though Melusine checks her email every fifteen minutes, uncaring if Felix notices.

Oh Gunther, she wants to say, we were just a few days of

magic. And you changed my life and brought me such joy and yes, we both had hopes, but what could we really expect? Yes, we both hoped, at least I did, but what could we expect? I love you, I admit it, I fell in love with you then and even more over this past year. I know I said writing isn't real but it is, you helped me through tough times and brought me love every day when everything went wrong.

Later that night, as she sits around the kitchen table with her family, with everyone laughing and joking except for her, she feels the sharp pain of heartbreak.

Gunther had sent her one final message: *You're right, let's not be hasty or hurt one another. I'm going to the Bahamas for a photoshoot for a few of days, it'll be good for us to take a bit of time to think about things. I'll email you when I get back.*

Melusine feels sick and she pushes her food around her plate.

"Are you okay?" Nika asks and Melusine smiles at her.

"Yes, dear, I'm fine. I look around at you lot and my heart is so happy. But I'm sad for the things that have passed, the things that will never return."

She knows they all think she's talking about Hans and she doesn't correct them.

She looks at Jonas who's holding fat little Tommy, their Buddha baby, and her spirits lift.

"We have treasures and gifts in each other. I'm so grateful for this," and she waves her hand around.

Jonas comes and gives her a hug.

"Everything will be fine from now. It's been the hardest of years but the worst is behind us now."

She hopes he's right.

"Oh my," she says. "I just remembered. We haven't told Ana anything about this. It's been our secret. She's going to kill me."

The others laugh. "Oh yes, she will," Jonas says. "A story this gigantic and you held out on her. Yes, Mami, you're going to have to pay big time!"

"Call her now and see if she can come over," Felix says. She loves Ana. "Say there's a lot of takeout food and that we have the most incredible story to tell her."

Melusine does exactly that and in less than fifteen minutes, Ana is knocking at the door.

Six
now the journey is ending

45.

SEVERAL MONTHS LATER, it is early spring and the train pulls into the station. A tall woman with long dark wavy hair gets off and stands on the platform, looking around with uncertainty.

She has no idea where to start. The town is small but to a stranger in search of one man, it is a vast landscape.

She finds a cab driver who speaks English and asks him to take her to the part of town where the homeless men hang out.

When the driver looks at her curiously, she tells him that she is looking for someone. "Hans Meier? Perhaps you've heard of him? There were lots of stories about him in the newspapers, a year or so ago."

"Everybody knows Hans. But what do you want with him? Rumour has it he's very dangerous these days. He walks around screaming and trying to strangle ghosts."

"I believe I can help him."

"Do you want me to take you to meet his wife? She runs a local café near the university. She can tell you more about him."

"No, I just want to see him. Please. Take me there now."

The cab driver shrugs and takes her to the park. He points out Hans who is striding up and down, throwing his hands out in front of him and shouting.

"Oh my. I wouldn't have recognized him."

The driver glances in the rearview mirror. "When did you know him?"

"I really thought I could help him," she replies vaguely, not answering his question, "I really did. I can see that I'll need some time to think about this," she adds.

"I told you, he's in a bad way."

"Is there a fairly decent place to stay within walking distance of this park?" she asks, and he drops her off at a cheap but respectable hotel.

"Thank you," she says, paying him.

"Lady, you want to be careful with Hans," he calls out but she is walking up the steps, pulling her small piece of luggage on wheels and either she does not hear him or she chooses not to answer.

The cab driver shrugs again and drives away, thinking about his mistress who is demanding that he leave his wife. *Women.*

The Reverend Juditha Estima checks into the hotel and lets herself into her room.

She pulls the curtains closed and does a long meditation for guidance.

Although she firmly believes that no one person can save another, she cannot help but feel responsible for having played a part in Hans's demise. She had understood that he was in pain but she had not acknowledged or seen the degree of vulnerability that lay beneath his organized exterior.

After he stopped calling and seemingly vanished, she continued to focus her meditations and healing prayers on him. Having no way of contacting him, she searched the Internet, certain it was a fruitless enterprise and was horror-struck to read the news of what he had done to the schoolgirl as well as his subsequent homeless condition.

Dismayed, she had tried, in the year that had passed, to find peace with what had happened but she could not let it go; she had to find Hans and try to help him.

And she had been so confident in coming here, certain that she could bring him back from the brink but, having seen the degree of emotional erosion and the thorough decay of his sanity, she is less sure. Nevertheless, she has to try.

She meditates for an hour, has a shower and then meditates again. Then she readies herself to leave. By now it is late, it is close to ten p.m., but she cannot wait until the morning; she feels that the time is right for her to see him now.

She leaves, and quietly closes the door behind her.

46.

THE FOLLOWING MORNING, Melusine and Felix are in the café, taking turns to feed Tommy who is ravenous. "You'd think we never feed him," Felix says. "Our little butterball." She wipes his chin and he beams at her.

The door chimes, and Melusine looks up. The early morning breakfast rush has come and gone and she is surprised to see Jürgen Klein.

"You should have let me know you were coming. I would have baked your favourites."

He shakes his head and she immediately knows that something is terribly wrong.

"Hans?" she asks and he nods.

Melusine sits down and Felix feeds Tommy quietly. They both wait.

"I feel responsible," Jürgen says. He looks haggard and tired. "I should have listened to my instincts and found a way to have him locked up. But he hadn't committed any crimes, so I couldn't but now, look what's happened..."

"Jürgen, just tell me, what has happened?"

"Hans killed a woman," he says, heavily, sitting down. "A woman named Juditha Estima, a Reverend from the Healing Lives Ministries. According to a cab driver who picked her up from the train station, she thought she could help Hans. He dropped her off at a hotel and then she must have gone to see Hans later."

"What? The Healing Lives Ministries? Where did she come from? Who is she really?" Melusine fires questions at Klein.

"I'll tell you everything," Klein says, "but first you need to know that Hans is in hospital, in very bad shape, he most likely won't make it."

He looks at Melusine and Felix. "Some kids walking through the park found them this morning on their way to school. Hans strangled Juditha Estima. He was sitting on the ground, rubbing her feet and singing to her. The kids phoned the cops."

"And he's in hospital?" Melusine feels numb.

"Yes. The Sisters of Mercy. He was half frozen to death himself. There was a cold snap last night and he wasn't dressed for it. He's got pneumonia and the prognosis isn't good."

"Why was she here?" Melusine asks. "I don't understand. What was she even doing here? He doesn't have anything left to give her. I don't understand."

"From what I gathered, from her sister who I spoke to, she felt very bad about having failed Hans," Jürgen says. "Her sister said that Juditha was quite obsessed about what had happened to Hans and she wanted to try to fix things. She was convinced that she'd made things worse for him, and who knows, maybe she did, but she certainly did not deserve to die."

"So she came to try and help him? She really was trying to help him? Who'd ever had thought that? And now she's paid with her own life."

Jürgen nods.

"What will happen to her now?"

"Her sister's coming to get her and she'll take the body back home to the States."

"She came all this way to try to help Hans? Oh my god." Melusine's eyes fill with tears. "Is there no end to this affliction? When will it end?"

"Perhaps it's ended now," Jürgen says gently. "Perhaps this is the end."

"I must see Hans. Can you take me to the hospital? Felix, will you be all right here by yourself?"

"Of course, yes. If I need to, I'll call Emily to help me with the café. Melu, shouldn't you call Jonas?"

"Oh yes, of course, thank you, Felix. I'm not thinking straight at all."

She calls Jonas and tells him his father is in hospital and asks him to meet her there. She will tell him the rest in person.

An hour later, she and Jonas are staring at the man who used to be Hans Meier. He is breathing with the help of equipment and bears no resemblance to his former self.

Jonas is calm; he stands with his arm around Melusine who feels as if she can hardly breathe.

"We don't think he's got long to live," a doctor informs them. "His body's in such a weakened state."

"We'll stay however long we need to," Melusine says and she puts her hand out and touches the sheet.

She hasn't yet told Jonas about Juditha. "Oh Jonas," she says, "I should tell you..."

"I know, Mami." He gets her a chair. "I know about the woman from the Healing Lives Ministries."

"But how?"

He shrugs. "Richter told me. He called me this morning. I was trying to think how to tell you but then Jürgen arrived at you first. And I'm glad he did. I didn't know how to tell you."

That explains Jonas's unearthly calm; he had already known the whole story.

"Jonas, are you okay? I'm sorry, I've been so selfish, only thinking of me."

He sighs. "Papa died to me the day he attacked Kateri. He tried to kill a woman and that's when I knew my father was gone."

"And yet I only know it now. I guess I was waiting for him to come back all this time, even though I never realized it. We'll have a proper burial. Your father and I bought a plot in the cemetery years ago."

Jonas is surprised.

"Your father," Melusine says and her voice gets caught in her throat, "used to be the most thoughtful man. He always used to think consequentially, about everything." She is crying now and Jonas hugs her.

"Can I get you a nice hot coffee?" he asks. "Let me get you something. I've got to go and update Nika, she's in the waiting room."

"Coffee would be good," Melusine says, not really caring.

Jonas leaves. In reality, he is the furthest thing from calm; he is in a cold sweat and he is sick with fear but he cannot let Melusine see.

Because it is not true. He had not learned about Juditha Estima from Richter.

For some time, Jonas had been paying Kristian, one of Hans's homeless friends, to keep an eye on Hans and to phone him if the situation changed or if anything went wrong.

And, the previous night, Kristian had phoned to say that a woman was trying to talk to Hans; a tall woman with dark hair, that he had never seen before. Jonas had told Kristian that he should be there in a matter of minutes and he had rushed over to the park.

He dragged the woman away from Hans and tried to talk some sense into her but when he learned that she was from the Healing Lives Ministries, he was filled with violent anger.

"It's all your fault," he shouted, his voice vicious. "You and your crap pushed him over the edge. Any normal person would have told him to get on with his life and be happy with his lot but no, you had to phone him every day, spewing nonsense into his ear and taking all his money."

The words poured from him, startling him with their venom. "You bitch," he said, "you ruined my father and broke my family."

"I only ever wanted to help him," the woman said. "I was only trying to help. And I'm here to help him now."

Jonas had gestured rudely towards the crazy man who was drawing pictures on an invisible wall in front of him and shouting expletives.

"So, go and help him then," he spat at her, knowing he was sending the woman to her death. "Go. You think you can fix this? Well, go ahead and try." He walked away without a backward glance and went home.

And in the morning, it was true that he had spoken to Richter. The young police officer had called him in the early hours.

"I'm really sorry, Jonas," he said when he came to the end of the story. "We're trying to fit all the pieces together as much as we can and as soon as we do, I'll let you know what we find."

Jonas had listened in silence, saying as little as possible and hoping that Richter would mistake his reticence for numb shock.

"I phoned Kommissar Klein as soon as I heard," Richter said. "He came over immediately and he's on his way to the café now to tell your mother. He should be there any minute."

"I must go, she'll need me," Jonas said. "I'll call you later."

He sat staring out into space, thinking, and minutes later, his mother called him and he rushed to the hospital to meet her.

And now, at the hospital, his thoughts are spinning and whirling like frightened birds and he is trying to slow things down and take stock of the situation.

He tells himself that no one had seen him in the park with Juditha and even if they had, who would believe a bunch of winos? He had left Nika sound asleep and returned to find her in the same position; he had nothing to worry about there. In fact he had nothing to worry about at all, except for the fact that he had as good as murdered the woman himself.

He makes his way down the busy hospital corridor to find Nika pacing in the waiting room.

"Not good," he says in response to her unasked question. "It's a matter of hours."

He sits down on the sofa and puts his head in his hands.

"Jonas." Something about Nika's tone makes him look up.

"Where did you go last night? You went out at midnight, where did you go?"

As if things couldn't get any worse for him.

"I couldn't sleep so I went for a drive." He knows it is stupid and lame as he says it.

Nika sits down next to him.

"No," she says. "We've never had any secrets, you and me. We always tell each other everything."

He sighs. "Kristian told me there was a woman with Papa, so I went out to see what was happening. But she wouldn't leave with me so I left her there and now what if they think I killed her? Because Nika, when I realized who she was, I've never been so angry in my life. I can't believe the things I said to her and then I left her there. What if someone saw me with her and the police think I killed her?"

"Jonas, everybody saw Hans try to kill Kateri and everybody knows you could never do anything like that."

"But everyone also knows how angry I have been with the people from the Healing Lives Ministries and how much I wanted to find them. I'm really afraid, Nika."

She takes his hand and chews on her lip.

"Let's work this out. Kristian phoned you and you went out at midnight and got back an hour later. Where was Kristian? Did he see you at the park?"

"No. He wasn't there. I didn't understand that. I thought we were supposed to meet there but he wasn't there."

"That's one good thing then. Who else was in the park?"

"No one. Well, no one that I could see. But who knows who could have been hiding in the darkness, watching. Any number of people could have seen me. That area is usually so busy that time of night, with the homeless guys and prostitutes. That's the thing, I can't believe that no one saw me."

"Well, let's not assume the worst. I can always say I couldn't sleep, that I was up reading and that you didn't go anywhere."

She rubs his back. "Jonas, are you listening to me?"

He nods but doesn't really seem to be hearing her.

"Nika, the worst thing is that when I heard she was dead, my first thought was that she deserved it, the bitch. She deserved to die and I was happy, I thought, *yes, you stupid bitch, how psychic are you now that you couldn't see this coming? Serves you right.* That's what I thought."

His face creases and he puts his head in his hands again and starts to cry; big wracking sobs, his whole body shuddering.

Nika says nothing but she waits until he is all cried out. She gets up, grabs a box of Kleenex on the coffee table and hands it to him.

He blows his nose vigorously and looks slightly calmer. "I keep trying to tell myself that there was nothing else I could have done. That she would have stayed with Papa anyway. But be that as it may, I should have called the police. Why didn't I call Richter? Why? You know why? Because I wanted her to die. There, that's the truth. I wanted her to die."

"Wishing someone dead isn't killing them," Nika tries to reason with him.

"But I didn't take any action that could have saved her. I left her to certain death."

"Jonas, she was a grown woman, responsible for her own actions. And who knows, even if you had called them, maybe she would have gone back at another time. We need to find out where Kristian was and if anyone else saw you. We can deal with everything else later. Come on, let's go and phone Richter. You can't use cellphones in here, let's find the payphones."

She pulls him to his feet and leads him out the room, stopping at the doorway. "But listen Jonas, the only thing you tell Richter is that Kristian phoned you, yes, be upfront about that but say you thought you'd deal with it in the morning. Okay? Nothing else."

Jonas nods. "Okay. Don't worry. Let's go and do this thing."

They find a pay phone and huddle in the booth, with Nika listening in.

"We've pieced it together as much as we can," Richter says, "So Kristian phoned you from the Mission where he was having the late night snack. And he waited for you there but when you didn't come, he went back to the park and he said that the woman was still trying to talk to Hans…"

"What time did he go back?" Jonas interrupts him; he is relieved to hear that Kristian had thought they were meeting at the Mission and not at the park and Nika nods too, knowing what he's thinking.

"Close to one a.m. He said he remembered the time because he had wanted to go and watch TV at that all-night doughnut shop near the Mission. The owner lets some of the fellows watch TV after midnight as long as they keep it quiet and Kristian was pissed off because he was missing his programs."

Jonas and Nika exchange a relieved glance and she puts her arm around his waist.

"So what happened then?" Jonas tries to keep his voice even.

"Kristian said he got pissed off with the woman, she was as stubborn as all hell and wouldn't leave with him, and he couldn't think what else to do, so he left her with Hans and went to the doughnut shop. He says he should have called me and this is all his fault."

"No, it's my fault," Jonas's voice is small. "I should have met Kristian at the Mission or gone to the park myself. Yes, Kristian phoned me, and I told him I'd go but then I just got tired, tired of it all, and I didn't want to leave Nika alone. I'm the one to blame. Kristian must be really angry with me for not showing up."

Nika shoots him a warning glance; he's saying too much.

"Kristian said he figured you fell back asleep, he said you sounded half asleep on the phone. And listen, you and Kristian both need to cut the crap. I know Hans is your father, but he belonged in a nuthouse and me and Klein should have found a way to put him there. I know Klein feels the same. We're the police officers, if anyone's to blame, it's us."

Jonas rushes to reassure him. "But you couldn't do anything because we wouldn't let you. Dieter wanted us to give you the support you needed but we wouldn't. So no one else saw anything? Didn't anyone see Papa kill her or even just see them talking?"

"Nope. No one saw a thing. Quiet night in the park I guess. We spoke to all the regulars and no one saw anything."

"Well, I'd better get back to my mother. Papa could go any minute and I want to be with her. Thanks Richter, I needed to talk about it."

Nika punches him again and signals hanging up the phone.

"No problem. You go and be with your mother and I'm sorry, Jonas, and please, tell your mother too. You take care, man."

Jonas hangs up the phone and turns to Nika. His T-shirt is drenched with sweat.

"Well," he says.

"You said too much," she is accusing. "But it's fine."

He nods. "I can't tell you how relieved I feel, Nika. That no one saw me is amazing. I tell you one thing, Papa ruined his life with all of this but I won't let it ruin ours. I feel like I dodged a bullet."

She hugs him close to her.

"Let's go and get Mami a coffee. Come and be with us, Nika, don't wait out here."

When they return with the coffees, Melusine gets up and gives Nika a hug.

"I'm glad you're here. Listen you two, I need to make a call too. You'll both stay with him?"

They nod and Melusine leaves. She does not say who she's going to call.

She digs in her handbag and finds a small notebook. She flips to a page and dials the numbers carefully. It is long-distance and there are lots of numbers to dial.

She is numb and her movements are mechanical and she is finally rewarded by the ringing of a phone.

"Hello?" a familiar voice answers, one that she has not heard in a long time.

"Gunther?"

"Melusine." She can hear his unmistakeable relief and happiness at hearing from her. "And here was me thinking that you were never going to call. How are you? What's going on?"

She tells him.

"My god." He is silent for a moment. "I want to come and be with you. Please, don't say no. Don't. Okay? I know all the complications and I know we can't promise each other anything, but just let me come; let me come, the man who loves you. Just let me come."

She leans on the same panel where Jonas had rested his head.

"Yes," she says. "Come."

Acknowledgements

Immeasurable thanks to my publisher and Editor-In-Chief, the wonderful, talented and incomparably hardworking Luciana Ricciutelli; I, along with every sculpted word, offer grateful thanks.

Thanks also to my entire Inanna family who help me realize my writing dreams. I'm very proud to be part of this inspiring collective.

Bradford Dunlop, thank you for bumping into the German woman in Las Vegas: were it not for that chance meeting, this story would not exist. Most importantly, I thank you for your endless patience, for your love and for your lovely way of seeing things. Your insightful photographer's eye sees so much more than most.

To Mom, thanks for daily support, encouragement and love; to Dad thanks for your stalwart belief in my writing and your view that writing really matters. My beautiful sister; I'm so proud of you. I thank my whole family for unceasing love and support and that includes my extended family on Bradford's side; Marci, Mark and Deb and Syd and Lorie and Ed and Patti, Greg and Barb — and everyone — you truly make me (and the books) part of the family.

Thanks to my adorable niece Tully and my nephew Grayson who was my muse for Tommy.

Thanks to Danila Botha for your big heart and faith in my writing.

Grateful thanks to Chris Bucci for immense generosity in guiding me with invaluable initial plot outlines and related feedback.

Thanks to Jason Logan for much appreciated cover design direction.

To all my patient and wonderful friends — thank you! I am so very blessed by this abundance of friendship.

Thanks to Bonnie McKee Staring for always making me laugh and also for introducing me to the art of objectifying the back story — without you, there'd be no Ingeborg Bachmann in this book and I also thank Ingeborg Bachmann for wanting to be a part of this book; I felt her presence strongly.

Thanks to Yoko Morgenstern for helping me get my German facts right.

I'd like to thank Kate O'Rourke for her support since the start of my writing and I'd like tell her that her feisty spirit still burns bright — she's greatly missed. And Julie Hope, also taken far too soon.

Brenda Missen, Dorothy McIntosh, Rosemary McCracken, Lisa Young, Donna Brown, Pam Mountain, Caroline Clemmons, Betsy Balega, Beverly Akerman, Kristin Jenkins, Pam Lofton, Richard Rosenbaum — it takes a village to bring a book into this world!

Poems and quotes:

The following quotes are from poems by Ingeborg Bachmann, With thanks.

Carefree be carefree ... Cheerful and with music (Advertisement)

I step outside of myself, out of my eyes, hands, mouth, outside of myself I step. (I step outside myself)

I am cut off from myself and from everything else. (I Should Disappear)

Where the others have a body, I had genius. (My Cell)

Your eyes, which administer heaven, I can only speak of darkness (Darkness Spoken)

When someone departs he must throw his hat,
filled with the mussels he spent the summer
gathering, in the sea
and sail off with his hair in the wind (Songs from an Island)

I with the German language
this cloud about me
that I keep as a house
drive through all languages. (Exile)

Mouth, that spent the night in my mouth,
Eye that guarded my own,
Hand —
and those eyes that drilled through me!
Mouth, which spoke the sentence,
Hand, which executed me! (Songs of Flight)

The loan of borrowed time will be due on the horizon...
(Borrowed Time)

I step, a bundle of goodness and godliness that must make good this devilry that has happened. (I step outside myself)

War is no longer declared but continued. The outrageous has become the everyday (Every Day)

Each half-baked feeling that passes by me … I have regis-tered for a life sentence with you that cannot be carried out. (Consolation Aria)

At an end is the beginning of daydreams (Tired and Useless)

A long, long love has seen its wings grow heavy (My Love After Many Years)

Now the journey is ending (Stay)

From the novel *Malina* by Ingeborg Bachmann:

"A woman has to shelter her real feelings in the ones she's invented, just to stand the whole business with the feet, but above all to stand the greater part that's missing, for someone who is so hung up on feet is bound to be greatly neglecting something else."

Website sources:

<marjorieperloff.com/tag/ingeborg-bachmann>
<weatherspark.com/averages/28994/11/Wiesbaden-Hessen-Germany>
<www.wiesbaden.de/en/tourism/index.php>
<www.winespectator.com>
<mybestgermanrecipes.com>
<www.germany-insider-facts.com>
<www.germany.travel/en/towns-cities-culture/towns-cities/jena.html>
<similarminds.com/personality_disorder.html>
<www.allthetests.com/quiz26/quiz/1229120796/Test-for-Schizoid-personality-disorder>
<www.photius.com/countries/germany/national_security/germany_national_security_federal_police_agenc~1448.html
legislationline.org/topics/country/28/topic/12>

Other Sources:

The Thunder From Down Under DVD: *Live in Reno*

Thanks to the Toronto Reference Library for many happy hours working with Ingeborg Bachmann's writing.

Photo: Bradford Dunlop

Originally from South Africa, Lisa de Nikolits has been a Canadian citizen since 2003. She has a Bachelor of Arts in English Literature and Philosophy and has lived and worked in the United States, Australia and Britain. As an art director, she has worked on *marie claire, Vogue Australia, Vogue Living, Cosmopolitan* and SHE magazines. Her first novel, *The Hungry Mirror,* was published by Inanna Publications in 2010 and was awarded the IPPY Gold Medal for literature on women's issues in 2011, as well as long-listed for the 2011 ReLit Awards. Her second novel, *West of Wawa,* was published by Inanna in 2011 and was one of four *Chatelaine* Bookclub Editor's Picks and was awarded the IPPY Silver Medal for Popular Fiction in 2012. Lisa lives and works in Toronto.